The *Star* Man

The True Story of Willie Kean, Journalist and Rebel

The *Star* Man

A NOVEL

The True Story of Willie Kean,
Journalist and Rebel

CONOR O'CLERY

SOMERVILLE PRESS

Somerville Press Ltd,
Dromore, Bantry,
Co. Cork, Ireland

© Conor O'Clery 2016

First published 2016

Designed by Jane Stark
Typeset in Adobe Caslon Pro
seamistgraphics@gmail.com

ISBN: 978 0 9927364 60

Printed and bound in Spain
by GraphyCems, Villatuerta, Navarra

LOTTERY FUNDED

AUTHOR'S NOTE

This is a historical novel about William Kean, a newspaperman and rebel in the 1790s, and of his newspaper, the *Northern Star*, which for a few short years outraged the gentry and propagated revolt throughout Ireland.

Willie Kean is a real person. He was caught up in an extraordinary drama of intrigue, violence and betrayal, as the mainly Presbyterian population of Belfast and the adjacent counties simmered with revolutionary fervour, inspired by events in France and America.

He tells the story himself in this imagined account of his turbulent life and loves during the years leading up to the rebellion of 1798.

Willie Kean, along with many thousands of his kinfolk, fought British Crown forces for liberty and equality, for all the people of Ireland, only to be undone by treachery and superior arms.

Their doomed rising, in which he played a leading role, is often overlooked in the grand sweep of Irish history. The narrative sits uncomfortably with the loyalism of the rebels' descendants, and is overshadowed in the historical memory of nationalists by the rebellion in the South of Ireland. But Willie Kean belonged to perhaps the most progressive and enlightened generation of Irish men and women ever. Their fight to the death for liberty and equality deserves to be remembered and commemorated.

Break the alliance of three million discontented Catholics and half a million disaffected Presbyterian republicans, deeply intoxicated with French notions and French practices, or Ireland is lost to Your Majesty

– Edmund Burke (attributed) in message to King George III

CONTENTS

BELFAST, 1790s

DONEGALL STREET

NORTH STREET

HERCULES STREET

SMITHFIELD

MILL STREET

CASTLE STREET

GRAND PARA

LINEN HALL STREET

DONEGAL SQUARE NOR

WHITE LINEN
HALL

1. ALEXANDER'S TAVERN
2. MURDOCH RESIDENCE
3. McTIER RESIDENCE
4, 5 & 6. PRESBYTERIAN MEETING HOUSES
7. DONEGALL ARMS HOTEL
8. EXCHANGE & ASSEMBLY ROOMS
9. BARCLAY'S TAVERN
10. FLANAGAN'S TAVERN
11. NORTHERN STAR OFFICE
12. BELFAST SOCIETY FOR
    PROMOTING KNOWLEDGE
13. ARTHUR STREET THEATRE
14. ARTILLERY BARRACKS
15. WHITE LINEN HALL
16. BELFAST ACADEMY

WARING STREET

BRIDGE STREET

HIGH STREET

WILSON'S COURT

MARKET

ANN'S STREET

RIVER LAGAN

N

MAP ARTWORK BY MICHAEL O'CLERY

ANTRIM

CAVE HILL

BELFAST LOUGH

PORT

BANGOR

D

GRANSHA

CO. ANTRIM

NEWTONARDS

BELFAST

COMBER

GR

LISBURN

KILLINCHY

BLARIS CAMP

MOIRA

SAINTFIELD

HILLSBOROUGH

P

BALLYNAHINCH

CO. ARMAGH

SLIEVE CROOB

STRANG

BANBRIDGE

DOWNPATRICK

CO. DOWN

N

RATHFRILAND

NEWRY

MOURNE MOUNTAINS

CO. DOWN

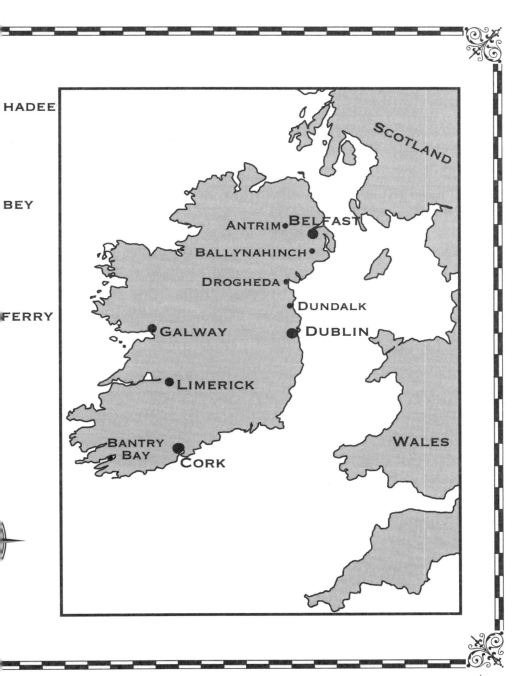

HADEE

BEY

FERRY

SCOTLAND

ANTRIM • BELFAST

BALLYNAHINCH •

DROGHEDA •

• DUNDALK

GALWAY • DUBLIN

• LIMERICK

BANTRY
BAY
• CORK

WALES

MAP ARTWORK BY MICHAEL O'CLERY

— ONE —

GUNFIRE AT THE ACADEMY

My name is William Kean. I live in Philadelphia. I enjoy prosperity but I find it hard to enjoy life. When asleep I suffer nightmares, and sometimes, when awake, my grief and self-pity becomes so intense I wish I were dead.

In fact I am not supposed to be alive at all. In Ireland I was sentenced to death. That was in 1798. The English military judge ordered that I be hanged and my head cut off and stuck on a spike on top of the Market House in Belfast. Imagine that! I'm sure my one-time rebel friends passing along High Street would have tried to avoid catching my eye, though from what I saw of the heads already stuck up there, the eyes were pecked out by seagulls.

How did I end up almost losing my head, and my eyes?

It all started, I suppose, ten years earlier, on the day I refused to take off my cap.

That was in Moira, the village in County Down where I was born. It's a pleasant place, laid-out around a broad main street with lime trees and stone houses for linen dealers. The village is dominated by Moira Castle, which belonged to an elderly nobleman called John Rawdon, the First Earl of Moira.

Like all big landowners, the family planted exotic trees and shrubs in the demesne. They erected a stove house, said to be the first in Europe, with lurid green glass panes, and kept it at tropical temperatures to propagate foreign plants, mostly from Jamaica. My father, like his father before him, was manager of this horticultural enterprise. As a boy I helped him count and catalogue the plants in the bedding trays. I would spend hours making sketches of orchids, bromeliad, hibiscus and poinsettia, and different ferns and cacti. I noted down magnolias from the Carolinas, lavender, bluebells, honeysuckles, sweet briar and jessamine. I learned from an early age when to thin, prick and water.

When I was still a child, old Lord Moira rented out the castle and moved to a new family mansion in Ballynahinch in the centre of County Down. Good riddance, everyone said. He was a member of the established Anglican Church, and seriously disliked Presbyterians, whom he regarded as 'very troublesome under the pretense of being godly men.'

His son, Baron Francis spent years away, fighting for the English in the American War of Independence and hobnobbing with the Prince of Wales in London. He visited the village of Moira occasionally, and one freezing December day he came riding by our school with his estate manager. It was my first time to see him. He looked tall, stately and athletic, sitting on a high-bred horse.

From early on I was told to doff my cap when the gentry passed. That day I didn't. I just stood and stared as other boys removed their head gear and tugged at their forelocks.

I had decided I didn't like landlords. I took in everything that was said when my father and his friends smoked their pipes around the turf fire in the evenings. They spoke of the injustices inflicted on Ireland by the landlord class, of evictions and forced emigration, and of Presbyterians like us being excluded from high office and forced to pay tithes to the Ascendancy church to which the big landowners belonged. Even then, just thirteen years old, I was fired up with indignation.

So I didn't take off my cap. I just stood there.

The agent asked, 'Where's your manners, boy?'

I said nothing.

He dismounted and smacked my head with his open hand, sending my cap flying. I picked it up and put it back on. I stared defiantly at him. He was a small fellow with a fat face and I was tall for my years. 'Take it off!' he barked, and reached for me. I clenched my fist and swung at him. The agent slipped and fell on his bum. Everyone laughed. The wee man got up and came at me with his whip.

Baron Francis called out, 'You've met your match, Claiborne, leave him.' So they rode off.

The story did the rounds. I was a hero. Nobody liked Claiborne. But my father was worried. He spent a day walking to Ballynahinch and back to plead with Baron Rawdon not to allow his agent to exact revenge.

He brought astonishing news. The son of Lord Moira had taken not the slightest offence. Apparently he had advanced ideas and didn't share his father's distaste for troublesome Presbyterians. He had asked a lot of questions about me. My father told him that I was fond of books and always first in my class at school.

The upshot was that the Baron suggested sending me to a new Presbyterian academy established in Belfast by the town's merchants and businessmen. He would pay the fees. He liked the idea of being a patron of promising youngsters. Even cheeky ones. He cautioned my father that he couldn't always control Claiborne and that I should keep out of his way.

So not long afterwards there I was, walking the fifteen miles to Belfast with my father, carrying as much oaten bread, eggs and butter as my mother could pack into a satchel.

My first impressions of Belfast were of broad streets, three-storey brick houses with slated roofs, coal smoke, pigs snuffling in the gutters, and the stink of horse piss and dunghills. And most of all the noise, the racket of cartwheels on cobbles and people shouting and horses neighing and seagulls cawing and screeching.

We found the academy in a dingy, three-storey building beside St Ann's Church on Donegall Street. The kindly old principal, the Revd Dr James Crombie, entered my name in a ledger.

'Every boy wants to study business,' he told my father. 'That is the way to get on in life. Belfast is a place of entrepreneurs and merchants, men of strong character. Do you have a strong character, boy?'

'Oh aye! He has,' said my father.

Revd Crombie put me under the charge of the mathematical master, Mr Dinneen. I was assigned a bed with a straw mattress and blanket in a dormitory with thirty other boys. I settled into a routine: prayers at seven in the morning and eight in the evening; classes all day for arithmetic, algebra, geography, astronomy, navigation, natural and moral philosophy, and book-keeping. Words came easily to me and I got the highest marks for my essays. I wrote up a diary every evening by candlelight in an exercise book I'd bought in John Hughes's bookshop on Bridge Street. I kept it up until the very day I was sentenced to death ten years later.

I read as much as I could. I discovered Shakespeare and memorised excerpts from his plays. I absorbed the contents of the political pamphlets which circulated in Belfast, and used them to argue with the teachers about the need for reform in Irish politics. Dr Crombie once remonstrated with me for talking back to the tutors.

'You are sharp as a nail,' he said. 'Challenge authority by all means, but be careful you don't get a name for yourself as a trouble-maker.' Then he winked, pinched my cheek, and sent me packing.

Old Crombie was a sick man and he died in 1790 when I was in my second year. None of us took to the new headmaster from Dublin, the Revd Dr William Bruce, a Trinity College-educated clergyman full of self-importance, who sweated profusely under his powdered wig and starched stock collar. He liked using the cane. His nagging wife Susanna bossed him around in front of the boys and called him a ninny. He was however a very important figure in Belfast society, with a great liberal reputation, and his sermons at the First Presbyterian Church in Rosemary Street carried a lot of weight.

Today the Revd Bruce still makes a great show of supporting reforms. But it is all talk. We rightly figured him from the start to be anti-Papist. He once said if Catholics got into power they would establish an inquisition. Well, we considered that the French Revolution proved him wrong. It was the Catholics of France who brought about the revolution that toppled the cardinals from their thrones.

In my final year, 1792, I was the first boy to get Wolfe Tone's sensational pamphlet, *An Argument on Behalf of the Catholics of Ireland*. I passionately agreed with Tone that the English were the ruin of Ireland and the only way to free Ireland from a corrupt government was to unite Protestant, Catholic and Dissenter. It made total sense to me. In spring I gave John Hughes a penny a week from my allowance until I had paid sixpence and could collect my own copy of *The Rights of Man* by Thomas Paine. Everybody was reading it. My friend and classmate George Gray, tall like me, with ginger hair, big ploughboy hands and a taste for political discourse, formed a debating group to discuss Paine's theory – that revolution is permissible when a government does not safeguard the rights of its citizens.

Some of the other boys couldn't have cared less about politics, or were loyalist, but I got on well with them. They liked to have me around when we sneaked out and confronted gangs of street urchins looking for a scrap. Because of my height I had little to fear from the scrawny Belfast kids.

Our antipathy towards Revd Bruce reached a pitch over Easter that year. He cancelled our holiday because we had taken up class time on the Catholic question. So a few of us decided to take action. It was the custom every year for a group of senior students to bar out a teacher from his classroom for one day to extract concessions. Usually the barring out was a bit of fun and the upshot was a treat or a day off. But this time eleven of us – nine boarders, Auchinleck, Stouppe, McMinn, the two Rialls, Atkinson, Verner, Arbuckle and I, along with two day boys, Crombie and Cunningham – decided to arm ourselves and make a stand that all Belfast would hear about. Crombie was the son of the former principal and the Rialls were relatives of the town sovereign, or mayor, the Revd William Bristow, so we were a well-connected bunch. George Gray had gone home to the country that day so he wasn't with us, which turned out well for him.

At six in the morning of Thursday 12 April we crept out of the dormitory, broke into the armoury and took five pistols and bags of gunpowder and balls. We raided the kitchens for bread, beef and milk. Then we barricaded ourselves in the mathematics room on the ground floor. We pinned a letter to the door of the outer writing room. The letter was headed 'Liberty Hall' and it informed Revd Bruce that we had taken up arms to gain by force what we had been denied by entreaty. We would surrender only if granted three days' holiday at Easter and two at Whitsuntide, and permission for boys to stay out on weekends until nine o'clock in the evening.

Bruce and his fussy wife arrived at half past six, highly affronted, and shouted through the open window that if we gave ourselves up in fifteen minutes he would take no action against us. But he wouldn't countenance our demands. One of my classmates grasped a flintlock pistol with a curved wooden handle, poured in black powder and a lead ball, and fired in their direction. The bang nearly deafened us and filled the room with smoke and the smell of sulphur.

Revd Bruce then broke down the door of the adjacent writing room and advanced through it, wielding a crowbar and egged on by his shrew of a wife. Our shooter fired through a hole in the door and the shot passed near Mrs Bruce's head. They made a hasty retreat. An hour later a mason poured water down the chimney. The room filled with steam from the coal fire. We called out that we would set the school alight. The water stopped.

We heard urchins in the street cheering us on. For once they were on our side. We ate our rations and did our business out the window when bladders grew tight.

Mayor Bristow arrived. He sent in a note to inform us that firing a pistol was a capital offence. He ordered us to surrender by command of the King. One of his nephews shouted back that we would send a ball through his wig.

As a country boy I was determined not to be found wanting before my town classmates when it came to being reckless. I took a firearm, rammed in powder and ball, and fired at the bottom of the door. We heard Bristow scrambling away, yelping as if he had been shot.

In the afternoon several patrons of the school arrived, among them some of the most important citizens of Belfast. We exchanged notes with them and got an agreement that we would surrender our weapons and retreat to our dormitory for the night. We had made our point.

Next morning we were paraded before the patrons and presented with a document to sign, expressing remorse and praying not to be beaten or expelled. We refused. Bruce sentenced us to twelve stripes each, to be administered in the presence of the esteemed benefactors.

He made an exception of 'the tall boy with the curly hair'. That was me. I was to get fifty lashes. He called me the ringleader, his chin quivering with outrage. Actually I wasn't, but one of my companions, I know not who, had obviously fingered me. Since I was the only boy not from a 'respectable' Belfast family I was a convenient scapegoat.

I was stripped to the waist, secured to a pole and whipped by a bailiff. I never experienced such pain. When I fell to the ground after being untied, two bailiffs set upon me with fists and buckled shoes. I was left lying semiconscious in my own blood. I couldn't see from my left eye. I have a dim recollection of boys helping me back to the dormitory. I passed out, face down on the bed. That's where my friend George found me when he came back to the school that evening.

'I'm not sure you'll do,' he said cheerfully. George liked to see the bleak side of things. As he cleaned the blood from my face, he informed me that I was to be out of the academy by the next day. I had been expelled.

I told George I couldn't go home to Moira in this condition. My friend invited me to stay at his father's house at Gransha, about twenty miles from Belfast, until I recovered. His father was a widower and there was just George and his sister Elizabeth at home. So there was room for a friend in need.

— TWO —

NORTHERN STAR

And so began my journey on the road that was to bring me to the scaffold.

On Monday George came with a chestnut mare. I mounted behind him. We set off to north County Down across the twenty-one arches of the Long Bridge. We kept to a steady four-beat walk. Every step was agonising. My head throbbed and my body ached and my back stung as if in contact with hot metal. Despite a chill in the air, I took off my coat and shirt to prevent the searing friction of the cloth on my skin.

We rode east around steep little hillocks, known as drumlins, picking our way through walkers, carts and cattle.

The bleach greens around Belfast gave way to potato and clover fields and patches of flax. We skirted Newtownards and turned north-east between ditches topped with hawthorn bushes. Five hours after leaving Belfast we arrived at the townland of Gransha and dismounted at a long white-washed thatched cottage at the end of a muddy lane.

George's father, Hans, a thin, wiry man, unshaven, in rolled-up shirt sleeves, was grooming a horse beneath a tree. George explained my damaged face and bloodied back. Hans greeted me cordially. Any friend of George was welcome in his house, he said. He sat me down at a table in the kitchen.

As we took milk and oaten biscuits, George's sister Elizabeth came in with a basket of eggs. She was about fifteen, with red hair down to her shoulders, blue eyes and a small pert mouth. 'I'm Betsy,' she announced. George told her my story. She laughed and said, 'Aren't you the fine rebel.' She warmed some water, wet a cloth, and washed away the encrusted blood on my back. It was painful but I liked the caress of her hands. She washed and dried my blood-stained shirt.

I was given a straw mattress in the half loft over the kitchen, with the thatch just above my head. How quiet it was after the racket of Belfast. I lay on my stomach and stared down at the pet lamb that reclined by the fire. It gazed back at me as if resentful of my presence.

The kitchen was just like my parents' in Moira, with a smooth earthen floor and a spinning wheel in the corner. A door at one end led into a bedroom where Hans and George slept, and at the other was a parlour where Betsy spent the night. A churn and wooden plunger stood in a corner by a brass-dial grandfather clock made by Wilkinson of Wigtown. Silverware and brass candlesticks sat on the dresser, along with pewter plates engraved with the initials H.G. and a brass guinea box inscribed 1684.

I remained awake for hours, worrying about my predicament. I felt sick in my belly at the thought that a fellow-pupil had betrayed me.

Next morning George left to go back to the academy. I spent a week in the Gray house recovering from my whipping. Every morning Betsy changed the dressings on my wounds and the puffiness around my black eye subsided. She was quite accomplished for a country girl, and proficient in grammar and spelling, having attended a school for young ladies and gentlemen in Linen Hall Street in Belfast. Hans Gray doted on her and was clearly intent on giving her every chance in life. She had a box of books which she let me look through. I found Shakespeare's *Sonnets*, the poems of Robbie Burns, Swift's *Gulliver's Travels*, *The Surprising Miracles of Nature and Art*, and a copy of *La Grammaire Française*.

'Did you study French?' I asked. '*Bien sûr!*' she replied. I nodded as if I understood. Then confessed that I didn't know what she meant.

I helped with chores. I drew water from the well fifty yards away, and weeded the vegetable and flower garden. I went for a walk on my own along the overhung lanes that connected to the neighbours' farms like verdant tunnels.

The Grays were well-to-do by the standards of tenant farmers. They had about seventy acres in potatoes, oats, flax and pasture, and five geese, six hens, two long-horned cows, a piglet that wandered in and out of the kitchen, a tethered goat that kept the grass down in front of the house, two horses, a half-crazed cock that crowed at dawn as if the world was coming to an end, and the pet lamb that lived on boiled potatoes and kept me company at night.

On the Friday Betsy produced *Caroline of Litchfield* by a Swiss author. We listened enchanted as she read to Hans and me the tale of the pains and pleasures of thwarted lovers.

George came back on Saturday morning. He told me I was viewed as a mighty man by my friends at the school, even by the loyalists.

He brought me to the blacksmith's forge at the crossroads to introduce me to the local men who gathered there. The big, burly blacksmith Matt McClenaghan was regarded as the local wit, and he sometimes sang old Irish ballads as he hammered out a horseshoe or mended a plough.

'You're the brave lad but you will live longer if you aren't so headstrong,' said Mat, after George explained why my face was black and blue. 'Pity you missed with the pistol,' said one ruddy-faced lad.

That evening several more neighbours came to have a look at the reckless youth who had taken a pot-shot at the mayor of Belfast. I protested that I only had fired at the door. The smithy arrived with his fiddle and we had songs and recitations. I saw Betsy watching me from the back of the room and I caught her eye and winked to make her blush.

My country idyll came to an end when a young man, stout, freckled, and sweating under his three-cornered hat, rode up to the cottage and asked for me. He introduced himself as Billy Templeton, a clerk at the *Northern Star* newspaper in Belfast. The proprietor, Mr Samuel Neilson, wanted to see me. I should call to the *Northern Star* office on Wednesday morning. There might be a job for me there.

'I had a hard time finding you,' said Billy, wiping his face with his hat.

I wished he hadn't. Not for a while anyway.

On the day I left, Betsy made breakfast of stirabout with goat's milk and fried me two goose eggs. As I went out the door she kissed me on the cheek, which I found very pleasing.

I set off walking and arrived in Belfast in late afternoon. I called into several taverns to seek accommodation. Mr Hugh O'Kane, the landlord at Kelly's Cellars in Bank Street, figured out who I was. He said I could use the stable loft if I swept up sawdust and rinsed jugs and tankards in the evenings.

O'Kane pointed me out to customers and I had to relate the academy story in every detail. One slapped me on the back, which made me cry out. I got a glass of whiskey for my pains and threw it back as if I was a hardy drinker. It burned my throat and made me retch. They had a good laugh at that.

On Wednesday morning I made my way to the *Northern Star* office. It took up one of a row of three-storey houses with slate roofs on High Street beside a narrow alleyway with thatched dwellings and taverns. There was a constant clatter from carts rattling over the big flagstones to and from the quays. Giant seagulls dived and squabbled over rotting scraps. Coal smoke curled down from the chimneys.

I found Billy Templeton working at a ledger in the front office. He took me to the editor's room upstairs.

Samuel Neilson bade me sit by his desk as he finished writing with a goose-feather pen. He was a good-looking man of about thirty with shoulder-length hair brushed back from a narrow forehead, and scraggy sideburns reaching down to his chin. He was dressed like a typically prosperous Presbyterian merchant in a fine frock coat, striped waistcoat and knotted silk cravat. On the wall above the fireplace hung a framed parchment with the words 'Hope for the future lies in France which has recently burst her chains, demolished the strong hold of despotism and laid the foundation of a noble pile, a Temple of Universal Liberty.'

Mr Neilson placed the pen in the ink pot and handed me what he had written. It was an editorial on slavery. He asked, 'What do you think of the last sentence?'

It said that the abuse in America must end but that there was an immediate need to achieve the freedom of the three million slaves in Ireland.

'I agree, sir,' I said. 'Wholeheartedly.'

'Do you think there should be immediate Catholic emancipation?'

'Yes,' I replied, 'the Catholic question should be settled.'

'There is no Catholic question,' he snapped. 'There is no more a Catholic question than a Presbyterian, a Quaker, an Anabaptist or a Mountain question. The true question is whether Irishmen should be free.'

He reached into a large wooden box behind his chair and took out *The Rights of Man*.

'Have you read this?' he asked.

'Yes, sir. I have my own copy.'

'You have?'

I explained I had studied Paine's definition of a perfect republic, where the poor are not oppressed, the rich are not privileged, the government is just and there is no cause for the people to engender riots and tumults, and that I longed for such an outcome for Ireland.

He raised an eyebrow. 'Indeed,' he exclaimed.

Opening a silver box, the *Star* editor placed a pinch of snuff on the back of his hand and lifted it delicately to his nostrils. He told me that the purpose of his newspaper was to publicise the aims of the Societies of United Irishmen, formed by himself and several notable patriots in a tavern in Belfast's Crown Entry the previous October. These were to unite all creeds, to promote religious liberty and equality, to stop landlords evicting honest farmers, to end the payment of tithes to the established church, and to throw out corrupt lords from the parliament in Dublin and replace them with good men elected by universal suffrage.

'In short,' he announced, 'this newspaper will educate the public in the ideals of the French Revolution.'

He got me to recount the story of the barring out of the mathematics room. 'Did you really take a shot at Bruce?'

'Ach, no,' I replied. 'It was at Bristow.'

He raised his eyebrow again with a half-smile. 'When can you start?' he enquired.

'Now,' I replied.

Next day, Thursday 26 April 1792, I began work at the *Northern Star*. Billy took me in hand. My new friend told me that the *Star* had been launched three months previously, that it came out twice a week, on Wednesdays and Saturdays, and that it was in competition with the long-established *Belfast News-Letter*.

'They are the enemy,' he said. 'Our goal is to overtake the *News-Letter* in circulation. People buy the *Star* mainly because we carry more news from France which everybody is mad to get. And we are more radical.'

The head printer, John Storey, expressed delight at meeting 'a real rebel boyo'. He saw me looking at his blackened fingers. 'The acid in the ink does that,' he said. 'It's got arsenic, to make the ink dry more quickly.'

In the printing room, over a constant clicking and clacking from the wood-framed presses, Storey showed me how a compositor fitted letters into a frame called a coffin at the base of the printing machine. A boy kept him supplied with tiny wooden letters from box shelves in a back room. I was astonished at the ability of Storey to read the upside-down words. A worker poured ink onto a polished slate table and rolled it on the letters, then brought down a frame called a tympan to hold the paper. The printed sheets were taken to a drying room where a coal fire burned day and night, then folded to make up a two-page newspaper. 'As many words as possible are crammed into the columns,' Storey explained. 'That's why we use small letters. *Brevier* type. No internal angles so they don't become ink traps.'

Storey interspersed his lecture with jokes. 'Hey, young fellow,' he said. 'What did the printer say to the compositor who wouldn't stop talking? Get to the point.'

I didn't quite know what my job would be, or what I would be paid. But from the start I loved everything about the *Star*, the noise and bustle and the smell of the paper and the ink and the acid, and the clowning around. Most of all I felt that I would be part of something that would change Ireland for the better.

Mr Neilson came in late and looked me over with a critical eye. 'We'll have to make you respectable,' he said. He sent me to a tailor's shop in Rosemary Street opposite the Old Sugar House, owned by his friend Joseph Cuthbert. There was a notice in his window advertising theatre tickets. *The Beggar's Opera* was playing; very apt in my circumstances.

Joe Cuthbert, fresh-faced and fussy, exclaimed in mock horror with his hand to his mouth on seeing the scars when I removed my shirt. After taking my measurements, he gave me a clean shirt on account. As I put it on, he quizzed me about the barring out.

'Bristow is not such a bad mayor,' he said. 'You shouldn't have fired at him. But by God I admire your spunk. Come back tomorrow.'

That evening I washed dishes and tankards in Kelly's Cellars until midnight. Mr O'Kane took pity on me and moved me to the spare room above the bar when everyone had gone. From the smell of sweat and perfume, I guessed the bed was put to good use several times a day.

Next morning Mr Neilson instructed me to acquaint myself with back editions in the reading room and to note well the names of the merchants who advertised their wares, as he relied on their money as well as their enlightened support.

The first edition carried a letter from the former African slave Gustava Vassa wishing blessings and joy to the *Northern Star*. I had seen him a few months earlier. Senior boys at the academy were brought to hear him speak in the Assembly Rooms about his book on the conditions of slaves in America. He was elegant and articulate and dressed like a prince. Ladies fluttered around him. I remember thinking, how could such a fine man be bought and sold?

In his editorials Mr Neilson excoriated Belfast's overlord, George Augustus Chichester, 2nd Marquess of Donegall, for treating Belfast as a rotten borough. Lord Donegall chose the twelve members of the Corporation who in turn elected the two Belfast members to the Dublin parliament. The town's grand hotel, the Donegall Arms, was named after him.

There were long columns about the triumphs of the French Revolution and the progress of the French armies in Austria, along with news of the latest Paris fashions, which introduced me to a whole new lexicon. Women's hair should be *frizzled* with full, large loose curls, five on each side, interjected with a garland of *coquelicots*, and set off by globular earrings. They should wear a gown of chemise of *nakara* satin, the top of the *flounce* trimmed with black satin and white gloves. Gentleman should have their hair divided at the crown, sliding down in a full *frisure*, ending at the bottom in a long curl, and they should wear a lapelled scarlet coat with white convex buttons and a sky-blue double-breasted waistcoat.

Some Belfast merchants listed their wares in every edition. Thomas Mullan regularly advertised that his grocery and haberdashery on the quays had cinnamon and French cordials, truffles, olives, anchovies, gherkins, capers, salad oil, best white wine vinegar, brandied fruits, Narbonne honey, lavender waters, Naples and Marseille soap, citron and vermicelli macaroni, French apples, plums, prunes, walnuts, cloves, nutmeg, cayenne, and other peppers, figs, raisins, lemons and oranges. Martin Tennent of Waring Street 'expected daily' in every edition a parcel of new hops but meanwhile he had Bordeaux brandy, strong whiskey, London porter, Red Port, claret, sherry, old Malaga wine in butts and quarter casks, vinegar, raspberry and cherry juice and Seltzer water. William Dawson, goldsmith and jeweller of North Street, offered diamond and pearl settings in clusters, hollow-backed and plain rings, bracelets, lockets, breast pins, paste and enamel borders, Venetian glass, watch chains and trinkets, braided hair rings and knee buckles.

I came across a survey of Belfast published the previous year giving its population as 18,320, the number of houses at 1,081, and the number of publicans licensed to sell spirits and strong beer 167. I did a quick calculation. That was one tavern for every 17 houses. Belfast floated on a sea of alcohol. It was not surprising, seeing the town water was so foul. Better to drink ale.

That evening Joseph Cuthbert outfitted me in high-collared frock coat, breeches buttoned at the knee, cotton stockings, and tongue and buckle shoes. In the street gentlemen bade me good day who would have ignored me before.

Next day Mr Neilson put me to work in the front office with Billy Templeton. Billy looked very important, with big, round spectacles clipped to his nose and a quill permanently behind his right ear. We perched on high chairs behind a wooden counter. Our job was to help merchants compose their advertisements, and to rewrite some of the foreign news that came in on the packet ships.

'The *Northern Star* is the engine of change. Change is ordained. Always remember that,' the editor told me. 'As mankind becomes more informed, it becomes more wise and virtuous. This is the consequence of knowledge, the effect of intelligence, the result of truth and reason.'

Word had evidently got round that the *Star* had hired the academy rebel. Some readers who called in looked at me askance, but others shook my hand for taking a shot at Bruce.

'Bristow,' I corrected them. 'And I only fired at the door.'

George Gray graduated and came round to say farewell before returning to the family farm to begin applying the principles of husbandry he had learned. He whistled at my new appearance.

'Crime pays,' he said, looking me over.

'It does,' I replied. 'Everyone treats me like I am Paul Revere.'

Pupils at the academy, and even some of the tutors, now referred to the mathematics room as Liberty Hall, George said. 'The bad news is that all your fellow-conspirators have also been expelled.' He invited me to come back to Gransha any time. It seems I had made a good impression. I gave him a note for his father thanking him for his hospitality and expressing warm appreciation for the nursing skills of his beautiful daughter.

'Make sure Betsy sees it,' I said.

'I'll have to keep an eye on you,' said George.

Mr Neilson called me up to his office a few days later. He told me to continue working with Billy for the time being, but that he would have 'special assignments' for me in due course. He had paid close attention to my rewrites. 'Do you know that one of the reasons I hired you was because the Reverend Bruce said you have a great talent with words.' 'Did old Brucie say that?' 'Indeed, yes,' he replied. 'He actually thinks you are quite smart but a bit of a ruffian and far too radical. And that's the other reason I hired you of course. I need someone like you. You will find out why soon enough.'

He gave me a guinea and said that my salary would be £25 a year. He produced a small book with the instruction to study it daily. It was a primer on shorthand by Samuel Taylor.

My editor also found lodgings for me, with a lady called Martha McTier, who had a spare room in her house in Cunningham Row.

'She's very well connected and runs a school for girls,' he said. 'Her brother, William Drennan, is one of the founders of the United Irishmen. He wrote the constitution. He lives in Dublin now. He has an accoucheur practice there.' I looked blank. 'He delivers babies. And Martha's husband, Samuel McTier, is ballast master at the Harbour Commission and he is also a founding member of the United Irishmen. These are very respectable, worthy people. Martha is a real society woman and likes to gamble at the card tables and she knows everything that goes on in this town. Make sure you get on with her. You might even meet Wolfe Tone there. He has graced her table more than once.'

I found the McTiers' two-storey thatched house just fifteen minutes' walk from the *Star*. Though early in the day, Mrs McTier was dressed stylishly with long brown hair tied back with a white scarf. 'So you are the academy boy,' she said, looking me up and down. Sam McTier shook my hand vigorously. He seemed convivial and good-natured. He showed me to an upstairs back room with a bed and a table overlooking the yard and invited me to dine with them that evening.

At dinner they made me tell the story of the siege at the academy. 'Your behaviour was reprehensible and you am lucky not to be in jail,' scolded Mrs McTier. But like everyone else she seemed more amused than outraged. Sam McTier chuckled and said, 'I like a good election riot myself.'

The Revd Bruce sometimes came calling and if we encountered one another I should pay him every respect, said Mrs McTier. I promised. But they didn't have much time for him either. 'The good Dr Bruce wraps himself up in self-importance and his wife is a shrew who apes his manner foolishly,' commented my new landlady. 'The better sort only like him in the pulpit and constantly snub him and his ignorant wife at genteel parties.'

How my life had changed in just three weeks. I had my own room, an exciting job, a salary, new clothes and a reputation as a firebrand which did me less harm than good.

Billy Templeton cautioned me not to take anything for granted however.

Over a now-regular tankard of ale in Flanagan's on the quays – I learned fast the ways of the newspaper world – he warned me that the *Northern Star* might not last. Sam Neilson had sunk all his money into it and had no reserve capital. The rival *Belfast News-Letter* was well funded and had been on the go for fifty-five years. People could afford only one newspaper and it was a devil to get them to switch to the *Star*. The *News-Letter's* proprietor Henry Joy paid lip service to the need for reform. We had to be more radical.

Billy and I began to have some fun together. We bought tickets from Mr Cuthbert for a performance of *Signor Spinacuta and His Performing Monkey* at Greg's yard in Arthur Street. The Signor wore a big turban and introduced his monkey as *Le Chevalier des Singes*. It walked a tightrope and did tricks with hoops and a wheelbarrow. There were loud boos when someone shouted that it was a child dressed up. Spinacuta and the monkey-child left in a hurry. We chased them down Arthur Street but they did a disappearing trick.

In the evenings I struggled by candlelight with Taylor's book on shorthand, and before long I was able to write 'the Right Honourable John Foster rose and said he wished to bring forward a matter of the utmost consequence to Ireland' as 'th rt Vnr jn fstr rs sd h wshd br-ing fr-ward mtr v Vtmst kn t rlnd.' It's silly, I thought. A whole book just to tell me to leave out the vowels.

— THREE —

THE MAN IN THE TOP HAT

Two weeks after I started work for the *Northern Star* John Storey took me into the printing room and invited me to join the Society of the United Irishmen. A thickset man with receding hair, John was immensely popular, always jesting and playing tricks, but he was deadly serious now. This was politics. I had been anticipating the moment with some eagerness.

And so it was that on the following evening, Friday 11 May 1792, in a room in Alexander's tavern, in the presence of John and other members, I was sworn into Belfast Society No. 69 of the United Irishmen. With my hand on the Bible, I agreed that the weight of English influence should be balanced by a union of all Irish people; that the sole constitutional way of opposing English influence was a complete and radical reform of parliament in Dublin; and that no reform was just that did not include Irishmen of all religious persuasions.

Amid the congratulations, John's brother, Tom, a pamphlet printer as burly as his brother, took my arm and gripped it hard. 'Come here,' he said, leading me to a bench at the back of the room. 'You are the type of person we need. Radical ideas, commitment, clever, all that. But if you want to change things, you have to keep a cool head. No more firing off pistols for devilment. That was really stupid, you know. You could have got yourself hanged. You are a liability if you are not disciplined.'

I hung my head and promised with sincerity to obey his instructions. But privately I thought to myself that everything good that happened to me came from my acts of impetuosity, first being insolent to Baron Francis Rawdon, then firing the pistol at the academy. I had an education that lads in Moira could never aspire to, and now I had a position in the *Northern Star.* So perhaps it wasn't that stupid at all. But I knew I was in a different category now and my luck could easily run out.

Around this time I was also forced to confront my failings as a son. Mrs McTier told me that the Revd Bruce had called for tea and mentioned that he had sent letters to my father and my benefactor about my dangerous behaviour and my expulsion. 'I presume you have written to your father?' she asked me. 'And Baron Rawdon? To thank him and explain yourself?' I stayed silent. She pointed to her desk with inkpot and quill beside it. I should be particularly grateful to my benefactor, she said. 'He is quite radical, you know, and the better type of landlord.'

So I wrote to Baron Francis in Ballynahinch. I thanked him for his patronage and apologised for not finishing my final year at the academy. I assured him that his investment in my education was already bearing fruit, though I doubt he would have approved of the radicalism of the *Northern Star.*

I owed it to my father and mother to go and give them an account of myself. A letter would not suffice.

A steady drizzle soaked me to the skin on the four-hour walk to Moira. My father shook my hand at the door. They had been very disappointed to receive the letter from Revd Bruce about my expulsion, though word had already got back to the village. I asked them for their forbearance and not to judge me too harshly, and elicited some sympathy when I showed them the scars on my back.

I could see they were actually quite proud of me. The *Northern Star* was all the rage among the progressive people in Moira. Workers gathered in barns to hear it read aloud. My father was concerned, however, that the campaign for reform and Catholic emancipation might stir up the prejudices of the anti-Papists. Most Presbyterians in Moira were behind reform, he said, but old hatreds died hard.

He reminded me of the bloody history of Moira. The biggest battle in Gaelic lore was waged in nearby pastures over a thousand years earlier, when Celtic kings fought for control of Ulster at Aughnafosker, the 'field of slaughter'. Then the English came and its soldiers were awarded land for subduing the natives. A vast tract around Moira was confiscated from the Catholic Irish and given to an English army major from Yorkshire called George Rawdon, the ancestor of Lord Moira. Hundreds of Presbyterians from Scotland, like my great-grandfather, came to settle and work as tenant farmers. They were wary of the Catholic neighbours who used to own the land.

'This is a new era,' I said. 'The French Revolution shows we can trust the Roman Catholics and unite with them to end injustices.'

'I hope so,' responded my father.

Uncles and aunts and cousins came round in the evening and we had a ceili. They saw me as a town boy now, and a bit of a lad.

Next morning I walked with my father through the demesne to the greenhouse where we had worked together planting out seedlings and cataloguing exotic plants. I was sad to see that the new tenant of the castle was not keeping it up. The stove was no longer lit. Old Lord Moira never visited his rented-out property, having made his home at a new mansion, Montalto, in Ballynahinch. My father had helped transport cuttings of rare plants there. Moira's son, my patron, Baron Francis, was away a lot, hobnobbing with royalty in London.

Their agent Claiborne rode over from Ballynahinch occasionally to collect rents and evict those who couldn't pay.

'Watch out for that man,' my father warned. 'He is a bad lot. He will never forget you made him a laughing stock. I don't want you coming to a bad end. You are our only son and we worry about you.'

I got a lift on a cart back to Belfast that afternoon, with butter and eggs for the McTiers. It was so hot the butter melted.

I arrived back at my lodgings to find Martha McTier had another guest. A tall man, with long curling side-burns, large black eyebrows and a top hat appeared on the stairs.

I had heard a lot about Thomas Russell in the *Star* office. He was an Anglican, descended from gentry in Cork, and had served as a British army officer in India, yet he was as radical as any Belfast Presbyterian and was a co-founder of the United Irishmen. He greeted me in a melodious up-country accent.

'Martha has told me about you,' he declared. 'I want to hear all about your *contretemps* with old Brucie.'

Over dinner I obliged and he laughed heartily. He recalled that he and Wolfe Tone once had a furious row with the Revd Bruce, at the same table where we were sitting. The academy principal had come out with wild notions about Catholics, saying they would revive claims to land titles and would form a government of scavengers incapable of enjoying liberty. Tone had been roused to a fury. He had called him 'an intolerant high priest', and Bruce and his wife had departed in a huff.

Russell, who to my astonishment didn't take off his top hat even at table, confided that he was thinking of giving up his job as a magistrate in Dungannon, because he objected having to administer oaths of allegiance to recruits for the English army. 'Dublin Castle will be glad to get rid of me,' he said. 'They regard me as a dangerous republican.'

'The people aren't republican,' he said, giving an account of his travels around the countryside. 'They love the King, but they hate the government.'

He believed that ownership of property by a few was at the heart of Ireland's corrupt and hypocritical governance. These few had corrupt morals: they held shameful views on adultery, gaming, duelling and luxury, and considered them honourable.

'This comes from the rich making laws,' he said. 'Property is put before life. Property must be altered in some measure.'

Martha asked him if his views applied equally to men and women.

'Has it ever occurred to anatomists to observe is there any difference in the brains of men and women?' he replied. 'Women in public office – queens, poetesses – are as clever as men. In merchants' houses they keep the accounts as well as men.'

Everything that this strange former officer said struck a chord with me. I found his conversation stimulating and insightful. I thought to myself that to be a dangerous republican was a worthy ambition. I resolved to become his friend.

After dinner, in keeping with a promise I'd made my mother to start attending church again, I asked the company for guidance. Belfast had only one Anglican church and one Roman Catholic church but we Presbyterians were spoilt for choice. We had five places of worship, three of them in nearby Rosemary Street, called the 'First', 'Second' and 'Third' Presbyterian churches. The Revd Bruce preached in the First Presbyterian Church so that was out. I opted for the Third Presbyterian Church as the most radical, though Martha called the minister, the Revd Sinclair Kelburn, 'a hypocritical little spitfire'. Kelburn made no secret of his distaste for the English connection, and in company he and his wife always refused to stand for a toast to the King.

Over time I came to appreciate that Martha had a great way of sizing people up and putting them down. She delighted in gossip. Every week she wrote a letter to her brother Dr Drennan in Dublin about the goings-on in Belfast and she would put on her oval tortoiseshell spectacles and read aloud his replies, detailing political intrigues in the capital. I learned from her how important William Drennan was as the chief architect, poet and balladeer of tthe United Irishmen, which he likened to a 'benevolent conspiracy'.

Sam Neilson was always eager to know what Drennan was writing to Martha, and I happily told him. I guessed this was partly why he arranged for me to stay with the McTiers. And Sam and Martha were content when I brought snippets of information from the *Star* office. I loved being first with the news and I happily conveyed the tittle-tattle back and forth. I had stumbled upon my true calling. Like Billy Templeton I found myself starting conversations by asking 'What's going on?' 'What's the latest news?'

Mrs McTier decided she liked me and that I needed to learn some etiquette. She brought me to the Assembly Rooms above the Exchange at the corner of North Street and Waring Street and started to teach me how to play whist, piquet and faro. Belfast society met there for coteries, dancing classes, drama groups and card games, or just for cakes in the coffee room. The building, designed by the famous English architect Sir Robert Taylor, was the beating heart of Belfast, and grand balls and town meetings took place in the main hall on the first floor, with its decorated eggshell-blue walls and arched wooden ceiling.

The younger ladies there were more concerned with my looks than my reputation. 'Isn't he a lovely lad,' one would say. 'Gorgeous,' another would respond, loud enough for me to hear. They tittered behind their fans and fluttered their eyes at me. I feigned not to notice.

I got a chance to call upon my friend George Gray when Mr Neilson asked me to ride out to north Down to see if circulation of the *Star* could be increased. The editor provided me with a list of subscribers and a plodding white mare from the office stables. It was called, as a joke, Eclipse, after the famous racehorse that inspired the phrase, 'Eclipse first and the rest nowhere'.

I bought brandied fruits and Naples soap from Thomas Mullen on the quays and a copy of William Cowper's anti-slavery book, *The Task*, to bring as gifts, and set out on a lovely June morning across the Long Bridge and towards Newtownards.

For two days I talked to subscribers and farmers and anyone I chanced to meet on the roads to assess the general mood. All the talk was of the big parade planned for Belfast on 14 July to celebrate the fall of the Bastille. The French Revolution had fired up the people. Everyone was eager to get news of the French invasion of Austria and the spread of Liberty.

Overnight I stayed in William McCormick's inn in Newtownards. The landlord told me the *Star* had become very popular but most folk could not afford it, even though we sold it at two pence a copy, half a penny less than the *News-Letter*. Labourers earned only six pence a day, he said, and many sympathisers had already paid an annual subscription to the *Belfast News-Letter*.

In the seaside village of Donaghadee I was told bluntly most people 'are too poor to gratify themselves with a second entertainment.'

At length I arrived at the Gray household. Hans and George were eager to hear the latest from Belfast, and Betsy wanted to know all about the progress of the French armies. I presented her with *The Task*, earning a sweet kiss on the cheek. 'They say Robert Burns carries it around in his pocket,' I told her.

Several neighbours came by after dinner. I was a bit more of a curiosity now as the man from the *Northern Star*. I was quizzed as if I knew everything going on in the Dublin parliament and the French battlefields. And I did know a fair amount from the dispatches we received from the packet ships, the columns we reprinted from the *London News* and from Drennan's letters to Martha.

Betsy, very pretty in a muslin dress, her red hair tied back with a ribbon, sat on the grass outside with her best friends, Eliza Bryson, a fair-haired lass with soulful green eyes and full breasts, and Willie Boal, a solid, dark-haired, taciturn lad, a bit younger than me. George whispered to me that Willie was Betsy's childhood sweetheart. That's that, I thought.

I stayed the night in the kitchen loft and was wakened at five by the crowing of the demented cock. Betsy provided a breakfast of stirabout with milk. I walked with her and George to the crossroads to buy dinner from a Donaghadee fishmonger, who stood by his cart singing, 'Herrings alive, fresh and stinking, Come to the cart and see them winking.' I declined to buy some for the McTiers – they really would have been stinking by the time I got to Belfast.

Betsy took both our hands as we walked back. 'My two big brothers,' she said.

'We will look after you if trouble comes,' I joked as I mounted Eclipse.

'Don't be so sure,' said George. 'When the bit comes to the bit, she'll be the one looking after us.'

Next morning Mr Neilson called a meeting of staff in his office. He announced that in future he would allow subscribers to pay the nineteen shillings annual subscription in arrears. No newspaper had tried that before. He worried we might have trouble collecting the money and instructed us to brook no nonsense from subscribers.

After slowly and deliberately inhaling snuff from his silver box, he informed us that the *Northern Star* circulation had reached 4,000, exceeding that of the *Belfast News-Letter* in just six months. He allowed himself a rare smile. 'Anyone who wants can join me in Peggy Barclay's,' he announced.

Peggy Barclay's tavern, round the corner in Sugar House Entry, was the paper's drinking hole. It was always busy, with a staff of more than twenty serving girls, waiters and potboys. As the *Star* workers crowded round the main bar counter Mr Neilson took my arm and said, 'Come with me.' He led the way up the creaking stairs and along a dark passageway to the end room. 'Welcome to the Muddlers' Club,' he said.

In the light from candelabra in wall holders I read the rules of the club displayed on the chimneypiece. 'Rule number one: The business of the club is jovial amusement.' 'In reality,' said Mr Neilson standing behind me, 'it is here that United Irishmen can meet privately and exchange information.' Several men sat at two long wooden tables on rough-hewn benches, clutching tankards of ale. Among them was Thomas Russell, still wearing his top hat. We joined them.

Neilson was in fine form and kept the bar girl busy running up and down the stairs. Russell got quite drunk and, with one arm around a buxom serving wench, recited William Cowper's poem, 'The Negro's Complaint':

Forced from home and all its pleasures
  Afric's coast I left forlorn
To increase a stranger's treasures
  O'er the raging billows borne.
Men from England bought and sold me
  Paid my price in paltry gold
But though slave they have enrolled me
  Minds are never to be sold.

Everyone shouted 'Bravo!' and banged their tankards on the table. I was to learn that Russell always ended up reciting 'The Negro's Complaint' when he'd had a few jars.

Shortly afterwards Russell and the wench disappeared.

Sam got quite intoxicated that evening. He had every reason to celebrate. The articles of partnership of the *Northern Star* had at last been drawn up and the directors came the next Monday morning to sign them. We lined up to shake hands with some of Belfast's most respected citizens: the merchants William Tennent, John Boyle and William and Robert

Simms, the shipbroker Henry Haslett, the publisher William Magee, the linen draper Gilbert McIlveen, the tanner William McCleery, the woollen draper John Haslett, the banker Robert Caldwell, our publisher John Rabb and Neilson himself, the town's wealthiest woollen merchant, at least until he ploughed his fortune into the paper.

Most of these Presbyterian gentlemen were in on the founding of the United Irishmen with Wolfe Tone. They had given the *Star* a sound financial basis. The company issued forty shares at fifty pounds each. Neilson took thirteen and the other directors divided up the remainder, which worked out at about three shares a head.

As they left, Robert Simms pointed with his umbrella at the English crown over the harp on the *Star*'s masthead above the door. 'When are we going to get rid of that?' he demanded. It wasn't clear if he meant from the masthead, or from Ireland.

— FOUR —

BASTILLE DAY

The biggest event in Belfast that summer was the commemoration on Saturday 14 July of the storming of the Bastille in Paris three years earlier. A huge turnout was planned, led by uniformed units of the Volunteers. It would signal to Dublin, and the world, our determination to follow the French example.

The Volunteers were raised by Protestant gentry ten years earlier to help defend the country against an invasion by Royalist France, at a time when Britain was heavily engaged fighting the Americans. They were allowed to carry arms but were not subject to government control. Lots of young gentlemen joined for want of anything better to do and paraded around in smart uniforms. But the Volunteers had become a thorn in the government's side, especially in the northern counties. They demanded reform of parliament, admission of Roman Catholics to the legislature and an end to unjust trade laws imposed by England. They began enrolling respectable Papists. It was the nearest thing Ireland ever had to a patriot army. Since the end of the American war, the viceroy and his cronies in Dublin Castle had been trying to stand down the Volunteers, terrified that they might rise up against them.

'Only here in Belfast are the Volunteers still a formidable force,' said Sam. 'We'll see a great show of strength on Saturday. Wolfe Tone himself is coming as representative of the Catholic Committee in Dublin.' 'How can he represent Catholics?' I asked. 'He's a Protestant.' 'Of course,' replied Neilson. 'Anglican actually, but none the worse for that. He is so enthusiastic about the Catholic cause that they have made him their secretary. He will address the Bastille Day crowd on the need for political and religious union. Some of our brethren from Armagh can't abide the thought of linking arms with the Papists, but it has to happen.'

To make sure Belfast would be *en fête* for the parade, a Harp Festival was scheduled for the two days preceding. It was organised by a committee of leading citizens, headed by Dr James MacDonnell, an Irish-speaking convert to Protestantism from County Antrim, who was an intimate friend of all the leading Belfast radicals.

On the eve of the Harp Festival, people began arriving in Belfast from every province. Wolfe Tone came on the mail coach from Dublin along with the head of the Catholic Committee, a silk merchant in his fifties called John Keogh. They were entertained at the Donegall Arms. The taverns that evening were full of people drinking to the sound of fiddles and flutes and stamping feet and endless toasts to Liberty.

In the Muddlers' Club I made the acquaintance of Henry Joy McCracken, one of the most respected Presbyterians in the town, owner of a cotton mill with a reputation as a good employer. A tall, good-looking man of about thirty-five, with small features and rust-coloured curls tumbling down over his forehead, he came over to shake my hand. 'I hear you are the *Star* man who fired off at the sovereign,' he said. 'I had a run-in with Bristow myself. I started a Sunday school in the Market House with a few members of the industrious classes to teach reading and writing to boys and girls, of all religions. Bristow arrived one day with a number of ladies, wielding rods as badges of authority, and closed us down for breaching the Sabbath. He said children should only read Bibles. What a foolish, ignorant fellow he is.'

Ten harpers were registered for the festival. Six of them were blind and most were ancient. They strummed and thrummed and twanged all afternoon to polite applause from semicircles of women in bonnets and men in powdered wigs perched on cushioned chairs in the Assembly Rooms. The rest of us stood at the back. There was a terrible crush when the famous Derry harpist Denis Hampson took the stage. Called the 'man with two heads' because of a large growth on his neck, Hampson was so accomplished that the other harpers refused to come on after he had played.

He was ninety-six and blind and was said to have sired a daughter in his seventies. We fell absolutely silent as he plucked out with long, crooked fingernails the haunting strains of 'The Dawning of the Day'.

During a break in the afternoon of the second day, Sam Neilson came to the coffee room with Wolfe Tone and introduced me as the 'young radical I've been telling you about.' The founder and inspiration of the United Irishman had thin lips and brown hair tied with ribbon in a pigtail and his forehead slanted in parallel with his nose. I anticipated approval from the great man, but instead I got a lecture on the careless use of guns. At Trinity College he had acted as second in a duel over a frivolous affair. As a result, his best friend was killed by a bullet in the head. 'It was foolish beyond reason,' he said. Red-faced, I nodded vigorously in agreement.

Tone was in a sour mood with everybody. 'I was given too much punch last night,' he complained. 'My head aches and I feel as stupid as a mill horse.' He was not enjoying the harpers. 'Seven of them are execrable. Only three of them are any good. It's just *strum, strum, strum*, and be hanged. There's no new musical discovery to be found here. Anyway, all the good Irish tunes are already written.'

Waddell Cunningham, the richest merchant in Belfast, came by in silks and powdered wig, his face wrinkled like a prune from his years in the tropics as a pirate and sugar plantation owner. He once tried to get Belfast merchants to invest in slave ships but a watch-maker called Thomas McCabe shamed him by declaring, 'May God eternally damn the soul of the man who subscribes the first guinea.' Not one did. Cunningham liked to boast that his Negro slaves in Dominica were happier than the lower classes in England. He added to his riches by speculating on the land of evicted farmers in County Antrim. 'Insufferable prig,' Martha called him. The whole town knew that he kept a whore in Dublin and that he had had triplets by a kitchen maid. The old lecher gave Tone a curt greeting and passed on in a little cloud of perfume.

'Be wary of him', said Neilson. 'He is trying to turn the Volunteers against the Catholics.'

'Oh I know all about Cunningham,' said Tone. 'He's a lying old scoundrel. I had a furious battle with him over dinner last year in McTiers.

It lasted for two hours. He can't abide the Catholics getting their rights.'

Walking back to the *Star* office with Sam Neilson, I took the opportunity to enquire how I should address him. I was still somewhat in awe of this dour, idealistic man, more than ten years my senior, who had elevated me from schoolboy to newspaper man. I had spent too much time drinking with him by then to call him Mister Neilson, but maybe he would think me impudent if I started to call him Samuel. What would he prefer? 'Call me Sam,' he said. 'But never Sammy.'

Next day Hampson had just finished playing 'Deirdre's Lament for the Sons of Usneach' when I heard a voice in my ear saying, 'I'm here too.' It was Betsy. She was with George. 'Don't you look the fine gentleman now,' she laughed, eyeing me up and down. I am sure I blushed.

In the coffee room we chatted about the latest news from Europe. George thought that war between England and France was inevitable, because of the French success in spreading revolutionary principles across Europe, and he feared that it would be used as an excuse to crush Irish aspirations for freedom.

'On the contrary,' I argued. 'Haven't you heard? – England's misfortune will be Ireland's opportunity.' 'Who said that?' asked George. 'I did,' I replied, laughing.

I tried to avoid gazing at Betsy. Her red hair shone. Her pale skin glowed. She smelled of lavender soap. She was barely sixteen, but was already an attractive and fully formed young woman.

A stout young man wearing wire-rimmed glasses and short-style breasted waistcoat came by and greeted Betsy merrily. 'How do you know Edward Bunting?' I asked as the portly young musician who had recruited the harpists passed on, shaking everyone by the hand. 'He gave me pianoforte lessons,' she said. George laughed and declared that their father was intent on making his daughter a refined young lady. I said, 'Sure she already is.' This time she blushed.

On the Saturday morning Sam Neilson gave Billy and me graphite sticks and paper to record the great commemoration of the liberation of the Bastille. It began at nine in the morning of a clear, hot day. I counted fifteen corps of Volunteers parading in full uniform on foot and on horseback along High Street, with green flags and banners proclaiming '*Erin go bragh*' and drummer boys keeping up a tattoo. One banner stated 'Our French brother was born on 14 July 1789. Alas, we are still in embryo.' Another, 'The Irish Bastille, Let Us Unite to Destroy It.' Peddlers sold French flags and Bastille Day jugs with an etching of the Paris prison being torn down. Wolfe Tone rode by in regimentals of white waistcoat and green uniform with gold epaulets. Units from Muckamore, Dromore, Larne, Bandalstown, Ballynahinch, Moira, Downpatrick, Carrickfergus and Broughshane were cheered by big crowds past the Donegall Arms, which was draped with French and American flags, and along Mill Street to the reviewing field on the Falls. Thousands were gathered there from all over the north.

The delegation heads huddled in an adjoining potato field to discuss the wording of the speech Tone would make that evening on behalf of them all. There was so much arguing and shouting it was difficult to take notes in my vowel-free shorthand. Tone said he planned to make a '*déclaration des droits de l'homme et du citoyen*' and to call for approval of the full and immediate emancipation of the Catholics. Volunteer captains from Armagh and south Down argued that this was too much for many of the Presbyterian Volunteers to swallow. Sam Neilson himself suggested such a call might be rejected and that it could set back the cause of unity. He revealed that he and Wolfe Tone had found Waddell Cunningham whipping up anti-Papist fervour among some delegates in his room at the Donegall Arms. 'I see some of you here,' he said, looking around.

As head of the Catholic Committee, John Keogh himself argued that a more moderate appeal would impress the government. Tone, in exasperation, agreed to drop the word 'Catholics'. Instead, he would call for equality of Irishmen of 'every religious denomination'. That settled the matter.

I was surprised to see Tone deferring to Keogh. Only later did I learn that he regarded the Catholic leader, whom he called 'Gog', as so insufferably vain and self-important that Tone thought it better 'to stand behind the curtain and to advise Gog' rather than to confront him.

I pushed through the crowds until I found Betsy and George. Betsy had tied back her hair with a green ribbon and George had laurel leaves in his hat. Betsy linked us, her eyes shining with excitement. We couldn't talk much, such was the noise of pipes and flutes and drummers playing tattoos.

We walked with the parade as it returned to Linen Hall Street, led by the Artillery of the First Belfast Company and standard-bearers with a portrait of Benjamin Franklin and the colours of five nations: France, America, Great Britain, Poland and Ireland. They were followed by a triumphal cart drawn by four horses with a big canvas depicting the release of the prisoners from the Bastille on one side, and on the other a shackled Hibernia and the motto 'For a People to be Free, it is Sufficient that They Wish It.'

I left George and Betsy and headed to the White Linen Hall where three hundred and fifty-four patriots sat down to a grand dinner at which Wolfe Tone called for religious emancipation. He was supported by a large majority, including several Presbyterian clergymen, though some south Down Volunteers walked out, whether in protest or simply because they had a long march home wasn't made clear. I scribbled down the toasts: 'Success to the French Army', 'Confusion to the enemies of French liberty', 'To the memory of General Mirabeau', 'To the people of Poland and success to their arms', 'To the rights of man,' 'To the union of Irishmen'. Sam Neilson proposed 'The liberty of the press'. Tone was overwhelmed and shouted 'Huzzah!' to every declaration. He broke his glass banging it hard on the table and splashed wine over Gog. Then he got up and sang a song addressed to Irishmen that he had written himself. The conclusion of the final verse brought everyone to their feet cheering:

Then let us remember our madness no more,
What we lost by division, let union restore.
Let us firmly unite and our covenant be.
Together we fall, or together be free.

After the ladies left, we gentlemen, for I could call myself that now, made loud use of chamber pots behind screens in every corner and continued drinking until the wee hours.

— FIVE —

WE NEED THEM AND THEY NEED US

'I have a special task for you,' Sam Neilson told me in his office the following Monday. Wolfe Tone was there, perched on the edge of his desk. They planned to ride to Rathfriland in south Down to broker peace between Protestants and Catholics who had been rioting in the streets. If such scenes continued and spread, they could never hope for an alliance against the government.

'One side is as bad as the other,' said Tone. 'An ignorant rabble of the Catholic persuasion has been misled into acts of violence equalled by the Protestant side.'

Sam said he was taking his wife Ann. 'I want you to make notes,' he said. 'And I want a handy pair of fists if there is trouble.'

We saddled up next morning at seven and made our way along the Dublin turnpike to Banbridge, and on through hamlets infested with dogs as savage as wolves. They snapped at our horses' heels but Eclipse cantered on, ignoring them. It grew hot and my nose was soon blocked up with pollen.

Not far from Rathfriland we halted at a two-storey slated farm house called Linen Hill to spend the night. It belonged to the Lowry family. Alexander Lowry was a strong Presbyterian radical and family friend of Sam Neilson, whose father had been a Presbyterian minister in nearby Ballyroney. Rathfriland's Presbyterian minister, the Revd Samuel Barber, came to dine with us. He was even taller than me. 'Here he is,' said Lowry, as the clergyman ducked his head under the doorway. 'Six foot two without a shoe.'

A courteous, scholarly countryman in his fifties with a ruddy face framed by a mass of untidy white hair and a ready wit, Barber had managed to calm the situation in Rathfriland and had organised a gathering the next day to start a process towards peace.

I had to tell my story of the barring out again. Neilson seemed to delight in my episode but Barber, like Tone, warned me about allowing anger to get me into trouble. He quoted Tacitus: 'He that fights and runs away, May turn and fight another day; But he that is in battle slain, Will never rise to fight again.' 'All very well,' I said. 'But he that fights and runs away may get caught and be slain anyway.' I had occasion many years later to remember this exchange.

At daybreak Lowry and Barber escorted us into Rathfriland, a pleasant little town on top of a steep drumlin adjacent to the Mourne Mountains. We met the Protestant and Catholic delegates in the Clanwilliam Arms, a hostelry on the town square built with stones from the ruins of a castle that was once the stronghold of the Catholic Magennis chieftains. They included local Protestant magistrates and Volunteer officers in uniform. The atmosphere was civil. The Catholics were headed by John Keogh, who had ridden from Belfast on Sunday.

After much debate, and not a few whiskeys, a consensus was reached that the Protestants were the aggressors because they had attacked the funeral of a Catholic schoolmaster, but that they had been provoked for weeks by Catholics marching about in military array. A deal was made, which I dutifully recorded. The Catholics would stop marching and the Protestants would not riot against them. Everyone shook hands. My fists were not needed.

We went that evening to the New Light Presbyterian Church to hear the Revd Barber give a talk on the French Revolution. A mongrel dog sat upright beside the minister as he began his sermon. The Reverend described France as a happy country now, a refuge and asylum for the brave and good, like a lily on a hill in the midst of Europe, shedding light, liberty and humanity all around. 'In France the rights of man are sacred. There is no Bastille to imprison the soul, no religious establishment to shackle the body.' He quoted Tacitus again. He must have studied him well. 'A desire to resist oppression is implanted in the nature of man.'

At this point the dog put its paws on the Bible and yawned, provoking some hilarity. Barber joked that it was a Catholic dog converted by his oratory, but that it didn't tolerate long-winded sermons. 'So I'll stop now,' he said.

Next morning, after an immense breakfast of fried bacon, poached eggs, soda farls and porridge in wooden bowls, Neilson left his wife in my care and he and Tone excused themselves to meet privately with two Catholic merchants from Dundalk. They returned at midday and we took our leave of the Lowry family and set off for Belfast.

As we rode side by side Neilson confided that the merchants they had met were actually leaders of the Defenders, a Catholic self-defence organisation that had evolved from a sectarian group in County Armagh into a secret oath-bound society dedicated to revolution. He passed me a card one of them had given him containing the Defender oath. It called for 'The dethroning of all kings and the planting of the Tree of Liberty in our Irish land, where French Defenders will protect our cause and Irish Defenders will pull down British laws.'

'We need them,' said Neilson, 'And they need us. I just hope we can trust them. But without the Catholic Defenders we are on our own, and without the Presbyterian radicals the Defenders don't have the North. That's why the government is stirring up old hatreds, to divide the people, and it is hinting at concessions for Catholics to make them think their best interests lie with the Crown.'

'What concessions?'

'Granting the vote to wealthy Catholics,' said Neilson, 'but without giving them the right to sit in parliament.'

'What about Keogh?' I asked.

'He's a United Irishman but he's no rebel,' replied Sam. 'He defers to the Crown too much for my liking. He wants equality more than revolution. He'll stop at concessions one day.'

Wolfe Tone stayed on in Belfast after that and was much sought after in the dining rooms of the most prosperous merchants. He often dropped into the *Star* office late in the morning, badly hung over and complaining about how much he disliked the card clubs and coteries to which he was invited, and the squires he met 'who can talk about nothing else but fox-hunting, hare-hunting and buck-hunting.' He was very ungracious about Belfast society women. 'They are ugly and wear too much heavy make-up.'

One morning Sam Neilson told the head printer to take Billy Templeton and me up to Divis Mountain overlooking Belfast to learn how to use flintlock pistols properly.

John Storey had training in firearms in the Volunteers. He taught us to fire in volley so sparks did not ignite the other's powder when loading, and to use the ramrod to extinguish embers; otherwise the powder might explode prematurely. He explained the need to clean the barrel thoroughly after use, as sulphur residue from powder could turn into sulphuric acid and corrode the metal. 'If necessary in the heat of battle you can piss down the barrel to wash out encrustations,' he said. I also learned how to speed up loading by measuring out powder in paper cartridges. By the afternoon I could fire two rounds a minute.

Soon I was told what this was about. The peace deal in Rathfriland hadn't worked out. The Protestants had found out about the meeting with the Catholic Defenders and were furious. Rioting had taken place again. Sam Neilson and Wolfe Tone planned to return urgently to plead for unity, this time without Ann Neilson. It would be dangerous. I was to accompany them, armed with a case of pistols.

We guessed something was awry when we arrived at the Clanwilliam Arms in the late afternoon to meet the local Protestant gentry. No one turned up. The landlord refused us entry. A hostile crowd gathered across the square. We remounted. I primed a pistol with shaking hands and held it high to warn them off as we galloped away.

We rode across the Mourne Mountains and took overnight accommodation in the Catholic village of Rostrevor. There we were treated as liberators and provided with a dinner of broiled salmon and potatoes. Our disappointment was eased by several draughts of Bordeaux. Tone had by this time taken a liking to me. When I ventured that what we had experienced boded ill for the future, he slapped me on the back and said,

'Rathfriland was an aberration, young Willie K, it will not stop the growth of the Tree of Liberty. You'll see.' We drank to that.

On the return ride to Belfast we detoured via Ballynahinch where Tone desired to call on Baron Francis Rawdon at Montalto House. I declined to face my benefactor, having let him down by failing to complete the academy education for which he had paid. I waited in a local alehouse, of which there were thirty-six in the town – I counted them.

On resuming our journey Tone mentioned that Rawdon was quite sympathetic to the principles of the United Irishmen but had declined to join them, even after Tone held out the prospect that one day he might become president of an Irish republic. The baron in turn warned Tone of the bigotry of some of the bigger landlords in County Down, in particular Lord Annesley of Castlewellan, who mistreated Catholics and wanted to crush the Defenders. Baron Londonderry, who owned much of the Ards peninsula, was cut from the same cloth.

Our arrival back in Belfast coincided with exciting news from Paris. The monarchy had fallen. King Louis XVI had been arrested and imprisoned. The French Revolution was entering a new phase.

We gave Tone a splendid farewell supper and next day a large crowd saw him off on the Dublin coach with cheers and a forest of fluttering three-corner hats.

— SIX —

GIVING UP SUGAR

In a few months I had changed from a gangling youth to a keeper of secrets and man about town. I could now hold my liquor. I often drank until late, mostly in the Muddlers' Club. I felt I had made my mark there when the serving lass Belle Martin took to calling me by my first name. Belle was popular with the United Irish regulars. She was in her twenties, very fetching, with yellow hair and a mocking way of smiling with one eyebrow raised. She wore a low-cut blouse that revealed her generous breasts. She made sure to give us a look when bending to lift our tankards. The wench stooped to conquer. She sat on my knee one evening and I got terribly aroused. Belle jumped up and said, 'Oh Willie!' Everyone laughed. She had a reputation for being obliging to a select few who caught her fancy. I became quite obsessed with the thought that maybe she would oblige me one day. I still had no experience in that department.

That summer we got an idea of how resistant the Anglo-Irish establishment was to reform. The Dublin Corporation sent a resolution to King George pledging to preserve inviolate the Anglican Ascendancy in Ireland, which they defined as 'a Protestant King of Ireland, a Protestant Parliament, a Protestant hierarchy, Protestant elections and government, Protestant Benches of Justice and Army and Revenue, all supported by a Protestant realm in Britain.' Protestant meant Anglican only. We Presbyterians were banned from public office, just as the Catholics were. We could not aspire to a place in the decision-making process by which we were governed. We paid tithes to a church in which we did not worship. We did not have a say in how we were governed.

But I did have a pistol. Sam Neilson let me keep a firearm after our trip to Rathfriland, on condition that I looked after it and never took it out of the office without his permission.

Belfast stagnated and stank in a late-August heatwave, so on a Sunday morning I saddled up Eclipse and rode to Gransha. As I neared the lane that led to the Gray cottage I came across Betsy and Willie Boal on the road. They were picking blackberries and giggling. The mare whinnied and they turned and saw me. Betsy called out, 'Why it's you, Mr Kean.' They approached me hand in hand. How arrogant to think I could arrive at any time and expect her full attention.

I proceeded to the cottage and found George. I mentioned I had seen Betsy and Willie Boal and they seemed very close. George sighed. He said their father wanted Betsy to do well for herself but she seemed set on Boal. 'He's a good lad,' he said. 'Quiet type. He's the sort of person who takes a long time to make up his mind but when he does, nothing will stand in his way.'

I declined George's invitation to stay. That night, more put out than I cared to admit, I got quite intoxicated in Peggy Barclay's. Belle Martin helped me down the stairs with her bosom almost fully exposed but I was not capable of anything and I ended up being sick on Mill Street.

The mood in Belfast varied with the progress of the French armies. We were plunged into gloom when the Prussians made gains in their effort to restore the French king, and we became delirious with joy when the French revolutionary army prevailed, the Prussians retreated, the French monarchy was abolished and the first French Republic was declared. Householders fixed transparencies to their windows declaring: '*Vive la Republique*', '*Vive la Nation*', 'Irishmen! Look at France, Liberty and Equality', 'We are taxed, tithed and enslaved – we have only to unite to be free', 'The Rights of Man Established – Despotism prostrate', and 'Church and State divorced – Liberty triumphant'. On the last day of October the town was illuminated with candles to celebrate news of a great offensive by the French in Germany and Flanders. Volunteers and citizens packed the dining room in the Donegall Arms to celebrate. Samuel McTier took the chair. Resolutions were passed 'publicly to declare our happiness at the glorious success of French arms against the enemies of the human race,' and 'to support full and immediate Catholic emancipation.'

That evening in the Muddlers' Club everyone was in fine spirits. Sam Neilson declared that with the rapid progress of the union of Catholic, Protestant and Dissenter in Belfast, it was time to take some action, such as refusing to pay the hated hearth tax and the tithes for the Established Church, though nothing came of that.

At noon the following day the two Belfast Volunteer companies fired three *feu de joie* outside the White Linen Hall to celebrate the French victories, sending the seagulls into a frenzy of screeching. As the boom of cannon rattled our office windows I called out, to nobody in particular, '*Vive la Liberté!*'

To my surprise Neilson turned on me. 'Don't you know the cry in Paris is no longer Liberty but Public Safety? Prisoners are being massacred and priests slaughtered. What will the Catholics think of that? They will be afraid their priests will be put to the sword here. So they will settle for minor concessions. Our unity will be smashed.'

With that he went out, slamming the door.

The town was nevertheless infected with the idea of Liberty, first gained in America, then in France. Would Ireland be next? There was a feeling that anything was possible and that change must come. Even the reactionary old physician Dr Alexander Haliday, who, like Waddell Cunningham, owned a slave plantation in the West Indies, mouthed platitudes about reform. They and several other notable Whigs passed resolutions in favour of liberty for all denominations at a meeting in the Donegall Arms. Sound men!

Martha was present and was having none of it.

'These conservative gentlemen just pander to the common mood,' she said over breakfast next day. 'Underneath it they are a little averse to giving up prejudices long nursed in secret. I know Haliday. He is secretly horrified the Catholics might get the vote.'

Martha was hardly a republican but she had no time for injustice or snobbishness. She put her principles first. There was never any sugar on her table. In fact, she and Thomas Russell refused to eat anything with sugar, because it came from the work of slaves in the British West Indies, a point she always made when the slave plantation owner Dr Haliday came to dine. I went along with this too. It changed my habits. Soon I couldn't abide the taste of coffee with sugar in it.

'There is a lot of hypocrisy in this town,' she maintained. 'We are all against slavery. But many good men here profit from it, selling soap and candles to the slave-masters and broad-fitting shoes for the slaves.'

The Belfast Volunteer Company organised a great meeting at the Exchange on Monday 24 November after news came in that the French had triumphed over the Austrian army at Jemappes in Wallonia. But the Battle of Jemappes meant only one thing. War between England and France was inevitable, as George Gray had predicted. The French were advancing on the Netherlands and the English had vowed to protect the Netherlands from the French.

The excitement was terrific. If it was war, might France use Ireland as a side door to attack England?

No one was more taken by this heady prospect than Thomas Russell, who arrived back in town the following weekend. I found him in McTiers' dining room, top hat in place as always. He was on his way from Dungannon to Dublin, having given up his post as magistrate in Tyrone. 'I could not reconcile myself to sitting on a bench where the practice prevails of enquiring what a man's religion is, before enquiring of what crime he is accused.' He viewed the coming war as an opportunity for great events in Ireland. I accompanied him and Sam McTier to the Muddlers' Club. The gathering there asked Russell to present a resolution to a Catholic Convention to be held in Dublin, calling on them to insist on the full rights of man and to reject half measures, the more so as their Presbyterian brethren were determined to recover those rights for *all* Irishmen.

'Don't you know what war will mean, boys?' said Sam McTier. 'They'll disarm the Volunteers. Mark my words.'

Russell disclosed that the Volunteers in Dublin planned to muster on the streets in new uniforms of green, and buttons with a harp but no Crown. 'We'll see how they like that,' he said.

Belle Martin gave me the eye late on as Russell was launching into 'The Negro's Complaint'. I went down to the yard and she slipped out after me. She took my hand and pulled me into the stable, then pushed me back onto the straw, unbuttoned my breeches and began bouncing up and down on me like a rabbit, all the time giving me a lopsided smile. I started to come and she rolled off me and finished the job with her hand. Before I could get my breath back she was running upstairs, a tankard in the same hand.

I slunk off to my room in Martha's rather than go back to the Muddlers' Club. I feared they would notice my flustered state and that Belle would give something away. I didn't know if I could trust her.

— SEVEN —

PRINTING SEDITION

One frosty December evening Martha took me to the Assembly Rooms to watch her play faro and learn a few tricks. The Revd Bruce was at one of the card tables. While everyone spoke excitedly of politics, Bruce refused to take part. According to Martha his antipathy towards Catholics almost cost him membership of a new library called the Belfast Society for Promoting Knowledge. He was initially black-beaned and managed to get in only on the third vote. Bruce's wife Susanna irritated everyone by sitting by him and telling him what cards to play, making his face redden. When supper appeared the Bruces ate voraciously of every dish.

'He's so stingy,' complained Martha. 'He makes a practice of calling on parishioners in the evening and sitting till he is asked to supper, and all the time the boys are left to tutors.'

Martha played faro well but lost two shillings and decided she had had enough. 'Always remember,' she said, as she took my arm on the way home. 'When you lose too much, you should quit.' I told her I would be in favour of making a big bet. All or nothing. 'That's what I like about you,' she responded. 'You have courage. But you still have to learn wisdom.'

Next day it was Sam Neilson who displayed real courage. A courier arrived on the evening coach from Dublin with a United Irish document for publication in the *Star*. It was an address to the Volunteers of Ireland, drafted by Martha's brother William Drennan. It called on the Volunteers to resist being disarmed. They should 'assert the common rights of the people of Ireland through arms, and if weak or wicked men force the people into extremity, let all the miseries of civil convulsion fall on them.'

Sam consulted his fellow-directors. 'They tell me this might be seditious,' he told us after they departed. 'But they left the decision up to me.' He handed the text to John Storey. 'Print it,' he said.

My stomach churned a little with fear – fear that this might mean the end of the *Northern Star* and of my own stellar career.

The Call to the Volunteers was published on Wednesday 5 December 1792. Crowds gathered as soon as the first copies were pasted up on the public boards. Illiterate citizens clamoured for it to be read aloud.

A week later the government moved against the Volunteers in Dublin. In a letter to Martha, Dr Drennan related how the Lord Lieutenant had banned the muster of the Volunteers and deployed troops on the streets to enforce his order. He issued a proclamation outlawing 'seditious meetings' and empowering magistrates to disperse all gatherings of people in arms under colour of the Volunteer institution. An act banning the carrying of arms in public was rushed through the Commons. The Dublin Volunteers caved in and called off their demonstration, ostensibly so as not to undermine a Catholic delegation that had just set off for London to petition the King for their rights. The delegation was actually on its way via Belfast. There had been token defiance. Archibald Hamilton Rowan of Killyleagh, co-founder of the United Irishmen and one of the better County Down landlords, defiantly strolled in the Dublin streets with side arms and in green uniform and was surrounded and cheered by the mob.

Martha asked me to take the letter immediately to Sam Neilson. 'The Belfast Volunteers will be next,' he said after reading it.

The following day, a Wednesday, the delegation of five prominent Catholics led by John Keogh arrived from Dublin *en route* to London with their petition to the King. Several Presbyterian merchants hosted them to breakfast in the Donegall Arms. They had already received a few concessions from the government, such as the right to become barristers and to set up Catholic schools without permission from a Protestant bishop, but the junto in Dublin would not give them the vote. They wanted the King to intercede. Keogh expressed thanks for this strong mark of affection from

Presbyterian Belfast, and declared their determination to maintain the union of Catholic, Protestant and Dissenter.

When they emerged and climbed into their coach, John and Tom Storey unharnessed the horses, and teams of men pulled the carriage down Corn Market, along Ann's Street and to the other side of the Long Bridge as a gesture of solidarity. There they hitched the horses again and bade the delegation God speed, with loud cries of 'Success attend you!' and 'Down with the Ascendancy!'

I thought as I watched them disappear that relations between Protestant and Roman Catholics had never been better. Keogh, the leading Catholic, was a United Irishmen and Wolfe Tone, a Protestant, was Secretary of the Catholic Committee. These were surely the cornerstones of a new Ireland.

I misjudged the tailor Joseph Cuthbert, who had dressed me respectably when I joined the *Star*. Joe seemed too gentle and effeminate to be a militant revolutionary. However, one day the following week he came to the *Star* and asked Sam Neilson to print one hundred reproductions of a pamphlet written by the radical Thomas Cowper of Manchester. It urged soldiers to defy their officers and not to prop up military occupation anywhere. He intended giving them out himself. That would be a courageous, even foolhardy act.

'I'll print it,' Sam said, 'but I will not reveal the *Northern Star* as the printer. And if you try to give them to the soldiery, you will definitely be arrested for sedition.'

As John Storey worked on the handbill he confided to me that Cuthbert was a leading Defender and a strong advocate of union between the Defenders and the United Irishmen. 'He's a hard chaw, I wouldn't want to cross him,' said Storey, a big, brawny fellow who could have knocked down the slightly-built Cuthbert with a single blow.

When Joe called to collect his pamphlets I asked him if he was afraid of being caught and imprisoned. He laughed. 'Go away out of that. Don't I provide riding dresses for all the officers' ladies? They will never let it happen.'

He was arrested the following day. Joe was reported by a soldier called James Rose, to whom he had given a pamphlet, and was charged with distributing seditious material. He got out on bail pending trial, which eventually took place in County Antrim Assizes in Carrickfergus. Neilson sent me there to report the proceedings. Cuthbert was found guilty by the jury and sentenced to the pillory and one year in prison. He winked at me as he was led away.

No one had been pilloried in Belfast in living memory. A big crowd gathered next day at one o'clock to see Joe Cuthbert placed in the stocks in High Street, with the cavalry in attendance. Upright citizens, including some noble ladies who were his best customers, stood in silent protest. Printers and compositors from the *Star* took up position in case any urchin was tempted to throw tomatoes. Joe was released after an hour and taken to Carrickfergus jail, from where he sent a note that we published in the *Star*: 'Joseph Cuthbert, Tailor and Ladies Habit-Maker, in prison. Begs leave to acquaint customers that orders will be filled during his confinement. Has engaged a foreman of skill and experience. Commands left in his house will be punctually attended to.'

If Cuthbert's fate was meant as a warning about the consequences of the written word, Sam Neilson declined to heed it. Soon afterwards I handed him a report of a meeting of the Belfast Jacobins in Flanagan's tavern, chaired by a baker and attended by braziers, weavers and tin menders, mostly Catholics. I included their call on citizens to use 'every means' to achieve reform. After taking a pinch of snuff and deliberating for several minutes over my report, Sam decided to publish it. 'In for a penny, in for a pound,' he said.

A few days later he redesigned the masthead of the *Northern Star*. Since the beginning it had featured two female figures in classical costume, one holding a harp, the other a sword, and in between a shield topped by a crown. 'Get rid of the crown,' he told the chief compositor. 'Replace it with an eight-pointed star.' The printers banged lumps of metal on the table to show their approval.

In defiance of the Lord Lieutenant, many Belfast men joined the Volunteers. At a gathering of the First Belfast Regiment in the Brown Linen Hall, Roman Catholics were for the first time invited to take part. Overall membership rose from 350 to 500. A resolution was passed that a cheap uniform be endorsed to facilitate the admission of working members, and that it should be green, not the red of the original Volunteers. The name was also changed to the National Guard in imitation of the French revolutionaries.

I joined the queue to sign up. I was just short of eighteen but I was big for my age and they asked no questions. I went to Joe Cuthbert's shop in Rosemary Street and bought a green jacket faced with yellow, a green waistcoat, white breeches, long black gaiters and a leather cap. Sam Neilson let me take his musket as a side arm for a parade next evening.

I lined up with several hundred Volunteers in High Street at the head of a section of clerks and shop assistants. We marched by lamp-light through slush to Flanagan's tavern and back, then cheered a resolution proclaiming our right to seek our goals through force of arms. I found myself shoulder to shoulder with Henry Joy McCracken. We discussed the likelihood of war with France. He mentioned that he was proficient in French.

'Should we all take it up?' I asked.

'No harm,' he replied.

I enquired politely if I should call him 'Henry', or 'Henry Joy'. He used 'Henry Joy' as his first name because, he said, he was proud of the Huguenot name of Joy on his mother's side. Her grandfather was one of about a hundred Protestant Huguenot exiles who had settled in Lisburn at the start of the century and developed the linen industry.

'The trouble is,' he said laughing, 'I'm sometimes confused with my cousin Henry, editor of the *News-Letter*, whose surname is Joy. 'So my friends call me Harry. And you?'

'Willie,' I said.

Henry Joy, the *News-Letter* editor, unlike his cousin Harry and most of Protestant Belfast, espoused only modest reform. So it greatly relieved Sam Neilson when he saw in the *News-Letter* that his rival had also published the text of the United Irishmen's call to arms in its report on the Volunteer meeting. 'That means they won't touch me, because they would have to arrest Joy as well,'

He worried however that other methods might be used against us. In England a mob had been egged on by the authorities to wreck the offices of the *Manchester Herald* which was campaigning for parliamentary reform. 'What's the matter with Manchester?' he asked. 'They rioted against Paine's *Rights of Man*. They hung Paine in effigy on the street. Common folk raging against the champion of their own interests, to the benefit of their oppressors. What dupes!'

On Christmas morning, a Tuesday, I walked to Moira, carrying a bottle of Bordeaux. It was cold and dry. Lumps of old snow lay in the ditches. My occasional companions over the sixteen miles had great expectations of war. Many seemed to welcome the idea of the French landing in Ireland.

At my family home I was in great demand as the man from the *Northern Star*. The men who came to smoke pipes in the kitchen wanted to know everything. I stayed one night and returned to Belfast next day feeling guilty for abandoning my parents again so soon. In truth I couldn't wait to get back to town and the excitement, and the McTiers' Christmas feast, to which the most important citizens had been invited.

Martha had decorated the house with laurel, holly and ivy and several people came on the Thursday for a dinner of roast goose stuffed with herbs and fruit, veal chops and mashed potatoes with butter and ham, and ribs and sirloins done rare. First to arrive was the wealthy banker John Brown, whose establishment on Ann's Street was known as the Bank of the Four Johns, because all the partners were called John. Next came the elderly ex-mayor Stewart Banks, founder of the Poor House and a former Volunteer. The pompous Revd Bruce and his nagging wife couldn't be kept away and barged in to pay their compliments despite not being invited – they could smell a hot meal from across town. They ignored me and I them. I retired to my room, stuffed like the goose.

Next day a big crowd assembled in the Second Presbyterian Church on Rosemary Street to elect delegates to a convention of Volunteers in Dungannon. It was organised by twenty-five prominent Belfast citizens, including Sam McTier.

The mood was very belligerent towards the government. In the chair the banker Charles Ranken said only a nation of slaves could tolerate three-quarters of the inhabitants – the Catholics – being excluded from the legislature, members of parliament appointed by a few individuals, places and pensions acquired through corruption, taxes levied to purchase votes to levy more taxes, peerages put up for sale, and subjects deprived of trial by jury. Those seeking to preserve this corrupt system were deranged. '*Quem Deus vult perdere, prius dementat*,' he said. 'Whom God determines to destroy, he first makes mad.' To deny reform was to invite anarchy. He demanded a just system of King, Lord and Commons where the Commons really represented the people.

The Revd Bruce, sitting with Henry Joy, stayed silent, his sour face crumpled in disapproval at even talk of reform. The meeting elected a committee of sixteen to represent Belfast at the convention, headed by Sam Neilson. Bruce and Joy were rejected as too obviously out of step with the radical mood.

Martha as always had the measure of the bankers and merchants who sought to dominate the meeting with cries for reform. 'No one now dares to venture a word against the present radical views of the people, but underneath it is all prejudice,' she said as we left. 'Many hate the light that now exposes the narrowness of mind that has long disgraced them. They vent their gall in croaking forebodings of mobs and carnage, which they would rather see verified than be perpetually disappointed.' For every radical, she said, there was a reactionary, like Waddell Cunningham, Dr Haliday, the Reverend Bruce, and Henry Joy.

'They are in a minority,' I said. 'They cannot hope to prevail.'

Neilson read my report on the meeting while inhaling snuff from his wrist. 'Anarchy is indeed what they fear,' he said. 'It threatens their businesses. They will nevertheless be snubbed by the government, which now seems to regard even moderate calls for reform as sedition.'

The Volunteer Convention, held in Dungannon Presbyterian Church in County Tyrone, voiced support for Catholic emancipation but, to the disappointment of the radicals, it vowed to resist any French invasion and republican form of government.

Over a jug of punch in Barclay's on his return, Sam Neilson declared, 'We do have to think now in terms of a republic and separation.'

He was desperately worried by a warning from William Drennan in a letter to Martha that the government had got it in for the *Northern Star* for printing the call to arms. The Castle junto saw Neilson as a real firebrand, he wrote, and was fabricating rumours of riots and barricades in Belfast. The high official behind the denigration of Belfast was the Lord High Chancellor himself, John FitzGibbon, the worst kind of Protestant bigot. He had been born in Dublin to a Catholic father who converted to the Anglican religion to practice law, and he now despised Catholics and loathed those who espoused their cause, even moderate parliamentarians like Henry Grattan and Lord Moira. He rode around in a fashionable carriage imported from England, and acted as if he were the sultan of Ireland.

On the last day of the year the Castle junto made its move against us. Two law officers arrived on the night coach from Dublin with arrest warrants for the proprietors of the *Northern Star*, issued by Lord Chief Justice of the King's Bench, Viscount Clonmel. They took rooms in the Donegall Arms and ordered Revd Bristow to send bailiffs to convey the directors to their presence.

Sam was furious at being treated like a criminal. Half the staff accompanied him as he walked to the hotel. Inside, in armchairs by the coal fire, we found the law officers. One was plump and perspiring under his wig, the other thin, with a beak nose that dripped sweat. Both were very nervous. The portly one's voice trembled as he informed Neilson that the *Star* owners must come to Dublin to face charges for publishing the Address to the Volunteers.

'We must hear first what bail terms will be set by the judge before we leave for Dublin,' said Neilson.

'That will take two days,' they said.

'Fine,' said Neilson. 'It's New Year's Eve. We'll look after you while we wait, and ensure your safety from insult.'

That evening he and his directors wined and dined the law officers in the Donegall Arms. The government's men expressed surprise at the genteel behaviour of the Northern Presbyterians. They had been led to expect riot and tumult. After a few drinks they hinted that the prosecution would be dropped if Neilson undertook to moderate the policies of his paper.

As midnight and the New Year approached, and the dining room filled with noise and tobacco smoke, the sharp-nosed one became quite friendly. He said some of our own were misrepresenting Belfast in Dublin. They were told the town was in open rebellion, though they hadn't seen a symptom of that, other than French flags hanging from windows. They let slip that it was Bristow, upholder of the law, who was behind the treacherous reports of a lawless Belfast.

Neilson, his fellow-proprietors, and two bleary-eyed King's men, departed by coach for Dublin on the morning of Wednesday 2 January 1793. I remember the date well. It was my birthday. Sam left Billy Templeton and me in charge of the editorial content while he was away.

Here I was, just turned eighteen and jointly in charge of Ireland's most popular newspaper.

In Dublin the *Star* directors were arraigned at Clonmel's house in Harcourt Street. By Sam's account, the Lord Chief Justice reeked of whiskey, and could not produce a warrant nor tell them what the charges were, other than a vague incitement to arms. He imposed bail of £100 each and ushered them out without setting a trial date.

'The holder of Ireland's highest legal office is a wilful, fat drunkard,' Sam told us on his return. 'His face is so red from drink they call him 'Copper Face Jack'. But he is a clever bastard. The whole thing was a ruse to give me time to repent my temerity at the *Northern Star*.'

'On the road back we passed artillery heading north,' he added. 'And I hear that the Belfast Port Collector has purchased a quantity of gunpowder. The Collector does not deal in merchandise of any kind. This must have been by order of the government. I fear they are sending in the military against us.'

— EIGHT —

BAD-MOUTHING BELFAST

Sam's premonition was correct. A company of the Royal Irish Regiment of Artillery under Captain Lucius Barber rode into town next day with three field pieces and two wagons loaded with ammunition. Their officers burst into a coterie in the Assembly Rooms and demanded the ensemble play 'God Save the King'. The musicians obliged and played the anthem over and over. 'That's the way to baffle them,' said Martha. Belfast's district commander, Major General Richard Whyte, was in attendance, boasting that he had eight regiments he could call upon at short notice if Belfast did not mind its manners.

Soon we received reports that some of the street riff-raff were being enticed into the barracks on Ann's Street and given free whiskey to do the soldiers' dirty work. The following Sunday, four drunk ruffians emerged from the barracks shouting, 'Death to the Volunteers!' They beat up a merchant called Greg and a visiting American by name of Willcocks who happened to be nearby. Greg had a thumb put out of joint. The American was so afraid of getting his fine teeth damaged, he lay with his face in a soft dunghill as he was kicked. One of the assailants was caught. He confessed he had been given whiskey in exchange for oaths of loyalty.

The assault scandalised the town. It was brought up at a dinner party in the house of the High Sheriff, Chichester Skeffington. The sugar refiner Francis Jordan made some critical remarks about officers plying low fellows with drink to have them assault Volunteers. Revd Bristow banged the table with clenched fist in the most violent and unprovoked passion his fellow diners ever saw and roared, 'Must a set of men be condemned for declaring loyalty in a barrack! No town in his majesty's dominions is more loyal than Belfast!'

Martha was outraged. 'Bristow is an ignorant and bigoted zealot who is playing an insidious role in vilifying Belfast by conveying to Dublin every old woman's idle tale,' she said.

What really agitated the Ascendancy and the Crown Forces was the idea that Northern Presbyterians might support France in a war. The old order was outraged. Lord Downshire, an absentee landlord, felt it important enough to travel from London to give his subjects a warning about disloyalty. He called a meeting in Denvir's Hotel in Downpatrick, then kept everyone waiting. He was shocked to be treated with contempt. There were derisory cries of 'How's Molly?' a reference to his mistress, Molly McPherson from Banbridge, whom he had married off to a revenue man but with whom he still enjoyed naked romps in Hillsborough Castle. When Dr Joseph Little of Killyleagh berated Downshire for not supporting reform, the elderly marquess tried to put him down by saying, 'Dr Little, you are growing less.' He was mortified when Little replied, to cheers, 'My Lord, it is not to make little people less that we come here, but to make great people little.'

The following week news from Paris that King Louis XVI had been executed by guillotine somewhat dampened the enthusiasm for the French. Dethroning a king was one thing; beheading him was quite another.

On Friday 2 February 1793, republican France declared war on Great Britain. The government in London aligned itself with all the royal houses of Europe against democracy. The prospect of French backing for an insurrection in Ireland became real. No one removed the French tricolours hanging from the Belfast windows but an air of anticipation gripped the town. The government clearly saw us as a French revolutionary Trojan horse in the north of Ireland. The parliament in Dublin swiftly brought in a bill to prohibit the possession or transport of arms and gunpowder.

In a defiant response, two hundred Volunteers marched in uniform and with side arms the following Sunday to Rosemary Street for church service. Another hundred came from the direction of Waring Street. Sam

McTier declared that the junto in Dublin would not be able to resist the force of the people.

Others preferred to leave before the storm broke. At supper that evening Sam McTier bemoaned the fact that many principled men were talking about emigration – among them John Boyle, a shareholder in the *Star* – and he confessed that if he were not in his fifties he himself would set sail for America.

Later we adjourned to Flanagan's tavern. There, over tankards of ale, Thomas Russell said he believed the wars raging on the continent were connected to the promise of the coming millennium; that they would be long and bloody and the last to infest Europe, and that they would end in general republicanism. We drank to that.

Martha was scornful of the idea that the French might rescue Ireland from oppression. 'The French are a light, frivolous, aspiring people and I wish them well,' she declared, 'but if we cannot obtain liberty by ourselves we are not worthy of it.' Sam Neilson was of the same mind. 'The United Irishmen should abhor the idea of any foreign interference,' he asserted. 'It is up to us in the Irish nation to correct abuses in government.'

But he didn't rule out an alliance with France 'when all constitutional means are removed.'

During these fraught weeks the Crown forces intruded on many aspects of our daily life. On 25 February a new theatre opened on the corner of Arthur Street and Ann's Street, a grand semicircular arena with elegant boxes and brilliantly lit by glass lustres. Sam McTier was a £100 investor and possessed a silver admission ticket with which he brought Martha, me and several friends to a box overlooking the stage. To my dismay we had to share with three dour-looking army officers, who, Martha whispered, looked as if they had been sent to Coventry.

When 'God Save the King' was played, the officers stood and clapped noisily and Bristow and Bruce and the other Whigs in the stalls joined in. The crowd in the gallery heckled and called for the French revolutionary tune, '*Ah! Ça ira*'. Suddenly the air became thick with nuts, orange peel and apple cores. Michael Atkins, the theatre manager, took over the orchestra and got it to play the less contentious Volunteers' March. Everyone settled down to enjoy Sheridan's *The School for Scandal*. Afterwards Atkins threatened to close the theatre and take his troupe of actors to Derry if the audiences were not more respectful.

That week the military began barging into houses and workshops, searching for arms under the new Gunpowder Acts. They seized all but six of the cannons of the Volunteers, which remained hidden.

On the morning of 9 March, a Saturday, four troops of the 17th Light Dragoons arrived in Belfast. They were English soldiers, stationed in Ireland since being humiliated in the American War of Independence. In keeping with their boast to be the 'Death or Glory Boys' they wore a death's head insignia on their helmets.

At midday they came galloping along High Street in bright red coats and white cross belts. As they passed Grand Parade a group of urchins got a blind fiddler to play '*Ah! Ça ira*'. Two cavalrymen dismounted and prodded the fiddler with bayonets and forced him to play 'God Save the King'. People gathered at the corner of Grand Parade and Corn Market cursing the soldiers. Major General Whyte arrived and ordered the dragoons to disperse to their billets. Seemingly they spent the afternoon getting drunk. We stayed on late at the *Star*, fearing there was trouble in store.

About a quarter to seven, a body of dragoons and artillery men suddenly rushed out of the barracks in Ann's Street with sabres drawn and ran towards the *Northern Star* offices shouting 'God Save the King'. We slammed the door and turned the heavy iron key. Neilson came running down the stairs. Billy pushed us away from the windows, just in time. With a loud crash, shards of glass flew across the stone floor. The soldiers broke twenty more panes in the *Star* printing office before doubling back up Bridge Street.

I went to follow them. Neilson grabbed me by the arm. He would not let go until I had calmed down and promised to observe only.

The Dragoons split into parties of ten, each under orders of a sergeant. They cut at anyone that got in their way and left several people lying on the ground bleeding. They slashed the face of Charles Rangen, a justice of the peace, and stabbed the surgeon Mr Campbell.

Two soldiers with a ladder climbed up and tried, unsuccessfully, to pull down the copper sign of Benjamin Franklin hanging over the door of Barclay's tavern. Others vandalised John Hughes's bookstore. They broke the windows of Sam Neilson's two-storey house in Waring Street, then attacked the alehouse where the French Revolution was celebrated with a crown suspended upside down on a gibbet, and slashed with their swords at a memorial sign commemorating the radical French writer Gabriel Riqueti, comte de Mirabeau. They laid siege to Johnson's tavern and brought down the carved figure of General Francois Dumouriez in gold-trimmed uniform and white wig, that Johnson had put up to celebrate the French victory at Jemappes. They broke the windows of Watson's alehouse on the quay and Sinclair's public house in North Street and Miss Wills's hat shop, which had green cockades and caps in the window.

I watched with fury as they raided Thomas McCabe's watch and jewellery shop on North Street. They tore down his shutters, smashed the windows, and defaced the signboard declaring 'Thomas McCabe, Licensed to Sell Gold and Silver'. Fortunately, the proprietor was not there.

As word spread of the outrages, scores of armed Volunteers in uniform gathered in Grand Parade. I ran back to the office to get my Volunteer uniform but Neilson again stopped me. 'You observe, you observe, you don't get involved!' he shouted. So I observed, hot with anger. I observed four hundred and fifty armed Volunteers confront the dragoons. One shot could have started a war. But the English soldiers had done their work and retreated to barracks, laughing and cursing. The town's two corps of Volunteers mounted a guard of sixty men on the streets. It was all quiet by dark.

Next day hundreds more Volunteers poured in from the countryside. A thousand milled around the Third Presbyterian meeting house in Rosemary Street. Forty new recruits came forward.

In a panic at the possibility of armed conflict in the streets, Mayor Bristow called a town meeting at three o'clock. He nominated a committee of inquiry into the dragoons' behaviour, of which the only members were himself, the high constable and five magistrates. They met General Whyte, who promised that the dragoons would be dealt with (so help him, God) and a strong guard of the 55th Regiment was deployed immediately to – his own words – prevent further outrages. The committee then sent a deputation to the Volunteers requesting them to stand down. Surrender more likely! Some Volunteers wanted to stay on the streets but most were tired, hungry and wet because it had started to rain quite hard. They dispersed.

I was disappointed and frustrated. I believed the whole episode was a trick to test the strength and determination of the Volunteers and see who their leaders were.

When the Bristow committee began hearing witnesses on oath at ten o'clock the following morning, a weaver testified to finding a card dropped in the street by a captain of the dragoons. On it was a list of the premises to be attacked, headed by the *Northern Star,* beside which was written 'Encourages sedition'. A shopkeeper swore that he overheard an officer say the list was compiled by Lord Downshire. Even the magistrates were agitated to see that Thomas McCabe's shop was on it. Few people were more respected. McCabe was the jeweller whose moral force stopped Waddell Cunningham starting a slave trade from Belfast.

During the hearing a young boy was brought into the room with blood on his face. He had been beaten up by dragoons in Ann's Street. I went out and saw several soldiers daubing houses with white paint. They weren't finished. This stimulated even the Bristow committee to pass a resolution condemning the actions of the military. General Whyte announced that he would order the dragoons to leave town instantly – if the Volunteers stayed off the streets.

So that evening, their dirty work done, the dragoons left Belfast. They were jeered as they cantered towards the Long Bridge in the dusk, brandishing General Dumouriez's wooden head as a trophy. One of them slashed at a young man with his sabre making a deep cut in his side. Not one would be punished. We knew that and they knew that. As they passed, an officer was overheard saying, 'The Presbyterians of Belfast are in their heart Americans, and they are the same bastards we fought in Boston and New York.'

When I mentioned this to John Storey, he remarked, 'You know what they say in the United States about the fighting spirit of the Ulster Scots: 'Brewed in Scotland, bottled in Ireland, uncorked in America.' It will be uncorked here now. They will get their due.'

But I felt a great opportunity had been missed to make a stand. Even Martha McTier, who had loved intrigue but abhorred confrontation, remarked over dinner, 'There is a tide in the affairs of men and Ireland has not taken it.'

The raid on Belfast was a ruse cooked up in Dublin. It was followed by the arrival of a government messenger with a proclamation from the Lord Lieutenant to be published in the *Northern Star* and the *News-Letter* in every issue for two months.

It stated that, 'as several bodies of men have been collected into armed associations and have been levied and arrayed in the town of Belfast, and that as arms and gunpowder to a very large amount have been sent thither, and that as bodies of men and arms were drilled day and night with the obvious intent to overthrow parliament and government, all armed assemblies are henceforward banned.'

It was the Volunteers who faced arrest now, not the dragoons who rioted.

Fearful of disturbances, Colonel Barber ordered the closure of the new Arthur Street theatre.

A magistrate came to the *Star* office at 9 o'clock next morning with two bailiffs to search for arms. One opened a drawer, looked at my flintlock pistol, and closed it again with the slightest wink in my direction. They left empty-handed. As soon as they had gone I secreted the pistol in the flue of an unused fireplace. We received reports of arms searches outside Belfast and of a woman killed by the military in a raid in Banbridge.

Bristow's whitewash committee disgraced us all. It claimed that the riot of the dragoons was quelled by the active exertions of Captain Bourne, aide-de-camp to General Whyte. It alleged a rabble had tried to prevent a fiddler playing 'God Save the King', and that stones were thrown at the dragoons, provoking them. It lavished praise on the general for 'his vigilance, his judicious orders as commander-in-chief, his ready compliance with the wishes of the inhabitants, reflecting honour on his prudence and humanity.' The town committee met and refused to accept the report.

Neilson published his own succinct account in the *Star*. He wrote, 'This town is in a state of perfect peace at present: that tranquility was instantly restored when the dragoons belonging to the 17th Regiment were ordered away.'

In between pinches of snuff – his intake increased with his agitation – he told us that ridicule and satire were the only weapons of the defenceless, and we must now wield them as mercilessly as the dragoons wielded their sabres.

He started with definitions from a hypothetical political dictionary:

Freedom – an obsolete word

Aristocrats – tyrants who abrogate to themselves privileges, amass the wealth of a country and keep all in subjection by force and corruption

Government – the ruling party who by means of the purses of a nation and a standing army do as they please

The Irish – the Helots of Europe.

'Who are the Helots?' I asked.

'Slaves,' he replied. 'Slaves who never revolted.'

He also published, under the headline 'Spies and Informers', a warning to betrayers of our cause: 'Whosoever bears witness against his neighbour out of a principle of malice and revenge, from any old grudge or hatred, such a man is a false witness in the sight of God.'

'They can't charge us with sedition for printing this,' he said. 'It's from Dean Swift, quoting Exodus 20:16.'

He also reprinted a line from the Proclamation of the Commune of Paris: 'To arms, citizens, to arms. If you delay all is lost.'

— NINE —

WINTER OF DISCONTENT

On the morning of Monday 1 April John Storey gave me a letter to take to Robert Hunter on Hanover Quay. 'United Irish business,' he said. 'Top secret.' Hunter read and resealed it and told me to bring it to Billy Dawson, the goldsmith on North Street. Dawson did the same, told me to pass it on to the vintner Martin Tennent on Waring Street. Tennent told me to take it to the notary John Tisdall on High Street. On the way this time I opened it. The note said, 'Send the fool on.' I returned to the office to cries of 'April Fool!'

An hour later I got Billy to give Storey an item for typesetting. It was a new government order that all Presbyterians must grow their hair at least twelve inches long to show they did not sympathise with French revolutionaries, who cropped their hair. Inspectors were to be appointed and armed with rulers.

'The bastards,' said Storey. 'Well dare anyone come near me with a ruler! I will cut all my hair off rather than obey such a law.'

'And wouldn't you look a right eejit,' I said from the doorway, adding 'April Fool!' as a shower of wooden letters hit the back of the door.

The joke with the letter led to an encounter that marked the beginning of a crucial friendship in my life. While passing along North Street I had seen a young man on a ladder giving the final touches to a new sign over a shop damaged by the military. Instead of 'Thomas McCabe, Licensed to Sell Gold and Silver' it now read, 'Thomas McCabe, *an Irish Slave*, Licensed to Sell Gold and Silver'.

'Good on you,' I called up to him.

'Damn their eyes,' he replied.

William Putnam McCabe climbed down and introduced himself as the son of the owner. He said his father would not allow the broken panes to be repaired, so everyone who passed would see the evidence of the riotous behaviour of the foreign soldiers.

I took an immediate liking to him. He was eighteen, same as me, educated as a mechanic, and recently returned from Manchester where he had been apprenticed to the cotton business.

We met later that day for a tankard of ale. In the meantime his father had told him of my revolt in the academy. I had to tell the story once more. He roared laughing. 'You're the boy,' he said. 'Bristow must have shit himself.'

He told me that his father, a founding member of the United Irishman, was always going on about how foreigners had seized most of the land of Ireland, a foreign church had been planted to which other denominations had to pay tithes, a foreign military was allowed to act with impunity, a foreign country prevented free trade, and a foreign government denied the vote to the Catholics.

'I never listened to him – until now,' said the young McCabe.

The Putnam in his name, he told me, came from a relative, General Israel Putnam, who fought the British in America, including the regiment whose dragoons had wrecked the shop.

A few days later, William Putnam McCabe, standing beneath a bust of Voltaire in Kelly's Cellars, was sworn into Belfast Society No. 69 of the United Irishmen.

Clutching the Bible to his breast, he affirmed his support for a union of all Irish people to oppose England's influence, and a complete and radical reform of parliament in Dublin to include Irishmen of all religious persuasions.

William Putnam McCabe became a regular member of our group. We took to calling him Putnam. There were too many 'Willies' in Belfast. Shout 'Willie!' and half the street would turn around. I sometimes got 'Willie K.' but for obvious reasons Putnam didn't entertain being called 'Willie P'.

It was becoming evident that the government was following a policy of coercing the Presbyterians and placating the Catholics. We got word from

London that the Catholic Committee delegation had got some concessions from the King. Wealthy Catholics would get the vote but they were still barred from sitting in parliament or holding any political or judicial office.

'It's an effort to placate Catholics and dissuade them from making common cause with Dissenters,' was Sam Neilson's conclusion.

The coercion of Belfast continued. In mid-April the 38th Regiment arrived in town in a spring snowstorm to reinforce the military garrison. Their officers acted in the Assembly Rooms as if they were lords of the manor. They proclaimed in loud voices their intention of teaching Belfast another lesson.

At eight o'clock one evening a party of the regiment, accompanied by artillery men, emerged from the barracks and used a metal bar to dislodge the figure of Hibernia from above our door. They pulled down the copper image of Benjamin Franklin, which had defeated the dragoons. An angry crowd gathered. Mayor Bristow arrived with some officers, and the signs were returned.

That evening Henry Haslett, a linen merchant and one of our directors, dined with Colonel Lucius Barber of the Royal Artillery. Barber boasted that the military would put the *Northern Star* out of business next day. We mounted a picket outside our premises, whose numbers included my new friends, William Putnam McCabe, and Harry McCracken.

As darkness fell, several artillery men emerged from the barracks. Colonel Barber was behind them, smirking. There was some pushing and shoving and a soldier was knocked down. Barber made as if to draw his sword. McCracken pushed his way to the front.

'Don't draw it,' he commanded.

Barber cursed him as a ringleader and a rascal and asked, 'Who do you think you are?'

Harry retorted, 'I am your equal. Mr Bristow will tell you who I am.'

Several voices were raised to attest that Harry was a cotton manufacturer and respectable citizen.

'This doesn't end here,' said Barber. He ordered the soldiers to withdraw. The printers stayed at the *Star* all night, armed with cudgels. Billy, Putnam and I kept them supplied with ale from Barclay's.

Mayor Bristow sent for Harry the next morning and asked him to make an apology to Colonel Barber. 'I will not,' said McCracken. A Colonel French was present, who warned him that he would burn down the town if anyone shot at his soldiers through a window. Harry expressed his outrage at such a threat.

This Colonel French clearly believed he could act with impunity. When the respected elderly physician, Dr Alexander Haliday, chairman of the Whig Club, timidly ventured at a social dinner that the people of Belfast wanted reform and would get it 'by application in every way', the colonel shouted that they would never get it, and threatened to order three more regiments to Belfast, bring back the dragoons, and billet seven soldiers in every house.

Meanwhile Colonel Barber allowed the theatre to reopen. I went with my friends to see Shakespeare's *Richard III*. When the actor playing Richard paused after the first line, 'Now is the winter of our discontent', Putnam shouted, 'Aye, it is indeed'. Officers in the boxes stood up and booed. The following week we turned up for a performance of a new play called *Guillotine* which favoured the French Revolution. As the curtain was raised some officers shouted, 'Off!' 'Off!' We responded from the gallery, 'Go on!' 'Go on!' Michael Atkins quietened everyone by ordering a musician to play a hornpipe. He got the actors to do a quick change of costumes and perform instead a farce by Barnaby Brittle.

We were now beholden to the military for our very entertainments.

Thomas Russell arrived in Belfast at the end of May with the same message as Colonel French – we could indeed forget about reform because we were not going to get it.

Russell had been without employment since giving up his job as a magistrate in Tyrone. His clothes were those of a gentleman but threadbare. His top hat was battered. His shoes were split open. He confessed he was so broke he had pawned Wolfe Tone's watch and sent the proceeds to his impoverished sister in Enniskillen.

'Reform is no longer on the agenda,' he announced in the Muddlers' Club. 'The parliamentary liberals have become reactionaries, the French are retreating in the Netherlands, the Catholics have been bought off with concessions, and the military are being used to intimidate Belfast. The government is about to raise a militia. They intend to arm the peasantry of one county to subdue the peasantry in another.'

'Don't be so despondent,' countered Neilson. 'Derry, Tyrone, Antrim and Down are burning with indignation against the government. The spirit of the North has never been higher. I'm getting reports every week from parish meetings, Masonic Lodges and town conventions, calling for radical social change.'

'We've had our day and we let it pass,' declared Russell. 'We have no plan. The most active men around the country are emigrating to America. If the Catholics don't unite with the United Irishmen for reform, I might emigrate myself.'

I must have looked pretty down in the mouth. Russell punched me on the arm and said, 'Don't despair, young fellow! Things will come around! It's divinely ordained!'

He ordered whiskeys, which of course we had to pay for.

Before long Russell was bellowing out 'The Negro's Complaint' and asking where he could find a wench for the night. I didn't help him on that score – I was keeping Belle Martin for my own gratification later.

Usually Belfast ignored the King's birthday, which fell on 4 June. That year the old slave owner Waddell Cunningham got the idea that the town should be lit up to show its loyalty to the Crown. Mayor Bristow obliged and ordered every house to be illuminated. The inevitable happened. The soldiers went on the rampage, breaking the glass panes in every window not lit up, wounding several citizens, and leaving a man called Birnie for dead.

Worse was to follow, when soldiers fired on people protesting against forced recruitment to the new militia at Castlereagh, a village south of Belfast.

Unlike the Volunteers, the militia were to be controlled by titled officers answerable to Dublin Castle. Across the thirty-two counties, young men whose names were drawn in a ballot were taken from families and farms, with harvest time almost upon them, and forced into units that served in distant counties. The United Irishmen in the North encouraged big rallies against forced recruitment in Ballynahinch, Rathfriland, Greyabbey and Castlereagh.

As the *Star* reporter, I joined a thousand protestors at Castlereagh House, a small, whitewashed country mansion, where a recruiting table had been erected on the lawn. Putnam came with me. Some men tried to overturn the table. A body of dragoons pushed them back. Lord Downshire's son, the Earl of Hillsborough, appeared at a window, aiming a musket. A shot rang out. A man fell near me with blood gushing from his neck. The dragoons lowered their firearms and discharged a volley. There were bangs, sparks, smoke, screams. Several people fell. The crowd fled in every direction.

Five men were killed and twenty maimed. Putnam and I helped lift the dead into a cart. He was very quiet as we made our way back to Belfast. 'This changes everything,' he said. 'My father is right. We have to get rid of the foreign army that keeps Ireland in subjection.'

My hand was shaking as I wrote my report. The printers could barely read my writing. It was the first time I had seen a man killed. Hillsborough committed murder that day, as far as I am concerned. He would never be held to account.

Even the old Whigs were outraged. Dr Alexander Haliday came to dinner at Martha's the following Saturday and launched into an angry tirade.

'The establishment is corrupt and a financial drain on the country,' he asserted. 'I fear for Ireland. We will have either a future of gloomy servitude, or a dreadful explosion. I fear the latter.'

I held my tongue. There would inevitably be an explosion. It was at this moment in my life that I knew for certain that I would help ignite it.

— TEN —

A BAD INFLUENCE

Belfast that July was intolerable. The gentry fled to the countryside. The heat was oppressive and the dunghills hummed with wasps and horseflies. There were no meetings, no politics. Sam Neilson was furious that the Catholics in Dublin had been bought off so easily. Even the ebullient John Storey was uncharacteristically subdued. He told me of rumours that Sam and the directors were so disillusioned and intimidated, they considered selling the *Northern Star* to the government, though thankfully that came to nothing.

So I was very content when the editor encouraged me to accompany Russell on one of his frequent long walks into the countryside, in order to take a measure of political sentiment. Putnam came along too.

Russell's encounters with country people always revived his enthusiasm and provided new opportunities for amorous adventures. After a tour of the Mournes he had raved about the beauty of the girls in Bryansford, which made me think he had found accommodating quarters there.

In our outing north of Belfast we found everywhere a desire for Liberty. The people were favourable to the French, though upset by the execution of King Louis XVI, and very irritated at English soldiers being billeted in their houses without a by-your-leave.

One encounter made a big impression on us. A Presbyterian weaver invited us into his cabin to drink whiskey from a stone jar. He told us, 'Catholics won't rise now because the priests are content with what reforms they have got, but for my part I'd risk my life for Liberty.' He had two children – one was climbing onto his knee. 'It grieves me to breed up these children to be slaves,' he declared.

As we left, Russell reflected, 'Here is a peasant interested in the freedom of mankind, but one doesn't hear such sentiments from the rich. The rich put property before life.'

'It is the lower orders who will achieve Ireland's freedom,' responded Putnam. 'When the people feel their strength, then adieu to property! *Tant mieux!*'

As far as he was concerned, the land of Ireland was confiscated, century after century, so that the sovereign in London could gratify the avarice of their favourites. Their descendants boasted of their foreign origin, while their Anglican Church establishment preached doctrines contrary to the beliefs of the people from whom they demanded tithes.

'Why, the Mohammedans use their minarets to call the faithful to prayer, but the Anglican spires flaunt a foreign flag.'

Bastille Day, Sunday 14 July, came and went that year without commemoration. The country was at war with France, the Volunteers were proscribed and public meetings were banned. A group of us, including Russell, Putnam, John and Thomas Storey and Billy Templeton, toasted the French in the privacy of Flanagan's back room. The mood was bleak. I relayed Drennan's comments in his latest letter to Martha that it was better to emigrate than persevere in a pettish silence, when our rights were torn away and our countrymen every day murdered before our eyes.

Russell was what my mother would call 'a bad influence'. We fell into a pattern of heavy drinking, following which we would go in search of 'impures' as he liked to call them. Sometimes I satisfied myself with Belle Martin but I was not averse to new experiences, and more than once I accompanied Russell to establishments where whores were available for six pence.

One afternoon we went to Drew's alehouse to play billiards. Tom went to a room upstairs with a Mrs Studdard, an old flame who turned up looking for him. Her groans of pleasure were audible throughout the building. Happily her husband didn't appear.

Next day in Barclay's, Russell was contrite and implored the heavens for forgiveness for his licentiousness. During this bout of self-loathing he confided in me his great and unrequited love for a young woman of exquisite beauty called Eliza Goddard from Newry, the daughter of a loyalist customs officer. He had spent some rapturous days walking with her in the Mourne Mountains. Then she broke it off because Russell was impoverished and her loyalist father would never agree to her marrying a democrat. With a sigh Russell confessed that perhaps he was only besotted with her, as she was actually a bit simple and not up to his intellectual standards.

There and then that day we pledged to forgo alcohol. After sitting a while in silence, Russell told me about a country man who vowed to stop drinking, but who got drunk every day by dipping his bread in whiskey and claiming to eat it rather than drink it.

'So should we order some bread?' I said.

'Aye, what's holding you back?'

That evening we went to the Promenade Club, which met every Thursday in the Assembly Rooms and romanced two girls from Coates the hairdresser. We brought them to Drew's tavern and took one each in turn to the room upstairs.

In mid-October the government began sending the new militia to different counties to keep order and prevent rebellion. Belfast was assigned the Fermanagh Militia, which was dominated by loyalists. On the first day of November, All Hallows Eve, drunken Fermanagh militiamen ran riot in the streets. They cut four citizens with bayonets, mortally wounding a United Irishman called Hugh Bell. The fatal blow was delivered by a militiaman called Smith who was sent back to Fermanagh to escape justice in Belfast. Our correspondent in Enniskillen reported that Smith was apprehended there by patriots and brought before a magistrate, but instead of committing him for trial, the magistrate released Smith and berated him for not using his bayonet to kill the 'rebels' who had arrested him.

At the Exchange coffee house, militia officers in uniform elbowed and jostled merchants and traders. One evening, they stopped a promenade where twelve gentlemen and their ladies were performing a dance and required the musicians to play 'God Save the King', not once but three times. During a coterie in the Assembly Rooms, an officers' guard made loud disparaging comments about disloyal Belfast and the lying *Northern Star*.

81

In Martha's opinion, the Fermanagh Militia were as much inclined to insult us as the troops we got rid of, and the problem was that this militia might not be got rid of at all.

Russell bristled at the attitude of the militia officers. One evening, as we emerged from a formal dinner in Bridge Street, one of our number shouted, 'Long live the United Irishmen!' A patrol of the Fermanagh Militia confronted us. Russell went up to their officer and stared at him from a few inches, eyeball to eyeball. The stare would have intimidated an ox. It was worse than any verbal insult.

The officer flinched. 'Do you know who I am?' he stuttered. 'I am Lord Cole. Don't you know I am Lord Cole? I am Lord Cole.'

Putnam's father Thomas McCabe called out, 'You are very fond of that title. Take care or it may not be long till you lose it.'

One of Lord Cole's officers recognised Russell as a former military man and challenged him to a duel, the time and place to be arranged on the morn. Tom accepted. I wanted to talk him out of it but he disappeared into the darkness.

Russell didn't return to his lodgings until the early hours. Next morning he was, typically, full of remorse. He had been with a prostitute after confronting Lord Cole and now he might soon find himself in the presence of God. 'How terrible,' he cried. 'I wish and desire for virtue, yet relapse into vice at the slightest temptation.' At times like this, he confessed, his longed-for love Eliza was uppermost in his thoughts. He cited Francis Bacon: 'Love is most powerful when we experience either great prosperity or great adversity.'

I reminded him that the first time we met in Martha's he had listed adultery and duelling as the honourable vices of the rich.

'What I said is that the rich think these vices honourable,' he said. 'I don't.'

We persuaded him to write a letter of apology to the officer.

'Your life is more important to us than a stupid test of your honour,' I told him.

'You are one to talk,' he said.

But he agreed, and just as he took up a quill pen, the officer came to the door to express his own regrets for his part in the affair. They shook hands and that was that.

Martha voiced her concern about Russell when I somewhat dramatically related the affair to her. (How she thrilled to hear all such goings-on around the town.) 'He lives on a pittance,' she said, 'and I fear he relies too much on people beneath him. But I have never heard a word from him that did not do him honour as a religious, moral man and as a polite finished gentleman. He is very agreeable, very handsome and well-informed, and possessed of the most insinuating graceful manners.'

Russell had a strong effect on middle-aged women like Martha. Harry McCracken's young sister, Mary Ann, who taught poor children at the Market House, was quite besotted with him. I heard her describe Russell as 'a model of manly beauty with the manners of a finished gentleman combined with the native grace that comes from superiority of intellect.'

These virtuous women never saw Thomas Russell in the wee hours.

In truth the whole town loved Russell and a decent job was soon found for him. Robert Carey, librarian of the Belfast Society for Promoting Knowledge, decided to join the exodus for America. Dr MacDonnell, founder of the library and a close personal friend of Russell, proposed Russell to succeed him. The salary was only £50 a year but it came with accommodation. He accepted and rented a house for the library in Ann's Street and moved all the books and himself there.

Then my new friend suffered a tragedy which affected him deeply. His older brother Ambrose, an army captain, died in India. In the following days Russell behaved strangely. He went out socially and even joined in the dancing at the house of the linen merchant John Ferguson, but suddenly left the company and went to his lodgings where he was heard weeping long into the night. Martha worried that Russell could not even afford a black coat for mourning. One evening Tom joined us in Flanagan's, looking wretched. He confided that he was haunted by the image of his brother enjoying the vigour of health and beauty and gaiety, and then being suddenly arrested by the hand of death. He constantly imagined in his dreams the funeral in India that he could not attend, the solemn music vibrating among the towers of the fort, the salute echoing over the grave.

Within a few weeks he recovered his spirits sufficiently to take part in a play reading in the McTiers' to entertain Martha's lady friends. In dashing fashion he performed Hotspur, a doomed rebel against the king, from *Henry IV, Part 1*. I read the part of the debauched, hard-drinking Prince Hal. Both of us excelled, if I say so myself. But Russell got the adoring looks.

Martha one morning chided me for my own drinking. I wondered had she picked up gossip about me and Belle Martin. Little in the town escaped her. I decided it was time to look for other lodgings. I was friendly enough with Sam and Martha by then to know I could still call regularly and exchange snippets of gossip from the *Star* and pick up information from her brother's letters.

Within the week I found a first floor back room in a house in Hercules Street, five minutes' walk from the *Star* office. The owner was a Mr Hamill, one of the butchers with stalls on the street and a strong supporter of the United Irishmen. His wife was a terrifying Amazon in blood-stained apron who wielded her cleaver like a woodsman, but inside the house was the soul of consideration and kindness.

Putnam helped me to move on a day when the streets were slick with snow. We loaded my box of possessions onto a makeshift sleigh. It wasn't very heavy. In my nineteen years on earth I had accumulated a Volunteer uniform, a pair of buckled shoes, a frock coat, two linen shirts, spare breeches, three candle-holders, one pistol, several books, a large jar of blackberry jam that Martha gave me, and the clothes and boots I was wearing.

Despite my increasingly dissolute life with Russell, I never missed a day at work and I developed a close relationship with Sam Neilson. I tried to anticipate his ideas and he took me completely into his confidence. I became known around town as his right-hand man.

Which explains why I was tapped on the shoulder one wet morning by a stout, middle-aged man with beetle eyebrows as I was hurrying to the *Northern Star* after breakfast. He thrust a sealed letter into my hand and walked away. It was addressed to Sam Neilson.

The letter was signed 'A sub-constable' and it informed Sam of the most flagrant falsehoods being deliberately circulated about the *Northern Star*. The chief culprit was a 'certain agent of the Crown' in Belfast who went door-to-door collecting taxes. When anyone expressed a grievance, whether it concerned the price of clothes, the behaviour of the soldiers, the unemployment of weavers or the starving of the poor, the tax collector would invariably blame the *Northern Star*.

'I know to whom he refers,' said Sam. 'It's George Murdoch. He's the hearth tax collector. A despicable rogue. He hates the United Irishmen.'

'What we should do?' I asked.

'What should we do?' echoed Neilson. 'We should publish it.' Which we did.

Going through the lower bar in Barclay's with Neilson a few days later I spotted the sub-constable, standing alone at the crowded bar. I caught his eye. He winked. I quietly pointed him out to Neilson, who paid for a large measure of whiskey and asked Belle Martin to take it over to him, no questions asked.

Despite the efforts of people like Murdoch, and the wealthier merchants who bided their time to see how things might develop, the majority of bourgeois Belfast remained steadfast in the radical and independent spirit. The *Northern Star* continued to outstrip the *News-Letter* in circulation, and as a consequence the rivalry and enmity of the respective editors became the talk of the town.

The *News-Letter* editor, Henry Joy, heard one day that the *Star* had received from Sam McTier an important document from the United Irishmen in Dublin. Joy sent his messenger boy to Neilson to pretend he had been sent by McTier to retrieve the paper for a short time. Neilson of course agreed. Later he learned he had been deceived. When Joy's lad came to return the document, Neilson seized him by the collar. 'How dare you come with such a lie in your mouth,' he said. 'You are like your master, a dirty little rascal and beneath my notice.' The boy fled with a kick up the backside.

We printed all sorts of stuff to win the circulation war. Sometimes we gave the readers a laugh. Martin Tennent, the alcohol merchant, allowed us to publish a story against himself. A woman came into his premises in Waring Street with a bottle and asked for it to be filled with a shillings-worth of whiskey. She got the whiskey, put the bottle in her bag, and handed over the shilling. Tennent saw that the coin was a forgery and demanded the woman hand back the whiskey. She reached into her bag and produced a liquid-filled bottle, apologising profusely. Only when she left did he discover that the bottle she'd returned was filled with piss.

We lived on the edge of course, expecting daily another attempt by the government, as Sam put it, to prosecute us out of existence for promoting the ideals of the United Irishmen. We were again served notice of trial on sedition charges, only to have it postponed again, to an indeterminate date. That way, they let us know that we were being watched.

— ELEVEN —

LOVE OR FRIENDSHIP

At the end of December I set off on Eclipse to celebrate the New Year, and my birthday, with my parents. Neighbours crowded into the cottage to smoke pipes and hear the news at first hand from the *Star* man.

On the first day of the New Year, 1794, I walked with my father to the greenhouse of Moira Castle, where many of the glass panes were broken and the remaining Jamaican imports had died from cold. The previous month old Lord Moira had expired, an occasion of local indifference to the Presbyterians for whom he had so much contempt, but regarded by the Ascendancy as a national event. He was given the biggest funeral ever seen in Ireland, with eight hundred carriages bearing four thousand mourners wearing black hatbands clogging up the village and roads for miles around.

My patron Francis Rawdon inherited his title. One of the first things the new Lord Moira did was to get rid of his land agent. My father explained that the younger man had always disliked Claiborne for his bigotry and cruel attitude towards the tenants, a factor which explained his lenience towards me when I stood up to the agent as a boy.

We encountered Claiborne on horseback as we walked back from the demesne. His fat face turned red when he saw me.

'Well, well,' he said. 'If it isn't the young Kean all grown up. I hear you are a big man in Belfast now.'

'What of it?' I replied. I was by then six feet tall and had no fear of the diminutive former agent. 'I venture you are not such a big man yourself any longer.'

'Just watch your back,' he said. 'You Papist-lovers are not wanted here.'

'You watch yours,' I said.

He reared up the horse and rode away.

Next day, for my nineteenth birthday, my father gave me a fob watch with the Kean family motto on the back: '*Felis demulcta mitis:* A stroked cat is gentle.'

'It's like what they say about the Irish wolfhound,' he remarked, 'Gentle when stroked, fierce when provoked.'

I recalled for him that Benjamin Franklin once described British policy towards America as like 'stroking a horse to make it more patient while the reins are drawn tighter and the spurs are set deeper into his sides.'

America's founding father wrote this comment, I explained, after Lord Downshire had entertained him at his Hillsborough mansion twenty years earlier. Franklin didn't like the lecherous old fart, regarding Downshire as 'conceited, wrong-headed and obstinate'.

'How do you know all that?' asked my father. I explained that I had read the English translation of the *Mémoires de la vie privée de Benjamin Franklin* in the new library, the Belfast Society for Promoting Knowledge, where I spent much free time discussing books with the librarian, my friend Thomas Russell.

My admission to the library had been approved during a committee meeting at which I was instructed that members were to confine themselves to arts, natural philosophy and literature. In other words, no politics. But there was plenty of good reading there. It had 150 volumes by authors such as Fielding, Swift, Pope, Defoe, Goldsmith, and Voltaire, and many books on the Scriptures, and more were being donated every week. I loved especially Shakespeare's plays, and I would lace my conversations at Martha's table with quotations to show I wasn't just a country boy.

It was always interesting to see how outsiders perceived us and I spent some hours at the library perusing with fascination *A Tour of Ireland* by Arthur Young. He saw the Irish as infinitely cheerful, with none of the incivility or sullen silence typical of the English, and he observed how they would take snuff and talk without tiring until doomsday. He had a rosy view of our local nobility, noting with approval that Belfast entirely belonged to Lord Donegall and that his lordship's royalties were the 'greatest of any subject in Europe'. He criticised Lord Antrim for renting out his land for only £8,000 a year and allowing tenants who had perpetuities to re-let it for £64,000 a year, which was 'perhaps the cruelest instance in the world of carelessness for the interests of posterity.' Though he praised the new buildings in Dublin and Belfast, he opined that half a century before there were no more than ten dwellings in Ireland 'fit for an English pig to live in'. He considered the game of hurling to be cricket for savages. Apparently this haughty and patronising Englishman was making a good living writing such balderdash.

On my return to Belfast I called into John Hughes's bookstore. There I purchased for Betsy *A Vindication of the Rights of Woman* by Mary Wollstonecraft which had been provoking much comment. I believed it would appeal to her, with its theme that woman should be educated and be the companion of man rather than his servant. Perhaps she might get my hint that she should not accept being spoken for at such an early age and to be more independent.

I was becoming a regular visitor to Gransha and always arrived with a gift of some kind, usually brandied fruits or walnuts from Mullan's or sherry from Tennents. Their cottage was like my second home now. I loved the ticking of the grandfather clock at night when everything else was silent, though I wasn't so fond of the cock that announced the rising of the sun before it peeped above the horizon. I sometimes helped with potato gathering or turning hay, trying not to look if Betsy's open blouse provided a glimpse of her lovely breasts. She had turned seventeen and had grown her red hair down to her waist.

Betsy was becoming more radical and she spoke passionately about the ill-treatment of men and women by government and landlords, so the Wollstonecraft book was perfect for her. She joined in the political conversations with Hans and George and Willie Boal. Willie did not contribute much or show his hand. He was a deep one. Betsy's bonnie friend Eliza Bryson would come across the fields and she flirted with me, and I with her. Once when I caught her eye she smiled and undid her blouse a little.

One evening, after everyone had gone, I told George and Betsy that I felt I was like a brother to them, in spirit and in kind. 'Perhaps one day we will be brothers in arms,' said George.

Next morning I woke in the kitchen loft to see Betsy at the table below reading *The Rights of Woman*. When I climbed down she pointed out a sentence: 'Love and friendship cannot subsist in the same bosom.' She said nothing but I got the message. She knows how I feel about her but I must subdue my feelings. I never felt closer to her at that moment, or further apart.

I spent pleasant hours at McClenaghan's forge. It served as a local meeting place. Betsy would bring the *Northern Star* there twice a week to read aloud to those who could not afford it or could not read. Local people got to know me as the '*Star* man'. They always wanted to know whether the French were coming and the general opinion was the sooner the better.

At last Joe Cuthbert was released from prison. The society ladies of Belfast queued at his tailor's shop to welcome him back. His wife had carried on business but nobody could match Joe's solicitous manner and his notions of the latest Paris fashions. He was given a less formal reception in the Muddlers' Club where we got him quite drunk.

Russell came to the printing office next afternoon and, flinging himself into a chair by the coal fire, began flagellating himself again over his morals, all because he had taken a woman home the previous night. As always, he moaned that he wished to be virtuous but still lapsed into vice at the slightest temptation. What really bothered him was that he had been to see Eliza Goddard in Newry and she told him she wished to see him only as a friend.

'Catch yourself on,' I said. 'I fancy someone like that myself, but I too have no hope, because she is spoken for. There's nothing to be gained blethering on about it.'

I refused to say who she was, judging it best to keep Russell, and everybody else, away from Betsy.

He cheered up after a few ales in Barclay's and we ended the evening with a sing-song, during which Russell lustily belted out a bawdy ditty, 'In Praise of the Sporting Plowman'.

Should maids agree I still make free
Yet never love to tease them o
When they are bent or give consent
I do my best to please them o.

Then as always, he headed off into the night in search of a maid who would bend and give her consent o, and become a cause of renewed soul-searching the next morning.

— TWELVE —

COPPER FACE JACK

The Crown prosecutors kept postponing the trial of the *Northern Star* until early in the New Year when Lord Chief Justice Clonmel ordered a hearing for 28 May. Apparently we had not sufficiently repented of our temerity. The specific charge was publishing a call to arms by the Irish Jacobins in Belfast in a report I had written, though of course my name was not attached.

Sam Neilson sent me to Dublin with the *Star* directors to take notes in court. Martha gave me a letter and a packet of oaten biscuits to deliver to her brother in Dublin.

We set off from outside the Donegall Arms a week later on a chaise and four and stayed overnight in Dundalk, paying two shillings for salted meat the consistency of leather. The Dublin coach, the Cock of the North, was very uncomfortable, with ten of us inside and a similar number clinging on outside. We passed the hundred-mile journey with liberal shots of bad whiskey and ribald jokes. To loud cheering we recklessly overtook the rival coach, the Old Cock, just before we arrived in the capital.

The city we entered was indescribably filthy. People in rags picked their way through unpaved streets. Beggars assailed our coach. The stench from dunghills and refuse was overpowering. Around College Green, however, another Dublin existed. The streets were paved and lit with lamp globes, and lined by magnificent four-storey houses, with grand entrance steps, fanlights and large ground-floor windows. Four-horse carriages and phaetons jingled by, and elegantly dressed ladies were carried back and forth in sedan chairs.

I was lodged in a modest house in Fishamble Street, and next day set off to deliver Martha's letter.

Dr William Drennan, about forty years of age, with long, dark hair carefully brushed back from a narrow forehead, welcomed me with instructions to wash my hands in a basin by the door – to guard against infection, he said. He ordered coffee from his serving girl, and quizzed me about affairs in Belfast. Drennan said he feared he might find himself in jail soon. He himself was to be tried for seditious libel for the publication of the Address to the Volunteers of Ireland.

As we munched Martha's oaten biscuits, Drennan postulated that the difference between Presbyterians and the Catholics was that 'we love the French openly and the Catholics hate them secretly because they have overturned the Catholic religion.' I took issue with him, suggesting it was the Catholic clergy, not the ordinary people themselves, who feared the French. I also took offence at a comment he made about Sam Neilson being 'self-opinionated and obstinate'. And for a great champion of Catholic emancipation he rather took me aback with an observation that Newry, where he had practised for some years, was 'full of pigs and Papists'.

That evening the *Northern Star* delegation dined at the grand house in Rathfarnham of barrister John Philpot Curran, who had been engaged by United Irishmen to defend the *Star* and was also counsel for Drennan. Curran was short in stature, with black hair combed down over his forehead, a high-pitched voice and a protruding lip, and I noticed he never looked one in the face. His eyes swivelled from side to side in a peculiar manner. He was a liberal Protestant like Wolfe Tone and a member of parliament and had a formidable reputation as an advocate.

Curran called his rather ill-kempt house 'The Priory' because, he boasted, he was 'prior' of a lawyers' drinking club called 'The Monks of the Screw', the word screw being an abbreviation of corkscrew.

As the evening drew to a close and port wine was poured, the conversation turned to the dramatic escape from prison of the leading United Irishman Archibald Hamilton Rowan. He had been arrested and lodged in Newgate prison for distributing, at a street corner in Dublin, the

United Irish appeal to the Volunteers. Fearing for his life he resolved to escape. He made up a story for his prison guard that he had sold a parcel of land but the purchaser was withholding payment because a document signed in prison had no legal status. On the promise of a handsome reward, the turnkey escorted him secretly to his home in Dominick Street late at night to witness the legal signature outside the precincts of the jail. Of course the buyer did not turn up. Rowan gave his keeper 100 guineas and got his permission to embrace his wife in the bedroom before returning to the jail. From the bedroom he climbed down a knotted rope, took a horse from the stables and rode it to the home of a patriot in Sutton, north of Dublin who arranged for two fishermen to take him to France. One of the fishermen produced the *Dublin Evening Post* with a wanted notice and asked, 'Is it Hamilton Rowan we are to take to France?' Told that it was, he replied, 'By Jasus, we will land him safe!' Hamilton Rowan reached Roscoff where he was arrested as an English spy but released when he produced the newspaper that declared he was an escaped United Irishman.

The trial of the *Northern Star* proprietors proceeded at the bar of the King's Bench in a massive new domed building on the northern bank of the Liffey. The judge was the Earl of Clonmel, Copper Face Jack, his face the colour of a penny. The charge was publishing, on 15 December 1792, a 'wicked, malicious and seditious libel', namely a call to arms by the Irish Jacobins in Belfast. The jury was made up of Ulstermen brought to Dublin by special coaches, selected for their loyalty.

Curran argued that the proprietors could not be held responsible for they were not involved in the workings of the newspaper. It would be like prosecuting the owners of a ship whose captain had turned pirate. The jury, to everyone's surprise, and Clonmel's fury, returned a verdict of not guilty against every director, save John Rabb, our publisher. Copper Face Jack sent John to prison for two years. Sam was very upset. He had made the decision to publish, not Rabb.

The Dublin citizens treated us to a victory banquet in the Star and Garter in Essex Street. Curran made a speech. One phrase stuck in my mind. 'Evil prospers when good men do nothing.' He told us that the old Whig Edmund

Burke, had been to London and had warned the King that the government must break the alliance of three million discontented Catholics and half a million Presbyterians, or Ireland would be lost to His Majesty. He warned Sam that the Crown would bring new charges against the *Northern Star*. The government wanted the paper stopped and Clonmel would seek revenge.

I was seated beside his junior counsel, William Sampson, a rather untidily dressed Belfast man with beetle brows and locks of brown hair hanging down over a high forehead. Like Tone he was an Anglican educated at Trinity College Dublin and a strong United Irishmen. Sampson commented that publication of the call to arms was bound to provoke a reaction. 'But arms are not the only means by which a subjugated people may expel tyranny and regain liberty. The press is often more salutary in establishing a people's rights than the bayonet.' He advocated the use of ridicule to expose the gentlemen of the Crown. Samson addressed Neilson across the table. 'Perhaps you might let me write a piece for the *Northern Star*?' 'Send us something,' the editor replied.

Back in Belfast after twenty bruising hours in the Old Cock, Sam Neilson gathered everyone in his office for a tot of whiskey. He assured the printers, compositors, and other staff that we would continue publication. But he warned us that Belfast was being vilified in Dublin and those who disliked Belfast would not rest easy until the town was destroyed.

'Who are they, that so dislike Belfast?' asked the young lad who fetched the type letters for the printers.

'I'll tell you who dislikes Belfast,' said Nelson, nodding at me to start writing. 'A gang of corrupt courtiers, who build their fortunes upon the ignorance and religious disunity of this country – they dislike Belfast. A gang of prostitutes and base mercenaries who persuade simple people to perjure themselves at elections and laugh at conscience and integrity as a state joke – they dislike Belfast. A gang of dissolute and avaricious bishops who own a great portion of the land and despise the poor – they dislike Belfast. The whole gang of tax gatherers and sycophants – they cry out against Belfast. The gentlemen of the standing army who act as they are commanded – they swear they will burn Belfast to the ground. Booby squires, Protestant

Ascendancy boys, guzzling corporations, old, idle card-playing tabbies who complain that the mob have raised the price of chair hire, the disinterested tribe of lawyers – they are the ones who rail against Belfast.'

'Print that,' he said. 'Word for word.' It appeared on Friday 13 June, with his addendum: 'There is no spot on earth than Belfast where better morals, more decent conduct, more real virtue, or more of the light of reason prevails. '

Thomas Russell had a good laugh when he read that. 'Better morals? Is he serious?'

In Dublin, John Philpot Curran worked his wizardry again and got Drennan acquitted. He argued that while Drennan had *written* the Address to the Volunteers, he had not *published* it. Curran and Drennan were chaired through the streets by supporters, all shouting huzzahs.

Martha was overjoyed, but her gratification was tempered by forebodings about the fate of Belfast. 'It is commonly said in Ascendancy circles that the country will never know peace until Belfast is in ashes,' she said. 'Let them beware of one remaining spark in those ashes lighting a conflagration.'

The military had already crushed local insurgencies in Louth, Meath, Cavan, Monaghan, Sligo, Leitrim, Derry, Limerick and Wexford. It was important for Belfast to stay calm and for us to avoid arrest. At a meeting of my Society No. 69 in Kelly's Cellars, we were told it would be prison now for anyone found administering the United Irish oath.

We worried that the frequency of executions in France was making people disillusioned with the prospect of revolution in Ireland. Robespierre, who used terror to create a republic of virtue, was himself guillotined in Paris. The French writer Jacques Mallet du Pan observed, 'A revolution devours its children.'

I wondered if we would be any more civilised towards each other if we were to survive a successful rising in Ireland, carried out by Protestant, Catholic and Dissenter.

— THIRTEEN —

THE TRIAL OF THE HURDY GURDY

William Sampson was as good as his word. The barrister spent that August in Bryansford writing a satirical offering for the *Northern Star*. It was an account of an imaginary trial, 'The King versus Hurdy Gurdy'. The offence of the hurdy gurdy was to play the French revolutionary anthem, '*Ah! Ça ira!*' The chief witness to the crime was a French horn.

It was a parody of the trial of the Scottish radical Thomas Muir in Edinburgh, where the hurdy gurdy was described as a seditious organ.

It became the talk of the town. Neilson persuaded us to act it out at a soirée in the Assembly Rooms. All society was in attendance, even Haliday and Bruce, sitting on padded chairs in the front row. Thomas Russell acted as defence counsel and William Putnam McCabe as prosecutor. The French horn was played, appropriately, by the Revd Dubourdieu, a skinny little man of French ancestry who was rector of Annahilt and married to Sampson's sister. I was assigned the role of jury foreman, Tallyho Turncoat.

Putnam was at his brilliant best explaining to the court why playing '*Ah! Ça ira!*' was a dastardly crime.

'The truth of this libel is a very high aggravation,' he declared in the pompous tones of a Crown lawyer. 'The first word, *ça*, is a French pronoun, that – and *ira* is the third person of the future tense, of the indicative mood, of an irregular verb, and means will go – taken together it is that will go… God help us, gentlemen, if they meant that the present order of things will go – it is an insinuation which beyond measure swells the enormity of the crime. I appeal by everything sacred and profane for a guilty verdict to teach a lesson to these abominable, ambitious, atheistical, atrocious, anarchical, barbarous, brawling, babbling, brainless, blasphemous, cruel, conspiring, contemptible, cursed, confounded, damnable, dangerous, destructive, diabolical, deistical, demagogical, execrable, egregious, extravagant, excommunicated, frantic, fanatical, furious, factious, ferocious French.'

My role was brief. As jury foreman, I pronounced the hurdy gurdy guilty and sentenced it to exile in Botany Bay.

Within a month Sampson and Russell collaborated on another satire. It was aimed at the Whig Edmund Burke, whom we despised for his polemics against radicals in his *Reflections on the Revolution in France*, and in particular for his assertion that a 'swinish multitude' – the common people – were not worthy of a final say in politics.

The satire took the form of a mock literary review of an imagined poem called 'The Lion of Old England'. The Lion, representing King George, was depicted as an oracle, whose unintelligible roarings were translated into a manifesto by his prophet, Burke. The manifesto declared that the swinish multitude was born only to labour and be governed, and the means of governing most consistent with true glory was a standing army, national debt, tax-gathering, ecclesiastical patronage, tithes and bribes. The idleness and voluptuousness of absentee bishops was essential to this true glory. The duty of a subject was to despise peace, prosperity, domestic endearments, personal danger, private judgement, and public tranquillity, and to fly off if commanded to the remotest corner of the earth, to kill anyone obnoxious to his mayor, including fellow citizens. In this kingdom, the poverty of the Irish people was the fault not of the government but of the ignorance, bigotry and profligacy of the Irish people themselves, who, despite having no shoes or stockings, happily sent flannel shirts to the British soldiers.

'The Lion of Old England' was a big hit when published in print. Burke apparently read it in Dublin and the King in London, and both were outraged. Martha said she was delighted to see wit and ridicule the order of the day in Belfast. The 'Belfast laugh' she called it. A powerful weapon.

My amateur acting career blossomed. Martha recruited me to read the part of Sir Lucius O'Trigger, an impoverished Irish baronet, in a rendering for her lady friends of Sheridan's *The Rivals*. We sat around a table with green cloth in her parlour, and declaimed while musicians played the viola and piano. Everyone laughed knowingly when I had to aim an imaginary pistol at the gentleman playing my rival in love, Mr Bob Acres. I got to kiss a lovely girl playing Lucy the maid. Martha rewarded us with fruit cake and wine.

The *Star*'s reward for publishing Samson's satires was another subpoena. A fresh charge of seditious libel was lodged against the proprietors. The trial was set for 17 November. We all had to take the road to Dublin again.

We arrived there two days before the trial, after a most unpleasant journey through rain and sleet in a leaking carriage. That evening we once again found ourselves at the dinner table of our defence counsel, James Philpot Curran. He raised our spirits by promising he had something up his sleeve.

Over plates of mutton and pork, Curran spoke of his deep dislike of FitzGibbon, with whom he had fought a duel with pistols some years earlier, the most common reaction to which, he added with silky self-deprecation, was that unfortunately both missed. He detested judges even more, Copper Face Jack in particular, whose smile he likened to the silver plate on a coffin. He liked to tell anecdotes in which he outwitted their lordships. Once, when he and a notorious hanging judge were dining together, the judge asked, 'Is that hung-beef?' To which Curran replied, 'Do try it, my lord, then it is sure to be.'

Once more John Philpot Curran outwitted the judge when our trial for seditious libel began. The prosecution exhibited the *Northern Star* for Wednesday 5 December 1792, with the Address of the Society of United Irishmen calling on Volunteers of Ireland to assert the right to carry arms. With a flourish Curran produced the *Belfast News-Letter* of the previous day, 4 December 1792. It also carried the Address to the Volunteers. Curran addressed the jury. 'To convict the *Star* of seditious libel, the court has to prove malice. Now the *Belfast News-Letter* is no friend of the United Irishmen, and indeed is loyal to the Crown, therefore, there can be no malice in their publishing the Address. The same must apply to the *Northern Star*, which only reproduced the Address *after* it had appeared in the *Belfast News-Letter*.'

The jury retired at a quarter past seven. It returned at nine with a verdict of guilty of publishing the Address, but not with malicious intent. The judge refused to accept this and sent them back. They returned with a verdict of not guilty.

We had confounded the attorney general again. 'We will be made pay for this,' said Sam.

At the next meeting of United Irishmen in Belfast he urged the utmost secrecy in our activities. We must do 'mole work' in future. Everything must be underground.

Tom Russell took the lead, riding around the countryside on a big roan mare he had acquired, encouraging new societies under cover of digging up old fossils. He found a thirst for news in the humblest quarters. 'I saw a little girl with a paper in her hand in a wild part near Ballynahinch,' he said. 'I asked her what it was. She answered, "the *Northern Star*". They read it with avidity.' His military experience and bearing, and his enthusiasm for the cause, made him a natural leader. Everyone deferred to him. The more militant of the younger men trusted Russell to act when the time came. Some of the more 'respectable' radicals were more wary of him. They were not yet ready to contemplate taking the field. I suspected they might never be.

One chilly early December morning I rode with Russell to Lisburn to attend an inaugural meeting of a United Ireland society in the Assembly Rooms in Castle Street, which was well supported by the town merchants. At dinner afterwards I made the acquaintance of their most prominent advocate, a prosperous silk and linen merchant called Henry Monro, who owned a drapery store in Lisburn Market Square. He was in his mid-thirties, small in stature and with deep blue eyes, and was a member of the established church, though more radical than most Presbyterians. Sam Neilson had spoken of him as a 'sound man'. Monro impressed me as a man of action rather than words. He had military experience as a leader of the Lisburn Volunteers.

Harry, as everyone called him, told me the spirit of friendship was so strong in Lisburn that on a recent Sunday the former Volunteers, all Protestants, attended services in both Presbyterian meeting houses and in the Catholic Church.

Monro's business took him around County Down and he knew like-minded linen suppliers and merchants in Banbridge, Ballynahinch and Lurgan. I was intrigued to learn that he had been acquainted with the late Lord Moira, who used to host dinners in Ballynahinch for cloth buyers every market day. He respected the new Lord Moira for speaking out for radical reform. I told him that I shared a regard for him as he had paid for my education.

Monro's equally militant sister, Peggy, enjoyed the reputation of being the first woman to ride a horse alone from Lisburn to Belfast. She joked that Monro liked to think of himself as an athlete. 'He jumped over a row of barrels for a dare last week,' she said. 'He's a blockhead.'

I struck up a rapport with this 'blockhead' and we agreed to remain in close contact.

That New Year's eve I rode to Gransha, on George's invitation, to be one of the first to cross the threshold after midnight. I equipped myself with a flagon of whiskey from McGibbon's of Waring Street and a box of salt from Standfield's grocery on High Street, and made my way to Gransha. I spent the evening in a nearby hostelry.

As midnight approached, I made my way by lantern light down the lane to the cottage where I met Willie Boal, who was carrying a pail of coal as a symbolic gift.

We banged on the door at twelve. George opened it. Betsy kissed me on the cheek, then clung onto Willie. I presented the whiskey and salt to Hans. He joked that with Willie's coal and my whiskey we would be warmed in body and spirit.

The room was already crowded with neighbours and thick with smoke from candles, pipes and turf. They all knew me by then. 'Make room for the *Star* man,' they cried as I approached the fire to warm my hands.

In the small hours we sang sad songs of Ireland. I mentioned that next day was my birthday. More whiskey was poured and toasts were made to me and Liberty. The door was opened to let the fumes escape. Betsy and Boal stepped outside and I affected not to notice. The blacksmith Matt McClenaghan played his fiddle until too drunk to continue. Eventually I passed out.

I woke in the morning stretched out on floor with Matt and two or three others and the pet pig – the lamb had long since been disposed of in the traditional manner. Betsy emerged and made breakfast of stirabout with cream. We sat at the table nursing our hangovers. Matt started playing the fiddle again and sang in his surprisingly sweet voice. I took my leave to get back to Belfast before dark.

As I departed, George, with his usual irrepressible pessimism, remarked, 'Unless there is a miracle, we are in for bad times. The men around here are getting very edgy. They are ready for anything.'

'That's good news,' I said, 'not bad.'

— FOURTEEN —

THE JUNTO PREVAILS

And then there was a miracle, or so it seemed at first. The New Year had hardly got under way when the Earl of Westmoreland, the boorish, anti-Catholic King's representative in Ireland, was recalled to London. He was replaced as Lord Lieutenant by Earl Fitzwilliam, a high-principled reform-minded Whig. Prime Minister William Pitt gave him the post because he needed Whig support for the war with France, which was then going badly for him.

The Whigs were in favour of granting full Catholic emancipation, if only to prevent Ireland from slipping into the arms of France. Henry Grattan, the long-standing Protestant champion of the Catholic cause in the Irish parliament, went so far as to predict that the British government would now relieve Roman Catholics of all their remaining disabilities.

Truth to tell, we at the *Northern Star* were dismayed. We feared that concessions would dilute the national ardour for revolution. 'They will settle for half a loaf, Willie K, you'll see,' predicted Billy Templeton as we wrote up the dispatches from Dublin and London. Indeed, the country was jubilant at the prospect of reform. When Earl Fitzwilliam arrived in Balbriggan on 4 January 1794 to take up his post he was greeted by enthusiastic crowds. Right away he started getting rid of the old junto. He sacked Beresford, the powerful head of the Revenue Department and number one champion of the Protestant Ascendancy. He dismissed Solicitor General John Toler, Attorney General Wolfe and the English Under-Secretary, Edward Cooke, who was responsible for the military and secret service. The new Lord Lieutenant and his wife – who in Drennan's words was 'a fright, with a waist as long as your arm' – became the most desired guests at dinner parties. They snubbed the Ascendancy landlords. At a grand banquet for the Anglican Archbishop of Dublin, Fitzwilliam dined with the Archbishop in one room, ignored the nobility in another, and went off without speaking to them.

Drennan wrote to Martha that the Catholics were happier now than at any time. They conveyed an appeal for emancipation to Dublin Castle with nearly a hundred carriages, and got a favourable response. Drennan warned, however, that the great aim now of the government was to rally all sections against France.

The rush to Catholic emancipation alarmed Irish Whigs, who were less principled than their British counterparts. The Revd Bruce, terrified at the prospect of Papists exercising the rights of man, travelled to Dublin to plea for gradual rather than immediate reform. He still had an important ally in high places. The arch-bigot, John FitzGibbon, who loathed Catholics and despised those who espoused their cause, was unaccountably allowed to remain as Chancellor.

The political excitement created great demand for the *Northern Star*. Subscribers gathered at our office to get copies still damp with ink. Labourers crowded into candle-lit taverns in the countryside to hear the news read out, braving bitter temperatures. Martha said that the lower orders so ardently sought news, she was considering the institution of a free reading room in Belfast with fire and candles. That winter was the coldest in a hundred years. The Lagan froze. Everyone worked, ate and slept in coat and gloves.

Before the end of the month Grattan lodged a bill for Catholic emancipation in the Irish Commons. If approved, it would mean Catholics entering parliament in Dublin. Its seconder was a County Down man, Robert Stewart of Mount Stewart, whose father, Lord Londonderry, owned large estates on the Ards Peninsula.

Billy and I were right to be wary of what London was up to. The price of reforms – which hadn't yet materialised – was capitulation to British war interests. Martha's brother warned that invective against the French had become the order of the day in Dublin 'with Robert Stewart leading it in his diffuse drawling manner.' Stewart and Grattan voted for £300,000 from the Irish budget for the British navy.

Thomas Russell gave vent to the fury we all felt at Grattan's abrupt transition from a champion of liberty to patron of a war against liberty, 'lavishly granting the treasure and blood of his countrymen.' He warned us that the Ascendancy would not be easily thwarted in its efforts to prevent Catholic rights being granted. On a visit to Hillsborough, south of Belfast, he heard that the young Lord Downshire – the old holder of the title had passed away – was rallying anti-Papists among his parliamentary colleagues in Dublin to defeat the Catholic relief bill. Downshire was the landlord, then known as Lord Hillsborough, who had fired at the crowd at Castlereagh. Prominent Anglican clergy and gentry were signing round robins excoriating Fitzwilliam personally and calling for his removal. In London, friends of Beresford and FitzGibbon were lobbying King George against him.

The King allowed himself to be swayed by the argument that the presence of Catholics in the Irish parliament would violate his coronation oath by which he had sworn to maintain Protestantism. It was said that he asked Pitt what the devil he was thinking of, sending a Whig to Ireland and allowing him to lose the run of himself.

The obduracy of the King determined Ireland's fate. Fitzwilliam was told to settle his tradesmen's accounts and return to London. Beresford and the old crowd came back into favour. Reform was dead. Henry Grattan was so outraged that he called for the removal of these old task-masters, 'who galled the country with their tyranny, insulted her by their manner, exhausted her by their rapacity and slandered her by their malice.'

I took the view that if a coronation oath in England stood in the way of liberating four million Irish citizens, then he who took that oath must not be allowed to exercise sovereignty in Ireland. I said this, standing on a bench with a tankard in my hand, at a rowdy gathering in the Muddlers' Club. Neilson wasn't pleased. 'Don't be making a show of yourself,' he hissed when I sat down. 'You are supposed to be a newspaperman, not an agitator. You're no use to me locked up in a prison cell.' Of course he was right. I apologised. But I found it hard to keep my political emotions in check.

By mid-March the old junto was in place again under a new Lord Lieutenant, Earl Camden, an anti-Romanist who cared little for Ireland or the Irish. Beresford was reinstated amid rumours that Pitt was planning a union of Britain and Ireland, with eventual Catholic emancipation as a sop to reconcile Catholics to British rule.

With Belfast in an uproar, an emergency town meeting was called in the Assembly Rooms on 19 March. Almost everyone of consequence turned up, though the Revd Bruce stayed away, wary that the meeting might adopt a prayer for the total emancipation of the Roman Catholics, which he could not countenance. The *News-Letter* editor Henry Joy did appear, looking shattered. He had consistently supported the government while advocating Catholic rights in the *News-Letter*. Now, like Grattan, he felt basely betrayed and so disillusioned with politics he was of a mind to sell the *News-Letter* and retire. The meeting resolved unanimously to send a letter to Fitzwilliam thanking him 'for seeking the complete liberation of our Roman Catholic brethren from those penalties and restraints which have so long fostered suspicion, envy and hate, created perpetual disorder and weakened and debased the nation.' It was also resolved that all shops, warehouses and establishments would shut on the day of Fitzwilliam's departure.

Martha was the only woman present. As we left I saw tears of frustration in her eyes. 'The masses should not allow Fitzwilliam to leave but should elect him president, and wouldn't that take the Castle by surprise,' she said. Martha was typical of the respectable radicals. She was outraged at the injustices inflicted on Ireland. As we picked our way over the frozen slush in Rosemary Street she said she feared that refinement, liberality, and even humanity, were dead, and the victims of any commotion would be the dissenters. 'If there were only one religion on this island a struggle would be worth venturing, but there are three, all naturally striving for superiority, and two of them dread and abhor the religious sentiments of the third and biggest, and fear it would swallow them up.'

'Many good men will now conclude the time for talking is over,' I replied.

She looked at me sharply and asked, 'And would you be among them?'
I just shrugged.

Not a shop or factory opened in Belfast on Wednesday 25 March 1795, the day Fitzwilliam departed from Ireland. The streets were deserted. No carts clattered along High Street. The looms of the weavers fell silent. Only the seagulls kept up their interminable squawking. I wrote in the *Northern Star*, 'There was not a shop or counting-house open during the whole day, all was one scene of sullen indignation.'

We all felt strongly that this was a defining moment in the history of Ireland. The die was surely cast. Revolt was now openly talked about. Before the end of the month several new members were enrolled in the societies, including Henry Joy McCracken, who had been in on the founding of the United Irishmen but hadn't taken the oath.

'With men of such intelligence, ability and daring as Harry,' I remarked to Billy Templeton as we worked together on rewrites from the English papers, 'who knows what we can achieve.'

Lord Camden arrived from London on 1 April to take up his office and was hissed through the streets of Dublin. Every store window was shattered in a riot, during which FitzGibbon was hit on the head with a stone when he stupidly peered out of his carriage.

Camden was the stepfather of Robert Stewart, son of Lord Londonderry of Mount Stewart estate in County Down. In a naked display of nepotism, Camden gave him an important post in the Castle administration. Stewart had won election in Down with the help of reformers such as Sam Neilson, and had spoken from the opposition benches. He now showed his gratitude by switching sides and throwing in his lot with those who sought to protect the Ascendancy at all costs.

Sam was increasingly inclined towards revolution. He published a quotation in the *Star* from the English philosopher, John Locke: 'The people retain the supreme power to remove or alter the legislative body when they find it acting contrary to the trust reposed in them.'

I remarked that the people never reposed any trust in the parliament in Dublin in the first place.

I spent a half hour romping with Belle in the stables on the evening of Fitzwilliam's departure. She said that, in her opinion, we brave men who met upstairs were the only hope for Ireland and she swore she would fight with a pike in her hand if there was a rising.

'Meanwhile I'll have to do with this rising,' she said with her lopsided grin as we got down to business.

— FIFTEEN —

THE OTHER HALF

I had grown to over six feet and was at this point in my life considered a real hard man and Sam Neilson's minder, though, at his insistence, I kept my head down. When Sam and *Star* director Robert Simms set off for Dublin to catch up with developments in the wake of Fitzwilliam's sacking, they took me with them on the rattling Old Cock, not just to take notes but to look out for them. That's how I found out how well the 'other half' of Irish society lives, albeit it's a tiny 'half'.

Neilson and Simms stayed with William Drennan while I found more modest lodgings in Hyde's Coffee House in Dame Street. Next day we went to a great meeting of Catholics in Francis Street chapel. Several speakers advocated unity with Presbyterian Dissenters in the light of recent events. Many crowded round to shake the three northerners by the hand. The Catholic leader, John Keogh, declared to loud applause that the Catholics of Ireland, refused this time, would never again seek the favour of the British cabinet.

Keogh invited the three of us to dinner at his home next day. He remembered me from Rathfriland. The silk merchant lived in considerable splendour in a fifteen-room house at Mount Jerome in Harold's Cross, south of Dublin. As he showed us into a large room with sofas, mirrors and lustrous candelabra, he made a point of mentioning that he had two thousand tenants on his estates in County Roscommon, but he was anxious to assure us that he was not a land-grabber. He had purchased the land since restrictions on Catholics buying property had been lifted ten years before, and not an acre had been confiscated from the ancient Irish.

Wolfe Tone arrived to join us for a dinner of brisket of beef, roast leg of mutton and boiled cows' heels, washed down with claret from Lisbon. As secretary of the Catholic Committee, Tone spent many evenings here planning strategy.

Keogh voiced what we all feared, that there would be an attempt by Pitt to create a union with Britain to dispense with the parliament in Dublin. That would end the prospect of majority rule in Ireland. The sop would be emancipation for Westminster elections. But the Catholics would have none of it, he assured us.

'I have devoted thirty years of my life for the purpose of breaking the chains that bind my countrymen,' he said. 'The way to do it is to make common cause with the Northern reformers.'

Keogh's wife stayed aloof during this discussion. I got the impression she didn't like Protestants of any stripe.

There were separate bedrooms for us in Keogh's, each with a spring mattress on a four-poster bed, linen covering, a chamber pot made of china and a rope to summon a servant. And this in the house of a Catholic!

At breakfast Tone told us that he would be attending a soirée at Francis Rawdon's Dublin residence at Usher's Island on the south bank of the Liffey, and we should accompany him to pay our respects. It took me a second to realise he was referring to the new Lord Moira. He mentioned that we should not be put off by the rather haughty manner of his mother, the Countess of Moira. While she was a real English blue-blood, being a baroness in her own right, she was in fact quite sympathetic to the United Irishmen.

The Moira mansion was a magnificent three-storey building with tall chimneys. We entered through a walled garden. I tried not to stare at the statues and busts and elegant panelling in the hallway. Obsequious footmen in embroidered liveries showed us into an octagon-shaped room with a high window reaching from floor to ceiling and sides inlaid with mother of pearl.

Upon greeting the Belfast delegation, the Countess announced, 'I do hate the North. And I detest Ballynahinch. Our rich neighbours there are so vulgar and illiberal, I have to say I was never tempted to exceed the limits of formal civility.' I warmed to her immediately.

Lord Moira, taller than I remembered him, thin-faced, with his hair sticking out in curls, embraced Tone, saying, 'Ah! The Irish Lafayette!' On being told who I was, he asked with a smile, 'Are you still creating mischief?' 'I am, sir,' I replied. 'Good, good,' he said. 'But be careful. These are troubled times.' I thanked him for providing me with an education and said I trusted my expulsion from the Revd Bruce's academy had not reflected badly on his choice. 'Matty McTier speaks very highly of you,' he said. 'You must have turned out all right.' He added that he never warmed to Bruce himself.

He turned to greet Henry Grattan, a surprisingly short, effeminate-looking man with extraordinary long arms, who entered looking around distractedly.

Robert Stewart next strode into the room, tall and imperious, with deep-set blue eyes and full, moist lips, nodding graciously to some and pointedly ignoring others. He passed Sam Neilson with his face deliberately turned the other way.

In my frock coat, breeches and cotton stockings I felt poorly dressed in this company of Dublin's finest gentlemen and ladies. Many of the men were attired in satin suits and embroidered knee bands, and sported wigs covered with pomatum paste and powder. Women of all ages wore voluminous silk dresses with bosoms in full view and paraded around under piles of ornamental hair held up by wire.

There was an enormous fuss when the Lord High Chancellor appeared, decorated with stars and garters and with a dressing on his head where he had been struck by a stone during the riot on 1 April. His face had the ruddy redness of a heavy drinker, and his eyebrows seemed permanently arched. FitzGibbon greeted us coldly.

'The *Northern Star* is the engine of rebellion,' he snorted. 'One day we will make the seditious press as tame as domestic cats.'

'A stroked cat is gentle,' I said.

'What, what's that?' he barked.

'It's my family motto,' I replied. He glared and turned away to receive the bows and courtesies of other guests.

I marvelled at how sworn enemies could mingle so easily in each other's grand manors. Moira loathed FitzGibbon for his bigotry, and FitzGibbon hated Moira for his shafts at the castle junto, but they accepted invitations to each other's houses. Everyone in the room hated someone else. The poet Henrietta Battier came to talk to Tone. 'How I loathe FitzGibbon,' she said. 'He's a glittering snake, an evil man.'

Miss Battier in turn introduced us to Margaret King, the daughter of the Earl of Kingston, a pretty woman with long hair in ringlets who asked us penetrating questions about northern politics and who, as Tone informed us later, was one of the only women members of the United Irishmen. Her loyalist brother, George King, with a reputation for mounting more than his horse, looked bored, enquiring only if the northern ladies were *amenable*.

As we left, I asked Tone if Lord Moira might one day become a United Irishman himself. 'Moira is sympathetic to us,' he replied. 'I have told him more than once if he would only lead the coming rebellion he could become the greatest man in Europe. But he won't listen.'

I reflected that if we Presbyterians had the support of Catholic leaders such as John Keogh, and of members of the aristocracy like Moira and Margaret King, then there indeed one day might be a truly united Ireland. At the same time I didn't feel comfortable in the grand houses of Dublin. The hearth by the turf fire at Gransha was my social and spiritual home. I wondered how these rich and titled patriots would coexist in a future Ireland with the tenant farmers and the labourers who so avidly read the *Northern Star* and yearned for a better life.

Neilson and Simms took the mail coach back to Belfast next day, leaving me in Dublin to report on the trial of the Revd William Jackson on a charge of being an agent for France. Jackson was a native of Newtownards who started life as a preacher in England, took refuge in France from a financial scandal, and wrote pamphlets in Paris attacking England. Aged about sixty, with a balding dome and bushy white hair combed round his sideburns, he appeared in the dock in a frock coat decorated with frogs. He looked quite weird.

The trial was really a vehicle to portray Wolfe Tone as a felon. Jackson had sent letters to the revolutionary government in France. One was intercepted. It contained a copy of Tone's assessment of the condition of Ireland.

There was absolute silence in court as Tone's critique of the British administration in Ireland was read out by the prosecution.

'There are three sects in Ireland, the Established Church, the Dissenters and the Catholics,' it began. 'The first, infinitely the smallest portion, have amassed all the profits and honours of the country exclusively, and a very great share of the landed property. They are of course aristocrats, averse to any change, and decided enemies of the French Revolution. The Dissenters, who are much more numerous, are the most enlightened body of the nation; they are steady republicans and, devoted to liberty, and through all the stages of the French Revolution have been enthusiastically attached to it. The Catholics, the great body of the people, are in the lowest degree of ignorance and are ready for any change for no change can make them any worse. They are a bold, hardy race and make excellent soldiers. In Ireland, a conquered, oppressed and insulted country, the name of England and her power is universally odious, save with those who have an interest in maintaining it. The great bulk of the people of Ireland are ready to throw off the yoke in this country, if they see any force sufficiently strong to resort to assist them. The Dissenters are enemies of the English power from reason and from reflection, the Catholics from a hatred of the English name. The government of Ireland is a government of force. The moment a superior force appears, it will tumble at once, as being founded neither in the interests nor in the affections of the people. The people of Ireland are ready to rise. There is scarcely any army in the country because of the war with France and the bulk of the militia are Catholics and would certainly refuse to act against a force that came to support them.'

Jackson was found guilty. He looked terribly ill when brought into the courtroom for sentencing. Steam was rising from his head. His coat was stained with vomit. He clutched at his stomach and shuddered in agony, then collapsed on the floor and, right there in front of us, expired. It turned out he had poisoned himself to avoid being pronounced guilty of treason, which would have barred his widow from inheriting his property and pension.

The Crown did not have the original of Tone's letter so there was no direct evidence of treason against him, but the message was clear: he could be seized and hanged any day if the Crown was so minded.

The government had given the United Irish leader no alternative. Tone could escape the hangman only if he left Ireland.

— SIXTEEN —

PARTING OF FRIENDS

Wolfe Tone chose to spend his last days in Belfast before taking sail to the United States. In early June he arrived by coach with his wife Matilda, their three children and his sister. Matilda was very pretty and clearly devoted. I could understand why Tone had eloped with her when she was sixteen.

Belfast society competed to host the family, and they were treated to dinners and entertainments every evening. There was a lot of drinking. After one bawdy night Russell, as usual indulging his hangover, complained he was in the 'blue devils', and that he was losing his faculties. 'Glad you have any to lose,' retorted Tone.

Near the date of his departure, Tone expressed a desire to climb Cave Hill, which overlooked Belfast, to take a last look over the northern counties of the land he loved.

Sam Neilson, Robert and William Simms, Tom Russell and Harry McCracken set off with Tone for the summit, with me tagging along to carry wine and provisions. We walked along North Street on a clear bright morning and took a well-trodden path through a carpet of bluebells under ash and sycamore trees, then trudged our way through thick bracken and bright yellow whin bushes to the top.

The outline of Cave Hill was an inspiration for *Gulliver's Travels*, Russell informed us as we climbed. Jonathan Swift imagined it as the head of a sleeping giant. He added that it was known in Gaelic as *Beann Mhadagain*, meaning Madigan's Hill, after an ancient king of Ulster.

At the summit we rested at McArt's Fort, an ancient structure with a steep precipice on one side and a ditch on the other. Here, it was said,

Madigan's nephew McArt was killed in a battle with the old enemies of Ulster eight centuries earlier.

We stood in silence, taking in the view. Beneath us were the chimneys and rooftops of Belfast. To the east across the Irish Sea lay the low hills of the Isle of Man and Scotland. To the south the grey ribbon of Strangford Lough and the purple line of the Mourne peaks, shimmering in the heat. To the west Lough Neagh glittered in the sun. To the north lay the deep Glens of Antrim.

After consuming bread, cheese and claret, Wolfe Tone made a short speech praising the people of Belfast for their kindness and affection. 'Even those we scarcely know have entertained us with parties and excursions for our amusements, and this for a man who is now driven into exile,' he said. 'Let us make a solemn obligation never to desist in our efforts until we have subverted the authority of England over our country and asserted her independence.' We stood and repeated his words. As we embraced, I felt there could be no turning back. The connection must be broken. We were going to have to go down the American route. Never before or since did I feel such an intensity of patriotism and love of Ireland as on that hot, still day on Cave Hill.

The McCrackens hosted a magnificent final supper for the Tone family in their house on Rosemary Street. All radical Belfast society crowded into the drawing room and dining room. Toasts were made to Liberty and to Tone's return. There were melodies from fiddles and dulcimers. The musician Edward Bunting, as round as a barrel from the sugar plums and sweets with which he liked to be rewarded, played several ancient Irish airs on his harp.

Among the guests were an affluent Catholic linen merchant of Anglo-Norman stock from Lisburn, called Luke Teeling, and his son Charles, who, though barely seventeen, was 'up and up', being a Defender and a United Irishman at the same time. They were well connected with both the gentry and the rebels: Luke was a personal friend of Robert Stewart of Mount Stewart, and his son-in-law was John Magennis, the leader of the County Down Defenders.

Harry McCracken's brother, a maker of ropes and sails, ventured over dinner that the Irish could free themselves without French assistance. Tone reacted sharply. 'If you act on that principle you may pursue your sail manufacturing long and prosperously enough, for there will never be an effectual struggle in Ireland without invasion.'

As Bunting played 'The Parting of Friends', Matilda Tone cried softly. Wolfe too shed tears, though I recalled his dismissal of harp music as 'strum, strum and be hanged'. Dr James MacDonnell plucked awhile at the harp; he was taught by the famous blind harpist Arthur O'Neill. Tone once called him jokingly the 'hypocrite', after his medical oath. The tall, handsome doctor had embraced Russell and Tone as dear friends but he had declined to embrace their United Irish principles. I didn't trust him a bit. He complained in my hearing that he had tried, but failed, to talk Tom Russell out of his involvement in the dangerous schemes that had become 'part and parcel' of his existence.

Everyone embraced at the end. Russell consoled Wolfe and Matilda with considerable gentleness. He said the Tone family would surely return in happier times.

On Saturday 13 June 1795, the Tones boarded the 225-ton American brig *Cincinnatus*, bound for Wilmington, North Carolina. Several of us went on board to furnish his small state room with sea stores, sweetmeats, wine, porter, spirits, books and games for the children. Dr MacDonnell presented him with a small medicine chest with written instructions.

Neilson, Robert Simms and Charles Teeling were the last to confer with him on the wharf before the ropes were cast off. Teeling's presence was important. He provided Tone with the confidence to assert that he could speak abroad for the Catholic Defenders as well as the Dissenters.

We stayed on the dockside waving handkerchiefs until the ship with its three hundred passengers slipped into Belfast Lough and out of sight.

That evening, with the *Cincinnatus* well on its way, Russell disclosed to us that Tone considered his compromise with the government to extend no further than the banks of the Delaware. He planned to travel from there to Paris. In France he would apply in the name of Ireland for the assistance of the greatest military power in Europe to assert Irish independence.

This meant, said Russell, that we should now plan in earnest for a rising, but there should be no attempt to achieve independence until we were sure of French help.

'What if it doesn't come?' I asked.

'Then we are on our own,' replied Russell. 'God protect us.'

— SEVENTEEN —

UP AND UP IN DOWN

After Tone's departure I spent some days riding around County Down to make contact with new societies that were springing up like mushrooms after rain. Billy Templeton did the same in Antrim. As *Star* men we had a good alibi for our movements. I relished the role of newspaperman and rebel. I was now a trusted member of Neilson's staff and a senior United Irishman, having been elected to the Belfast Committee at a meeting of Society No. 69 in Margaret Magee's public house on Mill Street, after which I was provided with a pistol in a case.

I was happy to saddle up Eclipse and get out of town. Belfast people were coming down with fever. The town was filthy. In the countryside I rode by blazing yellow whin, snow-white blackthorn, and banks of violets by whitewashed cottages with red geraniums in the windows.

My first stop was naturally Gransha, where I spent a pleasant afternoon helping George and Betsy Gray weed their patch of gooseberry and raspberry bushes. As always, I couldn't take my eyes off her. That evening Willie Boal and others came to hear the latest news. A lot of the conversation was guarded. George was openly for the United Irishmen. Willie was not so sure.

Betsy had no doubts. When the visitors had departed, and I was about to climb up to the open loft to spend the night and had already said good night, she whispered to me, 'There is nothing left now but the pike.' I was taken aback. That was what Belle Martin had said.

I was up with the crowing of the demented cock and set off towards Bangor.

For a week I criss-crossed the county. Everything appeared normal. People tended potato and turnip fields and patches of flax; cattle and horses grazed in clover patches; dogs barked and snapped at riders; geese cackled, bullocks lowed, goats foraged, weavers wove. Young women carried spinning wheels on their heads on their way to spin and sing together. Cock-fighting and bull baiting and horse racing were the talk of the villages.

But in every conversation seething resentments emerged, against the government, against tithes, against high rents, against loss of family members to America, against forced conscription into the militia. In the evenings, farmers, labourers, weavers, apprentice boys, young women and wives met in barns and taverns to debate the rights of the government versus the rights of the people. Reading societies were founded in many places as cover for United Irish activity. Most had heard Russell speak at one time or another and they worshipped him.

More than once I heard a prediction among country folk: 'We have had a frosty winter and a cold spring. We will have a bloody summer and a headless king.'

Most everywhere I got a great welcome as the *Star* man, as everyone assumed that I wrote the paper myself and knew all the latest news.

I was greatly heartened to meet again the Lisburn draper Harry Monro. He too had been travelling round the county buying webs for bleaching and had found great enthusiasm for the cause. He had contact with linen drapers in the south of the county who were also leading Defenders. Many Defenders were ready to join the United Irishmen. Quite a few were already up and up. His sister Peggy, who defiantly wore a green ribbon in her hair, had started a weekly quilting club at which she prepared the fashionable ladies of Lisburn to support the patriotic movement and keep their secrets. Harry said that Masonic Lodge No. 193, where he was master, had become the centre of revolutionary discussion. Most important United Irishmen were Freemasons, he said. It was the one place where all religions could meet. Bartholomew Teeling, a Catholic and brother of Charles, was a member of his lodge. 'So too is your editor, Sam Neilson,' he said.

From Lisburn I rode to Saintfield to confer with another key figure in our ranks, the dissenting minister, the Revd Thomas Ledlie Birch. A dour, craggy character with white hair swept back over his ears, Birch was a firebrand. He had created the first United Irish society outside Belfast and radicalised his congregation. We were joined for cold beef and hot apple pie by the Saintfield agent for the *Star*, David Shaw, a prosperous merchant with scrubbed cheeks who made his money as a grocer, spirit dealer, leather merchant, woollen draper and cotton manufacturer.

As we tucked into the pie, Birch explained how the Scriptures shaped his political views. 'True religion can flourish only if there is civil liberty,' he said. 'The struggle between France and the counter-revolutionary powers is the literal accomplishment of the Prophesy of the Battle of Armageddon in which the Beast and his Adherents are to be cut off. According to the Books of Revelation and Daniel, a millennium of peace will begin in 1848.'

'Not till then?' I said. 'Sure we'll all be dead.' 'Unfortunately so,' he replied, failing to note the mockery in my voice.

Saintfield Presbyterians had nourished grievances for decades. When leases expired, landlords put up rents, forcing many to emigrate, especially when there was a bad harvest. Hangings for agitation were not uncommon. One Samuel Jamison of Saintfield survived a hanging at Downpatrick jail by wearing a special collar made by his friends. He was found still twitching after an hour and was rehanged without the collar. Since then, said Birch, hangmen throughout Ireland had been instructed to bare the neck of every condemned man.

After lunch I watched from the gallery as Birch addressed the Saintfield and district Masonic brethren in his church. 'Kings are the butchers and scourges of the human race,' he thundered. 'They revel in the spoils of thousands, whom they have made widows and orphans. According to the Scriptures, the time is coming when wars will cease and mankind will become a family here on earth. Amen.' He looked up at me and I fancied he winked.

I reported to Sam Neilson that the men of County Down would surely rise when the circumstances permitted. He worried, however, that Catholics and Protestants were not yet united enough to contemplate rebellion.

Tom Russell took to heart the need to convert Catholics to our cause. He began to study Gaelic with Patrick Lynch from Loughinisland, who rode up to Belfast every week to conduct an Irish class at the academy. He persuaded Sam Neilson to publish a journal in Irish, *Bolg an tsolair,* which featured a grammar for learners and poems by Oisín, son of the mythical warrior Finn McCool. I told him the only Protestants keen on learning Irish were ministers who wanted to convert Catholics in Irish-speaking areas in the Mournes and the Antrim glens.

Meanwhile that autumn we began to reconstuct our societies into a secret army with military titles. Delegates from seventy-two societies in Belfast, County Down and County Antrim, mainly Presbyterian farmers, manufacturers and shopkeepers, met in Flanagan's to approve a new constitution. Each Society was to be split up into divisions of no more than thirty-six members. If more, it should divide into two societies with at least eighteen in each. The societies should send delegates to lower barony committees, whose members would be captains. The captains would elect upper barony committees, whose members would be colonels. The colonels would elect county committees that would elect provincial committees that in turn would elect a national executive.

We were given a revised wording of the United Irish oath. It was ambiguous enough to encompass reform or rebellion, requiring a member to endeavour simply 'to obtain an equal, full and adequate representation of all the people of Ireland'.

Around this time Sam and Martha McTier went travelling in Scotland but, alas, Martha returned a widow. Her husband of more than twenty years died of the fever in the Lowlands. Sam McTier was a few years off sixty. He had treated me well and I had got to love him like an uncle.

I called at the house as soon as I heard the shocking news. A big crowd came to offer sympathies, despite fear of contagion from the fever that had brought death to many doors in Belfast.

Martha was inconsolable. I spent as much time as I could with her, helping make arrangements for the funeral, serving drinks to visitors, doing messages.

She had spent her years finding ways to please Sam and now she was bereft. 'I have lost my even-tempered morning comforter, my daily companion, the generous provider of my comforts, my evening friend,' she said.

I was surprised Dr Drennan did not make the journey from Dublin to be by his sister's side. Martha said she did not encourage her brother because of the fever in Belfast. 'Death is busy here,' she said. Still, he should have come.

— EIGHTEEN —

MEETING THE LONDONDERRYS

In early October I was back on the road again on a special mission, this time to Greyabbey on the Ards peninsula.

Eclipse carried me at a canter from Belfast to Newtownards, then south past the sand flats of Strangford Lough. The shore was populated by large flocks of birds, some with gold-spangled upperparts, others black and white with orange bills, and ducks with dark green plumage – patriot ducks! Overhead a multitude of starlings wheeled across the sky making fantastic shapes. The sun shone weakly and the Mourne Mountains took on pastel shades along the horizon.

After a few miles I glimpsed, through a thicket of beech trees, a higgledy-piggledy mass of low buildings, one with a grand portico big enough to shelter a carriage from rain. Workmen were making an embankment on the lough shore. They told me that this was Mount Stewart, estate of Baron Londonderry and his son, Robert Stewart, the rising star in the Ascendancy government.

The men were wearing green kerchiefs. One recognised me as the *Star* man. They freely expressed their contempt for his lordship.

The little town of Greyabbey, a mile or two farther on, lived up to its name, with grey stone walls, grey houses, grey and black crows cawing in the trees and among the ruins of a Cistercian monastery, destroyed five hundred years before by a Celtic leader to prevent its use by English colonists.

I sought out the house of the Presbyterian minister, the Revd James Porter, a radical clergyman, noted far and wide for his brilliant lectures on astronomy and natural philosophy. He also had a reputation as a great

124

wit, and Sam had published the caustic letters he sent to the *Star* against injustice, signed 'Sydney'. My errand was to persuade him to write more extensive political squibs for the paper. To become part of the Belfast laugh.

A handsome man of about forty, with aquiline features, large twinkling eyes, a prominent nose and long hair hanging in strands welcomed me into the manse. The Revd Porter's parlour was cluttered with books and strange-shaped jars and bottles and shelves laden down with scientific instruments. He made me welcome and bade me stay the night. That evening with my host and his wife Anne I enjoyed a merry dinner of fowl with celery sauce, beef, blackberry tart and good Bordeaux. Their eight children ran in and out all the while.

Over the cries and squeals of the young Porters, he told me why he was a zealot for the cause. The lot of Presbyterian tenant farmers on the Ards was comparable to that of the serfs in feudal Russia, he said. 'Londonderry is the supreme arbiter of justice, even of life and death, here. His magistrates make the laws. His agent, the Revd John Cleland from Newtownards, is one of the most hated men in County Down. Three years ago he began to collect tithes for the Anglican Church which no one has had to pay for the last hundred years. If he doesn't get the money, he forces them off the land. They go to America or the poorhouse. Cleland puts on a show of meekness and humility but he is cruel and avaricious. Worse, he is an informer and a thief. He insists on being paid in gold coin, and everyone knows that he sweats the gold by rubbing the coins on canvas and saving the dust.'

Porter had grown up in Donegal where his father had a flax-scutching mill. One day he had taken two shirts from the thorn hedge where they were drying and left home to seek his fortune. He acquired an education in divinity at Glasgow University, a centre of radical sentiment, and eventually received a call to be minister at the dissenting Presbyterian Church in Greyabbey.

He would be happy to work on some satirical material for Sam Neilson. He would bring a squib himself to Belfast to see how we liked it. 'And I might commit myself, like I presume you have,' he said, his eyes holding mine across the table.

'There's many in the Society would like that,' I replied.

125

When I mentioned I had heard about his wondrous lectures, Porter boasted that even Baron Londonderry came to his talks on the latest scientific discoveries. He expected them to turn up for a performance in his church the following day. 'You must come,' he said.

We ended the evening singing ballads, some of which Porter had written himself. He was mightily pleased that I knew the words of his 'The Exiled Irishman's Lamentation', which recalled the wretched fate of small farmers forced into emigration. We recited it together, our arms out-stretched:

Green were the fields where my forefathers dwelt
Tho' our farm was small, its comforts we felt.
At length came the day when our lease did expire,
And fain would I live where before lived my sire,
But, ah, well-a-day, I was forced to retire...

By the time we retired to bed we were fast friends.

Next day I stood behind Porter at the door of his church as he welcomed the arrivals for his lecture.

Baron Londonderry, a skinny figure with domed forehead, fat cheeks and pointy chin making a perfect triangle of haughtiness, arrived in a carriage with the ladies of his family. Behind him came Robert Stewart, in top-hat and moleskin frock coat with a silk stock round his neck, followed by a pious-looking cleric with receding forehead and sharp nose, dressed in ruffle-fronted shirt and high-collared frock-coat. This was Cleland. He met no one's eyes, and as he took his seat those near him moved away.

Porter was a dazzling performer. His experiment with an electric machine evoked gasps of amazement. He used what he called a Leyden jar to create and store electricity, then made the legs of a frog twitch by jolting it with a spark from an electrostatic machine to show that nerve muscles work by electricity. He forecast that electricity and engines driven by steam would one day transform society and unite communities. 'Ignorance is the curse of God; knowledge is the wing wherewith we fly to heaven,' he said in conclusion, quoting Shakespeare's *Henry VI*.

While the church emptied, Porter introduced me to Robert Stewart as the representative of the *Northern Star*. He looked at me dismissively. 'Abominable publication,' he said. As he turned away, I decided to show him I was no stranger to the exalted circles in which he moved. I remarked that I had been at a reception we both attended in Lord Moira's house in Dublin. He looked at me sharply. 'Call tomorrow at Mount Stewart,' he said. 'Breakfast. Seven o'clock'. He turned and climbed into his carriage without waiting to see if this was convenient for me.

'I used to be a favourite in Mount Stewart,' Porter said, as I set out next morning. 'Lady Frances still invites me for tea on occasion, but his lordship knows I see him for what he is, a land-grabber and exploiter of the tenant farmers. Good fortune to you.'

As I entered the gardens of Mount Stewart I passed a gazebo and fish pond, and dismounted to inspect the plants in a nursery garden. 'Mediterranean cypress,' said a voice behind me. 'Actually, no,' I said. 'These are cedars from Goa, *Cupressus lusitanica*.' 'Well I'm damned,' said Stewart. 'Aren't you the clever fellow!' I told him I had once helped catalogue Lord Moira's plants. 'Is he still trying to plant the Tree of Liberty?' asked Stewart scornfully.

He brought me through a large hall with waxed and polished flagstones, littered with fishing tackle, antlers, foxes' tails and boots. On the wall hung a portrait of Stewart wearing a top hat and holding what he called a golf club. In the dining room the *Northern Star* and *News-Letter* were folded on a sideboard, along with the *New Peerage*. The table was set with cold meats and hard-boiled eggs. Cleland was sitting there. Stewart introduced me.

'I know who you are,' said Cleland, offering a limp handshake.

'And I you, sir,' I replied.

'I've made enquiries,' said Stewart. 'Bit of a firebrand at the academy. And Cleland here tells me you are turning up everywhere around the county where there is sedition. But Martha McTier, for some reason, has spoken up for you.'

I replied that I travelled on *Star* business and it was inevitable I would turn up where there was sedition, for the people were discontented everywhere.

Stewart proceeded to lecture me on the dangers of revolution, as a liveried servant poured black tea, which I affected to relish.

'I have been to the continent and I have seen both sides exhibiting scenes of savage barbarity that would disgrace a tribe of Cherokee Indians,' he said.

I reminded Stewart that he himself had said that the American and French revolutions were caused by the obstinacy of governments in resisting reforms. Hadn't he also declared that the connection between Britain and Ireland should not be preserved through abuse? And that the vices of the existing system had driven the public mind into a state of agitation?

'Reform is a wise and necessary measure,' said Stewart, 'but those who so loudly applaud the French Revolution should beware of imitating it. If Ireland were indeed to separate from Britain, we would cut a sorry figure in Europe, clad in our insular dignity and abstract freedom. It is absurd and romantic to think we can exist for any length of time as a separate and independent state.'

I said it was absurd to think that Ireland could exist for any length of time when the smallest portion of the population had amassed all the profits and honours of the country exclusively, and a very great share of the landed property.

Stewart laughed knowingly. 'I recognise the words of Mr Wolfe Tone,' he said.

'I am proud to repeat them,' I replied.

'And what will become of a government of Catholics and Presbyterians which you fellows are promoting? Only tumult and convulsion.'

'The *Northern Star* is intent on achieving reform, not revolution,' I said.

Cleland wasn't buying it. He gave a snort and interrupted, 'Why then has Sam Neilson taken the crown from his masthead?'

'You've got spirit, though I suspect you are gullible and easily led,' said Stewart. 'By the way Mr Porter is a brilliant philosopher but you are in dangerous company there. He has notions that will rise up and bite him.'

Just then his wife, Lady Emily, tall, fat and jolly, romped into the room.

'Take this young fellow to the garden,' said Stewart. 'He will tell you what the new imports are.'

'Good-oh,' she said.

As I left Stewart called out, 'Tell Sam to take himself off to America if he wants to live in a republic.'

On my return journey I cantered along the sea coast road by Portavogie and Ballywalter, then cut across the peninsula to Newtownards, and from there up the winding hill to Gransha. After dining with the Grays I took my leave.

Betsy gave me apples and pears from her little orchard. She hooked my arm as I went to untie Eclipse.

'Why don't you come more often? George misses your companionship,' she said.

'And you,' I asked. 'Do you miss my company?'

She blushed and ran back to the house. I was furious with myself. I had overstepped the mark. But I couldn't help the way I felt. And why did she take my arm if she didn't feel something for me? I was falling hard for Miss Betsy. I spent the ride to Belfast indulging in wild fantasies of kidnapping her and running off to America, or, better still, of young Boal emigrating himself and leaving the field clear for me.

Sam Neilson said nothing at first when I recounted my conversation with Robert Stewart. He put some coal on the fire and inhaled a pinch of snuff.

'Stewart once sought the assistance of men such as me to win election,' he declared. 'Now he sees the United Irishmen as Jacobins and would gladly have me locked up as a revolutionary.'

He pondered for another minute, then added, 'He says reform is wise and necessary, yet always remember, when Stewart speaks of reform, it is with England's interests in mind.'

— NINETEEN —

SPEAKING IN TONGUES

As the winter approached, my friends braved every type of weather to rally the people. Tom Russell was away riding around the north, ostensibly studying rock formations as an amateur geologist but in reality creating societies far and wide.

That December he made a lengthy tour of Counties Antrim and Down, trying to encourage Defenders to enroll in the United ranks. He arrived back in Belfast one day on his big roan mare, soaking wet and shivering with the cold. On his last night he had taken refuge in a public house in Loughinisland because of heavy snow. Silent men smoking pipes around the fire indicated with smiles and winks that they knew and approved his mission. The landlord, Andy Lemon, refused payment for his bed. When he left that morning, the snow turned to sleet, then pelting rain.

I told him of my encounters with Robert Stewart and how detested were the big County Down landowners, Londonderry, Annesley, Downshire and Savage. Downshire, in particular, was loathed for his callous nature; everyone knew he had fired at the militia protesters and it was said he gave a woman the pox and refused to support her as she lay dying.

Russell cautioned me that it was wrong to assume that all gentry were unpopular. He had stayed on Rathlin Island as a guest of the landowner, Robert Gage, on the pretence of studying geological structures. He secretly gathered a hundred of his tenants in a cave and persuaded them to take the oath. They did, he said, but they insisted on a clause that no harm would come to Mr Gage.

William Putnam McCabe was also on the go all that winter, travelling around the southern counties to drum up support for the United Irishmen. He returned to Belfast on 3 January 1796, just after I celebrated my twenty-first birthday with my parents in Moira. He told me how he had often turned his gift for mimicry to good use, adopting different disguises to avoid arrest.

He gave the *Star* an order to print a hundred hand-bills. They advertised the appearance of a converted Papist at a barn in Cottown the following Sunday who would explain how he became convinced of the true doctrines of Presbyterianism.

'What's this about?' I asked. 'Are you doing the Lord's work now?'

'Come, you'll enjoy it,' he said.

Cottown was close to Gransha. I said I would bring some local people. I gave him directions to the Gray homestead and asked him to drop off a note there to expect me on Sunday morning. 'Just mention my name and they will treat you well.'

The fields were white with hoar frost and Eclipse's breath made puffs of steam as I rode to Gransha on the day of the event. Betsy was in the kitchen reading a copy of William Cowper's *The Task* which she had obtained from an itinerant packman.

'This is you,' she said, quoting aloud lines she had marked with charcoal.

He comes, the herald of a noisy world,
With spatter'd boots, strapp'd waist, and frozen locks,
News from all nations lumb'ring at his back.

'So what news do you bring, *Star* man, with your frozen locks?' she asked.

The incident when I had embarrassed her was evidently forgiven. I looked over her shoulder and read out the next bit:

He whistles as he goes, light-hearted wretch,
Cold and yet cheerful: messenger of grief
Perhaps to thousands, and of joy to some.

'I fervently hope I may never bring grief to this house,' I said.

George, Betsy, Willie Boal, Eliza Bryson, Eliza's brother Andy and I set off across the fields to the Cottown barn. Betsy wore a green frieze cloak which she had made to display her patriotism. Coming on nineteen, she was now a striking, self-confident and very desirable young woman. How I longed for her attention.

People converged from all directions to hear the converted Papist. Near the barn a strange figure on horseback appeared in the twilight, clad in long black cloak like a priest's soutane and wearing a Quaker-style broad-brimmed hat and green-goggle spectacles. He tethered his horse and strode into the barn behind us. Candles were lit and the doors closed.

The man in the cloak climbed on to a table and began speaking in a low voice. He underlined the theological differences between Catholics and Presbyterians, while emphasising the sufferings of both. His voice gradually rose to fill the barn.

'Good people of Down, looking around me here I see Presbyterians, and even some Anglicans, and maybe a Papist or two. Now we all live together in this blessed part of Ireland, Protestant, Roman Catholic and Dissenters. And we all owe a duty of forbearance to each other. We are all Christians, are we not? We are all God's creatures no matter what religion we profess. And if a neighbour has wronged us we owe a duty of forgiveness. There is great evil in the world around us. We must fight against it, together, as brothers and sisters. What must the righteous do? Why, we must forget our differences, we must unite against injustice, we must all unite. Unite against those who would allow our different creeds to be used to divide us in the face of terror. We must unite in the face of repression. Come forth to me and make a pledge to be true to each other, to be true united Irishmen and Irish women.'

I gave a loud 'Aye!' Others joined in.

There was laughter and a few hoots as the country folk realised that the gathering was really to promote the cause of a United Ireland, though most had guessed that was the idea. The preacher was of course my friend Putnam.

I pushed my way forward and affected a country accent. 'Gie me a pike and A'll no see ye stuck,' I said, pulling my forelock. He gave a wink. 'Ah ha! A true patriot!'

George interrupted to say that three men known to be loyalists had just slipped out. I was about to chide him for worrying too much, as always, when there was a loud whistle and several dragoons burst into the barn.

The captain called out that no one might leave without an order from him. He pointed at the preacher with his musket and ordered him to surrender himself.

Putnam took off his hat with a theatrical flourish and extinguished the candle nearest to him. Every candle was snuffed out in the barn. We were left in darkness. Everything went quiet.

An English-accent was heard: 'Captain, I have left my musket outside.' The officer replied, 'Get it!' We heard a man go out, loudly cursing the blasted rebels.

The dragoons lit their lanterns. The preacher had disappeared.

From outside a voice cried, 'Liberty for all!' There was the sounds of hooves galloping away. The soldiers rushed out of the barn, furious at being tricked.

We grabbed Betsy and Eliza by the hands and ran out past the infantrymen as they lunged out with their musket butts, and made our way in the moonlight to the Gray household, stumbling and laughing. Eliza kept holding my hand. She was very fetching, with long fair hair, big eyes, full lips and a body shaped like an hour glass. I played along. If I attached myself to her I would at least have a reason to stay close to Betsy.

To my delight Putnam was waiting for us at the Gray farmstead. He knew I would be there. He confessed that he was sure they had him this time. Hans said he was welcome to stay, especially since he was a friend of the *Star* man.

Putnam looked at me and raised his eyebrows mockingly. 'Is that what they call you?' he said. 'Oh noble Willie K,' he intoned like a ham actor, "You are as constant as the Northern Star, of whose true-fixed and resting quality there is no fellow in the firmament." That's from *Julius Caesar*.'

'I know,' I retorted, punching him on the shoulder, 'Here's a line for you: "Compared to me you are all unnumbered sparks, you block, you stone, you worse than senseless thing!"'

Over supper Putnam said we should all be learning French. Betsy replied, '*Je suis d'accord.*' She had been studying *La Grammaire Française.* I promised I would. I said I was acquainted with a Frenchman in Belfast and would ask him to teach me.

Late in the evening, as Putnam, George, Hans and I were sitting round the fire drinking whiskey, George said, 'I know you're both sworn in. Time we were too.' He meant himself and Hans.

'What say you?' I asked, looking at Hans, who was the type of taciturn Ulster Scot who kept his thoughts to himself.

'Aye,' he said. 'It's time.'

'What does Betsy think?'

'She bullied us into it,' said George, laughing.

'And what about Willie Boal?'

'He's not the joining type. But if he ever does, England watch out!'

Hans fetched the family Bible and Putnam and I swore in the two Gray menfolk and taught them how to recognise a fellow United Irishman through a series of questions and responses: 'What have you got in your hand?' 'A green bough.' 'Where did it first grow?' 'In America.' 'Where did it bud?' 'In France.' 'Where are you going to plant it?' 'In the crown of Great Britain.'

Putnam and I slept in the loft that night. Betsy made stirabout for us in the morning and gave us oatmeal cakes for the journey.

As I was saddling up Eclipse, Betsy came out behind us. She pressed a small parcel into my hand and said, before running back in, 'For your birthday. Do you think I forgot?'

I put it in my pocket.

'I think you have a hankering there, *Star* man,' said Putnam as we set off down the lane.

'Not a chance,' I said. 'She's spoken for.'

I opened the package in my room that evening. It was her copy of *La Grammaire Française.* There was a note inside. 'To dear William, our best friend, who lifts our spirits always. I hope you get to use this well. *Rester en sécurité.* Betsy.'

Next day I started learning French. I joined an adult class conducted by Philippe Carmenthan who, like me, was a member of Society No. 69. Before the evening was out I could say, albeit with a Belfast accent, '*Je suis Irlandais*', and '*Nous sommes vos amis*'.

Perhaps I should have been learning Gaelic too.

That winter five companies of the Highland Regiment of Reay Fencibles arrived in Belfast from Scotland, their pipers making a dreadful skirl as they marched along High Street. They wore kilts and, apart from their officers, spoke only Scots Gaelic.

How ironic, I thought, that Gaelic-speaking soldiers from Britain, who didn't understand English, should find themselves in Ireland, keeping down English-speaking rebels, who didn't understand Gaelic, and who were learning French.

A grand ball was organised in the Assembly Rooms for the Highland Fencibles on their first Saturday in town. They came dressed in belted plaids with their hair plaited at the back and tied. The dancing continued until after midnight.

Dr James MacDonnell, who spoke Irish Gaelic, heard a private berate an officer in Gaelic for desecrating the Sabbath. The officer replied, '*An tir am bithtir, Se nithir* – In the land we be, so do will we.'

They soon made themselves very unpopular, detaining anyone out after dark. Even the new proprietor of the *News-Letter*, Charles Gordon, was taken to barracks one night and not released until he could prove his identity. The officers daubed slogans on walls stating 'Scots rule'. Someone went round writing underneath: 'Scots don't even rule Scotland.' (That was me.)

The Limerick City Militia, a body of 450 men, also arrived to garrison rebel Belfast, which by then, under the command of Brigadier General Nugent, contained detachments of the Royal Irish Artillery and the 64th Foot and Third Light Infantry, backed by a garrison of York Fencibles in Newtownards, the Cavan Militia in Dromore, the Drogheda Militia in Lurgan and the 22nd Light Dragoons in Lisburn. The Limerick men were paraded around the streets in scarlet cloth with yellow facings, shouldering Brown Bess flintlock muskets. Most of them were English-speaking

Catholics chosen by ballot to forcibly serve the King and many were rebels at heart. With their differences in language, religion and national identity, they and the Scots had little time for each other. It wasn't long before they began brawling in the streets. The generals realised that they had blundered and the Limerick Militia was ordered to leave for Derry.

Before they departed, the Highland Fencibles, bellowing out curses in Gaelic, attacked the Munster men in High Street with sticks and cudgels. The officers intervened, much to the disappointment of the crowd.

The Limerick Militia was replaced by the Monaghan Militia, which contained many loyal Protestants who called themselves Orangemen, after our historic benefactor William of Orange.

Societies of Orangemen had begun springing up in County Armagh which had the worst record for sectarian conflict in all of Ireland. Since the government's decision two years earlier to allow Catholics to become enfranchised forty-shilling freeholders, landlords had begun renting land to Catholics and this had driven up the price of leases in Armagh. Once in place, Catholics were getting into the textile trade, which the Protestants had monopolised, as weavers, spinners and bleachers. This had driven down the income from piecework. Resentment and religious differences formed a toxic mix. Nightly outrages were common. Protestant bands known as Peep o'Day Boys attacked Catholic homes and smashed their looms. Defenders raided Protestant houses and seized arms. Magistrates took the side of Protestants and many thousands of Catholics had to flee to the west of Ireland.

That September the Protestants won a pitched battle at a crossroads in County Armagh called the Diamond. Their leaders wore Volunteer uniforms which no doubt had been on display at the great Bastille Day celebration in Belfast. These were my co-religionists and decent folk but they were badly infected with anti-Papist rhetoric. They began forming Orange societies to counteract the designs of the United Irishmen. Like us, they modelled themselves on the Freemasons, with lodges, grand masters and oaths. They vowed to support the constitution, give allegiance to the King, oppose societies of a rebellious and treasonable nature, and join the government in protecting the country in case of foreign invasion. Catholics were excluded.

The Ascendancy had its protectors at last among the common people and didn't hesitate to use and arm them. We now had to face a formidable opposition within our own Presbyterian ranks.

— TWENTY —

THE BELFAST LAUGH

Sam Neilson, his face red from laughing, inhaled a wrist of snuff and said, suddenly serious, 'You know you will be persecuted if ever they find out you are the author?'

'So be it. I have no fear of them,' replied the Revd James Porter, warming himself by the coal fire in Sam's office.

The squib he promised when I visited him in Greyabbey was more like grapeshot. It was a dialogue between a 'Squire Firebrand' and his agent 'Billy Bluff' which ridiculed and exposed the system of feudal tyranny in Ireland better than any historian. It ran to several thousand words and satirised one of the most obnoxious landlords in County Down, Hugh Montgomery of Greyabbey Estate, and his bailiff, William Lowry.

Sam punched his palm with his fist, as he always did when excited. 'It's very long but I intend to print it all,' he said.

As I perused an extract, I wondered if the objects of Porter's rollicking humour would recognise themselves. If they did, he would surely suffer. It went like this:

'Well, Billy, what news?' says Squire Firebrand.

'Troth, sir, plenty of news, but none very good,' says Billy Bluff.

'What's your neighbour on about now?'

'Well, please your honour, he's at the old cut; railing against the war, against the tithes and against the game laws and he's still reading at the newspapers.'

'He's a damned villain and must be laid fast by God. But what more do you know of him, Billy?'

'Why, bad enough and please your honour. Him and the Popish priest drank together last market day till all was blue again with them; they shaked hands, so they did, drank toasts and sung songs.'

'Pretty work. By heavens, did you overhear them?'

'Ah, that I did too, and listened like a pig.'

'What were the toasts?'

'First, the priest drank Prosperity to Old Ireland, and –'

'Stop Billy! The toast is infamous, the word Old never was and never ought to be applied to any country but England, and he who would apply it in Ireland is a rebel and ought to be hanged.'

'He ought, and please your honour, as round as a hoop.'

'Well what toast did the villain drink?'

'He drank Union and Peace to the People of Ireland.'

'Worse and worse, Billy, a damned deal worse, he who wishes union wishes ruin to the country. Union forsooth! That is, what never was and what never must prevail in this country; as to peace, 'tis flying in the face of government to speak of it, the devil send the ruffians peace, till their betters choose to give it to them.'

'Then sir, the priest drank Here's Every Man his Own Road to Heaven.'

'That, Billy, is a toast that no man would drink, but a republican and sinner, for it supposes all men to be on an equality with God, and supposes that a man may go to heaven without being of the established church, which is impossible…'

Neilson was so pleased with the dialogue he took us for lunch at the Donegall Arms. As we entered, Porter turned to me and said quietly, 'I am ready to commit.'

Next day I brought him to 68 Linen Hall Street, the residence of the surgeon John Campbell. In a room there in the presence of Harry McCracken, I proposed Porter as a member of the brotherhood of United Irishmen. Harry required Porter to read the oath aloud, which he did. Afterwards he kissed the Bible.

It was a risky business. The Insurrection Act stipulated the death penalty for anyone caught administering the oath. It also empowered magistrates to impose a curfew, enter our homes and search for arms.

Sam Neilson told me to make sure my new flintlock pistol was not found in the office. I wrapped it in oilcloth and concealed it in small gap between the chimneys above my lodging room, distant enough to disclaim ownership if found, but near enough for speedy retrieval.

The Squire Firebrand satire appeared in the *Star* on Saturday 21 May. At the Muddlers' Club that evening Billy Templeton and I acted out the roles of Billy Bluff and the Squire to a raucous audience, including Tom Russell, Harry McCracken and William Samson.

Belle Martin stayed to listen and joined in the laughter. As it got dark, I took her to an empty back room and we did it on the table. She said she loved the little play we had enacted. She asked who wrote it so she could give him a drink on the house, but I wouldn't tell her. 'State secret,' I said.

Belle really wanted to be one of us, I imagined. She got quite cross, so I left her there and went to my lodgings, keeping to the darkest shadows in Rosemary Street to avoid the fencibles.

Satire was to become our main weapon in the succeeding months.

Encouraged by the acclaim for his 'King versus Hurdy Gurdy', Sampson produced a fictitious *Chinese Journal* which the *Star* serialised. It was a parody of a popular book called *A Narrative of the British Embassy to China*. In Sampson's version a mandarin advised the English ambassador that his country's vainglorious boasting and tyranny had made it universally detested. Unlike British rulers, who had the insolence to call poor folk swine – another dig at Edmund Burke for calling common folk a 'swinish multitude' – the Chinese emperor was beloved by his people. The emperor prayed that if any insurrection occurred, the poor would not suffer death by military violence, but that the mandarins of the district would be shamed and punished, for 'in the negligence and corruption of the great originate the vices of the poor'.

A dream sequence in another installment had William Pitt and Catherine of Russia playing cards with human hides. Pitt and his war secretary Henry Dundas were transported to Botany Bay to mend old clothes – 'their first gainful employment'. They were then hanged from a tree until it fell down, leaving Habeas Corpus suspended.

In the last episode the Turkish ambassador in Peking said of the British that they talked of liberty whilst they engaged in bribery and corruption. The English ambassador retorted that the British were 'the perfection of reason', then floored the Turk with a punch.

'Samson is tops now at creating the Belfast laugh,' said Martha approvingly.

We did our best to keep the identities of Porter and Sampson confidential. But if Martha knew, so too did much of Belfast society. I worried that these brilliant satirists and polemicists would bring down the wrath of the powerful upon themselves, knowing how vindictive their agents could be.

As it was, most everyone knew that we at the *Northern Star* were all secretly sworn into the United Irishmen.

This was made clear when Edward John Newell, a Downpatrick Catholic, called by the office to place an advertisement in the *Star*. Newell described himself as a portrait artist, specialising in miniatures, who did 'strong likenesses in crayons, oils, compound colours and miniatures, the same sizes as other portrait painters but at half the price, at his studio at 27 High Street.' A good-looking fellow with hair combed down over his ears, and something of a miniature himself, standing at well under five feet, Newell asked me with a wink and a nod to join him for a glass of ale and a private conversation.

Sitting on a bench in Peggy Barclay's he wasted no time getting to the point. He was already a Defender and would like to get inducted as a United Irishman.

'Why are you asking me?' I asked.

'Sure, isn't everyone at the *Star* a United Irishman?' he said, nudging me in the ribs.

I told him someone would be in touch.

A few days after that I called at Eddie Newell's studio and told him to come to a back room in Margaret Magee's public house in Mill Street.

Several men were there, including John Gordon, Sam Neilson's nephew, a hard and rather unpleasant man.

The miniaturist told us he had served his time as a painter and glazier in Dublin. He had come to Belfast to make a living for himself as a portrait artist. He was ready to show his love for Ireland by any means.

Gordon leaned forward and said, 'I am concerned.'

Newell replied, 'So am I.'

'With whom?'

'The National Convention of France,' replied Newell.

'What is your design?'

'On Freedom.'

'Where did the cock crow when the whole world heard him?'

'In France.'

Gordon shook Newell by the hand. He has successfully responded to the Defender code. 'He's good,' he said.

I brought the miniaturist to the next meeting of Society No. 69 in Kelly's Cellars. He was sworn in, told the signs of the United Irishmen, and relieved of six pence for his dues.

Newell became a popular figure in the Muddlers' Club. I found him a likeable fellow, a bit pompous and argumentative, but an enthusiastic radical.

I introduced him to the social life of the Assembly Rooms. We played faro there one evening. Eddie successfully bid for banker and won handsomely because of an unusual number of splits. I lost heavily on calling the turn wrongly almost every time. I should have taken Martha's advice – when I started losing, I should have quit.

When Eddie had money he spent it. After the card game we went together to find a couple of obliging ladies in the dark shadows of Mill Street. This became a regular occurrence. 'Nothing like a bit of debauchery,' Eddie liked to say.

Before long I suspected he was shafting Belle Martin too. I was not such a fool to think I was the only one upon whom she bestowed her favours. One night I asked her in the stables if she was having it off with Newell too. She laughed and ran back up the stairs.

Eddie joined in the French lessons given by Philippe Carmenthan. We learned to say:

'I am an Irish patriot – *Je suis un patriote irlandais'*.

'You must give us arms – *Vous devez nous donner armes,'* and

'Let me guide you – *Laissez-moi vous guider.'*

'How do you say, "Let's get drunk?" I asked Philippe, after class one evening.

'*Passons à la bu,'* replied Philippe.

'*Trés bon,'* I said, '*Passons à la bu.'*

— TWENTY-ONE —

A STONE OF THE HEART

Up to this point in my life, the cause was everything. I was a United Irishman working for the United Irish newspaper. I was taking part in a great historical endeavour. I had made friends and acquaintances with the leaders of the finest generation ever to live and dream in Ireland. I had travelled to Dublin and been welcomed into great houses. I was respected and looked-up to in my own back yard. I was in love with life, my life. I was also forlornly in love with Betsy Gray, but the drink helped overcome that.

Though we were inspired by the noblest ideals, the incessant pressure on us from the authorities, and the accumulation of injustice and outrage, did something to us. I noticed in myself, and in my comrades, a hardening of attitude, a chilling of the heart, a desire to strike back with violence. Chief among our enemies were the worst and the lowest, the spies and informers in our ranks.

The first spy with whom I came face to face was a Franciscan friar who arrived in the *Northern Star* office one afternoon from the west of Ireland. Skinny, and aged between thirty and forty years, Father Michael Phillips sought out Sam Neilson and claimed that he had been sent by the Defenders in Roscommon to liaise with the United Irish Societies of Belfast.

Sam invited him to lodge in a room of his house on Waring Street. Neilson frequently gave temporary board to priests seeking cooperation on Catholic emancipation; so many had stayed there his children referred to 'the priests' room'.

Joe Cuthbert the tailor and I took Phillips to a tavern on the quays for supper. He said he was interested in learning the new structures of the

United Irishmen for the benefit of the Defenders in western counties. We agreed to arrange a meeting for him. However Joe, who was both a United Irishman and a Defender, was suspicious, and some lads were assigned to watch the Catholic cleric discreetly for a few days.

When Phillips got permission to say Mass in St Mary's Church, one of the watchers entered the sacristy during the service and was able to read a letter secreted in the lining of Phillips's great coat. It was written by Under Secretary Edward Cooke and addressed to the military commander in Belfast, with instructions to give the bearer all assistance.

Cuthbert rode out to Lurgan and recruited three trusted Defenders for a special task. Meanwhile I informed the friar that the meeting he wanted was scheduled for the following evening, at eight o'clock in Flanagan's on Chichester Quay.

Cuthbert and his Lurgan friends were waiting for him instead. They knocked Phillips unconscious as he approached Flanagan's, retrieved the letter from his coat, and threw him into the Lagan with a heavy stone in his pocket to make it look like suicide.

Phillips's body was next day found at low water near the paper mills. I attended the inquest on behalf of the *Northern Star*. No one could identify the dead man. A military officer was present throughout. I suspect he knew well the identity of the victim but he said nothing. The jury returned a verdict of accidental death.

During the hearing, a Scottish soldier, using the Gaelic word for stone, testified that the deceased was found with a heavy '*cloc*' in his pocket. The magistrate thought he said 'clock', so the official report said he had a heavy *clock* in his pocket. I copied it out verbatim and a delighted John Storey made sure that was exactly what we printed.

We sent the incriminating letter to Under Secretary Cooke in Dublin, without an accompanying note, to let him know that our intelligence, in this case, was better than his. Joe took particular pleasure at the confusion over the word 'cloc', telling us, 'We surely clocked him!'

We soon clocked another. A militiaman from Limerick applied for membership of the Belfast United Irishmen. A defector, Corporal Burke, warned us that the Limerick man had been sent by Dublin Castle to infiltrate our society.

Burke arranged for a party of a dozen men, including me and Eddie Newell, to spend a Saturday evening drinking with the suspect. When it became dark we took him out to the mall 'to have some fun'. At the bridge near the paper mill Eddie, realising what was going to happen, made to depart. Burke pulled out a pistol and said 'Nobody leaves.' He then turned and struck the militiaman hard with the butt, knocking him senseless. He pushed him over the bridge into the water and cried, 'It is done by God!'

We fled in different directions. I took Eddie to Barclay's where we drank in the main bar. The portrait painter was shaking. I was quite calm. 'The first time is the worst,' I said, as if I dispatched informers every day.

Belle Martin leaned over us, exposing her white, sweaty breasts. She seemed inordinately interested in Newell and caressed his cheek. 'Poor boy! What's wrong with you?'

Harry McCracken got information that yet another military deserter, Sergeant John Lee, was in fact a government agent who had been collecting the names of militiamen at Blaris Camp, near Lisburn, who had secretly taken the United Irish oath.

Harry and Joe Cuthbert and others met in my lodgings in Hercules Street. Two pistols were produced and made ready. Cuthbert told us he had asked Belle Martin to bring a package of pistol balls which had been left for him at Barclay's Tavern.

'Are you mad?' I said. 'She's too nosey to be trusted.'

The others laughed. 'You should know,' said Joe.

'We have to use people like Belle to carry stuff around,' said Harry.

Belle Martin arrived and handed in a bundle wrapped in cloth. 'Here's your bunch of berries,' she said. She gave me a cheeky look. I thought she liked being around hard men, in more senses than one. Joe shoved them into his pocket.

Next day Billy and I were working in the *Star* front office when Joe Cuthbert came in. He was perspiring. He took a copy of the paper and sat reading it in a corner. He said nothing. After half an hour a courier arrived with a dispatch from Lisburn. Sergeant Lee had been shot and wounded and his coat and weapon stolen. A great hue and cry was going on.

'Terrible business,' remarked Cuthbert, without glancing up.

'Terrible,' I responded.

'By the way,' he went on, 'I have acquired a military greatcoat, if you know anyone who is looking for one.'

Having fully composed himself, Cuthbert minced off to supervise the girls working in his drapery and ladies habit-maker shop.

'He's some boyo!' said Billy.

The authorities had every reason to worry about the disaffection of the men in the militia camp at Blaris.

Cuthbert and his wife and other couples regularly travelled there in a coach and four with loud liveries to bring money and presents to the soldiers to encourage them to take the United Irish oath. Nobody stopped them. There were few guards. Several militiamen by then were 'up and up', Defenders and United Irishmen. We grew confident that, in a rising, hundreds of these Catholic recruits, resentful at being dragooned into military service to the Crown far from home, would desert and join our cause.

Two artillery men who did desert told us their commanders were terrified the French would invade and the population would rise up. Before they were safely got away on a fishing boat to England, one warned us that an unidentified young woman in Belfast posing as a prostitute had enticed a militiaman to admit taking the United Irish oath and then had informed on him and he was put in chains.

Preparations for a rising were stepped up in anticipation of French support. Thomas Russell was appointed military commander of County Down at a meeting in the attic of the Second Presbyterian Church. An executive directory was set up for the North composed of Tom Russell, Sam Neilson, William Putnam McCabe, Henry Haslett and William Sinclair. We were instructed to make every effort to stockpile arms and recruit members of the militia.

We were also instructed to stay away from the Muddlers' Club. It had become too well-known as a meeting place. We should gather in John Alexander's on Peter's Hill, or in Kelly's Cellars.

In late May I rode to Carryduff, Lisburn, Dunmurry and Ballynahinch to update the Societies. In Armstrong's Hotel in Ballynahinch I was told the town was completely organised by the United Irishmen and numbers were increasing. Lord Moira's gardener and groom swore the oath in my presence.

Learning of my interest in horticulture, the gardener took me to see his work at Montalto. The two-storey mansion, small by Ascendancy standards, was approached along a long, curving gravel avenue flanked by cedars, hornbeams and cypresses. I noticed that he had planted *Rhododendron ponticum* to bring colour to the woods and I warned him that this new import might overrun the property one day. To my delight I saw that he had planted out some of the dwarf spruces that my father had nourished in the glass house in Moira.

On the way out I had a chat with the gatekeeper who assumed I was visiting on business. He complained that all his lordship's tenants had been corrupted by the infernal *Northern Star*.

'Yes,' I said. 'Terrible rag.'

— TWENTY-TWO —

CORONETS ON PISS-POTS

Mountmumble would put a fellow in jail, or in the stocks, just when he pleased – nobody said it was wrong. He would horsewhip a tradesman when he presented his bill – nobody said it was wrong. Shot dogs for barking, imprisoned Catholics for keeping arms in their houses, fined Quakers for not paying tithes, got a Presbyterian assassinated for voting against him in the vestry, and kept a farmer's son in prison till he died for shooting a partridge, nobody said – nobody dared to say – it was wrong.

Thus did the Revd Porter begin a subsequent lampoon for the *Star*, taking direct aim this time at Baron Londonderry of Mount Stewart, who was reputed to have done all the things mentioned. Everyone reading the *Star* would know Mountmumble was Londonderry.

Soon afterwards Baron Londonderry was elevated to Lord Londonderry. In an earlier life he had been known simply as Alex Stewart, a Presbyterian like ourselves, from the townland of Ballylawn, but he had become enormously wealthy through the judicial choice of a spouse. His first wife, Mary Cowan, was the heiress of Sir Robert Cowan, who had amassed a fortune as the corrupt Governor of Bombay. The ill-gotten gains of his father-in-law had now secured for Alex Stewart a grand aristocratic title and the right to expect lesser beings to tug their forelocks in his presence.

As a consequence, his son Robert Stewart became Viscount Castlereagh, and was thereafter known simply as Castlereagh.

Sam Neilson was affronted. The way he saw it, the Presbyterian Robert Stewart, who portrayed himself as a reformer and got elected to parliament with the help of Presbyterian radicals like himself, was being rewarded with the fancy title of Castlereagh for throwing in his lot with the ascendancy church and a government that would not countenance reform.

At dinner one evening Martha, who for the first time since Sam's passing had dispensed with the black satin mourning gown and black velvet cap and looked resplendent in a patriotic green gown, also expressed her contempt for Castlereagh.

'He has a constant sneer on his fat face, and takes on airs and speaks in a drawl as if trying to disport himself as a studied, tedious talker,' she said. 'For fifty years he was an honest and private man, but now he has bowed to the temptations of authority and the baubles of office.' She added, 'And his "what-ho" English wife, Lady Emily, has the personality of a colourless barn door.'

'Oh, come!' said Dr Alexander Haliday, who was sitting next to me. 'She's a fine, comely, romping piece of flesh. She's got her own notions. She wrote a witty verse once, with the line "I love Rob's spear in my heart". It fairly enraged those around her who despise Robespierre as the villain of the French Revolution.'

Haliday had been mentor to the young Robert Stewart and still occasionally went to Mount Stewart on Sundays to play cards with Londonderry's second wife, Lady Frances, despite incurring the old landlord's displeasure for advocating reform in the Whig Club.

'I've been practising the new nomenclature which changes in that family almost as often as it does in chemistry,' said the elderly physician. 'Lord, earl, m'lord, m'lady, your excellency, your worshipfulness, your cleverness….'

'We have Londonderry to thank for much of the disaffection in County Down,' I said. 'Castlereagh makes things worse by acting like a petty tyrant.'

To underline the point I quoted a line from Shakepeare's *The Tempest* which I had seen in the Arthur Street theatre: 'My lord…you rub the sore when you should bring the plaster.'

Haliday applauded. He turned to me and said that Londonderry had banned the *Northern Star* from Mount Stewart since he recognised himself as Lord Mountmumble. He had ordered his tenants to boycott the newspaper.

'I bring the *Star* to Lady Frances when I visit,' he said, 'which is only when the prig is away.'

'He will not like the next edition,' I said.

The Revd James Porter, who knew everything about the source of the Londonderry wealth, had been inspired to fire off another squib, in which Billy Bluff informed Squire Firebrand about the comments of a radical tenant concerning the honours bestowed on Mount Stewart:

"What a fine thing ,' says he, 'to see in one day, Mr changed into Lord, Mrs into My Lady, Jack-a-Dandy into My Lord Likewise, and all the little Misses turning into My Lady A, My Lady B, My Lady C, My Lady D, My Lady E, My Lady F.

'Did you ever see mushrooms growing on a dunghill?' said he.

'Many a time.'

'Then,' said he, 'you have seen what our new race of lords and earls resembles; they have rotten roots, flimsy stems, spongy heads, and start up when nobody expects it, in 24 hours. Then,' said he, 'comes the coronet painted on the coach, on the harness, on the dishes and plates, on the piss-pots, it is stamped on the cows' horns, on the bulls' horns, on the spades, on the ploughs, on everything, so that the coach will run without horses, the dishes will always be full of nobility, the piss-pots will never break.'

'Stop, Billy, I'll hear no more of that damned, seditious rascal's impudence, and do you hear, borrow me that damn'd lying seditious paper, the *Northern Star*, and to your blood don't mention to a mortal living that I read it.'

'Never fear, I would not disgrace your honour's character by such a thing, as to say you would endure to read the lies that is printed in that paper.'

'Lies Billy, it's all lies, from beginning to end.'

'I thought they copied sometimes from other papers, your honour.'

'No matter, what's truth in other papers is lies when put into the *Star*, it is just the very contrary.'

'Then your honour, what is lies in other papers is truth when put into that one.'

'No, no, Billy, no such thing. It's all lies…. Damn thinking Billy, 'tis putting the world mad. Oh what a happy country we had before men turned their thoughts to thinking! 'Tis songs that is most to be dreaded of all things. Singing, Billy, is a damned bad custom; it infects the whole country, and makes them half-mad; because they rejoice and forget their cares, and forget their duty, and forget their betters.'

— TWENTY-THREE —

THE SIEGE OF BELFAST

Stung by the shafts of our satirists, and fretful that the peasantry was of a mind to turf them out, the landlords, many of whom detested one another, began to unite against the common enemy – those who sought to mend the rift between Presbyterians and Papists that kept both in subjection.

Lord Downshire, the most loathed of the northern landlords, organised a cabal of County Down aristocrats in Newtownards where, as an eavesdropper put it, 'every ass there brayed assent to a proposal to raise an armed yeomanry to put down the dissenters,' the asses chiefly being Castlereagh, Annesley, Price, Savage and Downshire. Lord Westmeath was there braying too, as his regiment the Westmeath Militia had been brought to County Down to help put out the fires of liberty. Such an armed yeomanry would be different from the militias; their typical member would be a Protestant on a horse, stationed in his own locality.

Castlereagh had become particularly active. Everywhere I went in the county he had been there before me, inquiring about the societies and their leaders. I heard that a turncoat had given him some names, and that depositions were being prepared. There was also evidence that the landlords had been given huge amounts of cash for informers.

One morning James Hope, a prominent County Antrim United Irishman who had been recruiting in the south, called to see Sam with some disturbing news. Jemmy, as he was known, was a self-educated hand-loom weaver who had mastered ancient Greek philosophy and was revered among our ranks for championing the cause of the poor. He told Sam that the previous evening, in J. McDowell's public-house in North Street, a Crown attorney had offered him ten fifty-pound notes – sufficient to buy a farm – to swear to the identity of leading United Irishmen, and had mentioned Neilson in particular. He said the money was provided by Lord Downshire.

Neilson felt it was no longer safe to sleep at home. He moved into a room in the house of the barrister William Sampson. Harry McCracken was also nervous and set off to lie low in the Antrim hills. 'Watch yourself,' he said before leaving. For the first time I felt vulnerable. What if I were to be arrested? I would be no good to anyone in a dungeon.

Undaunted, Thomas Russell continued to stir up the people. In September he published a pamphlet under his own name entitled: 'A Letter to the People of Ireland on the State of the Present Situation in the Country'. It recommended that the people should unify, arm themselves, be brave, acquire knowledge, and remove the foreign power that upholds the fungus-like Ascendancy.' He told me he felt the country was ready to rise and that it would be triggered by a French invasion.

Indeed that month news of a great French victory over Austria at the battle of Castiglione brought crowds onto the streets of Belfast, cheering and dancing, with everybody shouting for the French and Napoleon. Horse riders entering town were made to dismount and join in the celebrations. Bonfires were lit on Cave Hill and on hilltops all over Down and Antrim.

As usual the latest bulletins came by way of a letter from Dr Drennan in Dublin. He reported that the French were giving lessons to the Turks at Constantinople, teaching the court of Denmark good manners, organising insurrections in Sardinia, Naples and Genoa, forcing Switzerland to defend herself, and pushing Spain and Holland into a defensive war. However he believed rumours about a French invasion of Ireland were being propagated by the government to provide a pretext to garrison Ireland with Englishmen and force a union with Great Britain.

The garrisoning of Belfast was already well under way. Two more troops of the 22nd Light Dragoons were deployed to Belfast, bringing the number of Crown forces in and around the town to five thousand. Dragoon patrols began jostling and beating anyone with close-cropped hair, calling them 'Damned Croppies'. The fashion for short hair had been copied from the French revolutionaries who had stopped wearing wigs to be anti-aristocratic. The idea of us too cutting short our hair originated with the radical parliamentarian from Cork, Arthur O'Connor.

My hair was curly and down to my shoulders and I was instructed to keep it that way to protect my 'mole work'.

The agitation for a rising became intense. Sam Neilson used the *Star* to warn of the need for discipline in localities where patience was running out. Local insurrections only furnished pretexts for additional repressions, he warned.

The landlords struck on 16 September 1796, a Friday.

In the morning a troop of horse came galloping up High Street from the Long Bridge under the personal command of Castlereagh, Downshire and Westmeath. Dragoons and artillerymen turned out of their barracks at the same time.

The door of our office was flung open and Castlereagh marched in, pistol in hand. He dispatched dragoons with firearms to search the building for Sam Neilson. 'Take these two,' he commanded, indicating Henry Haslett, who had called by, and foreman compositor Samuel Kennedy, before posting a guard and leaving, having ascertained that Neilson was not there.

I got out by the back window and ran down Wilson's Court, my heart thumping. Behind me, on High Street, officers with sabres in hand were ordering shops and businesses to close and shouting at country people in town for the fair day to go home. They tipped their carts over, strewing cabbages and potatoes into the gutters.

I raced to William Sampson's house to warn Neilson, but Lord Westmeath was already there with a troop. They knew where he was staying! But Sam wasn't in the house. When they left, Sampson emerged to say that they had searched every room, closet and pantry, including the bedroom where Mrs Sampson was in the early stages of labour. He had told Westmeath that she was not, as some ladies were, in the habit of 'lying with other men'. Westmeath has recently been shamed when it was publicly disclosed during a divorce action that Lady Westmeath had cavorted naked with her lover in a carriage being driven through Dublin. Sampson said he continued to ridicule the red-faced Westmeath in front of his soldiers by pointing out that they had overlooked a hat box where the editor of the *Northern Star* might be hiding.

We found Neilson in the Exchange. 'Sam, they are looking for you,' said Sampson. Neilson said he would give himself up and make his case at trial. He had no choice. We walked together to his house in Waring Street where Sam said a tearful farewell to his wife and children and went to surrender to Westmeath.

I set off to look for Russell. Astonishingly, I found him walking nonchalantly through a group of soldiers in Grand Parade. He told me he has been strolling around openly since the military arrived and no attempt had been made to seize him. 'They want me to escape abroad so as to get rid of me,' he said. 'I won't give them the satisfaction. I will give himself up and stand trial.'

He proceeded to Ann's Street, where the military had broken down the door of the Belfast Society for Promoting Knowledge looking for him. Castlereagh, Downshire and Westmeath were standing outside the library with state attorney John Pollock. Sam stood beside them, his hands bound at the back.

Russell strolled up to Castlereagh, and presented him with a copy of his 'Letter to the People of Ireland'. He was immediately seized and bound.

'All I ask for is a speedy trial,' said Russell.

'You will get it,' replied Castlereagh. We were to find out too late that he was lying.

Downshire spat at Sam's feet. 'I'll see to it that all the scoundrels at your infernal, lying paper are put in the dock,' he said. 'Aye, you and the shareholders and the printers, all of them.' I shrank back into the crowd that had gathered.

The Revd Bruce turned up and began to remonstrate with the landlords over damage to the library. Not a word about the despicable treatment of his librarian. Russell handed him the key.

At three that afternoon Sam Neilson, Tom Russell and eighteen other prisoners, all United Irishmen, and including our foreman compositor, were taken to Dublin in nine post-chaises, escorted by a large party of dragoons, to face charges of high treason. The military withdrew.

Neilson had nominated his lawyer Tom Corbett as his successor should he be arrested. Corbett was very soft-spoken and had a habit of taking his spectacles off and polishing them when speaking, but he was hard as nails. He was a family man who was rarely seen in a tavern. We idolised him, mainly because he rarely advised Neilson not to publish.

He addressed us that afternoon. 'We have only one effective weapon with which to retaliate,' he said. 'Words.'

He got Sampson to produce at short order a satire on the landlords' raid, under the headline SIEGE OF BELFAST. It portrayed Castlereagh as an apostate in 'a very entertaining puppet show' performed by His Majesty's servants. 'The part of the Youthful Apostate who betrays his friends and insults his benefactors was performed to the life. At one time we were almost persuaded that this Puppet was a real man.' Sampson recounted his jibe to Westmeath that, unlike Lady Westmeath, his wife was not accustomed to entertaining strange men in her bedroom.

We asked our readers 'to excuse the lateness of this day's publication, as our office was blockaded for three hours.'

Next day we learned that, before arriving in Belfast, Castlereagh had detained young Charles Teeling, the Catholic Defender who had seen Wolfe Tone off on his voyage to America. The manner of Charles's arrest shocked everyone. He and his father Luke Teeling were riding on Lisburn's Main Street at first light when they encountered Castlereagh strolling in the same direction. They dismounted and walked with him, exchanging pleasantries as old family friends. Luke Teeling had helped finance Castlereagh's election. They came to the house of Castlereagh's relative, the Marquess of Hertford. Castlereagh suddenly steered Charles into the gate house where he was seized by soldiers. His father demanded to know the cause of Charles's arrest. 'High treason,' came the reply.

Castlereagh rode to the Teelings' house to find evidence against Charles. He drew his pistol and forced fourteen-year-old John Teeling to give him all the family papers. Their mother begged to see her son but Castlereagh refused. She told him bitterly she was foolish to appeal to a heart that never felt the tie of paternal affection, as he was not a father.

Castlereagh had failed to produce a son in two years of marriage.

Only much later did I hear that when Castlereagh returned to Lisburn, tired from his exertions in Belfast, he came to Charles's cell with a plate of cold meat, a bottle of wine and two glasses. He treated him politely. When he told Charles he had taken up Thomas Russell, his captive replied, 'Then you have arrested the soul of honour,' and refused to speak with Castlereagh any further.

That evening Charles was placed in a post chaise to join the procession of Belfast prisoners on their way to Dublin. A dense multitude filled the Lisburn streets and the cavalry had to clear a way through a forest of hats waving in support of the prisoner.

After the coup, men from the countryside, all wearing green, poured into Belfast. The military stayed in their barracks. George Gray arrived with four fellows from Gransha. I asked after Betsy and Eliza. 'They are worried about you,' said George. 'We are all worried about you.'

I was worried about myself. I didn't know what to do. For the first time I felt at a loss. My hero and mentor, Sam Neilson, for whose approval my whole life was dedicated, was gone, in prison, uncontactable.

Within the month Harry McCracken was arrested in County Antrim and taken under escort to Kilmainham Jail in Dublin.

Then Habeas Corpus was suspended, which was dire news for Sam Neilson and Thomas Russell, who had given themselves up on the assumption that they would get their day in court. Now they would rot in their cells at the pleasure of Castlereagh.

Tom Storey, Eddie Newell and I huddled in a corner of Barclay's going over these disastrous events. As we drank from tankards of ale plonked down by Belle Martin, I confided that I felt there was a highly placed informer in our top echelons.

'How did they know to lift the most important leaders in our movement? How did they know Neilson was lodging with Sampson? How did they know how important Charles Teeling was to the cause?'

'Damned if I can say,' responded Eddie. 'It seems the dogs in the street know what we are up to.'

Tom Storey produced from his pocket a new ballad pleading for the French to come and rescue us:

Come, come, brave Frenchmen, and land in our Nation,
We are anxiously waiting until that you come;
And we are ready, determined and steady,
The moment we hear the first tap of your drum.
Here are four millions of gallant Republicans,
Able and willing to march and to fire;
And to the world we have declared,
Never to sheathe their swords till we get our desires.

'Who wrote that?' I asked.

'I did,' Tom replied.

'You're no Robbie Burns,' I told him.

We at least had the satisfaction of making the Earl of Westmeath a figure of fun again. We heard that the *Star*'s account of the Siege of Belfast had all Dublin laughing at him. Castlereagh himself was said to be 'excessively entertained' by the article, despite its severity on himself.

— TWENTY-FOUR —

DISLOYAL CLOVEN-FOOTED
PRESBYTERIANS

The countryside also came under siege that autumn of '96. The military began arresting farmers, smallholders and weavers and charging them with treason, frequently leaving their wives and children without a man to harvest the barley or potatoes.

Then something wonderful happened.

I was riding towards Greyabbey to call on the Revd Porter. It was a glorious late September day. Near my destination I encountered about a hundred men and women marching along the road, with spades, pitchforks and scythes shouldered like arms. All were wearing something green. They were marching in step. And they were singing *La Marseillaise*.

I spoke to a young man with short curly hair and sharp features in green coat and kerchief who seemed to be in charge. He introduced himself as David Bailie Warden, a schoolteacher in Greyabbey and probationer Presbyterian clergyman.

Warden explained that people spontaneously had got together the previous evening after a farmer had been taken up by the dragoons. They were going to harvest his crops, he said.

I joined them. They set to in the fields of their imprisoned neighbour and in two hours, working and singing together, they had stacked over 1,000 stooks of grain and twenty ricks of hay.

What I witnessed that day was the start of a phenomenon that became a great sport for the people of Antrim and Down.

Rowley Osborne of Belfast had forty ricks of hay stacked by an immense number in a short time without the formality of a horse or cart, and tradesmen slated a house he was building in seven hours.

William Weir of Dunmurry had 2,360 stooks of grain and thirty-eight ricks of hay carried in and completely stacked and thatched in three hours.

Mrs Clarke of Swatragh, whose son was in prison, had her harvest cut down in two hours.

A crowd of harvesters were observed marching through Ballynahinch with fifes playing and carrying banners saying '*Erin go bragh*'.

We saw a great opportunity. I was given the task by my society of riding around County Down to instruct colonels and captains to watch out for spontaneous harvest gatherings and to provide banners and musicians with drum and fife and turn them into displays of defiance. They demonstrated the strength of the United Irishmen and got country folk accustomed to assembling and showing themselves publicly.

A harvesting was arranged for Sam Neilson's three small potato fields at Skegoneill, just north of Belfast. Our Society resolved to make it a great show of defiance and support for the *Northern Star* proprietor.

The day before that event, when walking home from the office, I received a tap on my shoulder and heard a stern voice say, 'You are under arrest, Mister *Star* man.'

It took a few moments for me to recognise the stern, grey-haired gentleman in a high-collared frockcoat and ruffle-fronted shirt as my young friend William Putnam McCabe. 'I arrest you in the name of Castlereagh,' he said.

'I will offer no resistance,' I replied, 'but don't do that to me ever again.'

In Nicoll's whiskey house in Pottingers Entry, Putnam told me he had been moving around the south of Ireland, rallying patriots to the cause. He carried a satchel full of wigs and powders to adopt different personae. He once encountered a man six times in different places in Wexford who was convinced he was meeting six different people. He had returned north to help organise the harvest gatherings and use them to discipline the people. I invited him to come to the lifting of potatoes at Neilson's fields.

On Monday morning we rode to Skegoneill together in bright sunshine. I wore my Volunteer uniform. Though like me he was only twenty-one years of age, Putnam looked very much a figure of authority, sitting high on a black horse with a German saddle and attired this time in wide-brimmed hat with a feather plume and a smart blue double-breasted jacket.

A thousand people walked to Neilson's few acres, many of them young men with girls on their arms. They marched two abreast, with spades over their shoulders like muskets, to the steady rat-tat of a drum and the music of two fifers. A few carried white flags and banners proclaiming '*Erin go bragh*'. Everyone wore green kerchiefs or ribbons. We distributed some emblems which were eagerly snatched up.

I again came across David Bailie Warden, who led the first dig near Greyabbey. Davy was very enthusiastic for the cause now, and was organising harvesting wherever it occurred.

As we neared Neilson's property Davy led the peasants and farmers in singing *La Marseillaise*. The stirring words of the revolutionary anthem resounded around the fields: *Aux armes, citoyens, Formez vos Bataillons, Marchons, marchons!*

Everyone lined up along the rills and at a signal started work. The potatoes were all dug in seven minutes and gathered within an hour. A picnic of buttermilk and oat cakes followed. There was no alcohol. The joy in unity of purpose and comradeship was intoxicating enough.

My work with the harvestings gave me new opportunities to visit the Grays at Gransha. Matt McClenaghan the blacksmith would come with his fiddle and there would be dancing and drinking and pipe smoking till the early hours. Eliza Bryson would sit with me and one night we kissed outside. I got aroused as she pushed her thighs against me but I resisted taking it any further. I told her she should not get too close to someone who might be arrested any day. That made her all the more passionate.

When all had left, and Betsy and Hans had retired, George, Willie and I would stay up talking. Willie had not yet been sworn as a United Irishman but said he was leaning that way. He wanted to be sure, because if he did take the leap, he would put his heart and soul into it. He was the type of honest Ulsterman we needed.

George took his commitment to the cause very seriously. He often said we were a band of brothers and must look out for each other. He recited lines one night from Robert Burns, whose death that summer was surely mourned in every cottage in the North of Ireland.

'Then let us pray that come it may,
(As come it will for a' that,)
That Sense and Worth, o'er a' the earth,
Shall bear the gree, an' a' that.
For a' that, an' a' that,
That Man to Man, the world o'er,
Shall brothers be for a' that.'

At the Grays I encountered the Revd William Steel Dickson from Portaferry who had dropped by to visit his friend Hans. A balding man over fifty with florid face and long white sideburns, Dickson had been a United Irishman since 1791 and had played a prominent role in the great Bastille Day commemoration in 1792. He was not a republican but he was keen to see Ireland independent.

Dickson was very agitated. Castlereagh and Savage had ambushed his congregation the day before as they emerged from his meeting house in Portaferry and had seized several members of the greatest respectability. Castlereagh told Dickson they had information against him from a weaver called Carr, and that he should proclaim his guilt as a member of the United Irishmen or leave the country.

'That's the thanks I get for helping Robert Stewart win election five years ago,' he said bitterly. 'I spent forty hours in the saddle rounding up freeholders to vote for him. I rode one horse nearly to death, reduced another to nearly half its value and expended over fifty pounds, part of which I had to borrow. He is the unblushing betrayer of Ireland to a foreign Sanhedrin. I will not flee. I will stay and fight to save my friends in prison.'

He said that Londonderry had summoned hundreds of tenant farmers on his estate to Mount Stewart to take an oath of allegiance which would require them to inform on seditious activities. Forty Bibles were delivered to Mount Stewart for this purpose. Londonderry had also turned up at the Non-Subscribing Church in Newtownards to berate the congregation for their disloyalty, but had been met with cat-calls, hoots and laughter. He was overheard saying to his agent Cleland as he left, 'Damn these disloyal, cloven-footed Presbyterians.'

George, Hans and I drank a toast to all disloyal, cloven-footed Presbyterians.

Hans later confessed that he had taken the oath of loyalty required by Londonderry and the other landlords. If he hadn't, he would have lost his tenancy. And sure an oath sworn under duress was non-binding. He went to the sideboard and produced a copy of the *Star*. He ran his gnarled finger down to a line in the satire of Billy Bluff and Squire Firebrand: 'A man convinced against his will, is of the same opinion still'.

George took me to a meeting in Matt McClenaghan's forge of a dozen United Irishmen from Gransha and Cottown districts. Eliza's father Andrew Bryson Sr., took the lead. He said the most dangerous man in County Down was Londonderry's agent, the Revd John Cleland, who had been provided with money to give to informers. Something would be done about him. 'Not before time,' I said.

The following Saturday night someone attempted to assassinate Cleland as he rode home to Newtownards from Mount Stewart. Apparently the agent saw the flint sparking in the darkness and returned fire with his pistol. He was unhurt. The devil looks after his own.

On 1 November the Lord Lieutenant banned gatherings to save the harvest, describing them as military exercises designed to terrify peaceable and well-disposed citizens.

The next day a potato dig was to take place in Comber at the fields of one of Londonderry's tenants called Maxwell, who was in hiding. I rode out to warn the organisers of the ban.

They didn't care. Under overcast skies two hundred men and women, George Gray and Willie Boal among them, set off defiantly with flags and banners, all dressed in their Sunday best. They marched in military formation, with an officer at front and rear, each file having girls to collect the potatoes.

After they had gone a mile or so there was a great stir. Castlereagh approached on horseback with Lady Emily. To the horror of his wife, he brazenly caught up with the leaders and walked his mount alongside them. I hung back with the brim of my hat pulled down.

In a show of good humour Castlereagh asked them if they might happen to know the whereabouts of some arms stolen from soldiers in Comber the previous day.

'They left them behind in a whorehouse,' someone shouted.

'Will you take an oath of allegiance to the government of the King?' asked Castlereagh.

'Never!'

'What if you could take the oath while affirming the need for parliamentary reform?'

'Aye, maybe,' said one or two. 'Why not?' said another.

I couldn't let this dialogue continue.

'Would your honour not take an oath of allegiance to us, the people?'

Castlereagh turned round and recognised me.

'Does not the King represent the people before God?' he retorted. 'And may I ask what you are doing here? You know this activity is outlawed.'

'I represent the *Northern Star*,' I said.

Someone called out, 'Good on you, *Star* man.'

'You mean you represent a seditious organ,' said Castlereagh.

He was distracted when a voice called out, 'Any word of a wee one?' There was loud laughter. Castlereagh's marriage was still childless. Nothing missed the country folk. His expression hardened and he mounted up, joined Lady Emily, and galloped off.

Castlereagh actually had a boy by a serving maid called Nelly Stoal, one of the diggers told me. When she became pregnant the Stewarts arranged for her to marry the local postmaster. Castlereagh doted on his son and still visited Nelly for their mutual pleasure.

I was now a marked man, I thought. Castlereagh had cause to have me arrested. I fancied however that being a protégé of Lord Moira afforded me some protection. The fellow-peers disagreed on Irish policy but they mingled socially in Dublin.

The potato dig at Maxwell's holding went off without incident. Two acres were cleared in half an hour. Betsy and Eliza arrived on ponies with oaten biscuits, apples and milk. As we picnicked Eliza clung onto my arm.

On my way back I stopped at William McCormick's hostelry in Newtownards. There I met an eccentric Frenchman who was walking around Ireland, armed with an umbrella, with a view to writing a travel book. Chevalier De Latocnaye, a small, dainty fellow dressed in silk stockings and dancing pumps, had illuminating observations to make. He told me, in his heavily accented English, that he had heard much about the troubles in the North but was surprised to find the inhabitants perfectly calm. 'Indeed all over Ireland I found people delighted to walk with me or even put me up on their horse and walk alongside me.' He was horrified however to encounter public hangings. 'Far too many and very cruel to make a spectacle of a man facing death.'

He had lodged at Mount Stewart and witnessed Londonderry's attempt to make the peasants swear an oath of allegiance. 'They had much trouble getting the first ten or twelve to join,' he said, 'and in the days following, seven or eight hundred came forward. Man is sheep everywhere.'

When I informed him that this was done under duress, he confessed that, while he was a royalist by inclination, he had little time for the excesses of either side, here or in France.

He was amazed at the peaceable nature of the defiance against the government and in particular a potato dig he witnessed in the fields of a farmer arrested on treason charges, where the country folk sang the *La Marseillaise* 'and they knew the words!'

'A man on horseback with nothing special to distinguish him extracted obedience and directed affairs by signs with the hand,' he said. 'The whole time the work went on, men, women and children sang, accompanied by one or other kind of instrument. No one was allowed to drink liquor. The peasantry had on their best clothes. A spectator arriving would think it was a fête day.'

I told him these gatherings had now been forbidden by the government. 'Very wise,' he said. 'If allowed to continue, they might become dangerous.'

De Latocnaye did not think much of the United Irishmen. 'They have stirred up the peasantry to believe they have grievances about parliamentary reform, impediments to commerce, taxes on wine and the like, but what does the peasant care whether he lives in a monarchy or a republic, so long as he can enjoy personal liberty and the fruits of his labour?'

I excused myself and consulted my *Grammaire Française.*

I returned to the table and said, '*Votre anglais est très bon.*' He gushed, '*Vous êtes très gentil.*'

I asked him what I might say in French, if French revolutionary soldiers arrived in Ireland. He replied pertly, 'I suggest *Fixer vos armes*! Lay down your arms!'

Castlereagh threw a banquet in Newtownards to help persuade people to swear allegiance to the government. Many of our men turned up for the free mutton and whiskey. They paid the price by having to mouth 'Rule Britannia' and toast the King. Cleland lorded over the proceedings, arrogant and drunk.

The following Sunday a party of Dragoons and armed Orangemen descended on a potato dig in Stoneyford, north of Lisburn. They arrested forty-eight people who had marched there in formation.

TWENTY-FIVE

A BAD WOMAN'S OATH

I had three lives that autumn, a high life hobnobbing with Belfast society, a low life in the taverns, and a secret life preparing for a rising.

My society life as a *parvenu* revolved round Martha. I was happy to escort her to card games, fandangos and coteries in the Assembly Rooms, where she made cryptic comments on how the ladies were getting skinnier because of the slimming rage. She was content to hear the latest intelligence from the *Star* and relay the Dublin news from her brother. She was sure her replies to Drennan were being opened, and teased the censor by writing that she had much interesting political news, but did not want to waste the time of a government inspector with it, as his hands were probably full.

Martha was highly amused at her own wit. She was almost back to her old self, fond of a bit of mischief, curious to know what was going on. I told her everything and nothing.

One day in October Martha invited me to a high-class dinner in her house at which she said, mischievously, a special guest would command my attention. He did too. It was Lord Moira, my benefactor. He greeted me civilly. He spoke of intimidation of Catholics by anti-Papists on the eighteen townlands he owned around Ballynahinch. Eighty-nine Catholic families had been forced to leave. Many loyal Catholics who remained had joined the United Irishmen, he said, because they saw the government winking at the outrages of Orangemen.

Dr Haliday praised Moira for his dire warnings in the British House of Lords that the government's policies would lead to revolution. He replied, 'They call me over there Lord Longbow the Alarmist.'

Moira took my arm as we rose to leave and said, 'They have it in for the *Star*, young William. If I were you, I would be looking for other employment.'

The least said about my low life the better. It involved shafting Belle Martin and occasionally picking up wenches with Newell. I warned my miniaturist friend not to be boasting to any of his conquests about our secret life, since one of the women we picked up might be the *femme fatale* who had been luring militiamen into betraying their loyalty to the United Irishmen.

My secret life, the life that gave meaning to my very existence, revolved round the covert meeting places of the United Irishmen, which often included the attic of the Second Presbyterian Church.

As winter approached a national executive committee was set up in Dublin, headed by Lord Edward Fitzgerald and the parliamentarian Arthur O'Connor.

I was promoted onto the Belfast military divisional committee along with Eddie Newell, Billy Templeton and three weavers, three clerks, three shoemakers, two cloth merchants, a jeweller, a painter, a book-binder, a merchant, a smith, and a saddler.

We debated endlessly whether we should rise without the French or take the advice of the 'foreign aid men' and wait. Meanwhile our priority was to dissuade farmers and tradesmen from joining the yeomanry, and to convert Orangemen to our ranks. We started calling ourselves Liberty Men rather than United Irishmen, as a sop to the anti-Papists.

We worried constantly about informers, and dealt with them when necessary. William McBride, a cotton spinner, was stabbed to death in North Street. I wasn't in on that one. Wealthy citizens offered a reward of three hundred guineas for apprehension of the assassin. Our barrister friend William Sampson was incensed enough to complain in the *Star* about the size of the reward for killing a wretched informer, while in Armagh murder after murder was committed in cold blood in the name of religion but no rewards were offered.

Billy Templeton proved to be a good military operator. He organised a daring raid on a gunpowder store and then wrote about it in the newspaper: 'On Friday night a most daring robbery was committed. The King's stores in Callendar Street were broken open and ten casks of gunpowder taken out. And what renders it the more remarkable is that there were five casks of damaged powder left untouched and the ten casks that were taken were concealed behind a great deal of other goods'. Billy had changed. My chubby, cheerful colleague still laughed a lot, but behind the spectacles his eyes had become hard and calculating. I felt I had changed too, in much the same way.

Another assassination led to the exposure of the most dangerous spy of all.

Joe Cuthbert was tipped off that a butcher called Kingsbury, who had a stall near my lodgings in Hercules Street, was a dangerous informer. Over tankards of ale in the downstairs bar in Peggy Barclay's he outlined a plan to lure Kingsbury out of Belfast and take care of him. He shut up as Belle Martin wiped down the next table. On Wednesday 9 November, Kingsbury was knifed to death near Drum Bridge, outside Lisburn. Shortly afterwards Joe and Tom Storey and two others were seized at a nearby Masonic lodge by a military party led by Castlereagh and Lord Carhampton, commander-in-chief of the army in Ireland. They claimed to have arrested 'the assassination committee' of the United Irishmen. The four were lodged in Carrickfergus jail on a charge of conspiracy to murder Kingsbury. Harry McCracken's mother was informed by the indiscreet wife of an officer, that 'Cuthbert and Storey were betrayed by a bad woman's oath.' I recalled the militiaman warning me of a woman posing as a prostitute to betray deserting comrades and wondered if she was the same one.

We found out who spied on us when Joe Cuthbert was brought up for arraignment in Carrickfergus.

I had been half-suspecting it, willing myself not to believe it.

The whore who gave sworn testimony against Joe was Belle Martin.

Sampson brought the news from the courthouse where he represented Cuthbert. The treacherous bitch swore in court that she saw Joe plotting in Barclay's to kill Kingsbury. I remember the trollop hovering around us that night when Joe said Kingsbury had to be taken care of. I broke into a sweat. I was there too. She had also seen me with Harry McCracken and

Joe Cuthbert when she delivered the balls for Joe's pistol, with which he had shot Sergeant Lee.

There was blood on the hands of the woman with whom I took my pleasure. Belle Martin was not just an informer. She had posed as a prostitute to entice soldiers to disclose they had secretly joined the United Irishmen and have them arrested. She hadn't had me arrested but I was thoroughly compromised. I cursed myself for being such a simpleton. I quaked at the thought of what more might come out when Cuthbert was brought to full trial. What would my comrades think? Would I be blamed for leaked information, even though I had told her nothing.

Peggy Barclay told me in a fury that the 'spying, loathsome, lying bitch' disappeared the day before without giving notice. The attic where she lodged was empty.

I went to break the news to Eddie Newell, who was working in his studio. He called Belle Martin a treacherous, conniving cow and wished the pox upon her. When he had stopped spluttering I said, 'Think of anything you might have told her. Did she ask you anything when you were riding her?'

'You can talk, you frigging halfwit imbecile,' he shouted.

We calmed down and went up to his room to get drunk.

'May stinking vapours choke her womb and may the north wind bluster in her cunt and turn her arse up in the air and perish in a wild despair,' said Newell.

That's a quote from Rochester, I said, before passing out on the floor, full of whiskey, fear and self-loathing.

— TWENTY-SIX —

THE FRENCH ARE ON THE SEA

We got the first indication that a French fleet was at last on the way from Arthur O'Connor, the United Irish leader, who came to Belfast in November to campaign for election to a seat in Antrim.

A gaunt man with heavy whiskers and receding dark hair which he kept covered with a black silk handkerchief, O'Connor had a superior, sing-song Cork accent that offended my Ulsterman's ear.

'Will the French come?' asked Tom Corbett, at a lunch for O'Connor and staff of the *Northern Star* in the Donegall Arms.

'Yes, they will,' he replied; '*entre nous* of course.' He added, 'And if they do, I can get a message to any part of Ireland in five days to coordinate a rising.'

He had been to France several times so we presumed he knew something. He took a pinch of snuff, sniffed, and tipped his head back while we waited for him to continue.

'We are fortunate to have in the Presbyterian north the best-educated and enlightened peasantry in Europe. I trust they will rally to the French when they come.'

'They will,' we said.

'I must say I marvel that you people of the north, so long violently against any connection with the Papists, now show uncommon zeal for a union with Catholics.'

He proceeded to lecture us – veterans of newspaper wars against the government – on the importance of the press, the palladium of liberty as he called it.

'It was the press that made England celebrated over the nations of Europe,' he declared. 'It was the press that overturned the Catholic despotism of France through the writings of Voltaire, Rousseau and others. It was the press in America that routed tyranny. It was the press – the *Northern Star* – that illumined Belfast, the Athens of Ireland.'

His saving grace was a droll sense of humour. Regarding the several new yeomanry corps being raised in Dublin he quipped, 'The cavalry company of barristers know well how to charge, and the new core of customs officers will be adept at preventing a landing.' In the north, he added, 'The Orangemen will form yeoman companies and they will give you the pip.' Everyone roared laughing. He warned us however that some leading Catholic lawyers, champions of Catholic emancipation such as the young Daniel O'Connell, were joining the lawyer's corps of yeomanry and were becoming dangerous foes.

We arranged for O'Connor to lodge in a new house on Rosemary Street and for the better-off United Irishmen to take turns inviting him to supper.

Robert Simms didn't take to him. He told me that O'Connor's real name was Conner and that he was a commoner who pretended his family was descended from the High Kings of Ireland. Martha, an excellent judge of character, ventured that he had a very bad countenance and would never rest until he was exalted.

Four weeks later, on Friday 23 December, news reports struck Belfast like lightning bolts. A French fleet had appeared off the south coast of Ireland.

The Highland Fencibles immediately strengthened their pickets with men and cannon.

Lieutenant-General Gerard Lake, who had been appointed to head the garrison in the north, threatened to burn Belfast to the ground if there was any provocation.

My heart beat faster all that weekend. The time for action might soon be upon us. Before long, I thought, French officers might well be dancing the *Ça ira* with Martha's lady friends in the Assembly Rooms.

On Tuesday the divisional committee met in McCaul's public house.

We were instructed to stay calm and not to be provoked. If the French landed, fresh orders would be issued. All must be ready to take the field. Officers must make up lists and inventories of guns and pikes. Some 1,600 United Irishmen were ready to rise in Belfast and 70,000 more around Ireland. Secrecy was paramount. Deliberations of superior committees were not to be divulged to inferior committees. We raised a collection to pay for mounting six pieces of cannon, hidden since the Volunteers were disbanded.

From Sam Neilson in Kilmainham came the message: 'Keep publishing the *Northern Star* at all costs.'

On the streets young men and women took to sporting green ribbons.

On Wednesday Mayor John Brown received a letter from the Irish Secretary, Thomas Pelham, confirming that a French fleet had arrived into Bantry Bay in Cork. He called an emergency meeting in the Exchange.

Brown told the gathering that Lord Charlemont, founder of the Volunteers, had urged patriots to sign up as yeomen to defend Ireland, on the grounds that 'he could not refuse to lend a hand in stopping a leak from a sinking ship just because he hated the commander'. All gentlemen in Belfast should now take the oath to the Crown.

A large man with a Bible and stentorian voice shouted, 'We will never take an oath to defend repressive laws. We will not do violence to our consciences by swearing such an oath. Never!'

We had to stop some hot-heads throwing the town sheriff, Chichester Skeffington, from the window when he proposed gathering signatures there and then for a yeoman corps.

The mayor called for the matter to be voted on at a general town meeting on Saturday 31 December.

William Sampson, Arthur O'Connor, John Storey and Tom Corbett came up with a plan to stop Brown having a resolution passed which would legitimise the yeomanry. They would propose that a committee be formed to frame resolutions for another general meeting on Monday 2 January, then load the committee to frame the motions in our favour, and round up the discontented in the population to make sure they passed by acclamation.

It worked. A nine-member committee was selected. Five were United

Irishmen: Sampson, O'Connor, William Tennent, Gilbert McIlveen and Robert Simms. They were mandated to draw up resolutions to be put to another meeting on Monday.

Over the weekend we rounded up so many peddlers and urchins from the back streets that the crowd could not be accommodated in the Exchange, and the town meeting was moved to the public space outside the White Linen Hall. Sensing the pro-French mood, Brown, Bristow and Skeffington conceded defeat and left. Sampson climbed on a chair.

'The enemy is not the French,' he declared. 'The enemy is the gang of political zealots who threaten to destroy the town if we do not take their oath. We will not take their oath or swear fealty to their repressive laws. We treat with contempt General Lake's threat to have the town demolished if we do not take the oath. It was not Lord Charlemont that raised the Volunteers; it was the Volunteers that raised Lord Charlemont'.

Sampson put a motion urging reform of parliament under the King and for arming the people in the manner of the Volunteers. The cheers were taken as affirmation.

We ensured the meeting ended peacefully. On the way back to my office I saw artillery soldiers formed up in Ann's Street with Colonel Lucius Barber in command, looking disappointed that they had no rioting mob to disperse with clubs.

I mentioned to Billy that it was my birthday. He produced a small jar of whiskey and I drank on an empty stomach, the result of which was headache and nausea.

With the prospect of the imminent arrival of the French, I took to carrying Betsy's *La Grammaire Française* in my pocket.

Philippe Carmenthan noted my renewed enthusiasm. I was making good progress, he said. '*Tres bon.*' He taught me some useful new phrases, so I could tell a French officer, if the occasion arose, '*L'ennemi Britannique est là*', and '*J'aime vraiment le vin de Bordeaux*'. But I was deficient in grammar. Philippe once engaged me in simple French conversation in Flanagan's. He started with easy questions which I understood and required the answer, '*Oui*'. Then he asked me something I didn't understand, but I answered

'*Oui*' anyway. When he stopped laughing he explained that he had asked me, 'Am I boring you with these questions?'

'You know,' he said. 'You are a real chancer.'

The French did not land. Napoleon's fleet was kept offshore by a fierce north-easterly gale. The ships turned and set sail for home. Many were lost to the storm.

If they had landed I was sure they would have overcome the British in Munster, all Ireland would have ignited in rebellion, and separation from England would have followed. But they didn't. I was sick with disappointment. The wind went out of our sails. We were all despondent, deflated, angry.

Belfast was singled out for its 'treasonable' resolutions after the danger had passed. Lord High Chancellor FitzGibbon fulminated about our 'insolence'. He sent a military convoy to Belfast escorted by the Cavan Militia with forty tumbrils of ammunition. He had a handbill circulated, signed 'An Irishman', warning us that if we acted against our allegiance to King and country, we must be ranked as 'degenerate fellow-citizens and enemies'.

Sampson and O'Connor wrote a reply signed by 'A Townsman', accusing the government in Dublin of ensuring that the French would be welcomed because of its rotten system, its gunpowder bill, its habeas corpus suspension bill and its long catalogue of vindictive and hateful measures.

Sampson was in foul mood, having come down with influenza after standing hatless in the cold outside the White Linen Hall. He was getting anonymous letters from so-called friends, warning him that the Lawyers Corps was plotting to have him ejected for treasonous speeches. He feared imminent arrest.

Poor Philippe. His French class dwindled away as fast as it had filled up. He mourned the death at sea of his compatriots owing to an overpowering and unforeseen weather event. It was a brutal example he said of *force majeure* that would retard the history of his adopted country. He didn't have to translate when he held his hand to his breast and said, '*Mon cœur est brisé.*'

At the *Star* we returned to doing what we did best. We published more definitions for our imaginary political dictionary:

Treason – a field of potatoes

Purveyor of sedition – one who tells honest truths

Ireland – a nation of noble people who give their lives to defend England but whose grievances must never be met

Mrs Ireland – a fine old woman whose constitution has been impaired by quacks who profit from the continuance of her disorders and who bleed her furiously while their servants pilfer her belongings.

We were consoled by a visit from Lord Edward Fitzgerald. The head of the national executive of the United Irishmen arrived from Dublin on January 13. He was a surprisingly small, wiry, aristocratic man, handsome with dark hair cut in croppy style and wide sidelocks, and wearing short jacket and pantaloons with green kerchief round his neck. He was affectingly modest and greeted everyone at the *Star* in a light-hearted way. When a printer bowed low he protested, 'My good man, I regard myself as a Paddy and no more, and I desire no other title.'

Humorous and affectionate, Lord Edward made a big impression on us, though I thought he lacked the gravitas of a future statesman. He was a soldier first and foremost. Like Lord Moira he had fought in America on the English side and now wished he had led the American rebels. He returned there briefly to live with Indians who had made him a chief of the Bear tribe. 'I'm *your* chief now,' he said laughing.

He was accompanied by a black companion, Tony Small, a former slave who caused a sensation when we brought the pair to the Donegall Arms. Everyone wanted to shake his hand and hear his story. He had saved Fitzgerald's life when he found him desperately wounded and unconscious on a battlefield near Charlestown during the American Revolution. He had taken Lord Edward to his shack, dressed his wounds and nursed him back to health. He had since travelled everywhere with him as a personal servant, to Spain, Portugal, France, England, British North America and Ireland.

Tony was very unhappy with Fitzgerald's role in the United Irishmen. His skin colour attracted too much attention. It tipped off Castle spies that Fitzgerald was in the vicinity. Sometime his master left him behind as a decoy or sent him on a wild goose chase to fool the informers.

Fitzgerald told us at a dinner at Sampson's that rather than being downcast, we should be greatly encouraged by the fact that the French had tried to land. It meant they would come again and this prospect would lift Ireland into a fever of anticipation. He warned us too that a rising would be bloody and should be as brief as possible. After victory, a national convention would decide the form of the new republic.

I worried however that the failure of the French to land had left people confused. Martha was sure that if the French came to Belfast they would be victorious, but with things left hanging, everyone in society was trying to please both sides and being damned in the process. Oaths of loyalty were being taken under pressure and 'reconciled in the usual way by mental reservation.'

Her brother in Dublin, she felt, was losing touch with the leading radicals. After his narrow brush with imprisonment Drennan has become less keen on direct action. He had expressed disgust with the 'stupidity, ingratitude and barbarity' of the lower orders. I wondered, ingratitude for what? As a founder of the United Irishmen he was now being criticised by members for his curious silence during the crisis. They said that 'he had inflated the balloon but was reluctant to ascend'.

I escorted Martha to a guinea-a-head charity ball in the Exchange Rooms for coal for the poor. Seeing me greet John Gordon, she warned me that Gordon was getting a bad reputation. Mary Ann McCracken told her that he had beaten a servant maid in her house so badly she was ill for days. And he had been heard boasting how he would make some people suffer when the revolution commenced.

I found myself wondering if it was the case that revolutions attracted violent men, or was it that revolutions make men violent. We needed people like Gordon, but their usefulness should end when the time for governing and reconciliation came.

Bristow, Bruce, Brown and Skeffington, all the toady Whigs, were at the ball, rubbing shoulders with the United Irishmen Arthur O'Connor, William Sampson and the Simms brothers. In spite of their deadly political games, Belfast gentlemen and ladies, as did their counterparts in Dublin, still liked to dress up in their finery and eat, drink and chat together, sometimes a little warmly, but not so heatedly as to fall out or disturb the serenity of their coteries or games of whist and faro. Slave owners Waddell Cunningham and Dr Haliday regularly had wined and dined with United Irishmen Thomas Russell and Sam McTier who were devoted to abolishing the source of their wealth. I was part of this charade myself.

I wasn't surprised to hear that the Revd Bruce had taken the loyal oath and joined the yeomanry, one of only a hundred men to do so out of a population of 18,000. Bruce never did relish uniting with Papists, and he was a terrible snob: I heard he was getting the academy boys to distribute Hannah More's dreadful penny pamphlets warning the common people not to get above themselves.

So when a meeting of my society resolved to dock the horses of anyone who signed up as a yeoman, I couldn't resist the temptation.

I persuaded Billy to come with me to the academy one night. It was pouring rain. No one was about. Billy kept watch while I entered the stable, reached over the stall door, grabbed Bruce's mount by the tail and sliced through the dock. The mare whinnied and kicked. Bruce, the ridiculous yeoman, now had a draft horse.

We ran off sniggering like naughty schoolboys.

— TWENTY-SEVEN —

PICTURE PERFECT

'Greetings to the *Star* man,' said Betsy with her usual sisterly peck on the cheek when I arrived one day that January as wet snow showers drifted in from the Irish Sea. I presented Hans with a flagon of whiskey and he made hot punch.

'Now Elizabeth is nineteen, it is time for her to have her portrait done,' said Hans. 'Could you recommend a good painter in Belfast?'

We both contemplated Betsy as she sat blushing by the fire.

I told him about my miniaturist friend Eddie Newell, and undertook to make enquiries about his skills.

Willie Boal, Eliza Bryson and the two Andrew Brysons, father and son, came for dinner. Betsy produced a meal of salted beef and plum pudding. I sat beside Eliza and held her hand under the table. Everybody was happy about us. I tried not to show I wished it were Betsy, and I wondered if either or both knew that full well.

Eddie Newell had built up a good reputation as a portrait painter in his relatively short time in Belfast. He produced good-quality watercolour on ivory at a reasonable price. I called at his studio, as he grandly called a side room he rented at McKittrick's on High Street, and agreed a date for Betsy to have her portrait painted for a miniature.

On the appointed day Betsy and George arrived by horseback wearing frieze overcoats against the biting cold. They stabled their horses behind the *Northern Star* office. We took Betsy to Victor Coates hairdressers in Castle Street to wash and trim her hair. She walked between us, linking arms.

We arrived at Eddie's studio ahead of time and encountered a flushed young woman fondly taking her leave. Newell had no option but to introduce her. She was a client, the wife of Murdoch, the hearth tax inspector. I thought at the time that if he was having an affair with her he was in risky company. Murdoch was a dangerous officer of the government. He would relish destroying a United Irishman like Eddie.

Newell posed Betsy in muslin dress, quite low-cut. He got her to hold a cloak with her left hand crossed over beneath her bosom in classical mode, her red hair tumbling down to her left breast. He explained this was the Paris fashion; the French king once saw his mistress bathing and was so enchanted with the way her hair hung down that he made her wear it like that always.

Betsy had her own ideas. She asked Newell to paint her in the style of Sarah Siddons. She had a page from a journal with a drawing of the Welsh actress with loose hair and breasts half-exposed, over an account of her performance in the *Fatal Marriage* in Belfast twelve years before, which was said to be so brilliant it had ladies fainting and men weeping.

Eddie knew his trade. The sleeve pulled back was very fashionable, he said, fussing over her, a little too much for my liking, and the décolletage should be two hand-breadths from the base of the neck, down, front and back.

George and I watched from a bench as he made a charcoal sketch and then copied it onto a piece of ivory lodged in a shallow box on a trestle. His technique, he explained, was to let the ivory shine through as the skin tone, and use watercolours for the hair and eyes.

I could not take my eyes of Betsy. She posed without flinching for two hours. Before leaving, Newell explained that when he finished the portrait he would shape it into an oval to fit into a brass locket. He cut a lock of Betsy's hair to insert at the back.

Next time I saw Martha I asked her if she had seen Sarah Siddons when she performed in Belfast. She had, she said. The voluptuous actress had had an extraordinary effect on the men when she played Belvidera in *Venice Preserv'd*. She recounted with some glee how 'Dr Haliday swelled and Waddell Cunningham rubbed his legs and changed his posture.'

A few days later Newell presented me with a parcel containing the miniature of Betsy, wrapped in brown paper and tied with cord.

'Here, I want to talk to you,' I said.

We went to Flanagan's for a drink. I asked him straight out if he was intimate with Murdoch's wife.

'None of your bloody business,' he retorted, then added with a soppy grin, 'She's a fine damsel, isn't she?'

'Lord, you're not in love with her,' I exclaimed. I warned him that the hearth tax collector was a staunch loyalist who wore an orange ribbon on his watch and went around town bad-mouthing the *Northern Star*. He should take care. Murdoch was known to collect intelligence and pass it on to the military.

'Well what about you and the bitch Belle Martin?'

'And what about you and her?'

We left it there. 'Fine pair of rebels we are,' said Newell.

In my lodgings I undid the packet. Newell had done a competent job. He had Betsy looking straight at the beholder, not smiling, her hand under her breasts, her right shoulder bare. I gazed at it for a long time. I opened the brass backing. Newell had glued the lock of Betsy's hair to the enamel. I cut a few strands and put them inside my watch, beside the inscription of the Kean family motto, 'A stroked cat is gentle'.

There were snowdrops like a carpet all over Betsy's little orchard when I arrived with the miniature. Hans opened it as Betsy looked over his shoulder. She cried with delight when she saw her tiny likeness. George praised Newell as a great artist.

Hans put it in a safe box after a while. He paid for it, so he would keep it himself for the now. Betsy was the apple of his eye. There had been no other woman in his life since his wife died.

As the February sky grew dark, George took me to Matt McClenaghan's smithy. The glow from his fire guided our footsteps across the fields. Shadowy figures hung around the forge. Inside a boy operated a huge bellows as Matt hammered a piece of metal into a pike head. Matt was singing at the top of his voice. He grinned at us and kept going: 'Well Jimmy Murphy was hanged not for sheep-stealin', But for courtin' a pretty girl and her name was Kate Whelan.'

The weapon fashioned, he clasped my hand hard and said, 'How's about you, *Star* man!'

Matt was a fierce-looking fellow but with a witty turn of phrase. George teased him, saying, 'Isn't it dangerous and sinful work you are at!' The blacksmith picked up a perfectly shaped pike head and replied, 'Damn it, man, sure isn't everything beautiful in its season.'

One of the watchers slipped in to say James Dillon was approaching. The boy, Tommy Burns, threw a blackened sack over the pikes and Matt picked up a harrow pin with his tongs and thrust it into the furnace. They did not trust Dillon, a schoolmaster who operated a shebeen at Drumawhey.

A thin man with sharp nose sidled in. He said he was out for a walk and saw that Matt was working late.

George introduced me as an old school friend. 'Sure everyone knows you,' Dillon said. 'You're the *Star* man. Watch you don't fall to earth now, ha, ha.'

Later Matt took his fiddle from a shelf and locked up the smithy. We went back to the Grays' where several neighbours were gathered. Willie Boal sat by the fire with Betsy. The portrait was handed round and much admired. We sang verses from 'Paddy's Resource', a song-book that Tom and John Storey had published, and which Squire Firebrand had condemned in Porter's latest squib, as 'patriotic lies, national impudence, and united treason'.

I sat with Eliza and later, after much singing and dancing and drinking, took her outside and lifted her skirts and made love to her for the first time. There was no turning back now. Afterwards I half-apologised for having my way with her. She laughed and said, 'How can I call you my seducer when I met the seduction half-way?' She added with a giggle, 'I got that from *The Memoirs of Mrs Leeson*. Betsy bought it from a packman. Don't tell anyone.' She promised to let me read the book myself, with its bawdy tales of a Dublin courtesan. There was more to these innocent country girls than I imagined.

I told her again I didn't want to get too fond of her, or her of me, because I was involved in a dangerous business. So we made love again.

— TWENTY-EIGHT —

FALLING STAR

Dillon's jibe about the *Northern Star* falling to earth was close to the mark. We were named after the only star in the sky that never moved. Now we were on a trajectory that could end only in a crash.

Arthur O'Connor and Lord Edward departed for Dublin at the end of January but before doing so O'Connor left a bombshell. He gave the *Star* a copy of an address to the electors of Antrim, which was in essence a call to submit to the French when they came. He expected us to publish it in the paper and as a pamphlet.

Tom Corbett submitted the address to William and Robert Simms, our only proprietors not yet in jail, for their approval. The Simms brothers summoned the clerks, compositors and printers to the editor's office and advised us we might be closed down and all of us arrested if we published O'Connor's address. But we were going to do so. We were the United Irish newspaper. We might all suffer the wrath of the authorities. They would understand if anyone wanted to leave.

Not one of us did. But I was now very worried. I didn't want to be in jail when the rising happened.

The *Northern Star* published O'Connor's lengthy address on Friday 27 January 1797. It included the following: 'Why should Irishmen resist invasion when already under the invader's heel…? Fifteen thousand English and Scotch have been sent to invade us already. Could the French invaders do worse than establish a system of pillage and treason? Could they do worse than reject laws that a unanimous people had sought? Could they do worse than withhold trials from Irish citizens cast into dungeons?'

Martha McTier sent for me. 'What's going on at the *Star*?' she asked. 'This address will provoke the Lord Chancellor, and that half-breed attorney will shut you down. And you will get to see the inside of Kilmainham Jail. Who will then escort me to the Assembly Rooms?' She expressed amazement that the quiet, prudent Simms brothers had exhibited such courage, and wondered if O'Connor wanted to get himself arrested.

'I see alarm on every face in Belfast society,' she said. 'People in my circle say that if the French had landed, even without their artillery, they would have been successful. The Revd Bruce is full of gall and bitterness. Those who would call themselves gentlemen have now enrolled in the yeomanry, and the old moneyed men are paying the expenses.'

I expressed the opinion that the richer farmers and merchants who fawned upon the United Irishmen at the prospect of French success could not be trusted in a fight without the French. 'Quite so,' she said.

The big houses banned the *Star*. But the people were going mad for it. Kennedy of Cultra found his twelve-year-old son in the stable, mounted on the manger and reading it to all the listening servants.

Before dawn, a week after O'Connor's article appeared, our enemies struck back. Colonel Lucius Barber and soldiers from the Royal Artillery broke into the *Star* office and took possession of the premises. I arrived at nine. I was not allowed to enter. Barber informed Tom Corbett that he had authority to seize that day's papers and detain the proprietors. His soldiers loaded books, papers and back issues of the *Star* and *London News* onto a cart and took them to the barracks, leaving only the account books.

Barber told us to quit our jobs and that our government stamps were being withdrawn and he would arrest us if we published the *Star* without them. He posted a picket of artillery privates in brown clothes and armed with bludgeons, then proceeded to the premises of Robert and William Simms on Chichester Quay and arrested them. They were transported to Newgate prison in Dublin in two post chaises that afternoon with an escort of dragoons.

Matthew Smith, Sam Neilson's nephew and proprietor of a printing shop in Bridge Street across the road, came to our rescue. He published hundreds of nine-inch-square pamphlets with an account of the arrests, and our promise that publication of the *Northern Star* would resume.

We informed the readers that the raid was 'an act of brutality unparalleled in the history of the Goths and the Huns – seizing of reformers, dashing the printing materials of a popular newspaper, stopping up sources of information, intimidating innocent, illustrious workmen, extinguishing the last spark of freedom of the press.'

On a more practical note, the leaflet also announced that Matthew Smith would accept subscriptions due to the *Northern Star,* and payment for advertisements, at his shop in Bridge Street. Corbett was desperately worried that we would not be able to pay our bills.

Two days later a King's messenger came to the printing office with armed soldiers and removed the collated types from which the first impression of the paper was wrought. All the seized property was sent off to Dublin with a guard of thirteen dragoons.

Only then were we allowed back into our offices, after another warning from Colonel Barber that anyone publishing the paper without government stamps would suffer the penalty of immediate imprisonment.

Everything inside was in a shambles. Ink tables were overturned, tympans torn, acid poured on the floor. In the compositors room the galley rack and setting stone had been smashed and hundreds of type pieces were scattered about.

In such times you discover who your friends are. Machinists from the *News-Letter* came to help clean and repair the printing press. It was not just solidarity in the trade; they were sympathetic to the cause. Francis Jordan, the sugar refiner, came forward with a handsome investment to make the *Star* solvent again.

We located boxes of old type in Neilson's house, stored there since our first year of publication when the *Northern Star* changed to *Brevier* type. It was smaller and harder on the eye but that was immaterial in the circumstances.

Corbett sent Billy Templeton to Dublin to apply for a new government stamp. In the meantime we decided to start publishing again, in defiance of Barber.

On Friday 24 February the *Northern Star* reappeared with a demand that the military pay compensation for suppressing the newspaper. We hadn't lost our sense of humour. Everyone applauded as the first copy was taken off the press and folded. Billy Templeton returned from Dublin that evening. He had managed to acquire government stamps after all, with help from United Irish lawyers in Dublin, and he had successfully registered Corbett as the new printer and publisher. We had a breathing space.

Corbett inserted an advertisement to support the Simms brothers' business while they were in prison. It stated that their store remained open 'for the sale on the lowest terms of English and foreign oak, train oil, white oak barrels, pipe stoves, fresh flour and prime scale sugar.'

He warned *Star* subscribers that no paper would be delivered to any person whatsoever who did not pay in advance. We feared that subscribers were holding back to see if we would be closed down permanently.

I was dispatched to the countryside to make sure subscriptions and morale were being kept up. In many places men were drilling and cutting ash for pikes. Everyone wanted to know when there would be a turnout. Everywhere I was obliged to partake of a drop and make toasts to Liberty. In the cottages it was poteen, and in the grander residences mulled wine or port. Half the time my head was spinning.

North Down was more solid than ever for the cause, but there were pockets of loyalists who were arming themselves to protect the Crown connection. In Saintfield the fiery preacher, the Revd Thomas Ledlie Birch complained bitterly that the local squire, Nicholas Price, had enticed several of his parishioners to break away and form a more loyal Seceder Church. 'Cheats, hypocrites, defamers and revilers' Birch called them, his face turning purple.

Militarily we were far from ready. Our *Star* representative in Saintfield, David Shaw, owner of the main store, brought me on a night-time raid designed to relieve a loyalist yeoman, Joseph Harper, of his weapons. A hundred men assembled in the darkness, some with guns and pikes, and we set off walking in the moonlight towards the townland of Lisdoonan where Harper's farm was located. A man brought a tinder box and dry straw to start a fire. However a guide failed to turn up. A pikeman took his place but vanished into the darkness. It was a fiasco. Everyone went home. Shaw was mortified. He vowed that the next raid he planned, on the house of the loyalist McKee family in the townland of Craignasasonagh, would be better organised. It wasn't. Some days later Shaw and ten other members of Revd Birch's congregation were arrested on a charge of attacking McKee's residence. One was injured by gunfire from two Scottish soldiers guarding the house. The casualty was lucky. McKee's daughter Nelly took an axe to cut off his head and was only stopped by the soldiers.

I found much superior discipline when I rode across the low drumlins of north Down to the seaside estate of David Ker in Portavo. Ker was the biggest landlord in north-east Down, but considered a decent sort. He was hiding in his big house, waiting to see which way the wind would blow.

Men from Donaghadee were openly cutting down ash trees on his estate to make pike shafts. Two estate workers turned up, but rather than interfere they started a fire and produced a bottle of poteen. Portavo was solid for the cause they declared; not a single man on the five townlands owned by Ker had joined the yeomanry. The few who were so inclined were persuaded – much laughter – to change their minds.

There was no dissension in the Revd James Porter's congregation in Greyabbey farther south on the Ards Peninsula. I sat at the back of his church as he gave a sermon to mark Thanksgiving Day, designated by Dublin Castle as the day to celebrate the dispersal of the French fleet. He called his peroration Wind and Weather. The French were only deterred by the wind and the waves, he declared. Had the armaments but landed, no force would have withstood its progress. 'The French are still a great nation,' he said, to cries of 'Amen!' 'They might one day revisit our shores.' 'Amen!'

He pressed a copy of his sermon upon me for publication. 'They might lock you up for this,' I warned him. He also thrust a letter into my hands, which the *Star* duly printed, in which he said the King should know that the 'duplicitous, arrogant, wicked and nefarious junto in Dublin', who pretended to be His Majesty's friends, were his worst and most mortal enemies because they would bring the country to ruin.

I caught up with Davey Warden on the Cloughey Road, and he took me out in the darkness as he drilled a large body of men shouldering pikes and hoes by the light of flaming torches. 'We have the run of the countryside now,' said Davey. 'Mount Stewart has an armed guard, the ladies have been evacuated and Londonderry has put bars on the lower windows. No one pays rent.' Castlereagh, however, had secured more large sums for Cleland, the 'master of the croppy hounds', to pay informers.

Much as I disliked Castlereagh, I loathed the Revd John Cleland, who besides being his agent was vicar of Newtownards. The barrister John Philpot Curran summed up Cleland in court once: 'He ascends the pulpit with the gospel of benignity and peace to impress himself and his hearers with his meek and holy spirit. Then he descends, throws off the purple, seizes the Insurrection Act in one hand and the whip in the other, flies by night after his game, his belly to the ground, and he turns round and tells you that his mind is unprejudiced and his heart is full of humanity.'

I rode next to Newry in south Down where I met in the Globe Inn the Presbyterian minister from Holywood, the Revd Arthur McMahon, and the Catholic rebel leader, John Magennis. Together they were recruiting Defenders into United Irish ranks. They took me to observe a training session for two score men in the hills behind Castlewellan. All were armed with ash poles with metal heads attached. Some had straightened scythes.

McMahon demonstrated how a pike could be used to slash horses' bridles or make a mount rear up and unseat its rider if thrust at its nostrils. 'A single cavalryman is very vulnerable to attack by two pikemen at the same time,' he said. 'A line of pikemen can stop cavalry but must be protected from flank attack by musketeers. Remember, it is hard to turn around quickly with a pike in your hand. Remember too that Polish pikemen recruited from the fields defeated the Russian army three years ago. We too can overcome an army.'

I took a pike myself and found it heavy and unwieldy and easily parried by a swordsman. I took down McMahon's instructions for distribution.

I reported back to the military committee in Belfast that Down was never more ready and that United Irishmen were in control of the roads

189

at night, especially in the northern parts. Billy Templeton came back from County Antrim with the same message.

It was different in Belfast. Privates from the Highland Fencibles molested people on the streets, cursing Ireland and the Irish in Scots Gaelic. No attempt was made by officers to stop them. When the British defeated a Spanish fleet, the Fencibles fired a *feu de joie* to celebrate, and hogsheads of porter were provided for the soldiers. Inevitably riots followed.

Still and all, recruitment to the Belfast yeomanry stalled and twenty-three men who did sign up issued a statement to the *Northern Star* protesting that they had taken the oath not to uphold coercive laws, but with the sole motive of repelling foreign invasion, and that they continued firmly attached to the rights and liberties of all the people of Ireland.

Corbett published our response. They were defending a government of landlords that needed a foreign army already in place to uphold their privileges.

The majority of yeomen were Orangemen and anti-Papist. James Joy, a relative of Henry Joy McCracken, had to resign his commission as a yeoman officer because twenty Orangemen refused to remove orange ribbons from their uniforms. They accused him of croppy blood.

In March the trembling County Down landlords and magistrates met in the Saintfield mansion of Squire Price, who was a cousin of Castlereagh. Lord Londonderry raged about gangs of estate workers from Mount Stewart attacking loyalist houses. Savage of Portaferry complained that the lower orders were more impudent than ever. Earl Annesley from Castlewellan, the worst bigot, said the whole county was disturbed and should be placed under martial law. Downshire demanded that all laws should be suspended and cursed 'that damned sink of Belfast'.

With Thomas Russell in jail, the Ulster Directory met in McClean's public house in Randalstown and agreed that, upon victory, the United Irishmen and Defenders would form a directory modelled on the French directory and new laws would guarantee freedom of religion, press and labour. Though he wasn't present, we elected the Revd Steel Dickson of Portaferry as our adjutant-general for Down. I had formed a good impression of the Revd Dickson when we met at the Grays' on the day after Castlereagh arrested members of his congregation. He commanded great respect for his radicalism but I worried that he was not a military man.

As I left the tavern, I took the opportunity to confront John Gordon about the allegation that he had beaten a servant girl.

'I did. I gave her a good smacking,' acknowledged Sam Neilson's nephew. 'So what? She was gossiping with other servants about meetings in my room in Alexander's.'

'Now she has a motive to inform,' I told him 'Keep your temper for the real enemy.'

'Informers are the real enemy,' he said.

— TWENTY-NINE —

'DARING AND HORRID OUTRAGES'

On Saturday 13 March 1797, I escorted Martha to an evening coterie in the Assembly Rooms. She wore an enamelled green brooch in the shape of an Irish harp topped by shamrock to show everyone where her heart lay.

Several military officers were there, including General Lake, a tight-lipped man of about fifty with a huge mane of powdered white hair tied back in a ponytail, strutting around in a scarlet coat with gold epaulettes. A friend came over to relay a story going round that when General Lake was dining with the Skeffingtons, their parrot squawked at him, 'Are you up?' A mortified Mrs Skeffington blamed the servants.

'It's a wonder Lake didn't arrest the parrot,' I said.

We were interrupted by a Miss Sinclair who whispered behind her fan that we should take note that the general and his staff were wearing their swords. An officer had just told her that they had received orders to begin disarming the people of Ulster, and raids for arms would start in the countryside at midnight.

I thought immediately of Matt and his stock of pike heads at Six Road Ends.

I made my excuses, quietly slipped away and rushed to High Street and saddled up Eclipse. By God's grace, the evening was calm and the moon came up. I arrived at the Gray farmstead at eleven. A little ceili was going on. Matt McClenaghan was scraping away at the fiddle, and two men were playing flutes. Everything stopped when I appeared, dressed for the coterie with riding cloak over my shoulders.

I called Matt and George outside. We ran down the road to the forge and gathered up two dozen pike heads from his back shed and moved them to a ditch across the fields. George assured me there were no pike shafts or heads at his house. He set off on horseback to warn other United Irishmen in the district. After midnight a patrol of soldiers with burning torches approached the forge. I watched from behind a hedge as they broke down the door and ransacked the building. They left empty-handed.

I sat up with the Grays until dawn. George was his usual pessimistic self. 'We will never prevail; they will find all our weapons,' he said. Hans chided him, saying, 'The darkest hour comes before the dawn.'

'*Notre jour viendra*,' said Betsy.

'*Ce sera*,' I replied.

As I rode back to Belfast I hoped that she was right, that our day would come, and soon.

Martha forgave me for abandoning her at the coterie. When I called to apologise next evening she said that the officers had left for their night's work soon after I did. A tone-deaf Whig lady went around saying, 'Don't you find General Nugent utterly *disarming*,' and tittering at her own wit. Several well-connected people there feared that General Lake was not quite right in the head, and that his search for arms would leave havoc in its wake. She still had her husband's musket and the military would never get that from her. 'Sam McTier bought it to defend the people,' said Martha, 'not to be used against them.'

The officers at the coterie were also boasting that the *Northern Star* would soon be stormed again, she warned me. Any night I needed to sleep away from my lodgings I could have my old bed back. I said I might take up her offer but had excellent protection in the form of my muscular landlady, Mrs Hamill, who grabbed a cleaver when she saw anyone nosing around.

Three days later General Lake imposed martial law on the north because of numerous 'daring and horrid outrages'. He assumed full authority to billet the King's troops in any houses they choose, to disarm the population, and to pay informers in strict secrecy. Only by surrendering their arms could the people rescue themselves from the severity of military authority.

That weekend Castlereagh came trotting proudly across the Long Bridge and up Ann's Street at the head of a procession of fourteen carts laden with arms captured or surrendered in County Down. A tender was brought into Belfast Lough to accommodate a growing number of prisoners. I saw dragoons marching six shackled men to the harbour. The captives defiantly shouted '*Erin go bragh*!' and street urchins ran alongside throwing refuse at the soldiers.

We played them at their own game. One night our lads, their faces blackened with burnt cork, visited the homes of several gentlemen in Belfast who had taken the yeoman oath and forcibly relieved them of their muskets and swords. Skeffington, Brown, Bristow and Waddell Cunningham expressed outrage at 'evil-minded persons putting peaceable inhabitants in fear of their lives.' I took charge of an expensive musket with a fine stock of German walnut, and wrapped it in canvas to hide beside my pistol between the roof chimneys.

County Down came under military occupation. Soldiers entered houses and cottages and beat and insulted people at will. Atrocities were reported from Loughbrickland, Saintfield, Greyabbey and Portaferry. In Saintfield a detachment of cavalry invaded the Revd Birch's Presbyterian Church looking for arms. In Newtownards the Revd Cleland led troops to arrest William McCormick at his inn.

We published a mocking letter from an imaginary County Down reader. 'We are in a bonny hobble now, in the Coonty Doon. O, the devil a gun nor pistol the English sojers have left us; we are as naked as the hour we are born, except pot-sticks and leadles.'

In Hillsborough the *Northern Star* carrier was stopped by yeomen and taken before Lord Downshire. His bundles were torn open and papers strewn on a table so the great man could make little of its contents. Our supporters seized and destroyed copies of the *News-Letter* on the roads in the vicinity of Hillsborough, Lisburn and Downpatrick.

The few reform-minded members of the Dublin parliament kicked up a fuss. The Kildare MP, William Brabazon Ponsonby, said it was fashionable to abuse Ulster 'whose people put William on the throne, bled at the Boyne and manned the walls of Derry, but have now committed two great crimes – they have turned their backs on religious bigotry and animosity, and they have realised that Ireland is ruled by a succession of English viceroys who have mangled and corrupted parliament in Dublin.'

That spring I was one of many arguing strenuously that we should rise without the French. Men were ready for action. The countryside was still bristling with concealed pikes and muskets. A French lugger landed a modest consignment of muskets near Kilkeel in south Down which were hidden in the Mourne Mountains. Scores of militia at Blaris army camp were said to be on the point of rebellion. More than seventy had secretly taken the United Irish oath. The iron was hot I said. We should strike before we were really left without 'the devil a gun nor pistol'. But the 'foreign aid men', the brave souls who would wait for ever for the French, prevailed.

In the High Street one afternoon a peddler wearing a Tam O'Shanter implored me in a wheedling Scottish accent to buy a belt or silk handkerchief from the box suspended from his neck. As I brushed past him he said, 'Are you still riding that whore Belle Martin?' Again it was William Putnam McCabe, master of disguises.

We met in a corner of the Donegall Arms ale room, after Putnam had transformed himself into a town gentleman with the assistance of a powdered wig, a cutaway coat with embroidered epaulettes and a starched linen collar. Where better to hide than in the most public place in town? Putnam was then a hunted man. He proudly showed me a crumpled notice circulated by the government putting a price of £500 on his head. It described him as: 'Height five foot eight inches; well made; walks smart; full face; black or dark eyes; dark hair; whiskers; good complexion; not corpulent but pretty lusty; a great deal of vivacity; wears pantaloons and boots.'

I looked across at the blue-eyed, clean-shaven Putnam. 'Pretty lusty? That's about right,' I said.

Jemmy Hope was with him, the curly hair of an aristocratic-looking wig resting on his shoulders. They had been given beating orders by the United Irish directorate to organise people across Ireland and had been recruiting in Wicklow, Wexford, Leitrim and Roscommon, often changing clothes and appearance to avoid arrest. They were in Belfast on a scouting mission to probe the defences of Blair military camp. They concluded that if Down and Antrim acted in concert, they could cut it off when a rising took place.

Putnam mocked me unmercifully about Belle Martin and about my penchant for quoting Shakespeare, teasing me with a line from one of the bard's sonnets: 'For I have sworn thee fair, and thought thee bright/ Who art as black as hell, as dark as night.' I learned from him, with some horror that, when she was exposed as a spy and *agent provocateur*, I came under suspicion at the highest levels, but my comrades testified to my trustworthiness and naïveté. It seemed everyone knew I was shafting her, and that Newell was too.

Putnam had survived several dangerous moments. Once when he was resting in a garret in Dublin on a cold, rainy night, he heard a patrol approaching, jumped out of bed, flung the window open and hid under the mattress. The soldiers assumed he had fled across the rooftops. In a village in County Roscommon he walked through a cordon by assuming the persona of the Scots peddler, pausing to sell trinkets to the soldiers as he passed.

They had just come from Roscommon where they pulled off one of their most daring escapades. Putnam donned the scarlet coat of a militia officer and, accompanied by Jemmy in the uniform of a sergeant, entered a room of Roscommon town jail where treason trials were being held. The first prisoner, Richard Dry, an important United Irishman from Dublin, was sentenced to five years for conspiracy to conduct armed rebellion. Putnam arose in his regimentals and announced that he was authorised to persuade gullible fools such as Dry to become loyal citizens and to devote their lives to the service of His Majesty, and that his recruiting sergeant would ask the prisoner to enlist. Jemmy approached Dry, ostentatiously pressed a recruitment shilling into his hand, and asked if he was willing to enter 'the only service fit for an honest Irishman'. Recognising Jemmy, Dry agreed. The judge released him into their custody.

Even acquaintances could not penetrate Putnam's disguises. He came to Belfast on the mail coach in the company of the barrister Francis Dobbs,

MP for Charlemont, known as Millennium Dobbs because he forecast Armageddon at the end of the century. Putnam put on an English accent and convinced the old windbag that he was a manufacturer from Yorkshire.

Like me, Jemmy wanted action. He feared that the better-off merchants would wait for ever for the French, and that they might not come in the end. The foreign aid men could not be relied upon to turn out and provide leadership if we decided to go it alone. 'They are like paper money,' he said, 'current for the time, keeping business afloat, but without any intrinsic value.'

'You should be proud to work for the *Northern Star*,' he told me. 'It's the moral force of Ulster. It sows the seed of truth.'

THIRTY

THE MAN IN THE MASK

Arming ourselves for a rising became an obsession. We listed the houses of loyalists in Belfast permitted to keep weapons at home with a view to raiding them. One of the most prominent was George Murdoch, the hearth tax collector and the cuckolded husband of Eddie Newell's fancy woman.

During an arms-procurement meeting of our military committee in John Alexander's whiskey house on Peter's Hill, John Gordon proposed we forcibly take guns from Murdoch's house at 61 Mill Street. He picked four men for a raiding party, including Eddie Newell. 'What if Murdoch resists?' Eddie wanted to know. 'He'll be dealt with,' replied Gordon.

What Eddie couldn't say, because his affair with Murdoch's wife was not public knowledge, was that he might be recognised by his mistress. 'Sure you'll be wearing a mask,' I said, as we walked home together, a remark I would later recall with bitter irony. 'And you can put on high heels, so she thinks you are a big fellow instead of her wee Eddie.'

Next day John Gordon brought Newell to his lodging room at Alexander's tavern, and they made plans for the raid. They were to post sentries, blacken their faces, then rush into Murdoch's home, make lots of noise, hold the family at gunpoint, seize the weapons and make off.

When the time came, however, Newell sent a message that he had come down with the fever and he could not join them.

Gordon decided to proceed without him. But the night-time assault was called off when a scout reported that a military guard had been posted at Murdoch's front door. That was strange.

We went looking for Newell. He was not at his lodgings. Next day he failed to keep appointments for portrait sittings. We concluded he had either been arrested or was lying sick somewhere or had left town for some urgent reason. I had a very bad feeling in my gut that the explanation might be more sinister. My apprehension was heightened when Mrs Hamill informed me that Murdoch had been in her butcher's shop enquiring who was lodging upstairs.

I decided it was time to take up Martha's offer of temporary use of my old room. I left my weapons hidden securely between the chimneys. Only the seagulls that made a racket overhead could spot them.

Several days later, on Friday 14 April, the military committee met again at John Alexander's tavern to prepare for the inevitable rising. Forty United Irishmen from two societies gathered in the upstairs rooms. At eight o'clock the door to the street was bolted and the proceedings began with a roll call. All the members of my Society No. 69 were there: Billy Templeton, John Gordon, Phil Kelly, Bobby Phillips, Robert Neilson, John McCann, Dick Magee, Jimmy and Ernie Corkran, Willie Scott, James Burnside, John Queery, John Shaw, John Tennent, Harry Speer, James Green, John Grimes, John Dunn, Alan Ingram, Robert Redfern, Bobby Montgomery, Alexander Kennedy and Hamill the publican.

When Eddie Newell's name was called there was no answer. We soon learned why.

Fifteen minutes after the start of our business, there was a sudden commotion below. The outside door was smashed in. Highland Fencibles, shouting and roaring in Gaelic, burst into our meeting. Some men jumped out the window onto the stable roof, but most of us were trapped. We were lined up against the wall facing a row of muskets and bayonets.

Colonel Lucius Barber entered with an officer called Fox and a Colonel Ellison of the Artillery who proceeded to gather up all the papers in both rooms.

A worse calamity could not have befallen us. The documents included the minutes of the military committee, reports from provincial and county committees, and resolutions of district societies. They included lists of names and arms held, and estimates of our strength: 68,000 sworn men in Ulster, of whom 22,922 were in County Antrim and 16,000 in Down.

Colonel Barber was accompanied by a small man dressed as a cavalry officer with black crape over his face and two small holes for his eyes. He went round the room pointing out members of the military committee by name, including me.

Barber hustled the informer into the next room to continue his treachery and then took him along the narrow corridor to the room where John Gordon lodged.

We were herded down the stairs, thrust into carriages and taken with a mounted escort to the Artillery barracks in Ann's Street. Crushed beside me as we rattled through the streets, Gordon said that the masked man had pointed out a concealed hole in the floor under the bed in his room. It was empty.

'That's as well,' I replied.

'Yes,' he said, 'but there is only one person to whom I ever showed that hiding place.'

'Oh no!' I cried.

'Oh yes!' he responded. 'Eddie shithouse Newell. He was the man in the mask.'

'Christ,' I said. 'I'm done for.'

I sank my head between my hands. I was struck dumb at this monumental act of betrayal.

'Do you know what,' I said. 'I think he was at Murdoch's all the time we were looking for him.'

He must be having a good laugh, I thought. Hadn't I talked to him about wearing a mask when we were discussing the raid!

At the barracks we were locked into a cold dungeon with straw on the flagstones. Other prisoners were brought in, among them Willie McCracken, Harry's brother. He had been drinking in Kelly's Cellars with two friends when Colonel Barber entered with a small 'cavalryman' wearing a handkerchief over his face who pointed him out. He recognised Newell right away.

I lay bewildered in the darkness, tortured by an awful thought: Were Eddie Newell and Belle Martin in league? Were they in it together all along?

A few days later I got my answer. They were.

William Sampson made the connection. He brought the news to me in the barracks when he was granted access as our legal representative. He had just come from Carrickfergus where he represented Joe Cuthbert in his trial for murder. Belle Martin had been summoned as the only prosecution witness. Sampson learned from other counsel that she had enticed four members of the Monaghan Militia to reveal they had taken the United Irish oath and had passed the information to Edward Newell, who in turn gave it to Colonel Lucius Barber.

It wasn't the planned raid on Murdoch's house that caused Newell to change sides. He had become an informer much earlier. I had sworn him in, we had played cards together, attended secret meetings together, got drunk together, gone whoring together. And he was reporting on our underground work. What an imbecile and numbskull I was not to realise that a United Irishman having an affair with a loyalist's wife should never be tolerated.

The trial of Cuthbert had been a debacle. Belle Martin suddenly left for Dublin and it had to be abandoned, though Cuthbert was rearrested and charged with high treason. Sampson believed the Crown had got wind that she was about to be destroyed as a witness by the Revd Steel Dickson of Portaferry, our commander-in-waiting, who was prepared to testify that, as a young woman in Portaferry, she had earned a reputation as a thief, liar and seducer of older men.

Sampson had also heard a rumour that she would be exposed as a prostitute and that Castlereagh feared being named as one of her past clients.

'My, God, was he?' I asked.

'I don't know,' said Sampson. 'But it is said, and I was going to ask him in court.'

When Sampson left I slipped down to the floor with my back to the wall and moaned like a child, full of self-pity and despair. I thought of my parents, and how the news of my arrest would leave them distraught.

After ten days in the barracks, eighteen of us were taken to Dublin in six carriages with an escort of the 22nd Regiment of Light Dragoons.

People came out in every town and village to wave their hats for us. In Hillsborough I was upset to see my father and mother by the roadside there, looking bewildered. They had walked the ten miles from Moira to get a glimpse of their neglectful son, and I do believe they failed to see me, though I waved at the last moment.

At Newry the coaches drew up at the White Cross Hotel so that the dragoons could refresh themselves and their horses. We were denied sustenance, but some girls pushed their way past the guards and pressed bread and milk upon us.

We arrived in Dublin at seven o'clock in the evening and were brought to the new Kilmainham Jail in the fields outside the city.

Kilmainham was gaunt and forbidding, with walls thirty-five feet high and massive wooden entrance doors. Inside it was cold and dank. We were taken along echoing stone passages with high vaulted ceilings from which water dripped. There was a constant creaking and banging of heavy doors, a clanking of chains and the shouting of prisoners and warders.

The resident prisoners were locked up in their cells before we arrived. Harry McCracken heard my voice and called out: 'Welcome *Star* man!'

We tried to keep our spirits up with songs and black jokes as we waited to be assigned to cells.

At three in the morning Lord Carhampton, commander of British forces in Ireland, an aristocrat in his fifties with a baby face set off by an expensive grey wig, came to inspect us. He asked the turnkey in a high-pitched voice why so many of us were not locked up, but were still 'at large'.

'If this be at large, what the devil would be restriction?' called out John Gordon.

'Be silent, or learn manners in the dungeon,' squeaked Carhampton, whom we despised as a murderous lecher who once, it is said, raped a 12-year-old girl in Dubln.

He was about to leave when he spotted a green ribbon attached to a foraging cap on a bench and demanded furiously to know who had brought such an emblem of sedition into the prison. Gordon put the cap on and said jauntily 'It's mine.' Carhampton ordered him to the dungeon.

We shouted we would go too. 'Let them be indulged,' he said.

As we were led off we sang defiantly the words that had meant little to us before when performed in the taverns, but now fitted the bill:

Though to the dungeon we go,
Where patriots dwelt before,
Yet in the cell or on the sod,
We're paddies evermore.

It was hard to keep our spirits up in the cramped and malodorous underground vaults. Rats ran across our feet, bed bugs came out of the walls to suck our blood, fleas colonised the straw on the stone floor.

After two days we were brought up and put in cells so small I could touch the walls on either side when I stretched my arms. There was no glass in the barred window above my head. My bed was a shallow wooden box with a straw bag. There was a stinking wooden bucket to use as a lavatory and to wash in.

Thus, duped by a whore, betrayed by a friend, deprived of a role in freeing Ireland from tyranny, I began the most miserable period of my life.

— THIRTY-ONE —

NOTRE JOUR VIENDRA

The distress of being in prison was mitigated somewhat by being reunited with my comrades, if only in shared hardship.

Sam Neilson embraced me – he had never done that before – and wanted to know everything about the *Star*. Always a bit morose, he looked haggard and had developed a fever from being kept for weeks in a dungeon at the start of his incarceration, subsisting on a penny's worth of milk a day. He was desperately worried about his wife and five children who were living on charity because he had sunk his fortune in the paper.

Harry McCracken, irrepressible as always, refused to let us sink into despondency. He had acquired a hoard of victuals and liquor. He fixed up a string and sent over two bottles of wine to our ward.

Young Charles Teeling told me he wrote several times to Castlereagh requesting permission for his father to visit, without reply. By contrast, the dragoon captain who escorted Charles from Lisburn presented him at the gates of Kilmainham with a silver snuff box, and expressed the hope that it would never be exhausted in prison.

There was something sweet and noble about Charles that made people love him. A Teeling family servant called Cotney walked the ninety miles from Lisburn and talked his way past the guards to offer Charles his cape and a leather purse of money, so he could walk out in his place. Charles of course declined.

We settled into a routine. Eight of us each got possession of a ward. There was but a single bench, so only three of us could sit down at one time.

I spent a lot of time comforting Billy Templeton, who was in a terrible state worrying about his widowed mother, who relied now on the kindness of others to support her three younger children.

Our cells were not locked during daylight hours which meant we could mingle. Billy and I doubled up, so one cell was free for use as a common room. We had access to a small circulating library with several works by Shakespeare, and had the use of a yard where we kicked around a stuffed leather bag.

I was given back the contents of my pockets, including my watch and Betsy's *La Grammaire Française*, which gave me enormous comfort.

We had some fun too. One night I heard scraping noises and the cell door was opened. Charles was there with two others. They had found a way to unscrew the locks from the doors. We had midnight parties with smuggled whiskey, until the guards found out and the locks were strengthened.

The turnkeys were simple fellows, without much malice. We were told that in January, when the French were expected, panic-stricken warders had mistaken the mighty thuds of snow falling from the roof for the sound of approaching cannon, and had begged the prisoners to protect them as they really were patriots at heart.

Within two weeks of my arrival more comrades arrived in shackles from the north, among them Joe Cuthbert who had been found guilty of treason. He brought needles and thread and was immediately appointed the prison tailor.

He told me that Edward Newell now strutted openly around Belfast with Murdoch, always accompanied by a military guard. They were both said to have been paid handsomely by the Crown. I wondered if they were sharing Mrs Murdoch. Or did the hearth tax collector still not know what others knew.

I learned that not long after our arrest, the *Northern Star* published an article about Newell, without naming him, in which they referred to 'a ruffian, who, with a handkerchief on his face, haunts the town to the ruin of peace and conviviality.'

A leaflet was circulated in response by Colonel Barber in which the masked man denied he was a villain who would barter his conscience and the blood of his countrymen for gold, as portrayed by the editor of the *Star*.

He claimed to be a steady and honest man who was ever active to promote the cause of Liberty and parliamentary reform, but 'when the assassination committee of Belfast would send their agents to murder a man who never gave them cause, what heart but must abhor that community who could plan and execute such premeditated villainy?' He was not seeking the bribes of government, but to expose the plans of the United Irishmen to butcher all the enemies of the constitution and to exterminate the government and allow anarchy and bloodshed to prevail.

Newell's anonymity was short-lived. His brother Robert wrote a letter to the *Northern Star* which appeared on Saturday 5 May, stating that he was horrified and mortified that his brother, a secret and treacherous informer, had for some time been going through Belfast, night after night, disguised as a light horseman with his face blackened and accompanied by a guard of soldiers pointing out certain individuals who in consequence were arrested.

The companionship of my comrades helped me bear the miserable food, the wretched accommodation, the flea bites, and the cold which, even as summer approached, chilled us to the bone. But I could hardly endure the mental torments and the questions that plagued me in the wee hours. Was our movement riddled with spies and informers? Could the rising take place when so many leaders of integrity and enlightenment were held in this stinking prison, or like Thomas Russell, languished in the hell hole that was Newgate? Would the rising take place without me? What was happening to my mother and father in Moira, and to George Gray and Eliza Bryson, and most of all to darling Betsy. More than once I opened the back of my watch and stroked the strands of her hair secreted there, and imagined I was back in Gransha listening to her read stories, only to fall into renewed depression at the thought that she was more likely cuddling by the turf fire with Willie Boal.

In mid-May the four members of the Monaghan Militia whom Belle Martin and Edward Newell had betrayed were sentenced to death. A newly arrived prisoner from Belfast told us how Daniel Gillan, Owen McKenna, William McKenna and Peter McCarron were marched through Belfast in procession with two priests and a guard of horse and foot composed of different regiments, then placed on cars and taken to Blaris Camp where they were shot by firing squad as they knelt on their own coffins. The whole camp, artillerymen, dragoons, infantry, militia and fencibles, were made to file past their lifeless bodies. The Scottish Fencibles refused to provide the firing party, and the executioners were drawn from the Monaghan Militia, Irishmen all. Owen McKenna's father refused to persuade his son to turn informer. He declared, 'The life of a son is of great value to the father, but if my son is spared to become a traitor, I would shoot him with my own hand.'

A week after that we got news that the *Northern Star* office in Belfast had been thoroughly wrecked by the military. Sam Neilson was distraught when he heard. I was pretty devastated myself. A full account of the crime was written up in the *London Courier* and a copy was smuggled to us by a turnkey.

The *Courier's* correspondent reported that on Saturday 19 May one hundred of the Monaghan Militia came from the New Barracks to Wilson's Court where they were joined by a party of artillery. A sergeant major of the Monaghan Militia led them into the printing office. He said to the workers, 'Don't blame us, boys, for what we are going to do, we are only executing the orders of our officers.' They proceeded to destroy papers, books, types and presses. They beat and severely wounded several printers and dispatch boys. Two clerks (standing in for me and Billy) ran to General Lake's house in Linen Hall Street to implore him to intercede. They were told the general was out of town. His aide-de-camp refused to let them appeal to the officer of the main guard, who was standing nearby. No city magistrate could be found. At length they located Colonel Leslie of the Monaghan Militia. He got the raiding party to leave and requested friends of the proprietors to take what they needed and make an account of the damage. They were only there ten minutes when a gang of sergeants from the Royal Artillery and the Monaghan Militia returned with hatchets and sledge-hammers. They broke the door and window frames, smashed the machinery and threw everything onto the street. Colonel Barber then went to all the printers in Belfast and forbade them to even think of printing the *Northern Star*.

The Monaghan Militia justified their excesses by complaining that the *Star* refused to publish an advertisement they had composed. Our investor

Francis Jordan had advised Tom Corbett not to print the item on the grounds that it insulted Belfast. Neilson said he was right. They were going to smash up the *Star* no matter what. Jordan was hounded out of his house for his decision and fled to the home of his friend Cunningham Greg. Soldiers found him, ordered everyone out and destroyed Greg's house. In my opinion Jordan's real offence was his refusal, as a prominent and wealthy citizen, to take an oath of allegiance to the government.

I wept for Sam and for myself. The newspaper in which I thrived was no more. The machinery which I loved to hear clicking and clacking was smashed. The rooms where I had worked with exhilaration and euphoria were desecrated. The colleagues I loved were dispersed or imprisoned. The proprietor, my hero and standard bearer, was stripped of his dignity and authority.

I was no longer the *Star* man. I was nobody.

Even worse, support for the cause had started to decline, according to Harry McCracken's sister Mary Ann. In a letter in June she wrote that assassinations had turned some away and the failure to rise had disillusioned others.

It was said in those days that the time of disturbances would be between the scythe and the sickle. The hay harvest was upon us and the timidity of our leaders still at large was nothing short of a betrayal.

I recalled bitterly the huzzahs for Liberty from the wealthy merchants who now drank toasts to the King with the officers who tortured and repressed their kinfolk. These fine-day patriots would regain their courage only if they saw Lake and Barber fleeing before a regiment of French revolutionary soldiers.

In my restless tossing and turning at night I tried to take comfort from the words of Betsy, '*Notre jour viendra*'. I began to use the phrase to revive the spirits of my comrades. Soon it was common to hear a prisoner shout to a guard, '*Notre jour viendra*', even if we were often consumed with the doubts that came to us when left alone with our thoughts. But when I soiled the bed at night with erotic thoughts it was Belle Martin I imagined shafting, and then I would loathe myself afterwards.

We tried to keep up our spirits with poems and stories and ballads.

Sometimes the prison yard was like a concert hall, and the roughest-looking villains often sang with the sweetest voices. Billy Templeton, the most unprepossessing of us all, had such oratorical skills that he had us in tears with his reading of a poem written by Dr William Drennan about the refusal of Scottish soldiers to execute the four Monaghan Militiamen.

When bid to take aim at the Irishman's heart
The stout Caledonian recoiled with a start
The first of my country, the first of my clan
E'er ordered to fire on a blindfolded man!
You'll find better tools to perform such a deed
And by Irish hands let the Irish bleed
In the spirit of Cain let them murder each other
And the United fall – by his United brother.

The worst days were when men were hanged. One morning a prisoner from the criminal wing was taken to be stretched. He saluted smartly three times as he crossed the yard and he called out, in an Ulster accent, that he was sorry to die for a crime he was ashamed of, and not for an act of rebellion. 'You will live to see the country free while I die for my folly,' he declared. 'While your tomb will be moistened by the tears of your country, mine will be marked by the finger of scorn.'

He was taken to the balcony above the main gate and shoved off with a rope around his neck. We banged our tin pots on the bars in protest.

There were good days too in Kilmainham that summer of 1797. I remember them vividly for the joy they brought us. The wife of a prisoner called Bond arrived with two immense pies one morning, one for the governor and a larger one for her husband. The pastry was made with the best butter. The governor was delighted. We took the crust off our pie to find letters, writing materials and foreign and domestic newspapers, and liquor. Charles Teeling became quite lyrical, calling Mrs Bond a 'ministering angel'.

Another angel was Henry Haslett's younger sister. She and her mother moved to Dublin to be close to him and were allowed to visit. Everyone doted on the little girl. She was the apple of everyone's eye, and when she performed party pieces for us, we were transported.

For me one of the very happiest moments was when I received a note from George Gray, delivered by the Revd Steel Dickson who was admitted as visitor. They were all well in Gransha, he wrote, and their house had not been raided. Hans, Betsy, Willie Boal and Eliza added their good wishes. Eliza wrote sweet endearments. Betsy prayed for my safe return 'to the embrace of your loving family'. How I treasured those words.

Dickson had come to Kilmainham because he was worried that the testimony of the informer Carr, kept in a separate wing, would land him in prison and cause four of his congregation to be executed. We resolved the situation for him. Joe Cuthbert made up a grave-folded clerical gown and we managed to get a comrade into Carr's cell posing as a zealous divine, with breviary and snuff-box in hand. The wretch complained bitterly to the 'minister' that he had been promised he would be treated as a prisoner of state, but for seven months he had been held in solitary confinement. Told that the door of forgiveness was never closed against the repentant sinner, and that his soul would reside in the blaze of perdition if he caused another man's execution, the wretched Carr grasped the visitor by the hands and implored his pious intercession and forgiveness. He would do what was right, he promised. When the case eventually came up at the county assizes, Carr was escorted there with a military escort, but refused to testify against the four men and they were acquitted and returned home in great triumph.

But these triumphs were as nothing compared to the relentless barrage of bad news brought to us by our lawyers and visitors.

County Down was ready to rise at the end of June but the Antrim men hesitated and as a result the role of our then military leaders, Alexander Lowry of Rathfriland and the Revd Arthur McMahon of Holywood, became known; they had to flee Ireland when General Lake raided Ballynahinch looking for them. Charles Teeling's brother-in-law, John Magennis, also had to take refuge. William McCormick's inn in Newtownards was burned down by yeomen under the command of Londonderry's agent Cleland, who said it was a centre for seditious talk;

fencibles in Newtownards torched the house of Dr James Jackson, taking care to steal his valuables first; the Revd Samuel Barber in Rathfriland was lodged in Downpatrick jail; in south Down a Welsh regiment, the Ancient Britons, shot and bayonetted to death up to twenty unarmed boys and old men between Newry and Kilkeel, an atrocity confirmed by the subsequent testimony of Captain John Giffard of the Dublin Militia; fifteen Catholic Kerry militiamen were killed by Scottish Fencibles and yeomen after they got into a sectarian fight with some Orangemen at Stewartstown.

We fretted that the longer the foreign aid men waited for the French, the more damage Castlereagh would inflict on our organisation. Already in Kilmainham about one hundred of the north's best men were behind bars.

In July Charles Teeling's father was at last permitted by Castlereagh to visit him. Luke Teeling was a broken man, his property and business destroyed for daring to send a petition to the King from the freeholders of Antrim to intercede with his corrupt ministers in Ireland.

Sam Neilson became emaciated and plagued with fevers. He refused to ask for Ann to visit him for fear it would distress her and that she would be humiliated by a minion in uniform. His wife came anyway and was duly distressed and humiliated.

And the prison killed our angel, Haslett's little sister. Her visits to the dripping, dark corridors of Kilmainham brought on a fever from which she died. Haslett was a broken man. No one could comfort him. Along the hundred miles of road from Dublin to Belfast, people turned out in big numbers to mark the passing of her coffin. The whole of Belfast attended the funeral. As Charles remarked, the enthusiasm of the people on these occasions was a bitter remonstrance to the government for putting us in prison, denying us the right of trial and suspending the laws of the land.

Men who are shut up together have too much time to dwell on slights, real or imagined. Our numbers were riven with petty spats and resentments. One of the worst arose between Sam Neilson and Harry McCracken, two men I loved.

Sam was one of the early group of prisoners who decided they would sink or swim together and would not undermine their solidarity by seeking

211

individual release through family or business or state connections. They didn't stick to it. Harry was furious when he learned that some of Neilson's friends had been pulling strings to get him out. He accused him of impropriety, which of course provoked a bitter retort. The two men stopped speaking to each other.

As Neilson's ally, Henry Haslett took serious umbrage with McCracken over this, which rather put me on McCracken's side because I never liked Haslett, who thought that, because he was a founder of the United Irishmen, he had the right to boss people around in a crude, arrogant manner. Mary Ann McCracken once warned us once that Haslett was a tyrant and universally disliked. But I was torn. Sam Neilson hired me when I was a nobody, and I would always be loyal to him, but Haslett was the first to invest in the *Northern Star* and Neilson could not forget that. I tried to stay on good terms with both Sam and Harry as the atmosphere grew poisonous.

Sam let the affair get to him. He drank too freely of the liquor that was smuggled in. He began to feel sorry for himself and he wrote a bitter little verse:

A year's not long, 'tis true, to spend
At liberty, with many a friend
But in these dreary walls enclosed,
Fretted at heart and much abused;
Assailed by every babbling tongue,
One year appears a hundred long.

The dispute came to a head one morning in August when Henry Haslett went for Harry with a saucepan containing boiling water and battered him until we pulled him off. Neilson looked on horrified but said nothing. McCracken was bruised more in spirit than body.

The bitter quarrel came to an end after Harry got a letter from Mary Ann who admonished her brother severely for allowing the discord to fester and pleaded with him to remove 'the envenomed dart in Neilson's bosom', saying their disunion afforded a triumph to their enemies, and vexation to their friends.

Harry invited Sam to his cell. They talked for an hour. Afterwards they appeared together in the yard, deep in conversation, looking at ease in each other's company. Everyone noticed. The relief was palpable. Then Neilson approached Haslett and sat with him on a bench talking earnestly. Haslett got up and shook hands with McCracken.

For me the lowest moment came on the last day of August when a turnkey threw down a letter beside my morning bowl of oatmeal and water. It was from my mother. My dear father had passed away from the fever. All those winter days spent in the greenhouse with its broken windows and unlit stove had taken their toll. I thought of him, lying on the bed where I was conceived, dignified in death as in life.

I was refused permission to attend my father's funeral. I can never forgive them for that.

Desperate to comfort my mother, on 3 September I submitted a memorial to Camden requesting bail for myself and Billy Templeton, citing the fact that we both were fatherless. My mother also applied on my behalf. We were turned down two weeks later.

We almost lost Charles Teeling that month. He fell desperately sick with the contagion. He was released on bail into the care of a Dublin family on security of £4,000 put up by his friends in Lisburn. He was carried out of the prison sweating and unconscious.

Charles returned to Kilmainham eight weeks later, but not as a prisoner. Having been restored to health, he had called at the Castle to give himself up and redeem the bail bond of his friends. He was invited into the chamber of Under-Secretary Edward Cooke, with whom he had a 'long and friendly' conversation, the outcome of which was his freedom, on condition he would not return to the north.

We bade him farewell. He told me he would of course return to the north, and I would find him there when our time came. 'And it will,' he said clasping my hands in his. '*Notre jour viendra.*'

— THIRTY-TWO —

REMEMBER ORR!

Of all the bad news that came to our prison nothing hit us harder than the fate of a *Northern Star* contributor from Farranshane in County Antrim. William Orr had turned up at our office one day with two excellent articles on the need for radical action. He was more than six foot tall, a model of symmetry and gracefulness, well-dressed, and wearing a green necktie. He had been active in the Volunteers and was an enthusiastic United Irishman. We took him for a glass of ale and found him open, frank and witty. He agreed to supply regular letters for publication advocating our cause. He declined an offer of a whiskey and a bed for the night, saying he wanted to be back with his wife and children before dark. He was as good-living a Presbyterian as he was mischievous as a writer.

Castlereagh wanted him behind bars and Willie Orr went on the run. In his absence, six hundred neighbours came and cut down his entire harvest in less than a day. Alas! He was seized by a force of twenty dragoons after he came out of hiding to visit his dying father. They found him concealed in a press and took him to Carrickfergus jail.

His trial began on Monday 18 September in Carrickfergus. We bribed the turnkeys to bring us daily reports.

Willie was charged with administering the United Irish oath to two Scottish soldiers in the Fifeshire Fencibles, named Hugh Wheatley and John Lindsay. It was the first trial for this offence under the Insurrection Act and a guilty verdict carried the death sentence. Willie's real offence of course was to lambast the government in the *Northern Star*.

It was unconscionable that this tall, gentle farmer from Farranshane should be hanged for his principles. John Philpot Curran and William Sampson, the best barristers in Ireland, were retained to defend him. The judge was Baron Yelverton, a Whig and a friend of Curran and a member of Curran's wine-drinking club, The Monks of the Screw.

The two soldiers swore that Orr administered the oath to them in Jack Gourley's barn in Farranshane. Wheatley claimed the men in the barn boasted that they intended to overthrow the government with the help of the French. Curran called witnesses who testified that Wheatley was a man of low character. Yelverton, however, praised Wheatley's evidence, which didn't bode well for the outcome.

The jury returned at six the next morning. The foreman, Archibald Thompson of Cushendall, said they were not agreed, and asked could they give a verdict qualified so as to save the prisoner's life. No, he was told, they couldn't. He asked might they leave the prisoner to his lordship's mercy. No, they couldn't.

The foreman then handed in a verdict of guilty, with a recommendation for mercy. The judge promised to pass this on to the government.

Two days later Yelverton betrayed all our hopes. He sentenced William Orr to be hanged on 7 October. He refused to admit affidavits from three jurors that they were drunk when they reached their verdict, having been supplied through the jury-room window with two bottles of whiskey to stiffen their resolve. He refused to listen to a complaint from the jury foreman that he was hard of hearing and had been intimidated by a loyalist juryman and now regretted the verdict. To the sound of weeping and wailing, the judge told Willie Orr that he was to be taken to the gallows, there to be hanged by the neck until dead.

Upon saying these words, the contemptible Yelverton himself burst out crying and sank his head in his hands for ten minutes.

Willie had to wait until the judge wiped away his tears to respond. He said he was innocent and was no felon. He could forgive the jury and was not afraid to die; but the witnesses who swore against him grossly perjured themselves.

Mary Ann McCracken wrote to Harry that even the greatest aristocrats in Belfast lamented the sentence on William Orr, and that old Archibald Thompson would lose his senses if Orr was executed, since he did not understand what he was doing and was threatened that he would not be left sixpence in the world if he did not find Orr guilty.

It appeared briefly that Willie had capitulated to his tormentors when the *Belfast News-Letter* reported that he had written a confession and acknowledged the justness of his sentence. Willie next day rebutted the *News-Letter* report. He wrote a riposte from his cell denying he had made any confession of guilt and contradicting the calumny.

It turned out that the false report was delivered to the *News-Letter* by the Revd William Bristow after he had visited Willie in prison and tried unsuccessfully to make him confess.

The execution was put off twice as influential figures, even Lady Londonderry, signed memorials asking for justice or mercy. Three gentlemen swore affidavits that Wheatley was a criminal who had admitted to rape and murder. Wheatley himself confessed to a Presbyterian minister that he had perjured himself at the trial.

All to no avail. Execution was set for Saturday 14 October. As Willie approached the scaffold he extracted a bundle of leaflets from his clothing and scattered them to the crowd. It was his 'Dying Declaration': 'If to have loved my country, to have known its wrongs, to have felt the injuries of the persecuted Catholics, and to have united with them and all other religious persuasions in the most orderly and least sanguinary means of procuring redress – if these be felonies, I am a felon, but not otherwise.'

On the scaffold he cried out, 'I am no traitor; I am persecuted for a persecuted country. Great Jehovah, receive my soul! I die in the true faith of a Presbyterian.'

The prison was a hive of rage. Pails and pans rattled furiously against the bars. When the noise died down we heard the distant rat-a-tat-tat of muskets firing a *feu de joie* to celebrate the defeat of a combined French and Dutch fleet by the British Royal Navy at Camperdown off the coast of Holland, which had likely been heading for Ireland with fifteen thousand French troops.

A newly arrived prisoner from Antrim told us that the administration of the United Irish oath for which Orr was hanged was conducted by William McKeever from Derry, who had fled the country. Orr was a bystander.

He also reported to us that just after the wooden types for William Orr's Dying Declaration were returned to Matthew Smith's printing shop in Belfast on the Sunday evening after the execution, Colonel Barber, attended by a guard of soldiers, burst in, walked directly round the counter, and seized them. Matthew was not there. Barber told his wife not to be surprised if soldiers came back to wreck the house and teach him a lesson. Next day she called upon General Lake and asked for his protection. 'Get out!' he roared. 'If I find Matthew Smith myself I will put him in prison in two seconds.' She went to appeal to the mayor of Belfast. Bristow told her not to be troubling him. She returned home to find a party of Monaghan Militia demolishing every article of furniture with sledge-hammers and smashing the doors and window sashes up to the third floor, leaving the house uninhabitable.

Having terrorised the Smiths, Colonel Barber went around the Belfast printing houses warning the proprietors that if they attempted to publish an account of William Orr's trial, their premises would suffer the same fate.

— THIRTY-THREE —

FROM *STAR* MAN TO *PRESS* MAN

After the judicial murder of Willie Orr and the defeat of the new armada at Camperdown, the cells of Kilmainham were rank with the corrosive feeling of despair. Almost all our best men were in prison: Henry Joy McCracken, Thomas Russell, Samuel Neilson, Arthur O'Connor, the Simms brothers, Henry Haslett. Good men like Lowry and McMahon and Magennis had fled abroad. Wolfe Tone languished somewhere overseas. The north was under martial law. Orangemen had taken over the yeomanry and United Irish funds had been exhausted in legal battles. We had been betrayed by informers whom we trusted as friends. The *Northern Star* was smashed.

Then on the morning of Friday 24 November 1797, a day so cold the perspiration froze in solid drops on the cell walls, I was set free, along with eleven others. Sam Neilson and the McCrackens remained behind but were told they would be next. No reason was given for our release after thirty-two weeks in jail.

Sam said I must get the message out, especially to our colonels, not to lose heart, to be strong and resolute, to endure, to rally the people, and prepare to rise up. I told him I would devote all my time and energy to the cause.

'They will regret locking me away,' I said, 'and they will regret setting me free.'

We walked across the rock-hard fields into Dublin and called at the house of William Drennan. He arranged for Billy Templeton and me to lodge the night in Kearn's hostelry in Kildare Street. He gave me a copy of a ballad he wrote called *The Wake of William Orr* and asked me to try to get more printed in Belfast.

218

Walking around the streets that evening we marvelled at the sounds and sights and careless languor of free men and women. The colour and noise of Dublin streets was overwhelming after Kilmainham. We had been given two pounds for our coach fare to Belfast and I spent two shillings that evening on one of the 'impures' who serviced all ranks in a house of ill repute in Pitt Street. She spread her legs for me on a creaking bed, and seemed delighted that the transaction lasted for only a few seconds, such was my pent-up desire for a real woman rather than the imaginary whores with whom I had tormented myself in the loneliness of the cell.

I had a caller next morning, a west of Ireland man in his thirties with red face and crooked teeth who introduced himself as Peter Finnerty, editor of *The Press,* established in Dublin by Lord Edward Fitzgerald and Arthur O'Connor to replace the *Northern Star* as the voice of the United Irishmen.

Finnerty knew all about me and my reputation as the *Star* man. He asked me to put my newspaper experience to good use and send him stories from the north. He proffered me five pounds advance and told me not to use the post but to find couriers, because all letters addressed to *The Press* were being seized. He recommended one of the coachmen on the 'Old Cock'. I agreed. We shook hands.

'You're a '*Press*' man' now, dear boy,' he said.

I found him a bit condescending. He called me 'dear boy' throughout. But he was a true radical, driven by a powerful sense of justice and righteousness, and resigned to whatever fate, or the authorities, had in store for him.

'Castlereagh is out to get me, dear boy,' he lisped, 'especially since I wrote last month that the administration is guilty of massacre, rape, military murders, desolation and terror. He acts like the prime minister of Ireland. He is ultimately responsible for all tortures and hangings, and that includes Willie Orr. Like Macbeth, he has waded so far in blood he cannot turn back.'

I couldn't resist showing off. 'They should remember that Macbeth also said, "Blood will have blood".'

In Belfast I found that dear patriotic Mrs Hamill had kept my room above the butcher's shop in Hercules Street. She had sealed the door after my arrest and my possessions were intact. Nor did she want back rent.

'Go on out of that,' she said. 'Am I not making good money selling beef and mutton to the officers who like to dine well and have meat every day, though I'd like to poison them all.'

I had a bath in her kitchen while she steeped my clothes in the tub to drown the fleas and bed bugs. She expressed shock at how my ribs stuck out and my muscles were wasted. 'You are away to scrapings,' she declared.

After a supper of beef and potatoes, and before collapsing on the bed, I climbed out the window and checked between the chimneys. The pistol and musket were still there in their canvas wrapping. I slept for a day and a half before rising and experiencing the joy of fresh clothes again, though they hung off my skinny frame.

Martha McTier was shocked to see me so emaciated when I called to bring her news of her friends still in Kilmainham. She poured out her pent-up feelings about what was being done to the town she knew so well.

'Belfast is now pervaded with fear of arrests, of house-wrecking by the military, of assault by the rabble, of a beating from soldiers. Ladies don't venture out at night except in chairs. General Lake goes around the streets stopping every fruit woman to enquire the name of any young man who passes. He seeks out the guests at every party to know what is going on in town and beyond. In the countryside houses are being burned and soldiers are inflicting tortures in search for arms. At present all here is detestable and low cunning, suspicion and ineffectual secrecy where both sides gain much true information yet both are betrayed. There is not a word or look on any subject other than the weather or the card table that is not noticed, and I believe there are few in any town who have not some sort of spy on them. It will be a long time before this devoted country recovers even the stupid contentment it enjoyed seven years ago.'

She got *The Press* from Dublin, she said, but worried that her house would be wrecked if the military found out. I confided to her that I would be writing for *The Press*. 'Don't tell anyone,' she said. 'You will be back inside before you know it.'

She insisted on giving me ten pounds which I promised to repay as soon as I could.

The *Northern Star* office in High Street was boarded up. The stables were empty. I called into Matthew Smith's shop in Bridge Street. He had just returned from Dublin and had been permitted to start his business again on condition that he refused all political material. He worried about his uncle, Sam Neilson, still languishing with rheumatic fever in a damp cell.

Matthew had sold the *Northern Star* horses and put the money aside for those who rode them. He gave me the twenty-five pounds he had got for Eclipse. The mare was getting old but I missed her.

That night we ex-prisoners were hosted by our comrades in Kelly's Cellars. Everyone was eager to supply us with ale and I was drunk after two tankards. I went looking for a prostitute and found the night streets full of wild-looking abandoned women, pulling men's clothes and shouting oaths. I ended up with a good-looking tart on Mill Street, though I again performed badly. I found out afterwards her husband was a patriot in Downpatrick jail and I engaged in a bout of self-loathing worthy of Thomas Russell.

When I had recovered enough strength, I set off walking to Moira under cold, grey skies. I had to rest frequently because of my weak leg muscles. I called on Harry Monro and his wife Margaret in Lisburn and they fed me scrambled eggs.

Harry assured me that in his business dealings with suppliers, merchants and weavers around County Down he found the resolve for action still existed despite, or because of, the brutality of the military. Pitch-cappings, half-hanging and house burnings had become common, but had not broken the spirit of radicalism. The Down colonels still wanted to wait for the French, however. At a county meeting held in Ballynahinch only a third of the delegates voted in favour of going at it now.

He feared that a high-level informer was at work in County Down. I wondered whom I could trust after my friend and my whore had both betrayed me.

I was shocked to see my mother in a black shawl when I arrived at Moira just before dark, though I should have expected that. She used to laugh and tease me; now her face was drawn and her body sagged. I begged her forgiveness for the pain I had caused her.

Many neighbours called to say sorry for my troubles on the death of my father and to share memories. They said the United Irishmen were still strong in Moira but a company of loyalist yeomen had been raised, dominated by Orangemen. My old nemesis Claiborne now rode around in yeoman uniform. Everyone said they missed the *Northern Star*. 'I do too,' I replied.

I visited my father's grave and to honour his memory trudged through heavy snow to the Castle, and stood for a long time in the glass house where he had spent his working life. The tenant was not good at keeping up the place. Most panes were broken now and the wooden frames had rotted. Snow drifted down on some brave orchids struggling to survive under the dead embrace of winter.

I spent a week with my mother, steadily regaining my strength. The day I left she gave me ten pounds from the family document box. 'Better you take it than the soldiers,' she said. I put it back when she was not looking.

I set off walking with a thawing westerly breeze on my back. I arrived at Saintfield in mid-afternoon and bought a coal-black mare and saddle from a dealer at Cow Green, where a fair was under way. I named her Shadow, because of her colour, and in memory of Eclipse, and rode her the short distance to the house of the Revd Birch.

My radical clergyman friend had also seen the inside of a prison cell. He had been arrested by Squire Price in April along with his congregation and they were taken in a cart, bound two-by-two, to Downpatrick jail and charged with high treason, but found not guilty at the autumn assizes. Our former *Star* agent and town merchant David Shaw joined us for supper. He too was held for several weeks after the failed attack on the house of the loyalist McKees, but was successfully defended by John Philpot Curran.

Before I left next morning Birch gave me an orange ribbon. 'Carry that in your pocket,' he said. 'It will be useful if you encounter yeomen patrols.'

— THIRTY-FOUR —

LIBERTY OR DEATH

Back in Belfast, feeling stronger, I loaded up with presents for a trip to Gransha. My heart beat faster with joy and also some trepidation at the thought of seeng Betsy again. For the household I purchased walnuts, raisins and French apples from Tom Mullan's grocery on the quays; for Betsy a copy of *Miss Williams's Tour in Switzerland* at John Hughes's bookshop on Bridge Street, and for Eliza an inexpensive green bracelet from Willie Dawson's on North Street. The colour, not the price, was important. It matched her eyes.

I was welcomed with warm embraces, and then smothered with kisses by Eliza who came running across the fields and almost knocked me down.

When I presented Betsy with *Miss Williams's Tour in Switzerland* she said wistfully, 'Maybe Miss Gray will do a tour of Switzerland one day,' to which I replied, 'I would happily take you there.' There was the briefest of silences before I added, reddening, 'You and Willie of course, and Eliza. Sure we will all go.'

Betsy laid the table with oaten bread, soda cakes, buttermilk, cream and cold meats. I told them of life in Kilmainham. They insisted on hearing every detail.

She said she couldn't bear to look at her miniature since she'd learned Newell was a traitor.

Though the countryside was in a state of perplexed calm, the radicalism of the Grays and their neighbours had hardened. Military raids had bred hatred and resentment. Two months earlier English dragoons searching for pikes had tied Matt McClenaghan's bellows-boy, Tommy Burns, to a gate post and whipped him with a cat o'nine tails until he passed out. They were about to cut off his ears with scissors when neighbours started a riot and the soldiers backed away. Betsy brought Tommy to her house and tended his wounds. 'I remember well your fine nursing skills,' I said.

I noted that the silverware and brass candlesticks were gone from the dresser. 'Did the dragoons take them?' I asked. 'No, they are hidden in the well,' said Hans, adding with a laugh, 'If they are stolen now, we will know who took them.' He said a neighbour woman, Mrs Moore, had buried her silver teapot because it bore the motto 'Liberty and Prosperity. Peace to America'. It was treasonable to own an article like that now.

George took me outside to show me a hiding place he had constructed in the turf stack by the gable if ever I needed it. It had a hollow section lined with straw which could be entered by removing a few bricks of turf and could accommodate a man.

Neighbours came by in the evening. I produced the copy of Drennan's *The Wake of William Orr* and recited it as we sat around the fire.

Here our murdered brother lies,
Wake him not with women's cries;
Mourn the way that manhood ought;
Sit in silent trance of thought…

Here we watch our brother's sleep;
Watch with us, but do not weep;
Watch with us through dead of night,
But expect the morning light.

Conquer fortune – persevere!
Lo! It breaks, the morning clear!
The cheerful cock awakes the skies,
The day is come – arise! arise!

As I finished, tears were running down Betsy's cheeks. 'Liberty or death,' she said. 'Aye, Liberty or death,' we replied as one voice. 'Remember Orr.'

Willie Boal had at last decided to join our ranks. The murder of Orr helped him make up his mind. Betsy might have twisted his arm but Boal was the type of fellow who goes all in once the decision is made.

We did the deed the following evening when several Gransha United Irishmen came to the Gray cottage, their wet cloaks dripping on the earthen floor. Among them was Eliza's father Andrew Bryson and his son Andy, who was then eighteen. Andrew Senior and I exchanged prison stories: he had endured seven months inside on a charge of treason. I was introduced to William Warwick, a young neighbour. Matt McClenaghan the smithy gave me a fierce embrace.

When Willie Boal arrived, Hans took him by the arm and announced that, having held himself aloof from the Society of United Irishmen, Willie now wished to join. He invited us into the bedroom adjoining the parlour and closed the door. Hans gave Boal a Bible and a pamphlet containing the oath and the constitution. I stepped forward and commanded Boal to recite the oath on the Bible. He did so, vowing to persevere in the goal of full representation and a brotherhood of affection among Irishmen of every religious persuasion, and never to inform on members of the society.

'Here's how you will know if a stranger is a United Irishman,' I said. 'If he says he knows 'U', you say you know 'N', then he says he knows 'I' and so on until the word UNITED is spelled out.

We stayed for some time in the room, discussing society business. Warwick was delegated to write a dispatch instructing the Portavo society to prepare for a call to arms, and it was given to a messenger to deliver.

When we emerged into the parlour, we drank steaming punch. Betsy recited a ballad honouring those who in Ireland's cause 'lift voice, or pen or hand'. She stressed the word *pen*.

'That's for you, *Star* man,' she exclaimed. Everybody laughed.

'Actually I'm the *Press* man now,' I said.

Inevitably Matt produced the fiddle. In his sweet voice he sang a new song about Ireland, 'The Shan Van Vocht', or 'The Poor Old Woman':

Oh the French are on the sea, says the Shan Van Vocht
The French are on the sea, says the Shan Van Vocht,

Oh The French are in the Bay, they'll be here without delay,
And the Orange will decay, says the Shan Van Vocht.
And will Ireland then be free? Says the Shan Van Vocht,
Will Ireland then be free? Says the Shan Van Vocht,
Yes, old Ireland will be free, from the centre to the sea,
And hurrah for Liberty!

We all shouted 'Hurrah!' and, with each succeeding verse, hit our mugs together, splashing punch.

Eliza recited a ditty composed locally, her eyes darting from side to side as she acted out the part of a hunted rebel:

The soldiers is coming! Run fast! Run fast!
With guns and with bayonets! Run fast! Run fast!
They're looking for guns and they're looking for pikes,
They'll show you no mercy, the blood-thirsty tykes!

As he was about to leave, Willie turned and said quietly to me, 'You know, there is no one like Betsy. She is always reading, always learning. She loves singing and reciting. She loves the land and nature. She is more of a patriot than any of those people up in Dublin.'

'You make her sound like a young Shan Van Vocht,' I said.

'She really likes you,' he said. 'She thinks of you as a brother. As do I.'

And that was it. Done nicely. I had no business thinking of her otherwise. I was confined to honorary kinship in the Gray household.

Hans confirmed my status next morning when he asked me to stay another day to celebrate his wedding anniversary. 'Sure you are family now,' he said.

Next day Eliza and I went for a walk holding hands. Her fingers were delicate and soft – the Brysons had a servant girl – and to be honest I lusted after her buxom figure. We made athletic love in the barn by her house in Ballygrainey, a mile across the fields. I found myself making promises to her I had no business to make. I told her I loved her, though in my heart I knew that was not true. I felt I could put off any commitment as long as

I was engaged in preparations for rebellion. 'Let's see if we all survive,' I suggested. 'Hush,' she said. 'Don't be a pessimist like George. You're the one we rely on to keep our spirits up.'

Betsy and Eliza prepared a special dinner to commemorate the day Hans had got married twenty-five years earlier. Many memories of Betsy's deceased mother were related around the table.

Hans had just finished making a toast when a neighbour rushed in to warn us that the dispatch Warwick had written had fallen into the hands of the publican James Dillon, who, as his former teacher, had identified Warwick's handwriting. Dillon had informed on him and soldiers were only five minutes away.

George managed to get Warwick into the turf stack before the patrol of York Fencibles arrived, filling the yard with their shouts and the creaking of leather and whinnying of horses. They pushed us up against the wall with their muskets. They turned over tables and the sideboard. One soldier smashed several plates. Another threw bedding on the floor. They lit pieces of bogwood from the fire and went outside to search the stable and the barn. We watched horrified as one of them casually set fire to the turf stack where young Warwick was hiding.

George shouted at the sergeant that they had not obstructed the search and didn't deserve to have their property burned. The sergeant told the soldiers to put out the fire. We ran to the well and conveyed pails of water to quench the flames.

I noticed that one of the English dragoons wore an Orange ribbon. I slipped out my orange ribbon, attached it to my wrist, and sidled up to him. Making sure he glimpsed it, I said softly, 'I see you are a good Orangeman, like myself.'

'Aye,' he said, 'a proud member of the York Fencibles, Loyal Orange Lodge Number 145. And you?'

'LOL 124,' I said, 'Newtownards,' hoping he would not know I had just made that up.

'Good lad, but thee art in bad company here.'

The soldiers marched off. Warwick came back into the parlour, shaking with fright. We suggested that, since he was now a wanted man, he should flee to Scotland.

'I can't,' he said. 'My mother is a widow woman and who will work the little bit of land?'

Next morning I saddled up Shadow before anyone had risen and rode back to Belfast. I dined with Martha McTier, and later, sitting by her blazing coal fire, I confided in her, for the first time, about my problematic relationships with Betsy and Eliza.

'What is it about Russell and you?' she said. 'Two good-looking men who fail to secure the women they love. You should be careful not to give one false hope, and brave enough to tell the other, this Betsy, your true feelings.' 'Would that it were that simple,' I said. But Martha sowed a seed of resolution. One day I would have to face up to my dilemma.

Upon relating my encounter with the York Fencibles, she told me the commanding officer, a pompous man in a ridiculous wig called Colonel Granville Anson Chetwynd-Stapylton, had come to her house in October to enquire about renting it. He didn't in the end. She had mixed feelings about that. Military occupation would mean it would not be wrecked by soldiers like so many others.

Next day, a Sunday, I escorted Martha to a performance of Irish music which had become all the rage. Several people in the Assembly Rooms came to shake my hand and ask after Sam Neilson and Harry McCracken, glancing around all the while to see who was watching.

To my surprise I encountered there the French émigré, De Latocnaye, who had returned to Belfast at the end of his long walk around the country.

'Ireland is no longer peaceful,' he told me solemnly. 'The signs of rebellion are everywhere.' He had seen a military notice on a tavern door in Newtownards. 'If there is another shot fired at the sentinels, orders will be given to burn the town'. He was taken aback however to find that the people of Belfast, reputedly ready to rise some time ago, appeared now to be 'in a sort of stupor hardly distinguishable from fear.'

He got a scare, he told me, as he walked the last stretch to Belfast. 'A man with a cart laden with turf asked me, "Will you push my cash?" I was terrified. I took this as a demand for my purse. But the poor man explained that "cash" is the word for a turf pannier. Whereupon I assisted him to move the turf, with all my heart.'

The diminutive French writer had been horrified to witness the military rampage in Belfast and said the people of the town would not for long forget the terror in which he found them. I put it to De Latocnaye that every country in Europe was at war, or about to go to war, with kings, and here it might all end with slaughter, so where did he think peace was to be found?

He replied that he knew one sovereign who had not been troubled, 'The Big Devil himself in hell!'

A few days later I heard the terrible news that Warwick was dead. James Dillon's wife had spotted him hiding in his widow-mother's cottage when she called for buttermilk. The young man was charged before Lord Londonderry in Newtownards Market House with writing a United Irish dispatch. Dillon failed to show up as a witness but Londonderry had him hanged anyway.

I wrote an account of the terror and of the execution of Warwick for *The Press*, and sent it to Dublin with the Old Cock coachman, as Peter Finnerty had instructed me.

— THIRTY-FIVE —

THE APOSTASY OF NEWELL

Since leaving Kilmainham I had one thing uppermost on my mind: to confront my betrayer, Edward Newell.

I didn't know what I would do if the opportunity arose. He was still in Belfast doing his dirty work under the protection of the military. Newell and his cuckold Murdoch were often seen guiding soldiers on search missions and terrorising the countryside. They wore masks but everyone knew it was them. One night they led dragoons to Holywood and pointed out houses to be burned. The troopers beat men so brutally, their womenfolk had convulsions from fright. They dragged a man called McComon and his wife from their bed and made them stand naked in the cold as they ransacked the house looking in vain for arms.

One morning Newell was spotted leaving Belfast in haste on a Dublin-bound coach, escorted by a guard of five mounted dragoons. There were rumours that Murdoch had discovered what everyone now knew – that Newell was mounting his wife – and that she had fled the house too.

I reflected how the hearth tax collector must regret taking the treacherous Newell into the bosom of his family.

Not long afterwards my new Dublin friend, Peter Finnerty, who, as a newspaperman like me, was a magpie for gossip, wrote to tell me that Murdoch had also arrived in Dublin but that he has been spotted walking arm in arm with Newell. 'However, the word is, dear boy, that the bold Murdoch is only waiting for a chance to destroy his wife's seducer.'

I wrote back that Murdoch must have read the Chinese saying, 'Hold your friends close but your enemies closer'.

Murdoch was indeed waiting his chance, as Finnerty's next letter revealed. He tried to shoot Newell one evening in his room, but the miniaturist overpowered him and took him to cool off in Newgate Prison. 'Newell can do what he likes, because he is the Castle's favourite toady and lick-arse informer,' wrote the *Press* editor. 'But he is out of control. He throws money around, acts in a disorderly manner in the streets, and even took a shot at a guard when returning to the Castle drunk one evening.'

One day, some weeks later, the printer John Storey and I were summoned to a back room of Kelly's Cellars where Henry Haslett and several members of the provincial committee were sitting at a table. One of them poured each of us a large shot of whiskey.

'You are going to need it,' said Haslett.

'I have received a letter from your pal Eddie Newell,' he said, looking at me. 'He wants to come back to our side.'

There was a silence as we absorbed this thunderbolt. My first reaction was disbelief, then bewilderment. This betrayer of our cause, the person responsible for my imprisonment and the incarceration and death of friends and patriots, had the gall to imagine he might simply return to our company.

Our revenge would surely be swift and merciless if we could get our hands on him. John was thinking the same. 'Let him come and we will reward him for his treachery,' he said.

'Did you reply?' I asked Haslett.

'I did,' he said. 'I told him that, from what I know of the disposition of the people, they would feel more real satisfaction in the forgiving of a penitent than the punishing of an offender.'

'Go on yourself! You are joking,' I said.

Haslett shook his head. 'Yes and no. He can be valuable to us. Read his letter.'

The letter was brief and to the point. Newell claimed to be suffering from pangs of conscience, to be disgusted at the perfidy of government, and to be ashamed of being despised by honest men and exposed in print.

'I am heartily sorry for my past conduct and wish through you to inform the people of it, and that if they will again receive me into favour and forgiveness, they will never have cause to be sorry for it, and though I know the injuries I have done them to be great, I think I can make some restitution by the exposure of the plans of government in which I have been connected.'

'What restitution can he make other than to offer us his neck?' asked John.

'He has letters and secret papers,' said Haslett. He is agreeable to have them published as part of his renunciation. You two are in the printing business. You can help him publish his confession for the whole world to see. It will mean they have to release many of our men.'

He added, 'We undertook that you wouldn't touch him. So don't lay a hand on him.'

Three evenings later John Storey and I found ourselves in an upper room of Flanagan's on the quays, sitting opposite the man whose base treachery had put me in jail for eight months.

I hardly recognised my once-lively and entertaining companion. He was a debauched and pathetic figure, cringing before us, looking up like a dog afraid of being beaten. His face was blotched and his hands were trembling.

'You're not so cocky without the mask,' said John.

'What have you to say for yourself?' I asked.

'I beg forgiveness of my old and trusted friends,' he said.

I turned to John. 'Should we just tie him up and dump him in the water?'

'I will personally attach the weights to his neck,' said Storey.

Newell leaned forward. 'I repent sincerely. And I know you can't touch me as I have a story to tell that can do great harm to the government.'

He handed over a sheaf of papers, some with official seals. 'It is all here,' he said with a conspiratorial wink. 'Publish all this and it will show my previous testimony in court to be worthless and scores of men will be set free. You can't deny that, so you must meet my concerns.'

'And what are those concerns?' asked John.

'That you and your friends do not harm me so I can testify to my false accusations, then take passage to America.'

We called for several extra candles and started reading.

And so began a series of meetings with the despicable informer, during which we helped him write a lengthy and detailed confession of his dissolute and treacherous life, exposing how the gullible and ruthless authorities used him to imprison anyone he named, without any evidence whatsoever against them – though truth to tell most of his information was accurate – while tolerating his drunkenness and plying him with gold.

His story began with an account of how he had developed a warm, brotherly relationship with George Murdoch and became 'intimate' with his wife, after going to the Murdochs' house to work on a portrait of the family.

When ordered to take part in the arms raid on the hearth tax collector's house, he had instead warned Murdoch, 'such was my respect and attachment to his family', telling him his life was in danger and that he should have armed guards posted at his door.

Murdoch in response informed Newell the military knew of his membership of the United Irishmen and of his role in the assassination of a Limerick militiaman. Newell agreed to a deal: if pardoned, he would turn informer. He became the masked man who betrayed us at the meeting of the military committee, and who night after night engaged in the sport of man-hunting.

'Weren't you an informer before that?' I asked.

'No, I swear,' said Newell.

'You passed on information from Belle Martin.'

'Never! On my oath!'

'You betrayed the Monaghan militiamen. Belle Martin gave you the names. You passed them on.'

'I swear I didn't.'

I knew he had, but given my own dalliances with the whore, I didn't press the point.

Newell professed that he now realised that Murdoch was 'a blood-thirsty cannibal, a fiend, who took care to blow the spark of resentment which glowed within my breast until it became a blaze.' He should have been a novelist.

After he started work as the masked man, Murdoch took him to Dublin to meet 'that arch-betrayer of every honest heart, the insinuating Crooke.' The Englishman, Edward Crooke, under-secretary to the Irish government, provided him with money, clothes and lodgings in Dublin Castle whenever he wanted, complete with 'breakfast, dinner, supper, wines, jellies, etc.', in return for compiling lists of United Irishmen, many of which he just guessed at.

When he was examined before a secret committee of the Irish House of Commons, sitting on a high chair for the benefit of being better seen, he deliberately exaggerated and fabricated stories to terrify them, said Newell. They swallowed everything he told them.

Cooke's instructions were to return to Belfast, to have anyone he fancied arrested without concerning himself about warrants, since these could be got afterwards when they knew the names. The under-secretary provided him with a letter instructing senior military officers in Belfast to 'allow him money or any number of men he may demand to obey his orders.' Newell dutifully guided soldiers to houses and cottages in the North. He examined lists of jurors for Colonel Barber and crossed out those he disliked.

And all the time he admitted that he 'lived in the habits of the most endearing intimacy with the Murdoch family.' Aye, I thought. Intimacy indeed, under the sheet when the master was out.

Then George Murdoch caught them at it. He beat up his wife and Newell fled to Dublin with fifteen guineas provided by Barber. Murdoch followed shortly and confronted Newell. 'After some hot words, Murdoch said he would not give the United rascals the satisfaction of thinking we had fallen out,' said Newell. 'We ate, drank, went to every diversion, arm-in-arm walked the streets.'

Nevertheless Murdoch was only biding his time and, sure enough, one evening when Newell had undressed and was preparing for bed, Murdoch drew a pistol from his pocket and snapped it at his head. Despite his diminutive size Newell easily overcame the portly tax collector and had him locked up in Newgate for the night. He provided Murdoch with reading material – several love letters his wife had written to Newell.

'What a nasty little man you are,' I said, feeling sympathy for Murdoch for the first time.

It was at this point, Newell said, that he determined 'no longer to be a tool of the government but to return to the principles of which deserting had been the cause of all his misery.'

He cadged a final payment of fifty guineas from Lord Camden, in gratitude for which he wrote to the Lord Lieutenant, 'I shall give you the truest information I have ever done – my Lord, the people execrate you.'

He then took the coach back to Belfast and fell back into the arms of Murdoch's wife. They ran away together, taking up lodgings on the Antrim coast. Hot on their heels, Murdoch scoured the countryside looking for them.

After twelve days in hiding Newell found his mistress 'inconvenient', as he put it, and decided to get rid of her. He sent word to Murdoch through a messenger where she was. He concealed himself nearby so that he could witness the 'pot-valiant hero' arrive and carry her home 'with every joy and forgiveness'.

Newell admitted to having condemned 227 men to prison or death. For this he calculated he took two thousand pounds in blood money, all of which he confessed he had spent on luxury and debauchery.

'That's less than seven guineas a head,' I said. 'You were bought cheap.'

From the names and dates it was evident he was an informer before the abortive raid on Murdoch's house.

'All that time you were pretending to be my friend,' I said.

Newell winked at me. 'We had a right old time of it, didn't we?'

I leaned forward and spat fully in his face. It took all of John's strength to hold me back.

'Bugger your soul to hell,' I said.

With trembling hand I wrote down his final plea to the United Irishmen. 'I hope the proof of my sincere repentance, by the exposure of government, will make me again worthy of your esteem and confidence.'

It turned out that Newell did not just betray his northern brothers. He did some felon-setting in Dublin. He swore a deposition that he had befriended Peter Finnerty in Matthew's Public House in Dame Court, and claimed that Finnerty had revealed to Newell that he was secretary to a society of Defenders, and even showed him a list of names.

'I made it all up,' said Newell. 'I never met Finnerty. Cooke wanted to keep Finnerty in prison if a libel action against him failed, because he was alarmed at the publication of Crown atrocities in the *Press*.'

Storey and I put Newell's confession, along with his lists and letters, into narrative form as quickly as we could.

John found it difficult to fathom the depths of deceit and self-delusion to which the despicable scoundrel had descended. 'He cuckolded and excoriated the man whom he professed to love as a brother. He betrayed all his former comrades. And for what? So that he could lie with Murdoch's wife, until she became "inconvenient". That's the only way it makes sense. Now he is disenchanted with her, and the junto has no more use for him, he has nowhere to turn to but back to us. Conscience my arse!'

Since Belfast printers were under the eye of the military, John took the manuscript to Dublin. It was printed there as *The Apostasy of Newell, Containing the Confessions of the Celebrated Informer, His reasons for Becoming, and So Long Continuing One, Written by Himself.*

John and I presented Newell with a copy in the same back room in Flanagan's. 'It's all right,' I said. 'You won't be harmed. This will save many good men from prison or worse.' He smiled and reached as if to shake my hand, saying, 'Have you bedded that red-head from the country yet?'

I grabbed his lapels.

'You can't touch me,' he cried.

I butted him full on the nose with my head. He fell back against the table, blood streaming from both nostrils.

'Did I touch him?'

'No,' said John, kicking him in the ribs. 'Neither did I.'

I leaned down and spat again on Newell's face.

'Consider yourself lucky,' I said.

We both kicked him again.

'We never laid a hand on him,' said John, after Newell complained to Haslett.

The informer was placed under our protection at a location near Portavo, waiting to be ferried out to a ship bound for America.

The moment arrived for his departure. He was put on a boat at Ballyholme Bay near Bangor by two trustworthy oarsmen, who rowed him towards a New York-bound ship moored in Belfast Lough.

The sea was calm, but somehow Newell fell overboard and somehow he drowned. Somehow too he left his money belt behind before falling overboard. He had only one hundred pounds after all his dirty work.

We drank a toast to the boatmen and hoped they would make good use of it.

— THIRTY-SIX —

NO TOWN AS LOYAL

After Peter Finnerty was imprisoned, on Newell's false evidence, *The Press* suffered the same fate as the *Northern Star*. Soldiers from the Cavan Militia were sent to destroy the types and presses and vandalise the rooms. The attack on *The Press* was timed to prevent publication of an article implying Castlereagh was directly responsible for the hanging of William Orr. Finnerty, a true hero to our profession, refused to reveal who the author was. He was pilloried in the stocks but no one threw anything at him and Arthur O'Connor held an umbrella over his head. Peter declared to onlookers, 'My friends, you see how cheerfully I can suffer anything provided it promotes the liberty of my country.'

Arthur O'Connor himself was arrested soon afterwards, in Margate, *en route* to France. He was brought back to England and charged with treason. There he wrote a 'recantation' in verse which Dublin Castle triumphantly published. Soon all Ireland was laughing at them instead. When the lines were read in different order it was a reaffirmation of O'Connor's loyalty to the cause of freedom.

    (1) The pomp of courts, and pride of kings,
    (3) I prize above all earthly things;
    (5) I love my country, but my King,
    (7) Above all men his praise I'll sing.
    (9) The royal banners are display'd,
    (11) And may success the standard aid:
    (2) I fain would banish far from hence

(4) The Rights of Man and Common Sense.

(6) Destruction to that odious name,

(8) The plague of princes, Thomas Paine,

(10) Defeat and ruin seize the cause

(12) Of France, her liberty, and laws.

O'Connor was subsequently acquitted by getting his highly placed Whig friends to swear he was not a rebel – they were furious later when the truth came out. At the same time, Harry and Willie McCracken and Henry Haslett were set free but Tom Russell and Sam Neilson were kept inside.

I was given orders to liaise with the societies among the mainly Presbyterian-populated areas of County Down, where I had a network of contacts from my time as the *Star* man. Billy Templeton was given the same task in Antrim.

Being no longer a newspaperman, I needed a reason for riding around the countryside at will. Matthew Smith kindly gave me a letter of appointment as a travelling salesman for his printing works at Bridge Street, and he supplied me with a stock of sample sheets and order forms.

I embarked on a series of excursions to towns and villages in County Down. I was dashed by hail, soaked by rain, pelted with sleet, confused by mist and blinded by the sun, sometimes all in the one day. In some places I found men were well prepared for battle. In others they were disorganised. In most villages men were drilling at night. A few had muskets they had stolen or bought from soldiers.

All the rural societies were united in their fury over military outrages and the execution of Willie Orr, though they could not agree on whether they should wait for the French before any rising.

As I rode hither and tither on Shadow, I wrote down details of pitch-cappings, hangings, half-hangings, floggings, burnings and arbitrary arrests, the result of the military being unleashed with licence to suppress dissent by any means.

It wasn't long before I saw for myself an act of savage brutality. Near Newtownards, I came across a small group weeping and wailing outside

Jack Sloan's blacksmith's forge at Gallows Hill. Dragoons were inside beating Sloan and shouting, 'Where have you hidden the pikes?' I happened to know that Sloan, while sympathetic, had declined to hammer out pike heads for the United Irishmen. A soldier took a remnant of coarse linen smeared with black pitch, suspended it over the fire until boiling hot, then slapped it down on Sloan's scalp. The blacksmith ran out screaming hellishly, whereupon the soldiers took the feet from under him. He crawled along the ground, tearing at his head, burning his hands. There was an awful smell of singed hair and charred skin. Black liquid oozed into his left eye. His hysterical wife, twisting and writhing and crying 'No! No!' was held back by two soldiers. A dragoon reached down and pulled off the pitch-cap, tearing the scalp away.

The soldiers mounted up and galloped off in high good humour. Someone threw a pail of water over Jack's head, but it was too late. He was dead.

I tried to end each day within riding distance of Gransha. The house was at the heart of north Down rebel country and conveniently located at Six Road Ends, so I could approach it from any direction. Thus I managed to stay a few nights in my old perch above the kitchen in the Gray household, in company with a new lamb which occupied the hearth, and Eliza. Lovely, green-eyed Eliza, whom I didn't love, would come over the fields at night and lie with me. Her house was too full of children for me to go there, not that I wanted to. After making love, I would feign sleep to avoid any exchange of endearments. The resolution I had summoned up after talking to Martha ebbed away. But my heart slumped when I saw Betsy looking at me over breakfast, almost accusingly.

On one occasion I arrived to find everyone in a state of agitation. Soldiers had tied a man onto a metal triangle outside Matt McClenaghan's forge and taken bets on how long before he would go into convulsions and shake the apparatus. It was a favourite trick of theirs.

George showed me a magnificent sword he kept hidden in the well, along with several pikes. It had a silver hilt, a handle of green-stained ivory, and a steel blade so fine it could be bent almost double without breaking.

Betsy said when the fight started she would be found in the thick of the men. Hans said he would forbid her to leave the house, for she would surely get herself killed. Willie Boal, George and I concurred, but we all knew it would be impossible to keep her away.

Back in Belfast, when I called at the McCracken house in Rosemary Street, I found Harry very weak and crippled with rheumatism but eager to get back to the business of the Society. Jemmy Hope was there, and we had an emotional reunion.

Jemmy was adamant that a rising should take place as soon as possible. 'Men of rank and fortune will never remove the grievances of the people,' he said. 'We have to do it.' He always saw things through the eyes of the working man. 'There are some landlords,' he said, 'who can pluck the last potato out of the warm ashes of a poor man's fire and force him to beg a cold potato from those who can ill afford to give it.'

'Aye,' said Harry. 'The rich always betray the poor.'

'Belfast is corrupt, hucksters become merchants, merchants become bankers and bankers become as pompous as provincial pashaws,' said Jemmy. 'These, Harry, are the men who will put a rope around your neck, and mine.'

'Are you afraid of being hanged, Jemmy?' asked McCracken.

'It would ill become one who has pledged his life to his country to shrink from death in any shape, and by the way, I have no desire to die of sickness,' replied Jemmy.

I said I would wish to be the one to hang the hangman.

I told them about my tour of Down and the military atrocities that were taking place there. 'And,' I said, putting on a nonchalant air, 'I am going to make a full report to Lord Moira himself to convey to parliament.'

'Are you indeed?' said Harry. 'Aren't you the well-connected Yahoo.'

I explained that the opportunity to brief Lord Moira had come through Martha McTier. She summoned me one afternoon with the news that Moira was planning to make a speech in the Irish House of Lords about the barbarity of the military, and was gathering information at Montalto House in Ballynahinch. She had told him I was better-informed than anyone about what was going on because of my role with the *Star*. He wanted me to call upon him at the first opportunity.

The Earl of Moira greeted me cordially when I showed up at Montalto next morning. I made a point of doffing my hat with a sweep of the arm.

'What, are you trying to make up for your childish insolence?' he asked, pretending to be affronted. He had not forgotten the time I had encountered him as a schoolboy and refused to tip my hat to him.

He walked me through his gardens and showed off a fish-shaped lake with trim little islands. I affected not to recognise the head gardener whom I had sworn in as a United Irishmen. Pheasants grazed unconcerned on the lawns and I glimpsed snipe and woodcock.

'These you will know something about,' Moira said, indicating plants native to other countries. 'Your father propagated many of them from seedlings.' There were, I noticed, several familiar species of orchids, marigolds, sunflowers and jasmine in a glass enclosure.

Looking around the meadow and the slopes of the big hill above the house I was able to identify Caucasian firs, Spanish chestnuts, Tasmanian blue gums, tulip trees, holm oaks, monkey puzzles, cedars of Lebanon, magnolias and azaleas.

'The house was built forty-five years ago so it is the same age as myself,' said Moira as we entered the two-storied mansion. He pointed out the stucco on the ceilings of fiddle-shaped arabesques, birds modelled in high relief, a squirrel, bunches of grapes and, in an alcove, a fox pursuing a cockerel in a chaise.

Flags and emblems from his campaigns as a British officer were stacked against a wall, and workmen in the library were packing hundreds of leather-bound volumes into wooden trunks. 'I had 25,000 volumes here, but I am shipping them all to London,' Moira stated. 'Terrible times are coming. I am more worried about what the Crown forces will do than you fellows. They don't like me, you know. Are you aware that General Lake raided this house looking for arms? And that he threatened to one day order soldiers to burn Ballynahinch, starting with Montalto?'

Over lunch of sirloin served by a French chef on silver plates, Moira showed me a copy of a lengthy speech he had already made in the British House of Lords about 'the absurd and disgusting tyranny in Ireland'. In it he condemned the suppression of the *Northern Star* by troops sent in broad daylight to destroy the whole property, types and everything. 'There is not one man in Ireland who is not liable to be taken out of his house, at any hour either of the day or night, to be kept in rigorous confinement, restricted from all correspondence, be treated with mixed severity and insult, and yet never know the crime with which he is charged... I have seen, my lords, a conquered country held by military force, but never did I see, in any conquered country, such a tone of insult as has been adopted by Great Britain towards Ireland.' There was much more in this vein.

For his next speech, in the Irish House of Lords, Moira wanted specific details of the atrocious behaviour of Crown forces in County Down. Two clerks appeared to write down my words with goose-quill pens. I knew that, like the gardener, they also had been secretly sworn in as United men.

My host steepled his fingers over his pursed lips as I recounted in precise and unemotional detail the death of Jack Sloan. I gave Moira names, places and dates of pitch-cappings, hangings, half-hangings, floggings with whips and bridles, burning of farmsteads and storage sheds, arrests, and death sentences carried out without due process. I told him of the practice of hanging a man by the heels and lashing him with belts as he whirled round to make him reveal where he had concealed arms. I mentioned the widespread outrage over the execution of William Orr and young Warwick, and the mischief of informers like Newell who had power to have anyone arrested they pleased.

When he asked about the strength of the United Irishmen in County Down, I replied, 'I know naught about that, except that the people are at breaking point.' I added that I had heard more than once the phrase 'We men of the north have a word to say, and when the time comes we will say it in our own dour way.' I caught one clerk's eye and gave him a slight wink.

Moira countered that his tenants had all taken an oath of loyalty. 'They appreciate that reform, not revolution, is the way forward.'

I recalled Lord Castlereagh saying something similar, though I had no doubt of Moira's sincerity.

'What good to the poor is breaking the hold of the Ascendancy on

Ireland if it is only to share out the patronage with other property holders?' I asked. 'The poor appreciate that radical measures must be taken to improve their condition.'

Moira looked at me hard. Perhaps he had heard similar talk from Thomas Russell and was making the connection.

On my departure he thanked me for my information, adding, 'I suspect you know more than you are prepared to let on.'

I again expressed my gratitude for his sponsorship of my education at the Belfast academy. He replied that he had no regrets.

I advised him to make sure his new *rhododendron ponticum* was kept under strict control because it had a propensity to grow fast and push out the species around it.

'Your father told me the same thing,' he replied. 'I might not be here to see it. Some of my rank feel that we landowners will be pushed out by forces that we can't control.'

A week later Moira made his speech in the Irish House of Lords. He charged the government with goading the people into rebellion through house burnings, imprisonment without charge or trial, and torture by means of pitch-capping and half-hanging. Ireland suffered the most absurd and disgusting tyranny that any nation had ever groaned under. Troops insultingly treated every citizen as a rebel. He advocated immediate reform, as 'procrastination *debauches* the minds of a disgusted and exasperated peasantry.'

I was taken aback by that word. Was it debauchery to think radical thoughts, to strive for justice and democratic rights by every means?

He concluded by proclaiming, 'There is no town as loyal as Ballynahinch,' citing the fact that his tenants, Protestant, Catholic and Dissenter, had all taken an oath of loyalty to King and constitution.

For once FitzGibbon was closer to the mark when he responded in the debate that 'Ballynahinch is one of the rankest citadels of treason.'

Somebody in the highest counsels in London was paying attention to Moira's warnings, and an attempt was made to bring the military in Ireland under control. At the end of February 1798, Sir Ralph Abercromby, a professional Scottish soldier, was appointed to the military command in Ireland to re-establish civil power and return the troops to barracks. To our surprise, and the junto's consternation, he issued a general order accusing the military of a state of corruption and licentiousness 'which must render it formidable to everyone but the enemy'. He stripped the old lecher, Carhampton, of his command, saying that every crime, every cruelty, that could be committed by Cossacks or Calmucks had been transacted in Ireland.

'This is the most wretched country,' he was quoted as saying. 'The upper orders are only occupied in eating and drinking. Their conversation betrays unrelenting hostility to the people and an ardent desire for the most severe measures unrestrained by law. They know they have been the oppressors of the poor and that the moment of vengeance is at hand.'

Of course he couldn't last. After barely two months Abercromby was forced to resign rather than have his reputation tarnished by the killings and torture still carried out by his troops. Lord Camden, advised by Castlereagh, had countermanded his order not to act without the authority of a civil magistrate. General Lake, who had no qualms about using fire, sword and pitch-cap indiscriminately, was promoted in his place.

The barrister William Sampson, visiting Belfast, was very downcast at the continued repression. He complained that 'Croppies lie down' was now the word 'and we do lie down'. He produced a crumpled handbill that was circulating among Orangemen.

Oh, croppies ye'd better be quiet and still
Ye shan't have your liberty, do what ye will
As long as salt water is formed in the deep
A foot on the necks of the croppy we'll keep
And drink, as in bumpers past troubles we drown,
A health to the lads that made croppies lie down
Down, down, croppies lie down.

Samson said it was composed by Camden's secretary.

'This,' he said bitterly, 'is the sort of thing they get up to in the Lord Lieutenant's office, when they have nothing better to do.'

— THIRTY-SEVEN —

FOREIGN AID MEN

As the days grew longer and the snow receded up the Mourne Mountains, leaving only white patches on Slieve Donard, there were signs of a thaw in relations between Dublin Castle and the United Irishmen. Almost all those taken up after being betrayed by Newell were now back in Belfast. Harry McCracken and Henry Haslett were free. The releases continued in County Down, among them the Revd Barber of Rathfriland – six foot two without a shoe. When I met him on my rounds he boasted how his daughter had got the better of Lord Annesley of Castlewellan. Annesley had told her, 'Your father, madam, is a rebel. I will commit him to the dungeon,' to which she replied, 'If attachment to country constitutes a rebel, my father is one, and the dungeon, my Lord, is now the seat of honour.' She sounded like Betsy, bold and brave.

To my great relief and joy, Samuel Neilson was allowed to walk out of Kilmainham at the end of February, having spent seventeen months in its interior. He elected to remain in Dublin to recover his health. Shortly afterwards I received an envelope from our friend, the coachman on the Old Cock. Inside was a blank sheet of paper. I heated it over a candle. It was from Neilson, written in lemon juice. He was staying in the Dublin house of the United Irishman John Sweetman. His wife had joined him and he planned to advance the cause in the capital. He wanted everyone in the north to be ready for the day of reckoning.

It was a false spring. In March, barely two weeks after Neilson's release, a new wave of arrests of our leaders in Dublin threatened to throw us off course. Sam Neilson and Lord Edward Fitzgerald remained at large and formed a new national directory.

Neilson sent William Putnam McCabe back to Belfast to liaise with Harry McCracken and report back. The three of us got together for hot punch in Barclay's.

Putnam recalled that two centuries earlier a reign of terror had been imposed on the Low Countries by the Spanish Duke of Alba, and burning, quartering, hanging, beheading and banishment became an everyday experience, and the smallest offence was considered worthy of capital punishment.

'All this was to deter men from insurrection,' he said. 'The horrors committed under Camden and Castlereagh are, on the contrary, designed to force the unfortunate people to a rebellion, so it can be crushed, and the leaders identified and dealt with.'

We contemplated this for a few minutes. Then I said, 'That means we must beat them at this game. The way to do that is to win.' We drank to that. But the idea lingered like a lead weight in my mind. I knew that it was infecting the minds of the foreign aid men, those of our well-off leaders who would not stir without the French.

Harry feared indeed that our chances of victory were slipping away. No date for a rising had yet been set by the national committee. 'We are all being asked to bear the shackles of tyranny a little longer,' he said. 'Seven thousand patriots in Antrim would rather be in the field like men than hunted like wild beasts with Orange yeomen riding roughshod over them day after day.'

A wave of patriotism was sweeping the country, he said. William Drennan's new term for Ireland, 'The Emerald Isle', was taken up everywhere. Everyone was wearing green.

Betsy's twenty-first birthday was coming up and it was most appropriate that I bought her, my idolised rebel heart, something green. I purchased a pair of emerald earrings at McCabe's shop in North Street. I would say it was from Eliza and me both. I hoped Betsy and Willie Boal wouldn't think I had crossed a line.

I arrived for Betsy's birthday late on the afternoon of 31 March, a Saturday. Betsy and Eliza were preparing for a ceili. I took Eliza aside and told her I had brought a gift for Betsy from the two of us. Eliza was very happy about that, because it reinforced our relationship in others' eyes. If only she knew.

Betsy kissed both of us and put on the earrings. As she raised her hands to pull back her hair I noticed she was wearing a gold ring. She smiled and said that Willie Boal had pledged his troth. They planned to go to Portpatrick in Scotland to make their betrothal official after the last harvest had been brought in.

I should not have been surprised but it was like a thump in the chest. In love, as in politics, one had to learn to sometimes disguise one's true feelings. I feigned delight and avoided Eliza's eyes. I would likely have to face that future myself with her, the way I had let things develop. To avoid spending the night with Eliza – I couldn't just then – I pleaded urgent business and set off to call on United men in the district.

In Greyabbey Davy Warden was still spoiling for the fight. He confided his concern, however, that there was a well-placed informer at work in County Down. The Revd Cleland had boasted to one of his congregation that he knew Davy had been promoted in the United Irishmen, 'and I had just been promoted a week before'.

Please God, not again, I thought. After my experiences with the whore Belle Martin and the traitor Newell, I wondered was someone else now waiting to betray us all, someone I trusted, someone I liked?

In Donaghadee I called on Francis Falloon, one of our colonels, at his hostelry, the Old King's Arms. He told us that, astonishingly, Wheatley, the false witness against Willie Orr, had come back from England to do some horse trading and stayed in the guest room. Falloon didn't realise he was the former soldier until he was leaving; otherwise, he said, Wheatley 'would have gone no further.' Francis poured whiskey and proposed a toast, 'That the wrong may cease and the right prevail.' 'Remember Orr,' I responded.

In Bangor I heard many stories of military outrages. In one instance soldiers had stopped a funeral, looking for hidden pikes. They prised open the coffin and tipped it over. The body of an old man tumbled out. It contained no weapons.

I returned to Belfast to find that Castlereagh had been made Chief Secretary of Ireland and martial law had been imposed in all thirty-two counties, on the grounds that Ireland was approaching a state of open insurrection. The Revd Dickson was in Scotland so County Down was missing its commander, but one of the *Northern Star* directors, the merchant Robert Simms, had accepted the rank of adjutant general for County Antrim.

I liked and admired Simms but I don't see him leading his fellow-merchants into the cannon's mouth. He was a foreign aid man. I have often heard him say he would prefer to see the French disembarking before he took up the sword.

To complicate matters further, public sentiment was turning against the French because of their aggression towards the United States. Their seizure of American merchant ships on the high seas was damaging trade for Belfast industrialists. Many of our kinfolk who had gone to America and fought the English were now fighting the French and sending letters home telling us to have nothing to do with them. How history can be turned on its head. Enemies one day, allies the next. Patriots one day, loyalists the next.

My society met on Sunday 1 April in the attic of the Second Presbyterian Church in Rosemary Street. An emissary from Dublin told us that a French fleet would be on the high seas in two weeks and would attempt a landing in both Ireland and England. The citizens of Dublin were prepared to seize the capital at any moment. Sam Neilson's health was restored and he was riding around night and day to organise the people in the south. No person ever knew where he dined or slept.

The French fleet turned out to be one lone frigate.

In early April we received word that a ship called *L'Amitié* was heading for the north-east County Down coast with a consignment of arms for the United Irishmen. Its destination was Cloughey Bay on the tip of the Ards peninsula. I was assigned to a company of men to greet the crew and unload and distribute the arms.

For two days we walked up and down the Ards shore, resting occasionally among the sea campion and lyme grass which grew in profusion, and chatting with the men forking piles of seaweed for manure, who knew better than to ask what we were doing. We stayed the night in a Portaferry tavern full of pipe-smoking Papists tapping their feet to dirges from uilleann pipes and fiddles.

A strong southeast breeze blew up. It became a gale. The local fishermen did not venture out to sea. They dreaded an east wind because it drove their boats onto the rocks.

That terrible fate awaited *L'Amitié*. Before midday on Sunday 8 April we heard that the French ship had been sighted in trouble off Sheepland Harbour near Ardglass, many miles to the south. We hastened to Portaferry and persuaded the ferrymen to row us across the choppy, dangerous waters to Strangford. There we acquired two mounts and galloped towards Ardglass.

Sheepland Harbour is a tiny bay fringed by grassland and basalt rocks. All we could see of the frigate were three masts protruded above the waves. Women gathered on a shelf of pebbles were crying and throwing their arms in the air. Several bodies of drowned French sailors had been pulled from the water and stretched out on the shingle.

Only one sailor had reached the shore alive. We found him sitting by the turf fire in a cottage, naked and shivering under a shawl given him by a local woman. I spoke to him in French. He grasped my hand and cried, "*Tous morts! Tous morts!*" He was the steersman of the brigantine which had a crew of a hundred men. The ship carried muskets, rifles and twelve cannon and ammunition. All lost.

The people there, mostly Catholics, undertook to shelter and look after the wretched sailor. A priest arrived and conducted a burial service for the dead.

I returned to Portaferry and rode back to Belfast through fields where farmers were busy sowing flax and barley and tending their cattle, as if all was well with the world.

One can imagine the despair that evening in Kelly's Cellars when we informed members of the military committee the bad news – that no French ship had sailed into Cloughey Bay. *L'Amitié* was wrecked and all arms lost. The cause too, I feared.

— THIRTY-EIGHT —

TRYING MEN'S SOULS

The shorthand I learned from my Samuel Taylor primer served me well in carrying around dispatches. I had added quirks of my own, so that only I could decipher what I wrote. To anyone else it would look like ancient Greek. I would translate the words back into readable English on reaching my destination.

For this reason I was delegated at a county meeting in Belfast to bring some messages to Sam Neilson in Dublin regarding weapons and men available. The intelligence was too sensitive to risk interception. Sam was always on the move but he sent word that he could be contacted through a barrister who lived on Usher's Island, next to Lord Moira's residence.

I arrived in Dublin on a Sunday, having travelled through villages where men stood around in groups and women huddled in shawls in an atmosphere thick with anticipation of something portentous about to happen. I jumped off the coach before its destination to avoid being spotted by Castle spies, and made my way to Usher's Island. The barrister took me out the back door of his house and directed me across the wall into the garden of Moira's mansion. He revealed the entrance to a subterranean passage in the shrubbery. I felt my way along it and emerged in the kitchen. A cooking maid there directed me to the library.

I found Sam waiting for me in front of a big log fire. He didn't look great and his face was blotched. We embraced warmly and a servant brought handsome measures of whiskey in crystal glasses.

'You have fallen on your feet,' I said.

'As long as I don't fall on my arse,' he replied.

251

Neilson listened as I read out my documents, all the while sipping his whiskey. We discussed Newell's apostasy. In his opinion, as an editor, Sam thought it was very badly put together. I had told him about my role in its creation, and felt chastised. 'It was a hurried job,' I protested.

Sam complained that the Catholic lower classes had been betrayed by the Catholic hierarchy, who had been bought off with an endowment for a seminary at Maynooth, and a vote for propertied Catholics. Yet still no Papist could sit in parliament and they could vote only for Protestants. The Catholic peasants on the other hand were straining at the leash, mad for revenge against the military. Sam and Lord Edward Fitzgerald had been travelling around Leinster in different disguises to rally United Irishmen for the coming fight.

I jumped up as Countess Moira appeared in the library doorway, dressed in a long green gown. 'Who have we here?' she demanded. I told her I was a beneficiary of Lord Moira's patronage and that I had helped provide information for his speech to the House of Lords.

'I don't remember you,' she said, waving a dainty silk handkerchief dismissively. After she glided on, Sam told me not to be concerned. She was a friend of the cause. She had banished Camden, Castlereagh and all the other members of the Castle junto from visiting the house, because of what she called 'their vicious reaction to what was only the truth'.

As for Lord Moira, having emptied his mansion in Ballynahinch of his books and valuables, he was now keeping out of the way in London.

When darkness fell, Sam and I left through the underground passage and made our way to the house of a feather merchant in nearby Thomas Street to meet Lord Edward Fitzgerald, who was residing temporarily in an upstairs room. With a price of £1,000 on his head he regularly changed his abode. With him was William Putnam McCabe. 'Hello again *Star* man,' he said, throwing his arms around me.

'You've come a long way since I found you up a ladder,' I replied.

Putnam had assumed the role of Lord Edward's bodyguard, and had saved his life just recently. They were waylaid by the Dublin constabulary in Bridgefoot Street. Putnam fought off the officers while Fitzgerald escaped, but Putnam himself was taken prisoner to Dublin Castle, where the blackened heads of executed rebels looked down from spikes above the Cork Hill entrance. He had been released after he convinced the Scottish guards, in a strong Lowlands accent, that he was an innocent Scottish weaver who had come to Dublin looking for employment.

I read out the documents I had brought to Lord Edward. He admitted that no date had been set for a rising, but instructed me to convey the news that it was imminent. The signal would be burning of the mail coaches from Dublin. 'That's Sam's idea,' he said.

We returned to Countess Moira's the same way, and I was given a bed in a servant's room. Two other United Irishmen were lodged in the same corridor. There were warrants out for their arrest and they were hiding there until they could escape.

I fell into a deep sleep, confident that there was no safer place for a rebel in these dangerous times than in a soft bed in the grandest aristocratic house in Dublin.

Next morning William Sampson appeared at the breakfast table in a bit of a state. He said he was being sought for treason and was making plans to flee to England.

'The terror in Dublin is so atrocious that no man can stand it,' he said. 'In every quarter the shrieks and groans of the tortured are to be heard. Men are taken at random and tortured by the lowest dregs of humanity. Torture centres are operating at the Beresford riding school, the Castle yards, the old custom house and several military depots. I know of a youth who was flogged to death for having a ring with the symbol of a shamrock. There's a Lieutenant Heppenstal who is known as the Walking Gallows, because he strangles victims by hanging them over his shoulder. Can you imagine! Such scenes are disgraceful to the name of man, and they are enacted in name of King and constitution. I can't stay here.'

I ventured that he was a marked man, not because he was a brilliant defence lawyer who had thwarted them at every turn, but because he had committed a great crime; he had subjected the government to ridicule and given us the Belfast laugh. How they must hate him for *The King versus Hurdy Gurdy* and *The Lion of Old England.*

On my return to Belfast I learned with dismay that Sampson did not get away. Our barrister-journalist was arrested in England and transported back to Dublin.

Worse was to follow. Lord Edward Fitzgerald was arrested at his hiding place. He was shot in the shoulder in a fight with officers who invaded his bedroom. He was lodged in Newgate prison. Putnam had escaped.

Sam Neilson took charge in Dublin. The former *Northern Star* editor was no longer wielding the pen but the sword, at the head of a national army-in-waiting of Protestants, Catholics and Dissenters.

On 21 May 1798, a Monday, we received word at last that the rising would begin in Dublin in two days. The failure of the mail coaches to arrive from the capital would ignite the whole country.

Wednesday came. The mail coach arrived. It arrived again on Thursday, this time with terrible news. Sam Neilson had been arrested and charged with high treason. He was spotted outside Newgate prison by a jailer and beaten and dragged inside. It seemed he was trying to reconnoitre the jail in preparation for an attempt to free Lord Edward to lead the rebellion. He had armed men waiting nearby. It would have been the Irish version of the liberation of the Bastille.

In Belfast it became difficult to move around. Harry McCracken had a narrow escape. He was coming to my lodgings in Hercules Street when he was attacked by a patrol of armed yeomen. The formidable Mrs Hamill ran from the shop in her blood-stained apron waving a butcher's knife. They retreated and Harry managed to get away. I met Harry later in Kelly's Cellars. He said we must act now or shut up shop.

At last on Friday 25 May the signal came. The northern mail coach was burned at Santry and all mail destroyed. Kildare and Carlow were already up.

The military authorities in Belfast imposed a curfew from nine at night to five in the morning. All arms, including pikes, were to be turned in immediately. Soldiers patrolled every street. I saw a tailor and a cotton printer given two hundred lashes for hiding arms. Colonel Barber arrested thirty-three men gathered at the sign of the White Cross in Pottingers

Entry, and marched them to the barracks, only to find that they were members of the Society of Tailors, demonstrating for better pay. General Nugent ordered the cancellation of Monday's race meeting at the Maze, and Mr Dumont suspended his Saturday dancing lessons for young ladies at the Exchange Rooms. What had the world come to!

Harry McCracken and several others came to my lodgings. Mrs Hamill stood at the street door with a butcher's knife in her hand to make sure we were not surprised. We agreed we must act now. Colonel Barber was picking up our men one by one. Harry proposed a bold stroke. 'They have beheaded our organisation. We should behead theirs,' he said. Every Tuesday evening military officers attended a promenade and music at the Assembly Rooms. Harry proposed that a party seize the officers and hold them as hostages. The idea was conveyed to the military committee. Several objected. The ladies would be in danger. There could be bloodshed. Harry was furious. Vacillation and lack of purpose and too much deference to society manners was now the curse of our merchant-class leaders. So long as it was a war of words, the higher orders in Belfast were militant and brave. They had little stomach for a real war.

'Maybe it is just as well, Harry,' I told him. 'There are so many informers in our ranks that we might have walked into an ambush.'

Harry quoted from Paine's *American Crisis*. 'These are the times that try men's souls. The summer soldier and the sunshine patriot will, in this crisis, shrink from the service of their country; but he that stands by it now, deserves the love and thanks of man and woman.'

I finished the quotation. 'Tyranny, like hell, is not easily conquered; yet we have this consolation with us, that the harder the conflict, the more glorious the triumph.'

I asked Martha for a bed on the Saturday. We talked around the subject of a rising. 'The people are down and the government is up,' she remarked. 'But both I think may be false colours.'

The rising in Dublin city collapsed. It was a shambles. Men appeared on the streets but, with no leadership, they dispersed, leaving behind stacks of pikes and muskets.

By Sunday Wexford was up but the news from Wicklow was terrible. Scores of United Irishmen were captured and slain by Crown forces.

Jemmy Hope arrived from Dublin and confronted Robert Simms at a hastily convened meeting in Flanagan's tavern. Blood was being shed in the south and the people of the north were becoming impatient and an irregular movement could not long be prevented, he cried. As Antrim adjutant general, Simms must now take the initiative. Simms said he would certainly call out the Antrim men, but not yet. He instructed Jemmy to travel back to Dublin to meet rebel colonels there and report on the progress of the rising.

Jemmy related this exchange to McCracken. Harry told him not to go, that it was a delaying tactic, that there were no colonels there to meet him because Dublin was finished and under military control. 'Simms is prevaricating; he has cold feet, he is letting us all down,' said McCracken.

Monday and Tuesday passed. On Wednesday McCracken returned furious from a meeting of the Ulster executive held in Campbell's pub in Armagh. The order to rise was deferred. Delegates voted to ask the Down and Antrim colonels to formulate a general plan for insurrection and to meet again on 24 June – nearly a month away! If there was no agreement, the executive members argued, then the whole thing should be abandoned and we should all go back to our regular occupations and not deceive the people any longer.

By this time the Revd Steel Dickson, who had been away in Scotland, had returned. After much toing and froing he agreed to honour his commitment to lead Down as adjutant general. We at least, and at last, had a brave, enlightened Presbyterian preacher to rally the United Irishmen of the county. Dickson would not wield a musket himself but would requisition food and quarters for the fighting men. He would stay in touch with John Hughes the Belfast bookseller at all times so we could contact him when the moment came. But the Down colonels insisted they would rise only if Antrim and other counties turned out at the same time.

As we wasted time, General Nugent took a platoon to the cow house of George Warnick on North Street and dug up two brass field pieces we had been hiding. Someone had informed. Two more cannons were given up in Lisburn and wheeled through the Belfast streets to the artillery barracks to rub our noses in it.

I had my first open disagreement with Martha McTier in six years. She expressed admiration for Nugent's use of 'prudent and gentle' means to procure the cannons, saying, 'Nugent is much liked and always was in this town, and I believe in my soul will act with all the forbearance the nature and difficulty of the situation will allow.'

When I demurred strongly and reminded her of the repressions suffered by Belfast and of the vile conduct of the military in the countryside, she expressed the opinion that the yeomen being under military law were already 'very much improved'. The one yeoman she couldn't stand of course was the Revd Bruce. He cowered in his academy, she said, and sent out a female scout to procure news who was deliberately given misinformation.

The days came and went. A week after the burning of the mail coaches our command continued to disintegrate. Robert Simms dithered and then resigned as adjutant general for Antrim, protesting he would only be leading people to slaughter. Twenty-three Antrim colonels met in Templepatrick, and only two resolved to act.

I was in despair. The fires of rebellion were ranging in the south and we, we who prided ourselves on our radicalism, our efficiency and our discipline – was any county as well organised as Down? – were still dragging our heels at the hour of destiny.

Four hundred rebels were massacred by Crown forces in County Kildare and we still sat idly by, waiting for the French, of whom there was no sign.

Harry McCracken, Jemmy Hope and I got together with a few others at Hay's tavern. Our best hope then was Steel Dickson, who had disappeared from his home in Portaferry. Harry tasked me and Jemmy to find him. If we got the Down men on the march, Antrim might follow.

We made our way to John Hughes's bookshop at 20 Bridge Street to establish Dickson's whereabouts. Hughes was in his bedroom, half-dressed and agitated, wringing his hands and crying, 'It is all over, our leaders have sold us out.' He grabbed Jemmy by the lapels. 'We should inform on them and have them arrested so we can pick new leaders.'

Jemmy produced a pistol and held it to the bookseller's breast. 'If you were not so near your wife and children, you would never speak such words again.' Hughes protested that he was only testing Hope and laughed it off. He told us we would find Steel Dickson at an address in Church Lane. We went. He wasn't there. We returned. Hughes asked us to give him two days to find where Steel Dickson was. Two days! What sort of an army did we have that we could not find our commander!

I saddled Shadow and rode around north Down to enquire about Dickson. No one in the Bryson or Gray households knew anything. Eliza and Betsy were busy preparing large quantities of food for the turnout which everyone expected at any moment.

Eliza ran to her house and came back bearing a green hat with cockade which she had made up for me. You have to look the part of an officer, she said. I told her I would wear it with pride and affection. I stayed the night with her and we made love as if for the last time.

I rode back to Belfast on Sunday morning, 3 June, to learn that Wexford was in rebel hands, though our comrades were being massacred in Wicklow, Kildare and Carlow. And all was still confusion in Antrim and Down.

The Antrim colonels had met again on Ballyboley Mountain and again a majority had decided against immediate action. But this time the more militant had walked out in disgust, and a bigger meeting was held at Ballyeaston where greater resolve was shown. These provisional United Irishmen decided to attack the town of Antrim on the seventh of June when county magistrates were due to meet, and to hold them as hostages. Five thousand Defenders were said to be in readiness to join the fray.

But County Antrim still had no commanding officer. And the Down commander was missing.

On the morning of 4 June 1798, a Monday, Jemmy Hope and I went back to John Hughes's house on Bridge Street to try again to locate Dickson. We arrived at a most dangerous moment. From the upstairs window we saw Colonel Barber and a company of yeomen approaching from High Street. A servant girl came running up the stairs crying that a

United Irishman was being whipped in High Street and telling all he knew.

Hughes panicked. He said he had a stone weight of musket balls and packets of gunpowder in a linen bag and if they found that he was done for. Jemmy told him to shut up. He grabbed the bag and ran down the stairs. We saw him emerge onto the roadway and join the yeomen as if one of their number, chatting and laughing, the bag over his shoulder. They all disappeared round the corner into Rosemary Street. There was no raid on the premises and I made my escape.

That day was the King's birthday and General Nugent was determined to show that Belfast was loyal. He organised a military parade of yeomen cavalry and infantry, led by the Monaghan Militia and the Fifeshire Fencibles. Royal Artillery musketeers fired a *feu de joie*, filling Linen Hall Street with bangs and white smoke. Several weavers and shop assistants were dragged off the streets for showing disrespect. Windows were ordered illuminated from 9 to 10 o'clock to honour the King. How things had changed since Belfast celebrated Bastille Day.

That night all social events were cancelled. The theatre was closed. Taverns shut their doors. Even a half a guinea-a-head celebration dinner for officers and aristocrats in the Assembly Rooms was cancelled.

Our anguish turned into despair. Lord Edward Fitzgerald died in Newgate prison from his wounds. The Revd Steel Dickson was arrested in Ballynahinch by Lord Annesley's yeomen and marched to Lisburn with a guard of fourteen soldiers, and then taken by carriage to Belfast and lodged in the Artillery Barracks.

— THIRTY-NINE —

THE FIRST YEAR OF LIBERTY

On Wednesday 6 June, a gloriously sunny day with not a cloud in the sky, everything changed.

At midday Harry burst into Kelly's Cellars. The Antrim colonels had elected him as commanding officer to replace Robert Simms. At dawn on the morrow they would lead assaults on military posts throughout the county and march to Donegore Hill five miles east of Antrim town. McCracken would rendezvous there and proceed to seize Antrim town and kidnap the magistrates.

There, in the tap room, Harry appointed several of us his officers. He produced a paper on which he had written a proclamation:

'Army of Ulster, tomorrow we march on Antrim; drive the garrison of Randalstown before you and haste to form a junction with your commander-in-chief. 1st Year of Liberty, 6th day of June, 1798.'

He thrust it at me. 'Get as many as possible printed,' he said.

Matthew Smith ran off dozens of the proclamation in short order and destroyed the type in case of a raid. There was much confusion in the streets. Frightened gentry were arriving from the countryside and yeomen and dragoons were on the move everywhere.

I fetched my pistol and musket from the chimney-block and stuffed them in a muslin bag along with a bunch of Harry's proclamations, my Volunteer uniform, and the green hunting hat with feathers given to me by Eliza. Having secured a supply of oats for Shadow, I set off at a four-beat trot for Donegore Hill, making the seven-mile journey in less than an hour and without incident. There were no military patrols on the roads. On the way I passed some Belfast men walking in their Sabbath clothes, wearing green kerchiefs, and carrying pikes.

The first person I encountered at Donegore Hill was Jemmy Hope. With great glee he told me how he had fooled the yeomen when he joined them carrying Hughes's bag of ammunition. He walked among them all the way to North Street where he slipped away, collected colours, two swords and a green jacket, stuffed the whole lot into a bigger sack, put it half-open on the back of a cart with a few weaver's heddles sticking out, and drove behind another corps of yeomen, gradually pulling away and out of town.

Harry was every inch a commander, six feet tall wearing a green jacket faced with yellow, and white breeches and a fine sword. He gave proclamations to runners to bring far and wide to the waiting colonels.

We had a few score muskets and one cannon that had been hidden under the floorboards of the Presbyterian meeting house in Templepatrick, in the charge of a patriot who had deserted from the Royal Irish Artillery.

Our horses were put out to graze, fires were lit, whiskey jars were passed around and ballads sung. When my turn came I recited a few lines from Robbie Burns's 'Scots Whe Hae'.

Lay the proud usurpers low!
Tyrants fall in every foe!
Liberty's in every blow.
Let us do or die!

Harry made a toast to Liberty, saying, 'If we succeed tomorrow, there will be sufficient praise lavished on us; if we fail, we may expect proportionate blame; but whether we succeed or fail, let us try to deserve success!' He held up his hand to display the words engraved on his gold ring: 'Remember Orr!'

The night was short and we hardly had time to sleep before the sun rose on another clear, still day. Harry raised the standard of rebellion by planting a green flag on a rise called Craigarogan Rath. Jemmy Hope and John Storey organised the men into divisions.

Then we waited. As the sun rose higher we scanned the fields stretched out below us, looking for the reinforcements called out by Harry's proclamation. All was quiet but for the dawn chorus of skylarks and meadow pipits and the plaintive mewing of a buzzard circling overhead. Nothing stirred. We waited some more.

We saw black smoke rising from Antrim town in the distance. Some youths came running to say an artillery officer had started a fire in the thatch of a house where pike heads were found and it had spread.

The minutes passed. We still waited.

At midday Jemmy called me over to look through his field glass. At first I saw nothing. Then – there they were! In the distance the sun glinted on hundreds of metal objects moving just above ditch level. Pikes! Long columns of men were approaching from the direction of Ballyclare and Templepatrick. As they came closer, we made out green banners, and a few white. Defenders too!

Jemmy and John set off to take command of the columns. Messengers criss-crossed the fields. McCracken issued instructions. Envoys came galloping up with news of risings in practically every town and village in the county. Randalstown was already overrun.

I was not destined to join the fun. Harry called me aside. He instructed me to ride hard and bring word to the Down colonels that the whole of Antrim was in our hands. 'If we rise together we are invincible,' he said. 'If we delay, we are lost. Go quickly! Take a boat across the lough.'

As Harry led his men towards Antrim, I rode off at a gallop in the other direction. Skirting Belfast I saw in the distance a body of red-coats trotting at a brisk pace with bayonets fixed towards Antrim. They had horse-drawn cannons.

At Whiteabbey village on the north shore of Belfast Lough men with pikes were guarding the coal pier. They told me that Carrickfergus was under siege by our forces and that the green flag had been raised on Islandmagee peninsula and in Larne.

I abandoned Shadow to their care and set off across the lough in a 'liberated' skiff, rowed by two muscular oarsmen. The water was as smooth as glass. We heard bangs and booms in the distance behind us. Three hours later they put me ashore at Holywood on the north Down coast. A crowd of nervous men watched my approach. They too were wearing green kerchiefs. The military had abandoned the roads and men had gathered here and there, but they had no orders.

They fetched a mare and saddle and I set off for Six Road Ends. The Bryson house was in turmoil. Eliza ran to greet me as I dismounted and fell weeping on my shoulder. Her father had been arrested the day before by the York Fencibles and taken to military headquarters in Newtownards.

I made the barn at Bryson's farm my headquarters and sent young Andrew and other volunteers to fetch any colonels they could find.

Before darkness fell I rode across the fields with Eliza mounted behind me to the home of the Grays. Hans and George Gray, Willie Boal and several Gransha men were there, fired up with anticipation of action. Betsy's glance of delight when I entered the crowded cottage, and her tight embrace, almost broke my heart, and certainly displeased Eliza, who nevertheless held her wheesht. We men bedded down on the grass outside. I lay awake for a long time, listening to the distant sound of cannon fire from Antrim.

— FORTY —

THE BATTLE OF SAINTFIELD

We were wakened by the cock at 5.00 am. Betsy and Eliza brought out bowls of stirabout with milk, and oatmeal bread and butter. My volunteer uniform, with the green headgear Eliza had made for me, caused much comment. Said Betsy, 'Isn't he our very own Napoleon!'

Davy Bailie Warden arrived on horseback, wearing a green coat and kerchief. He had tried to start the action himself the day before. He sent out word to the men under his charge to assemble at Scrabo Hill overlooking Newtownards. He waited all night. He could see lights blazing at the Market House in Newtownards where 300 York Fencibles were stationed. No one rallied to his call. 'Some of them are frightened of their own shadow,' he complained. But now men were gathering everywhere and the military had withdrawn from all north Down except Newtownards. Down was up! But we still had no leader. We needed someone with maturity and authority, at best a former Volunteer officer who would command respect and obedience.

Our best hope was Harry Monro in Lisburn, who had military training in the Volunteers and was widely known and respected. The Revd James Townsend from Greyabbey, a committed United Irishman, volunteered to ride the twenty miles there to persuade him to take command.

Meantime we decided to rally at Saintfield, the town just north of Ballynahinch where the United Irishmen were strong. Another group proceeded down the Ards peninsula to liberate Portaferry. I set off with Davy to get the men of north-east Down to join an attack on Newtownards.

Half an hour later we found ourselves in an astonishing world. The village of Donaghadee, a wide semi-circle of cottages and small houses round a sandy beach, with a harbour on the south side, was fully under the control of a rebel garrison. A Committee of Public Safety had been set up on the revolutionary French model, headed by a cart driver and a grocer.

Here, about eighteen miles east of Belfast, was an example to all of Ireland. The United Irishmen were well-disciplined and respectful of property. Though the landlord David Ker had fled to Scotland, Portavo House was not ransacked. The rebels requisitioned only camp furniture, some bottles of Madeira and a cello, and Ker's collection of erotica, which caused considerable distraction. The loyalist customs inspector James Arbuckle had run off to Dublin, but, rather than break into his house, the patriots sent a servant to fetch his spy-glass, which they promised to return.

Since the harbour was the Irish end of the passenger route to Scotland it was strategically important. Here men equipped with muskets had allowed thirty loyalist families to leave by boat. They had taken over a number of craft and sent out boarding parties to search for arms on Belfast-bound ships.

'My God,' said Davey. 'We have a navy.'

In their first engagement at sea they fired at a yawl bearing Ker's fleeing steward, John Catherwood, but he got away. Their second foray was more successful. A fishing craft manned by rebels boarded a small ship called *The Linen Hall*. They came ashore with two swivel guns, and several muskets, canteens and camp kettles, and also two prisoners, the former Belfast mayor John Brown and his wife. Brown was a wealthy patron of my old academy, one of the Johns of the Bank of the Four Johns, a yeoman officer and an occasional diner at Martha McTier's table.

The men asked me what should be done with them. 'Find somewhere to lock them up,' I replied. To Brown I said, 'You will be treated correctly. But as a yeoman officer you will be held as a prisoner of war.'

He looked at me coldly. 'You and your accursed, seditious paper. I told Martha you were up no good. You ruffians will be dealt with for this outrage.'

'You must bear some responsibility for the cruelties inflicted on the population by the yeomen under your command, and you will be court-martialed in due course,' I replied. I had no idea whether he would or not, but it gave him something to think about. 'You can read about your trial in the *Northern Star*, which we will soon be publishing again.'

Warden bullied and cajoled the local commanders to gather men for an attack on Newtownards, though they were understandably reluctant to leave their peaceful little French-style republic for action elsewhere.

We formed a column and rode to within a mile of Newtownards, where I parted company from Davy and turned my mare towards Saintfield, twelve miles to the south.

Along the way I passed men walking or riding in the same direction carrying pikes, pitchforks and muskets. The cheered when they saw my uniform. In Saintfield they gathered around the sloping triangle of Cow Green, where the mud had dried hard, and there was already a great noise of drums, pipes, fiddles and flutes.

I called at the manse of the Revd Birch, and found accommodation for the night along with a militant Killinchy apothecary, Dr James Cord. They told me that our best leader in that part of Down, the merchant David Shaw, had been dragged out of his store some days previously and taken away by the military.

Now that the most of the county had fallen into the hands of the United Irishmen, the gentry were taking flight. The previous day Squire Price had abandoned his mansion and Lady Roden and her family from Bryansford had come racing through the town in two rattle-trap chaises with military escort, heading for Belfast and most likely on to Scotland.

Next morning, Saturday 9 June, as the sun arose over the drumlins east of Saintfield, more country folk arrived – farmers, merchants, weavers, labourers – all in their Sunday best, and all wearing something green. United Irish officers set out to scour the countryside for reluctant warriors. I worried about the nerve and reliability of men who came because they were intimidated. I heard of one farmer, who always boasted how he would free Ireland with his blunderbuss, refusing to come because 'there's a wheen of birds about that will take all my shooting'.

As several colonels and captains conferred in Birch's house, a scout brought news that a military column was heading towards Saintfield. All was confusion as the word spread. Sometimes natural leaders emerge in such times. Two men, Colonel Richard Frazer from Ravara, and the Revd William Adair, a Presbyterian clerical student from Ballygraffan, assumed command. They rode around waving their swords and got the great body of men to move towards Oughley Hill to set an ambush for the Crown forces.

On the way a terrible tragedy occurred which bothers me to this day. David Shaw's brother, James, dressed in a green jacket and mounted on a grey mare, led a breakaway company towards the house of the loyalist McKee family at Craignasasonagh to secure their guns. Armed by the government, the family had been terrorising the countryside for months, spying on people and taking shots at known United Irishmen.

Their two-storey slated house was situated on a low hill. The McKees had barricaded themselves inside. Men with muskets, pistols and pikes surrounded it. Dozens of spectators gathered to watch. Shouts for the family to come out and join the patriot army were met with defiant yells from within. A shot was fired from a window high on the gable and a man fell wounded. Someone shouted, 'Smoke them out.' A ladder was fetched and propped against the back of the house where there were no windows.

A little fellow ran up – they said he was a fiddler from Saintfield – prised off a few slates and pushed a burning faggot into the rafters. Smoke seeped through the slates and curled downwards in the still air. It got thicker and blacker. Flames burst through the roof. The door opened and a man emerged. It was shut behind him. He tried to run but was piked through the chest.

From inside came terrible screams. With a crash part of the roof fell in. There was a horrible smell. Some girls from nearby houses began wailing. They said there had been eleven people in the house, Hugh McKee, his wife, his five grown sons, the youngest sixteen, his three daughters and a servant called Boles. It was Boles who had run out.

This could have been the undoing of us, there and then. Some men deserted in disgust, their fervour for revolution gone. One shouted up at me, 'We didn't sign up for murder.' But most were fired up with hatred.

'As you reap, so shall you sow,' a man shouted at the burning ruin. Shaw and I rode among the mob, and got them to continue to the gathering point at Oughley Hill.

At five in the afternoon, a scout arrived in a sweat to warn us that the military had already passed through Comber and were a mere three miles away. We hadn't spotted them because of the high drumlins that typify this part of County Down, creating a landscape like giant eggs in a basket.

Adair divided the United Irishmen on each side of the Comber Road. The musket men concealed themselves behind ditches overgrown with ferns and nettles. I helped deploy pikemen among the great oak trees in the demesne above and in a copse on the far side known as Doran's Wood. Frazer rounded up stragglers and urged the men not to take fright, warning what would happen to them in the event of the rebellion failing.

At length we were all in place, about a thousand men all told. I took up position in the demesne overlooking the road. Everything went quiet. The warm air, perfumed by summer blossoms and heavy with pollen, became absolutely still, as if nature was holding its breath. It was all I could do not to sneeze.

We heard a distant fife and drum, then the faint jingling of harnesses and the shouted commands of officers. The column stopped just out of sight behind a steep hill.

Two yeomen scouts rode right past the men lying in wait and cantered to the bridge at the demesne entrance. I recognised the Revd John Cleland, Londonderry's agent, and the Revd James Clewlew, the Anglican vicar of Saintfield. The two stopped, surveyed the almost-deserted village, and then wheeled round and rode back to make their report. No one gave away our position.

The military column appeared. At its head was Colonel Granville Anson Chetwynd-Stapylton, the pompous officer who tried to rent Martha's house in Belfast and who had imposed a reign of terror on north Down. He rode by at a leisurely pace. I could see drops of perspiration running down from beneath his powdered wig. Behind him a boy sounded a marching beat on a side drum. The officers, in large cocked hats and blue tailcoats, chatted as they passed. One said in a loud voice, 'It seems the Croppies have run away.' They numbered about three hundred, of whom fifty were yeomen from Newtownards in fur-crested round hats.

I recognised another minister riding with them, the Revd Robert Mortimer of Comber. He had just gone by with the lead cavalry when a shot rang out and Mortimer fell from his horse. Someone had loosed off before the order was given.

In an instant there was pandemonium. Our side opened fire on the cavalry at point-blank range. Mortally wounded men fell off their mounts. Horses crashed to the ground. Dragoons tried frantically to turn their mounts on the narrow road and retreat through panicking infantry. Acrid white gun smoke filled the air. A cavalry officer forced his way through a hedge and was stabbed to death.

I charged down from the demesne with more than a hundred pikemen to attack the supply train at the rear of the column. We managed to make off with some boxes of ammunition. I heard Richard Frazer shouting, 'Up and at them, boys! Liberty or death! Remember Orr!'

I fired my musket at a small, fat yeoman who fell clutching his leg. He turned his chubby face to me, red with outrage. It was Claiborne, the agent whose blow to my head ten years before started me on this devilish business. There was hatred in his eyes and I'm sure in mine. He struggled to stand up and aim his musket. Just then a pikeman came by and lunged at Claiborne's back. He fell on his face and lay writhing on the ground. I thought hysterically how I told him once that he should watch his back.

For several minutes there was desperate hand-to-hand fighting. Men on both sides fell with blood running from heads, arms, legs and torsos.

The English gunners managed to set up their six-pounders and fire a hail of grapeshot. On the marshy ground dozens fell. Our men pulled back. Dr Cord rode around recklessly on a white horse waving his sword and shouting, 'Damn you, are you going to leave me?'

It took us some time to realise that Chetwynd-Stapylton was retreating with his column back along the Comber Road. We began yelling in triumph. We had won! We had prevailed against the English cavalry, just as Polish pikemen recruited from the fields had defeated the Russian army. No matter that it was on a smaller scale. It showed we could do it.

We had some prisoners, a sergeant and his men who had been cut off. They were marched into the town and told they would come to no harm as long as our prisoners were treated well.

Though fired up with our victory we had to face the aftermath, for which we were little prepared. Wounded men cried for help where they lay. Distraught women came looking for their menfolk. People brought bandages, and supplies of milk and wine were requisitioned from the village taverns for the casualties of both sides. There wasn't near enough. I thought I was injured but the blood on my coat belonged to someone else. Four military stretcher-bearers approached with a white flag and we allowed them to take away their wounded.

I found the little drummer boy lying dead with a drumstick in one hand and a tuft of grass in the other.

I searched the pockets of a dead officer and identified him as Captain William Chetwynd, a relative of the colonel. A distressed farmer called Daniel Mellin stood beside him in tears. He kept saying in disbelief, 'I shot him. I killed a man.'

We let our men strip the dead fencibles and the yeomen of their uniforms and possessions, which led to some unedifying scenes. I saw two boys fighting to strip a dragoon of his trousers. The Revd Mortimer's corpse was left naked, propped up against a gate post.

About fifty bodies of United Irishmen were laid out side by side with cloths over their faces for burial the next day. Other casualties were loaded onto carts or draped over ponies and taken away by relatives. Maybe a hundred on our side perished. Frazer, Adair and Cord survived the battle.

We assembled in a circle of horses and resolved to surround Colonel Stapylton's remnants when it became dark, but at about nine o'clock, when still light, the Crown forces retreated towards Comber.

We dispatched runners across the countryside to spread the news. Fresh bodies of men armed with pikes arrived. Despite the deaths and injuries there was singing and dancing to the music of flutes and fiddles.

In the manse I found the Revd Birch weeping. His brother George had been commander of the Newtownards yeomen against whom we contended that day. But George's two sons had fought on the patriot side. One – the son of a Hindu woman from the East Indies – saw their father about to be piked and managed to save him. The other son, also called George, was killed by Crown forces.

'He was only a lad,' cried Birch. 'What can be worse than a civil war that divides families?'

Our sense of victory was rudely tempered by rumours that Harry McCracken and his men had fled into the hills after a calamitous setback in a battle for Antrim, although Ballymena and other towns were still under the control of United Irishmen. News circulated too of a terrible massacre in Scullabogue in County Wexford of over one hundred Protestants, burned alive by rebels in a barn.

One body of my countrymen discussed this heatedly before setting off home, unhappy about the idea of siding with Papists.

But the bulk of our men were up for the fight, and the battle of Saintfield made them believe that our cause could prevail. Almost all north Down and the Ards peninsula was in our hands. If we linked up with the Defenders of south Down we could yet ignite the flames in other provinces, and join a march on Dublin and start a new era when Irishmen, of all religions, would unite to control our destiny.

— FORTY-ONE —

PIKE SUNDAY

The morning of Sunday 10 June was cool with flying clouds, but it soon became hot again. As people began to rouse themselves from the streets and fields where they had passed the night, I went with Birch to have a look at Saintfield House which had been abandoned by the Price family.

Country folk roamed through the three-storey mansion gazing at oil-paintings of self-important land-owners in long wigs, trying out the plush sofas and armchairs, and wrapping themselves in fine, white linen. Some stretched out asleep, fully clothed, on four-poster beds. Volunteers were liberating camp supplies – pots, pans, sheets and hunting horns – and carting away large quantities of bacon, hams, tongues, salted beef, and mutton, and boxes labelled 'Lapsang Souchong Tea' from China. The wine cellar was well plundered but I managed to loot for myself two bottles of fine claret. Richard Frazer strode from room to room ordering that there be no wrecking or stealing of valuables, though I saw a man put a silver ink-well in his pocket after he passed.

At the First Presbyterian Church the grave-diggers were busy laying fallen rebels to rest. With my instincts as a newspaperman, I counted the enemy casualties on the battlefield – fifty-six dead fencibles and yeomen. Birch and his sexton organised volunteers to dig a deep pit for them on a river island beyond the graveyard. He rewarded his shaken helpers with large whiskeys in McCreery's alehouse.

The Crown forces would be back, that we knew. Frazer, Adair, Jackson and Cord and I decided to move our citizen army to Creevy Rocks, a large drumlin two miles south of Saintfield, and there to conduct drills and organise a proper camp and overall command.

All afternoon we herded the men towards Creevy Rocks. They walked in line, shouldering pikes, muskets, scythes and digging forks. Women on ponies brought panniers filled with provisions and barrels of water. A man called Henry Byers, mounted on Price's personal bay mare, drove the Squire's bullocks in our midst.

At Creevy Rocks the men organised themselves into work parties. They gathered kindling for fires and dug shit holes, though most just went behind ditches, and soon there were foul odours everywhere and you had to be careful where you walked.

On the back slopes of the drumlin came the distressed cries of cattle witnessing one of their number being slaughtered.

The Revd Birch came late in the afternoon, after personally supervising the burial of the child drummer. He stalked majestically through the crowd, climbed onto a cart and held up his Bible. Silence fell. His voice carried far in the still air. He took for his text Ezekiel IX, 1, and began:

'Cause them that have charge over the city to draw near, even every man with his destroying weapon in his hand.

'Men of Down are here gathered today, being the Sabbath of the Lord God, to pray and fight for the liberty of this kingdom of Ireland. We have grasped the pike and musket and fight for the right against might: to drive the bloodhounds of King George the German king beyond the seas.

'This is Ireland. We are Irish and we shall be free... Men of the south are in arms against the common foe. Let us go forward to the flush of victory when all hands will be joined in the bond of Irish unity.'

This produced loud and prolonged cheering from the mostly Presbyterian assemblage. Men raised their pikes and muskets in the air. I found myself wondering how many of the pike heads were cast by Matt in his forge at Six Road Ends, and where he and my Gransha friends were.

Birch had just descended from the cart when several men and women on horseback came riding up. Harry Monro was among them. Hallelujah! He jumped down from his horse and embraced me. Townsend had persuaded him to join us in Saintfield. They had ridden the ten miles from Lisburn without encountering any English troops.

'Truth to tell,' said Monro, 'We had to get out of Lisburn. The town is occupied by loyalists and Crown forces. I saw a neighbour, a good man, whipped in the street. The bastards were coming for me next, and for Peggy.'

Peggy, wearing a broad green scarf, dismounted from a grey mare. She had a sword in her belt. 'Do you remember me?' she asked. 'Of course I do,' I replied. 'You were the first Lisburn woman to ride a horse alone into Belfast.'

'That was me,' she said. 'Now I am ready to ride into battle.'

I had no need to introduce Monro to the half-dozen men who had acquitted themselves well as leaders the day before. They knew and respected him. Some had supplied his drapery business. We pressed Monro to take up immediately the role of County Down commander. After some hesitation he agreed, but he was well prepared.

From his saddle bag he unfolded his uniform as adjutant in the Lisburn Volunteers. In short order, with Peggy helping do up the buttons and smooth out the material, he was dressed in a magnificent scarlet coat with faced blue and silver lining, white breeches, furnished belt and pouch, knee-high boots and hat with white cock neck feathers hanging down over his black, ribboned hair. How clothes make the man! The not-so-tall linen draper from Lisburn was transformed before our eyes into an imposing military commander.

In the course of three days I too had been recast as a military officer by virtue of my hat with green cockade, velvet cutaway coat with ornamental buttons, green waistcoat, buckskin breeches, black gaiters and, of course, my possession of a musket and pistol.

Monro remounted, raised his Volunteer sword and addressed the gathering. 'The telling hour had come,' he cried. 'Only by unity and courage can the ideals of enlightenment be achieved and the yoke of military repression be removed. There will be no more pitch-cappings, no more floggings, no more hangings, no more burnings!' The Down men cheered.

I could not have been happier when General Monro – as we now addressed him – appointed me his aide-de-camp.

Before dusk a horseman arrived to tell us that the military had abandoned Newtownards and withdrawn to Belfast. Prisoners had been freed, including Andrew Bryson Senior. Our countrymen controlled the streets. The town was in chaos but a Committee of Public Safety had been set up in the Market House, headed by Bryson, to impose control. Young Andy had been sent out to destroy bridges and strengthen defences.

We held a council of war. Monro resolved to proceed to Ballynahinch five miles south, where we would be joined by Defenders from south Down, and make our stand. 'General Nugent will not be long coming to confront us,' he said. 'We must choose the battle-ground where we have the advantage. We will set up our headquarters in Lord Moira's demesne.'

Monro sent a dispatch rider to Newtownards with instruction to the men there to march immediately south, to reinforce our numbers for a decisive battle in Ballynahinch.

That evening the air was filled with wood smoke from fires all across the hillsides, which helped drive off the clouds of midges that were eating us alive. The multitude feasted on roast beef from Price's livestock. Music and dancing started up.

Would there have been such a big turnout in heavy rain? I didn't think so. Everything was now in our favour, even the weather, which had thwarted our goals so cruelly in the past.

As I turned in to sleep, a line about Ireland from Shakespeare's *Henry VI* ran through my head: '...the rebels there are up, and put the Englishmen unto the sword... the uncivil kerns are in arms, and temper clay with blood of Englishmen.'

That we surely were and that we were surely doing.

— FORTY-TWO —

BETSY AND ME

At first light next morning, Monday 11 June, a scout came to Creevy Rocks with news that several score men from Newtownards were approaching, led by Davy Warden. Monro and I rode to meet them. Davy was in great spirits. He joked that he had enough men now to dig all Ireland's potatoes in one day.

Then I saw her.

Betsy was in their midst, dressed all in green, with long, red hair spilling down over her shoulders. She sat astride a piebald pony harnessed to a block wheel cart laden with provisions. George Gray and Willie Boal rode alongside.

We all embraced. Eliza was not with them. She had stayed in Newtownards to be with her father and brother. That was all right with me.

'Now then, *Star* man, are you going to be our guiding star? Where will you lead us?' asked George.

'To Dublin, where a new Ireland will be born,' I replied in a ringing tone.

'God, you've got very pompous.'

Monro was magnificent. He treated everyone with kindness and respect, and gave orders for food for the exhausted arrivals. 'First time I've had fresh roast beef for breakfast,' said Willie Boal.

Monro, Adair and I drew up a list of developments in the previous twenty-four hours.

North Down was liberated.

Committees of Public Safety on the revolutionary French model were in control of Donaghadee and Newtownards.

A United Irish camp was established at Innishargie just outside Kircubbin. United Irishmen controlled the Ards peninsula.

Lord Londonderry and his family had fled and Mount Stewart was abandoned.

So far so good. Our only setback had been at Portaferry, where Crown forces killed several of our men before retreating across the Strangford narrows and fortifying Downpatrick.

Discipline was a serious problem. Davy Warden complained of the difficulty in getting his men – a mere country mob at the start, he said – to stand fast after six were killed by York Fencibles in the attack on Newtownards the day before.

'They ran a mile before prayers, entreaties, reproaches and threats induced them to halt.'

He led a second attack in the late afternoon, reinforced by a large group who had walked from Bangor under the hot sun, only to find that the military had abandoned the town, leaving behind ammunition, guns, provisions, uniforms and boots.

Monro's order to these men to march on to Saintfield came as they were celebrating the liberation of the town. All were exhausted, some were drunk, several wanted to return home considering their duty done, and a few were insubordinate. Only by cajoling and flattering them did Davy get the majority to stay together and bring their military booty with them.

A small committee was set up to distribute knapsacks and cartridge shoulder pouches seized in Newtownards. Some women were put to work filling paper tubes with gunpowder and lead musket balls. There was great interest in a captured self-priming carbine which had a short skeletal butt that rested lightly on the arm, and could be fired five times a minute. With these in one hand and emancipation in the other, we could be masters of out republican destiny!

To ensure order at Creevy Rocks, men were drilled and practised in the best use of the pike. I demonstrated how to cut the bridle of a horse and unseat the rider by stabbing the animal in the nose. When a farmer reacted in horror I said, 'What! Do you prefer to let a dragoon slice you open?'

A Lisburn native, wearing a beaver helmet turned up on one side with a large green cockade, spent hours drilling pikemen with the ramrod of a gun in his hand.

'Witness the Republican Army of County Down,' said Davy, sitting up on his mare and looking around at the drilling and the general commotion.

In my role as aide I made General Monro a rough shelter by tying canvas sheeting to tree branches, and I sent volunteers to Saintfield House with a cart to bring a table, chairs, candles, paper and writing materials.

Monro ordered James Townsend to take some of the best men and march to Ballynahinch a few miles farther south to dislodge any remnants of the military there prior to our occupation. Townsend set off with a sword in his belt and a carbine suspended from his saddle.

Before dark, a rider came back from Ballynahinch to inform the general that the military had abandoned the town, but not before hanging the only baker at his front door so that he could not make bread for us.

Monro sent three hundred more men under Davy Warden and a Bangor probationer, James Hull, to establish a base camp at Lord Moira's demesne.

We sent out scouting parties to requisition food and to bring in stragglers, especially those once-vocal radicals now skulking at home.

I contrived that evening for the Gransha contingent to pitch their camp adjacent to our headquarters, so that I could join them as they started a fire. Betsy produced eggs, buttermilk and oaten cakes. Men came around with pails of meat cuts from the slaughtered cattle. We ate fresh roast washed down with some of Squire Price's claret.

Having been the most reluctant to join up, Willie Boal was now the most militant of us all, and rallied the men around us with fighting talk.

When I was taking my leave, Betsy smiled at me and pulled back her hair. There was enough light from the camp fire for me to see.

She was wearing my earrings.

It was at that moment I decided that I could not live without her, and that I would have to make my intentions clear, come what may, when this business was over. I did not love Eliza. I was not being fair to her, or myself, or Betsy. I loved Betsy. And Betsy, I imagined, had a fancy for me. She must not marry Willie Boal just because they had been childhood sweethearts. It would break my heart if she did, and maybe hers.

Many good men died at Saintfield. Victory came at a high cost. More blood I knew would surely stain the soil in the coming hours. And death was capricious. George, Willie, Betsy and I had promised to look out for each other. I resolved to make sure that we did, that we get through this trial; after that, we could sort out matters of the heart.

— FORTY-THREE —

THE BATTLE OF BALLYNAHINCH

Tuesday 12 June, another glorious, cloudless day. The camp was roused early by men in forester green with bugle and horn. Monro sent a fast rider with a consignment of ball cartridges for Townsend and a note hoping the Defenders had rallied to him. The rider returned as we were moving out. The Defenders hadn't appeared yet. Our general sent another horseman towards Rathfriland to try to make contact with the Catholic forces.

Resplendent in his scarlet and blue coat and plumed hat, Monro led our citizen army in a long column along the narrow road to Ballynahinch, leaving a small force to protect our rear.

We proceeded in a cloud of dust through the hollows and saddles of central Down's green hillocks. Families came from cottages with milk and water as the long line of men passed carrying muskets, blunderbusses, pikes, pitchforks, turf spades, scythes, green flags and banners proclaiming *'Erin go bragh'*, followed by women with provisions on ponies and carts. Dogs yelped alongside, mad with excitement. Children ran with us as we sang *La Marseillaise* and Irish ballads. To hear *Shan Van Vocht* sung by hundreds of marching men heading for battle was thrilling beyond words.

And will Ireland then be free? Says the Shan Van Vocht,
Will Ireland then be free? Says the Shan Van Vocht,
Yes old Ireland will be free, from the centre to the sea,
And hurrah for liberty, says the Shan Van Vocht.

We entered Ballynahinch to the clip-clop of hooves, the thud of stomping feet, the beating of drums, and siren blasts from conch shells, hunting horns and tin trumpets. The inhabitants cheered us on. What now of Lord Moira's boast that there was no town as loyal as Ballynahinch?

We were greeted by Dr Valentine Swail, leader of the Ballynahinch United Irishmen. Monro appointed him adjutant because of his knowledge of the town.

Townsend had already organised defences under Samuel McCance, a new recruit who had taken up the cause with great enthusiasm. He placed musketeers and pikemen and two swivel guns behind the terraced ditches of Windmill Hill east of the Market House, to intercept the Crown forces that would inevitably pursue us.

We crossed the town and made our way west along Bridge Street to the entrance to Lord Moira's demesne, just a few hundred yards from the town square. There we scattered across a steep meadow known as Ednavaddy Hill, half way between the demesne entrance and the mansion, with a splendid view of the town from the summit.

I led some men to the mansion to secure tables and chairs for Monro's headquarters. Our boots echoed in the empty rooms of Montalto. All curtains, paintings, books and valuables had gone with Lord Moira to London, leaving only some basic furniture and a few tuns of whiskey, which had been well used, judging by the state of some of the advance party. I left a contingent to mind the gardeners who were hovering protectively around the orchids and hibiscus in the garden.

During the next, precious few, balmy hours, with the enemy still some distance away, and the midsummer sun climbing high in the sky, the scene on the vast hillside was quite idyllic.

Men and boys lay in the shade of trees, a few blissfully asleep. Others strolled around. Some read Bibles. Sweethearts went off into the trees. Fiddlers and drummers attracted small crowds. Former Volunteers in their fifties paraded around like peacocks.

Most of the patriots were in their Sunday clothes and everyone wore something green, whether a scarf, belt, coat, petticoat, hat or a sprig of the laurel which grew plentifully in the demesne. Some sported ornamental harps entwined with shamrocks, and brooches with slogans such as 'Liberty or Death', 'Freedom to Ireland' and 'A Downfall to Tyrants'. A few lads from the Presbyterian village of Broomhedge wore branches of yellow-flowering broom on their hats and called themselves the 'Broomhedge Boys'.

Women were treated with the utmost courtesy and gratitude. They brought fresh meat, salted beef and bacon, oatmeal bread, butter, rabbits hanging by their feet, pigs' heads, potatoes, bread and cakes. A feeding station was set up and orderly queues formed. Betsy was to the fore organising distribution from behind picnic tables carried from an outhouse. Pedlars moved around selling pamphlets, sweets and emblems. Farriers worked hard tending to limping horses.

Men showed off their pikes, the best of which had hooks for cutting bridles and pulling soldiers from their horses. Older men compared ceremonial swords and muskets. No more than three or four hundred had firearms but there was an abundance of ammunition from the government arsenals in Newtownards. I ordered the three barrels of captured gunpowder to be placed in separate locations in case one exploded.

Late in the morning a number of Defenders rallied to us. Hugh Jennings, a captain of the Dunmore yeomanry, switched sides and arrived with four hundred and fifty armed Catholics. Roger Magennis, dressed in green frock-coat with musket slung from his shoulder, came with a corps of Defenders from Rathfriland. This swelled our numbers to six and a half thousand men.

They brought word that my friend Charles Teeling, though still weak from the illness brought on by Kilmainham's damp cells, was helping to rally the Defenders in south Down, at Ballywillwill and Rathfriland.

Catholic Defenders and Presbyterian United Irishmen mingled and shook hands, though a few of our countrymen hung back, suspicious of the Papists and mindful of the massacre in Wexford. But uppermost in my own mind was the thought that this might be the first time in the history of Ireland that such a large army of Protestant, Catholic and Dissenter had come together to fight British Crown forces for Ireland's liberty.

Not everyone shared the festive mood. Some women in tears begged or harangued their menfolk to quit the field before it was too late. We had to accept that in a volunteer army – and some had not volunteered but had been 'persuaded' by neighbours – there would be defections. Only half-hearted efforts were made to stop them deserting us.

There was a stir just after midday when a Belfast yeoman arrived at the demesne, waving a green neck cloth. I recognised him. We had studied business and economics together at the academy. He told Monro he had deserted his unit to warn him that General Nugent had left Belfast at the head of a military force, bolstered by armed Orangemen in yeomen uniform, and was heading directly towards us. He said Belfast was under military control and guarded by yeomen.

'Incidentally,' he added, turning to me, 'the last sentinel I passed on the Long Bridge was that old bastard, the Reverend Bruce, holding a blunderbuss and looking quite ridiculous.'

For the first time we learned what we would be up against. By this man's account Nugent's line of march extended upward of three miles, and consisted of the Monaghan Militia, the Fifeshire Fencibles, the 22nd Light Dragoons, Royal Artillery and Belfast yeomen, with 12-pound cannons and howitzers.

We had no heavy weapons, only the one-pounder swivel guns mounted on common cars. Monro said we should make the capture of the British artillery a top priority. Ours were short range and no match for their cannon which could bombard us with exploding shells and grapeshot.

As the sun dimmed behind high clouds in the afternoon, we saw narrow columns of black smoke rising into the sky to our north, marking the approach of Nugent. His soldiers were burning farmsteads along the way. I thought with dismay of the terror being inflicted upon the women and children who had greeted us so gaily on the road that morning.

In the town below us many respectable citizens piled their belongings onto carts, from beds and chairs to clocks and ledgers, and made off into the countryside.

A pikeman told us that he recognised one of the milk-women in our crowd as a spy. We arranged to have her overhear us planning an imminent attack on Lisburn, and she made off. We hoped that would tie up Crown forces in Lisburn for a while.

The rear-guard that we left in Saintfield arrived in Ballynahinch five miles ahead of Nugent. They reported that he had shelled Price's mansion as he passed, though all our men had left but for one poor devil lying drunk in the wine cellar. They dragged him out and shot him at the front entrance.

Nugent's column was slowed down by trenches dug by men under Moses Montgomery, a Ballynahinch tavern owner.

In mid-afternoon runners came to tell us of a second Crown force approaching from Downpatrick, consisting of yeomen and Argyles under Lieutenant Colonel George Stewart. They reached Ballynahinch before Nugent and deployed to the south without coming into contact with our men.

The first sight of the enemy caused alarm. Everyone got to their feet to look in their direction, and the hangers-on, spectators and peddlers made their way hastily from the meadow. The order went round for women to leave but a few dozen remained, including Betsy.

Shortly afterwards, Nugent's forces came into view. The first shots of the battle rang out. Puff-balls of white smoke rose from Windmill Hill, where Sam McCance and his musketeers were firing on the military from behind the hedges.

The United Irishmen on Windmill Hill kept Nugent at bay for an hour. When we spotted Colonel Stewart's men moving to encircle them, Monro sent a runner with an order to withdraw. McCance could not see the trap closing and he obeyed with the utmost reluctance. Under fire, a brave youth called Peter Cranney brought the two swivel guns off Windmill Hill and over to us by horse and cart.

One of our colonels, Hugh McCulloch, was captured. The soldiers dragged him up the hill, put a rope round his neck and hanged him from a sail of the windmill for us to see. There would be no quarter in this battle.

Nugent set up camp on Windmill Hill and drew up his big guns. Then he opened fire on the town. The noise was tremendous. Shells smashed into the Market House. One crashed through the roof of Montalto. We fired our ships' guns in return but with little effect. A howitzer shell exploded among the trees at the entrance to the demesne, a bit too close for comfort. Horses and ponies shied and whinnied in alarm. The bombardment had a demoralising effect. Some men ran off. I overheard a conversation between two brothers who refused to join them. 'You see,' said one, 'we are deserted by our friends. If I be killed, first search my pockets and take what money you can find, and endeavour to save your life by flight, and if you reach home alive, tell my wife how I fell.'

A scout showed Monro a leaflet that the soldiers were scattering around. It contained a proclamation by General Nugent that if all persons did not return to their duties as peaceable subjects he would destroy their homes, burn the towns of Killinchy, Killyleagh, Saintfield and Ballynahinch, and kill everyone found in arms.

As darkness fell the Monaghan Militia entered the centre of Ballynahinch and began looting taverns. Soon they were roaring drunk and bawling out unintelligible words to the air of 'Lillibullero'.

'This is our opportunity,' said Dr Swail as we listened to the commotion. 'Attack now while the Monaghans are in no fit state to fight back. We can deploy two groups and advance from north and south.'

'No,' replied Monro. 'I scorn to avail of the ungenerous advantage which night affords. We shall meet them in the blush of open day and fight them like men, not under the cloud of night but in the first rays of tomorrow's sun. We will take the field at dawn.'

I could hardly believe what I had heard. I recalled Charles Teeling telling me once that Harry Monro's military talent was compromised by a mistaken feeling of honour. The argument became very heated. As Monro's aide I chose not to openly side with Swail but I knew the doctor was right. The discourse became so contentious that hundreds of men, including the Killinchy division, left Ednavaddy Hill in disgust. The Defenders, unfortunately, had not fully pledged themselves to Monro as commander, and a large contingent of Catholics also melted away. One said as he left, 'This is your fight, not ours.'

About two thousand men in all deserted during that night. It was hard to tell in the dark but I believe five thousand or so remained to fight, and a few hundred Defenders.

I went to find my friends from Gransha. They were sitting on the grass with their neighbours from Six Road Ends, none of whom had fled. They were disheartened by the defections.

'I fear we're done for,' said George.

'Shut up, none of that talk,' I said.

'Yes, enough of that,' said Willie. 'We're in this to the bitter end.'

'Take good care of this lady,' I said.

George laughed. 'Our Betsy's more likely to take care of us.'

'We will meet after the battle is won,' I said, embracing each in turn.

As I put my arms round Betsy I said, 'When liberty is secured, we must all be free to decide our future.'

If she detected a double meaning in my words, she took care not to show it. She sat down by Willie and looked at me sadly and I feared in my heart at that moment that I would never have her.

I left convinced that the coming hours would be crucial for Ireland, and for me. Everything had to be decided. Ireland's fate. My fate. As Brutus told Cassius in *Julius Caesar*, 'we must take the current when it serves or lose our ventures.'

At first light on Thursday 14 June, the battle of Ballynahinch began.

Monro gathered us in ranks, gave a short, stirring address, and led a charge of roaring men along the demesne avenue, out onto Bridge Street and into the centre of the town, under covering fire from our one-pounders. Roger Magennis and his disciplined Catholic Defenders took the offensive on the right at Mill Bridge. Nugent responded with cannon fire, and flaming fragments quickly set fire to rows of houses.

We were met with a murderous volley of musketry and grape and men fell all round us, but those behind kept pressing on, shouting encouragement to each other, taking the place of the fallen.

I recognised Colonel Ford of Seaforde through the smoke and heard him shouting over the din, 'God damn these stiff-necked Presbyterians. They won't run!'

We did run – towards them. We cried, 'Forward lads!' 'Remember Orr!' 'Liberty or Death!' By a miracle Monro and I survived the charge unscathed. So too did Monro's sister, Peggy, who rode beside us through the fray urging on the men.

The Monaghan Militia were in no condition to cope with the advancing phalanx of levelled pikes and we drove them back up Bridge Street and into the square. A musket shot felled the captain of the Monaghan Militia. In the furious tumult our men over-ran an artillery crew operating a cannon – the soldier putting a light to it was piked through the heart – and they turned the gun to face the army. But they didn't have the training or knowledge to fire it. They rolled it down the steps of a cellar instead to disable it.

In the fray I saw Willie Boal thrusting with his pike and Betsy, beautiful, foolhardy Betsy, beside him on her mare lashing out with a sword at any soldier who came close. I rode over and put my mount between them and the worst fighting. I continued to watch out for them as we conquered the square and pushed the Monaghans and the 22nd Light Dragoons down to the bottom of Meeting House Street. There my mount pitched forward and threw me to the ground. Monro too lost his horse. But we had the enemy on the run.

A tremendous cry went up from our pikemen: 'Charge!'

Just then a trumpet sounded. Our men stopped suddenly. What did it mean? 'Crown reinforcements', someone cried. Our lines broke in confusion and fell back. 'Stop, they are sounding the retreat,' someone shouted. 'It's the retreat.'

But it was too late. Before we could regain our momentum, the 22nd Light Dragoons turned and now came racing towards us. At the same time shells burst in our midst, fired by gunners to our south.

Reduced in number, our ammunition depleted, we turned to race back through the blinding smoke and flaming cinders of the town square, where men lay dead or screaming in pain. George and Willie each grabbed one of Betsy's arms and propelled her along Bridge Street. As we ran pell-mell towards Montalto demesne, we found that Stewart's soldiers had overwhelmed the Defenders who had been fighting bravely on our southern flank, and had cut us off from our gunpowder and ammunition stocks.

The men of our reserve force at Ednavaddy Hill scattered like sheep when they saw us racing towards them with the dragoons on our heels. Monro desperately tried to rally musket men to make a stand, but to no avail. Flight was the only course open.

I shouted to Betsy and her two protectors, 'Run, run for your lives. Get away! Look after yourselves! They will give no quarter.'

'Take care,' Betsy called out to me, as Willie pulled her along by the hand.

— FORTY-FOUR —

MURDER MOST FOUL

My duty was to Monro. I stuck closely by him as he organised a brave band of musketeers to cover the retreat. We then took flight ourselves. We leapt through hedges and stumbled across fields thigh-deep in grass and yellow-flowering weeds.

From his lifetime buying up flax, Monro was familiar with the network of narrow roads and laneways lined by hedgerows and brambles that curved and twisted around hundreds of small fields in these parts. When well out of sight we stopped behind a thicket of flowering blackthorn bushes, took off our green hats and uniform jackets, and started off again, stumbling up sloping fields to look out for pursuers, then running down the other side.

Behind us Ballynahinch was on fire. Ahead the noise of battle was replaced by the quiet of a still, sunny June morning. Song birds trilled, oblivious of the horror close by. Hares loped away at the sight of us.

We ran in circles and had put a mere two miles between Ballynahinch and ourselves by the time we reached a townland called Ballycreen. We hid behind the bank of a stream when we heard voices. Through the tall rushes I saw two soldiers, their hands and bayonets red with blood.

'Let's wash here,' one said. 'Don't bother,' said the other. 'We aren't done yet. Wait until the night when one wash will serve.'

We picked our way along the riverbed, past clumps of high reeds and prickly whin bushes heavy with yellow blossom.

Again we heard shouts and crouched down behind long grass. I glimpsed three figures running across a small field. Five or six yeomen were right on their heels, sabres drawn, shouting for them to give up. To my horror I saw they were Betsy, George and Willie Boal. Exhausted, they turned to surrender to the yeomen.

What I witnessed then will torment me for ever.

Willie leaned forward, his hands on his knees, trying to catch his breath. George shouted, 'Take us prisoner. Spare the lass!'

One of the yeomen responded by slashing out with his sword. It caught Willie's neck and he keeled over like a fallen log. Betsy ran back and raised her arm to shield her brother. A blade sliced through it. I stared in shock as her gloved hand fell to the ground. Betsy stayed standing, blood streaming from her arm.

There was a loud bang. A yeoman shot her through the eye with his pistol. She collapsed backwards onto the grass. There was another bang and George fell to the ground.

It was all I could do to restrain myself from crying out and running at the killers as they hacked at my dear friends with their swords. We had discarded our weapons. We were helpless. I bit my fist to the bone. How could I be there and do nothing?

A yeoman turned Betsy over, and pulled off her dress and green petticoat and stuffed it in his bag. A second ripped off her green earrings, the earrings I had given her, then lifted Betsy's severed hand, tugged at the glove and took from her finger the ring that Willie had given her.

They wiped their swords on the grass and set off again with whoops of triumph. I was violently sick. Monro wept.

'I know those bastards,' he said. 'They're from Annahilt. That was Thomas Nelson who shot the girl. Jack Gill was the one who cut her arm, and James Little who took her clothes. Blast their souls to hell!'

Three English cavalrymen came into view. They dismounted at seeing the bloodied bodies. 'Cursed murderers,' called out the officer, looking down at Betsy. He was referring to the yeomen, not their victims. 'Look! She's a real beauty! What cur would do that?'

They rode on. I ran to the bodies. All three were lifeless. We laid them side by side. I put my jacket over Betsy's head. We said a prayer and crept back through the whins and headed south-west for the Dromara hills.

For some hours we skirted around the higher drumlins, stung by nettles, blinded by sweat and tears.

Exhausted and dehydrated, we risked calling at a house to ask for shelter.

'Aren't you the draper from Lisburn?' enquired the tenant. 'Aren't you Monro?'

'I am. And I need to call on your charity.'

'I don't agree with you,' he said, 'but I won't betray you. Come on.'

He led us into a small barn containing a plough and some bales of hay. As he left, he barred the door. 'So they won't think to open it,' he said.

Lying in the darkness I was comatose with shock. I could not prevent the heinous murder of Betsy. I had failed to keep the promise we had made to watch out for each other. Our side had been defeated in a battle that we so very nearly won. And here we were, relying for mercy on a loyalist who had us locked in his barn.

I passed out and woke to hear Monro weeping in the darkness. I put my arms around him.

Next morning our host brought us stirabout with water, and news that the rebels had been defeated in Antrim and Down and everywhere else in the north. The dragoons and yeomen were hunting us down. General Nugent was threatening to hang anyone who sheltered fugitives.

'Thank you. We will leave,' said Monro.

For two hours we crept along the ditches. In the townland of Clintinagoold, halfway to Dromara, we came face to face with a farmer hoeing potatoes. He too recognised Monro. His name was Billy Holmes. He peered at me. 'Aren't you the *Star* man?'

Monro asked him to hide us until word of an amnesty. He offered him all he had – five pounds and his jacket. 'Willingly,' Holmes replied, taking the coins. He brought us water and opened the low door of the stone piggery. 'You will be safe here,' he said. We squatted in the muck as two sows rooted around us.

Shortly afterwards we heard Holmes say, 'They are in there, lads.'

A voice ordered us to surrender. We emerged to find four horsemen, each wearing a black cockade, the insignia of the black troop of loyalist yeomen. They tied our hands and roped us to two of their horses. And so ended our freedom.

As we were pulled away I turned to stare at Holmes and his wife. 'Damn you to hell!' I shouted. 'Your blood money will curse you.' The wife raised her hands over her ears and ran into the house.

Monro pleaded with our captors to let us go in return for money which he would get from wealthy benefactors. They laughed at him. For four hours we stumbled along, first to Hillsborough and then on to Lisburn. Labourers on the roadside took off their hats as we passed – sympathy for condemned men.

We were lodged under guard in the French Church in Lisburn's Castle Street. A pompous official came to confirm our identity. 'Why,' he said, 'this mighty general is indeed no other than the little hot-headed fellow who keeps a draper's shop in Market Square.'

A friend of Monro's brought us a clean set of clothes each from Harry's own shop and a pail of water to clean ourselves. We were given potatoes and butter by the Revd Snowden Cupples, the rector of Lisburn Cathedral. Cupples was a loyalist but he was Monro's pastor, as they were both of the established church. He sent word to Monro's mother in Lisburn and mine in Moira of our whereabouts and our likely fate.

Next day my mother was admitted to see me. She had walked nine miles but was permitted only five minutes with me. I pushed back her black shawl and wiped away the tears from her wrinkled face. 'Your father would be proud of you,' she said. 'I know I am.'

What she said broke my heart. My mother had never before uttered a word of encouragement about my rebel activities.

Harry Monro's wife was barred but not his mother. She told him to remain steadfast to the radical cause and not to betray his comrades. On hearing this, the dragoon guard threw the old lady out.

I wondered if Hans Gray was still alive and if the cottage had been wrecked by the soldiers who were burning rebel homesteads all over County Down. His wife died young. Now he had lost his only son and only daughter, and many friends and neighbours. He had no one left in the world.

— FORTY-FIVE —

OFF WITH OUR HEADS

Next morning, Saturday 17 June, our hands were tied and we were taken to a court martial in a house occupied by the military on Castle Street. I was consigned to a bench as Harry was brought forward. Lieutenant-Colonel Frederick William Walloston, commander of the 22nd Light Dragoons, attired in full regimentals and wig, formally charged him with treason and rebellion.

Two witnesses testified that they saw Monro at the head of the rebel army on the previous Tuesday. Harry looked at me and shrugged. Neither was known to us. An officer produced the note Monro sent to Townsend from Saintfield just before the battle for Ballynahinch as further evidence of his actions. How on earth did they get that?

In his defence, Harry pleaded guilty to treason and rebellion but protested that he had been coerced by Townsend into accepting the role of general. He threw himself on the mercy of the court and offered to make any discovery that might bring the rebellion to an end in County Down.

I could not look my general in the eye. He was fighting for his life but I found this hard to comprehend, especially after what his mother had said. And it did Harry no good.

Walloston read the sentence from a sheet of paper already prepared: 'The court finds him guilty of the crimes laid to his charge and by virtue of the late proclamation giving military power its full force does sentence him to death, in whatever manner shall be deemed proper by the commanding officer of this district.' He instructed an express rider to take the verdict to Belfast to have the sentence ratified by General Nugent.

I expected the same. However the colonel, having ascertained that I was a resident of Belfast, ordered that I be transported there for court martial by the Belfast military authorities.

We were hustled away without the opportunity to make our farewells and locked in separate rooms.

Four hours later a soldier unbarred my door to inform me that General Nugent had ratified the sentence and Monro was to be hanged immediately and I was to attend the execution.

With hands tied behind my back I was led behind Monro along Castle Street. The procession paused at the house of the Revd Cupples so Harry could receive the last sacrament, then resumed to Market Square where a makeshift scaffold had been erected outside Monro's shop.

To my horror I saw a head stuck on a spike on top of the Market House. One of our guards told me it belonged to a rebel called Armstrong who was found with a green cockade hidden in his hat and the words 'Remember Orr'. He added, to guffaws from his comrades, 'Your general will be sticking around with him soon.' A ladder was propped against the roof in readiness.

A big, silent crowd had gathered. Harry's mother and his sister Peggy supported each other by the shop entrance. Peggy had evidently escaped after Ballynahinch but she was risking exposure.

Monro asked to close his shop accounts. The ledger was brought out and placed on a barrel. He settled several bills with customers. One of them was Pointz Stewart, an elderly family friend who, as captain of the Derriaghy Yeomanry, formed part of the military escort. They disputed the sum involved, until at length they shook hands and Stewart resumed his place.

Monro closed the ledger, bowed his head in prayer as his hands were again tied behind his back, and then went to run up the steps to the scaffold. The two lower rungs broke and he fell back. He leaped up to the third step and announced, 'I am not cowed, gentlemen.'

The hangman, brought from the guardhouse with his face hidden by black crape, made fast the rope around his neck. Harry called out, 'Tell my country I deserved better of her.'

Two soldiers pushed him off the platform. A great sigh emanated from the crowd as Harry's body jerked, swivelled round and then became motionless. His neck was not broken but he lost consciousness immediately and slowly died of asphyxiation. I felt a strange detachment as I watched the last signs of life, a quivering of the hands and a slight curling of his feet. This was to be my fate too.

After ten minutes Harry's lifeless body was laid out on the platform and the executioner, a brute of a man with a cadaverous face, grasped an axe. He borrowed a chamois from a dragoon to wipe his sweaty hands, then severed Harry's head with a single blow. The axe stuck fast in the wood. The butcher grabbed the head by the hair and held it up, dripping blood. He called out, 'This is the head of a traitor.' He rammed it on a spike, ascended the ladder, and fixed it in position on the Market House alongside the unfortunate Armstrong.

I looked over at Monro's shop. Harry's mother and sister had slipped away.

My transfer to Belfast for trial was delayed because the military was overwhelmed with courts martial and executions. I was confined to a clammy stone room in the church with other prisoners. I was unable to sleep at night because of the constant noise of chains and boots and shouting, but the racket was preferable to the nightmares I endured when I did lose consciousness. They were always the same: my limbs turned to lead and the road turned to treacle as I tried to save the lives of those I loved.

The *Belfast News-Letter* was pasted up on a wall so we could see how hopeless our situation was. The United Irishmen were defeated everywhere and professions of loyalty were pouring in on all sides. General Nugent returned from the battle in Ballynahinch with eight captured swivel guns, two strands of colours, a jacket taken from one of the rebel chiefs who was killed – no name was given – a few pikes and three barrels of gunpowder. A detachment of the Fifeshire Fencibles and a party of the Monaghan Militia marched to the neighbourhood of Saintfield to destroy the houses of insurgents. They burned David Shaw's house and store. The *News-Letter* also reported that many of the soldiers returned loaded with plunder taken from the homes of rebels.

Days passed and I wished for nothing more than to get it over with. I could not bear life any more. All my friends were done for, my hopes for Ireland utterly dashed.

My mother came every morning with oaten bread and milk. We were never allowed more than five minutes together. She implored me to prepare well to meet my God. She told me the military had raided our house and ransacked everything looking for evidence against me. They took the few coins left in the document box. The United Irishmen in Moira heeded the turnout but were now lying low. The loyalists were cock-a-hoop and the Orange Order was growing. The killing of Protestants in Scullabogue had soured the town's Presbyterians against the Papists. Men who fought bravely were now saying that they had been coerced into taking up arms. My mother told me that Claiborne survived the battle at Saintfield but was crippled and would never ride again.

I asked her to go to Gransha and visit the houses of Hans Gray and Eliza Bryson, and to tell Eliza, if she survived, not to weep for me and to seek happiness with someone more worthy.

She managed to find them. Hans, she told me, sat by the empty fireplace all day, inconsolable, struck dumb with grief. The house was not raided. Eliza wore black and cried day and night. Andrew Bryson Senior and Andrew his son were on the run and Eliza fretted she would lose them both to the hangman.

Two weeks passed before I was summoned to stand trial in Belfast by order of Major General Goldie, on a charge of treason for acting as aide-de-camp to Munro. As I trotted and stumbled along the road to Belfast, tethered to a horse and escorted by dragoons, some people smiled at me, but many turned away. I was lodged in a windowless room in the Donegall Arms, which had been transformed into a provost's prison. Here I was to languish for several more days, waiting my turn to be brought to trial.

Gradually I came to learn who else was locked up in the building where we had enjoyed so many nights of revelry and made so many toasts to Liberty.

John Storey, my dear, droll, heroic, steadfast friend from the *Northern Star*, was in the next room, having been captured after the defeat in Antrim. David

Bailie Warden was imprisoned on another floor along with Billy Templeton. They hadn't been killed in battle but, like me, could only contemplate death at the hands of the hangman. I wasn't permitted to see them.

When I discovered that a rebel priest from Moira was locked in a servant's garret on the third floor, I asked to visit him, feigning a need for spiritual consultation. A guard brought me to his room and stood outside the door. The priest was a feisty, matter-of-fact man of about forty-five years. He had been arrested for membership of the United Irishmen, and feared he would rot in jail. We talked about my father, whom he knew well, and other acquaintances. I related my experiences and expressed a desire to join my dear ones in death.

'You must never give up striving for life,' he said angrily. 'If I were young like you, I would leap out of that window.'

'That's one way of ending it all,' I said.

On the morning of Thursday 30 June, John was taken and hanged and his head severed from his body and placed on a spike at the top of the Market House.

I had no tears left. I thought back to the day when he had welcomed me to the *Northern Star* as a 'real rebel boyo' and how his hands were always blackened and calloused from the ink, and how we had formed a great bond when we had work to do for the cause.

— FORTY-SIX —

BILLY

Next day was my turn. I was taken in irons to the Assembly Rooms for my court martial. It was a perfunctory affair in the card room where Martha had taught me to play faro. Four men called Petticrew, Fullerton, Keanan and Sinclare testified to my role in Ballynahinch. They said they had seen me with Monro and firing a musket. From the indifferent way they spoke, I guessed they had testified at other trials and were informing to save their own skins.

The presiding colonel read the precise same words that sealed Monro's fate: 'The court finds him [me this time] guilty of the crimes laid to his charge and by virtue of the late proclamation giving military power its full force does sentence him to death, in whatever manner shall be deemed proper by the commanding officer of this district.' It was as if they were talking about someone else.

I was to be executed at the pleasure of General Nugent, and next day I was informed that it was his pleasure that I should be hanged and beheaded two days after that, on Sunday 3 July. Even on the Sabbath the hangman and the axeman continued their busy work. My head was to be put on a spike beside that of John Storey.

I was told to make my will. I left my watch and my clothes to my mother, along with my few possessions stored in the Hamill's back room.

But the day that was to end my life as a rebel became the day I started the journey to another life.

Just before nine on the Saturday evening I asked to be allowed to visit the priest for his blessing. As a condemned man, I was granted my wish and a turnkey accompanied me and took up position at the open door. I entered the attic. The priest gave me his blessing with the words '*Salus, honor, virtus quoque. Sit e benedictio*'. Then whispering as if in prayer, he glanced at the window which he had opened and said, 'What's that slogan you fellows were always shouting? Liberty or Death was it?'

'Yes', I replied, 'Liberty or death!'

And with that I sprang to the window and swung my body round and released myself backwards. I fell feet first, not knowing where I would land. I crashed onto the sloping roof of a shed and slid and fell another distance into the yard. I was skinned and bruised and the breath was knocked out of me but I had survived with no bones broken. The guard appeared at the window and turned to slide down the wall after me.

I ran into the hotel through the back door and barred it behind me. I walked along the corridor to the front door, past the dining room where officers were making a great noise gorging themselves and laughing. I encountered a servant girl. I begged her not to open the back door which the guard was now pounding, and not to say she had seen me. She understood and ran up the stairs.

I walked out the front entrance of the hotel. At that moment the nine o'clock bell rang and the military tattoo sounded to announce the curfew. I turned left and came face to face with a sentry. He challenged me. 'Why are you still out? And without a coat or hat.' I pretended to be the worse for drink and said I lived just a few doors away and, putting my arm around his shoulder, started to sing 'Croppies Lie Down'. He pushed me away with a disgusted look.

Having ducked left into Legge's Lane, I lifted the iron grate of a drain, slid down into filthy waist-deep water and closed the grill above me. Seconds later the alarm was sounded. I heard boots and voices, 'He went this way!' 'No that way!'

I crawled along the culvert and came out at the River Farset that ran under a section of High Street towards Hanover Quay. The river was only two feet deep. I crawled down the riverbed, following the flow until I reached Joy's Entry by the *Northern Star* offices. And there I stayed for twenty-four hours, perched on mud and stones, until I guessed the search for me had been called off.

The next night, shivering almost uncontrollably and with cramp in my legs, I climbed out and made my way through pouring rain along Bridge Street and onto Rosemary Street. As I crossed Hercules Street looking for Mrs Hamill's house, I saw the flaming torches of a military patrol approaching. I couldn't run in the other direction because it led to a picket in Grand Parade. I rapped on the nearest door. A middle-aged man opened it, holding a candle. His face looked somewhat familiar.

'Would you take a man in for a minute to save his life,' I said.

He lifted up the candle. 'Are you Willie Kean?'

'Yes,' I replied.

'God in heaven, you are the most wanted man in Ireland.'

For a few moments he said nothing, then bade me come in, and locked and barred the door. The patrol passed.

I thanked him and made to leave but he said I was in no state to go anywhere. He insisted I strip off my clothes. He fetched a pail of water so I could sponge myself down and a cloth to dry myself. I lay on the floor and passed out. I came to, stiff and feverish, covered with a blanket. It was daylight but the curtains were drawn and the room was dark.

There was no sign of my host. He had left a clean shirt and breeches on a chair. As I dressed my heart sank. Hanging on a hook was a yeoman uniform. As I prepared to flee, its owner appeared down the stairs.

'Don't go,' he said. 'You don't stand a chance in the street.'

'Who are you?'

'Just call me Billy,' he said. 'If you are caught, it's better not to know my surname. Here read this.'

He produced the *Belfast News-Letter*. In it was a proclamation: 'William Kean, charged with treason and rebellion, made his escape from confinement on 2 July. General search immediately made through all the houses in the town. James Derham, Col. Commandant, called on inhabitants to assist in delivering up said Kean who is now concealed or harboured in some part of this town, and shall it be found hereafter that said traitor has been concealed by any person or persons of this town and its neighbourhood, or that they or any of them have known of the place of concealment and shall not have given notice thereof to the commandant of this town, such person's house shall be burned and the owner thereof hanged!'

'Don't worry,' said Billy. 'No one will suspect me of helping the likes of you. And if they find you, I will say you were trying to kill me.'

I slept all day in an upstairs room until Billy roused me. It was evident he lived alone.

'Why are you sheltering me?' I asked.

'Don't you mind me?' he said, raising his heavy eyebrows. 'I gave you a letter once, in High Street. It was I who warned you five years ago that George Murdoch was going around blaming the *Northern Star* for all Belfast's troubles. You published the letter. Remember?'

As he spoke I recalled the man who had tucked a letter into my pocket about the hearth tax collector. It was signed, 'A sub-constable'.

I peered closely at him in the gloom. 'Yes, of course. I mind you well. You're the sub-constable.'

'I am indeed. Or I was. I never liked Murdoch. He treated me like a vassal. He insulted people to their face, then stood behind me when anyone raised their fists. And I liked the *Star*. I enjoyed all that Squire Firebrand and Billy Bluff stuff. I had to join the yeomen because of my job, but don't be going thinking now that I agree with your crowd because I don't. I'm an Orangeman, by choice. But I won't give a man up to be hanged.'

And so began a strange friendship that was to last for five weeks.

Billy imposed a routine on me. I could not go near the window or draw back the curtains. If anyone knocked the door, and few did because Billy was something of a recluse, I was to hide upstairs. I lived in darkness, ready if there was a raid to climb out the upstairs window onto the roof.

It was a silent world but sometimes we talked in low voices. Billy kept me up to date with news. It was common knowledge among the yeomen, he said, that the United Irishmen had nearly won at Ballynahinch. The bugle call we heard at the height of the battle and which caused our men to flee did not sound the arrival of British reinforcements, but the retreat of Nugent's exhausted troops. He said four hundred United Irishmen and dozens of Defenders were slaughtered during and after the battle, and that the killing went on for three or four days in the fields. A week after the Battle of Ballynahinch the Irish uprising ended with the defeat of the rebels at Vinegar Hill in County Wexford.

Billy brought the *News-Letter* three times a week. It made for hard reading. Ballynahinch was in ruins. Of the seven inhabitants who stayed, three were burned alive and two were shot dead. A local called John McCalla recovered 1,236 muskets, pikes, pistols and swords from the battle scenes and organised the burial of the bodies which were being savaged by pigs and dogs. Montalto was partly burned by the dragoons. Lord Moira had put the estate up for sale.

I was tortured by thoughts of what might have been. What if we had overwhelmed them at Ballynahinch? Armies of Defenders would have joined us. Other counties would have risen. Betsy and George and Willie and Harry Monro would be alive.

Night-time was the worst. More than once I awakened to find Billy's hand across my mouth to stop me from shouting in my sleep. 'Who's Betsy?' he asked me once.

I thought of the hot summer's day three years earlier when Wolfe Tone, Sam Neilson, Thomas Russell, Harry McCracken, Robert and William Simms and I had climbed Cave Hill and solemnly vowed never to desist in our efforts until we had subverted the authority of England and asserted our independence.

Look at us now, I reflected: Tone in exile, Sam and Tom in jail, Harry on the run, Robert and William Simms behind bars, and I, a condemned felon, being sheltered by an Orangeman.

Some days the news was impossible to bear and I would spend hours in black depression.

The Revd James Porter, that learned and erudite man, the best of his generation, was hanged in Greyabbey. Thus did Londonderry and Castlereagh exact revenge for his lampoons. Billy too was appalled when I told him Porter was the author of the Squire Firebrand stories.

On 12 July, my host went off to join the Orangemen on a victory march along the same route as the Bastille Day parade six years earlier. He returned to tell me that two more of my comrades' severed heads had been displayed on spikes on the Market House. They belonged to Hugh Grimes – how he distinguished himself at Saintfield! – and Henry Byers, who was sentenced to death for stealing Squire Price's horse. Price was given the option of sparing Byers; instead he took him to the gallows himself, clapped him on the shoulder, pointed to the heads on the Market House, and told him to go boldly, as he would soon have plenty of his neighbours for company.

Billy could hardly contain himself when he came back four days later with the news that Harry McCracken has been captured in County Antrim and brought to Belfast. He was recognised by a yeoman as he tried to get to a foreign ship in Carrickfergus. The Revd Steel Dickson and the Revd Sinclair Kelburn were also taken up.

Next day Billy was called out to serve guard duty with the Belfast yeomen while Harry was tried at the Exchange. I waited with a heart as heavy as a cannonball to hear the outcome. He returned to tell me Harry was dead, executed for treason after refusing an offer of his life if he would betray Robert Simms. He was taken to a scaffold erected outside the Market House. He tried to address the crowd but the cavalry tramped their horses' hooves so that his voice could not be heard. Harry was then hanged. He was not beheaded and his sister Mary Ann sent for family friend Dr MacDonnell to try to revive the body, but he refused to come. I recall how Tone once called the doctor, who fawned all over the United Irishmen, 'a hypocrite'. He said it in jest, referring to the Hippocratic Oath, but I thought now it might well have been a joke with a jag.

After the execution Billy went with fellow yeomen for a drink in Whyte's Tavern. They made jokes there about Harry, he said. 'Where's McCracken?' 'He's hanging around outside!'

Thus they mocked one of Ireland's greatest heroes, who tried to save his country from oppression and disunity. Billy saw I was distressed and apologised.

He said he actually saw some of his fellow yeomen weeping at the hanging.

There was also a lot of scornful talk among his friends about a merchant called Alexander Orr who was accused by a colonel of being a croppy for having green curtains in his house on Linen Hall Street. Next day new curtains were put up, coloured orange. So that's what Belfast has come to, I thought.

General Nugent issued a proclamation offering fifty guineas a head for the apprehension of more than two score men on the run. Billy told me the biggest manhunt was for a United Irishman called James Hope. I rejoiced to hear that at least Jemmy was still alive and free.

On 24 July the *News-Letter* reported that James Dickey, a Presbyterian who had fought in Antrim, said before his execution that had the north been successful, they would have had to fight the battle over again with the Catholics of the south. Billy and I debated this late at night. He agreed. I disagreed. Neither of us could convince the other as to the rights and wrongs of the rising. He insisted that, having tried and failed, the Presbyterians would now become loyal citizens, realising that only in consort with England would they be safe from Papist domination – hadn't they narrowly escaped that fate when King William won the Battle of the Boyne against the Catholic King James in 1690? He told me of the story doing the rounds about a Munster Catholic deserter in charge of a rebel unit in the north who waved his sword in the air and cried out to his stupified Presbyterian colleagues, 'By Jasus, boys, we'll pay the rascals this day for the Battle of the Boyne.'

I tried to persuade Billy that only a union between Presbyterians and Roman Catholics would bring liberty and justice for all Ireland, but I bit my tongue at times out of respect for his hospitality.

We did agree on one thing from the start. I had to leave as soon as possible, not just Belfast but Ireland. My best hope was to take ship for America. Billy began making enquiries at the quays.

On 9 August an American ship, the *Harmony* of New Bedford, arrived in Belfast. I had a week to get on board before it sailed for New York. Billy came up with a plan. I should dress as a sailor and just walk to the quays with a couple of regular seafarers. I would get away with it, he believed, becausethe government's policy was changing. Castlereagh now preferred to get the rebels out of the country instead of executing them, and was turning a blind eye to the human manifest on outward-bound ships.

All I needed was a sailor suit and two obliging sailors. For this I needed money to give to Billy. I had only one item of worth in my possession, my fob watch. I removed the lock of Betsy's hair from the back and gave it to him to sell.

He went drinking with seamen from the *Harmony* and found two sailors who agreed to 'walk me' on board at a time when he knew the road to the dockside would be clear of patrols. And so on a wet and windy Monday evening, dressed in sailor's weskit of striped vest, blue and white trousers, tricorn hat and buckled shoes, and carrying a satchel with my few clothes, I bade a fond farewell to Billy, telling him he had restored my faith in human nature. At last he told me his surname but made me promise never to divulge it.

I was gripped on both arms by two sailors from the *Harmony* who told me to act like I was drunk. Almost blinded by the sun, I allowed them to half-carry me towards High Street and past the red-brick Market House.

'Don't look up,' said one. But I did.

There on spikes were the heads of Hugh Grimes, Henry Byers, James Dickey and John Storey. Birds had pecked out their eyeballs. I pulled my hat down over my face. One challenge from the military and I might be up there with them.

Twenty minutes later I was on board the *Harmony* and face to face with Captain Asa Swift, who got me to sign a promissory note for fifty guineas and hustled me into the cargo hold. Several figures were there in the darkness. No one spoke. I laid my head on my satchel as a pillow, and felt something hard inside. It was my watch.

I resolved that, if ever I could, I would reimburse my kind Orange friend and more.

— FORTY-SEVEN —

THE *HARMONY*

I didn't dare to consider myself safe until, on the following morning, Tuesday 16 August, the creaking and heaving of the ship told me we had left the quayside. We were not permitted to come on deck until the *Harmony* was far out from the coast of Antrim.

As we emerged blinking into the sunlight, I immediately found several of my fellow-combatants. We fell into a round of excited, emotional exchanges, punctuated with the cry of 'You are alive!'

The first to rush forward and clasp me to his chest was Eliza's father, Andrew Bryson. He had been taken after five weeks on the run and was being deported. His family had been destroyed, he said. Andy Junior was captured and sentenced to military service overseas with the British Army. Eliza had taken to wearing black like a widow, inconsolable that she did not go to Ballynahinch to perish with those she loved, 'and now she's grieving for you,' he said. His last image of Hans Gray was of a broken man, unable to stir from his kitchen chair, clutching the miniature of Betsy.

The bodies of Betsy, George and Willie Boal had been found by a teenage boy, Bryson said. They were lifted up by two local men and buried together in a boggy field on Armstrong's farm at Ballycreen. Their last resting place was marked with a log of black oak. In the weeks since their dastardly murder, people of all stripes had taken to calling them the Hearts of Down and paying their respects at the grave site. The yeomen killers from Annahilt, may they rot in hell, were being shunned by Orange and Green alike, especially since the wife of one of them was seen wearing Betsy's earrings, the precious earrings that I had given her for her twenty-first birthday. That hit me very hard.

Matt McClenaghan survived and was back at work at his smithy, but his young bellows-boy, Tommy Burns, died heroically. He was hiding from a patrol when he recognised the soldier who had whipped him the previous October. Stepping out, Tommy blasted the soldier's head off with his musket before being bayoneted to death.

I turned round and there was the Revd Birch, whom I had last seen in Saintfield on the day he preached at Creevy Rocks. He told me he was arrested after the battle of Ballynahinch and might have been hanged but for the intercession of his brother George, who was a commander of the Newtownards yeomen and Castlereagh's physician. When he was spared the hangman's rope, infuriated yeomen came to break him out and do the job themselves, but he was saved by the intervention of a troop of dragoons. He was interned on a prison hulk in Belfast harbour, the *Postlethwaite*, and was now being sent into exile, still inconsolable over the death of his son George at Saintfield.

Then I was smothered in the embrace of Davy Warden who emerged from the scores of men milling around on the deck. Davy had got back to Killinchy, but found that people were inclined to give him up as a sacrifice to prevent the village being burned. He surrendered himself to the military and was lodged in the Donegall Arms prison where, he said, all the prisoners celebrated news of the *Star* man's escape by stamping their feet on the floors so long and hard that the building shook. He had expected to die, but his hearing was fixed and put off four times. He was given the option of trial or banishment. The Bangor Presbytery refused him a licence to preach abroad and he was very bitter about that, blaming Castlereagh for intervening.

Minutes later I came face to face with Tom Storey and the tears flowed again. He too had seen his brother's head on the Market House as he was being brought to the ship. Tom also had a dramatic escape from execution. He was held in Carrickfergus jail pending trial for fighting alongside Harry McCracken at Antrim. A younger brother brought in a roast goose. He found a note inside saying 'Hide in the barrel'. There was an empty barrel in the assembly area. Tom managed to squeeze inside and cover himself with old clothes. The barrel was rolled out of the prison and collected by two comrades with a horse and dray and brought straight to the ship.

One of our youngest exiles bound for America was Alexander Porter, aged thirteen, son of my dear friend the Revd James Porter of Greyabbey. I remembered young Alex carrying a stand of colours at the battle in Ballynahinch and behaving very manfully, even when the flag was riddled with balls.

As we sat together on a coil of heavy ropes, Alex told me the full story of his father's execution. The Revd Porter was arrested and brought before Lord Londonderry at a court martial in Newtownards, on a charge of handling a military communication, a letter that was merely brought to him to read by illiterate pikemen. Londonderry sentenced him to death by hanging. In despair, Alex's mother took the seven children to Mount Stewart, in pouring rain, to beg for her husband's life. They were admitted by Lady Londonderry and her sister Lady Elizabeth, who comforted her and wrote a letter to General Nugent attesting to her husband's sterling character and imploring Nugent to change the sentence to deportation. Before they left Mount Stewart, however, Londonderry entered and seized the letter. In their presence he ordered Lady Elizabeth to write an extra sentence. This said that she was sending the letter only to gratify the widow, and that Lord Londonderry did not allow her to interfere in Mr Porter's case. Alexander said his mother knew then that there would be no mercy. Nor was there. A scaffold was erected outside their church. His father recited the 35th Psalm as the rope was put around his neck. 'But mine enemies are lively, and they are strong; and they that hate me wrongfully are multiplied. They also that render evil for good are mine adversaries; because I follow the thing that good is.' Despite an order from Londonderry that his tenants should attend, almost none did. Alex said his father smiled at him just before he was pushed off the scaffold to his death. He was now being taken to America by an uncle, because his mother was terrified he too would face arrest and execution for his part in the rebellion. For the length of the voyage we took turns comforting the lad and seeing to his welfare.

Dr James Cord, who fought so bravely at Ballynahinch, waving his sword in the air as he galloped round on his white horse, was also hanged, Bryson informed me. As he stepped onto the scaffold at Downpatrick jail, he told the crowd his spirit 'would not repair to the mansion of happiness, but would hover in the air, anxiously looking on till his country's wrongs were redressed.'

I gathered from fellow-passengers that Thomas Russell and Joe Cuthbert were to be deported on a later sailing, that William Sampson had been exiled to Portugal, that Charles Teeling had got away to the Mourne Mountains, and that the Revd Steel Dickson was still held on the prison ship but had been spared execution.

During the seven-week crossing we endured seasickness, scurvy, constipation, cold, soakings and a persistent stench. We were plagued by lice and rats and existed on a diet of over-salted beef and ships' biscuits infested with weevils. We were sixty-five passengers all told, some with business in America, but the greater number were United Irishmen like ourselves, stiff-necked Presbyterians, some of us being deported, others 'fifty-pounders' with a price of £50 on our heads.

I concluded that Castlereagh and Nugent and the rest had satiated their blood lust and now simply wanted to be rid of us. Why otherwise did they not search the vessel before it set sail? Perhaps we were marketable commodities. I wonder did the authorities know full well where I was, and even connived to have me exiled. Might Billy and Captain Swift have profited from getting rid of the troublesome fellow I had become. I tried to put such thoughts out of my head and believe in man's better self.

Our misery, mental and physical, was occasionally relieved by tots of whiskey and rum, and at such time we tried to piece together the events that followed our doomed struggle, and what might have been. I was among those who insisted that if we had won, our army in two days would have become forty thousand and would have been joined by the Defenders. But I also believed in my darkest moments that we were provoked into rebellion so we could be identified and isolated as a prelude to bringing about an Act of Union.

The military was given free rein to teach the rebels a lesson. They burned and plundered in the days after our defeat. I heard countless tales of murder: a man shot at his door because he could not provide them with bread and cream; two lads shot while hiding under a bed; a girl killed by yeomen for delivering buttermilk to the rebels. One story had us laughing and crying. As a cart arrived at a sand pit in Antrim piled with dead rebels, a yeoman officer asked the driver, 'Where the devil did these rascals come from?' A voice from the pile replied, 'Ah cum from Ballyboley.' The poor wretch was tipped into the mass grave with the rest.

On our Sabbaths at sea we did not want for preachers. There were seven Presbyterian clergymen aboard. Birch could be tedious with his biblical prophesies, but I prayed with him, for old time's sake, for a better future for Ireland and its exiles.

EPILOGUE

I am now well on in years. Since I wrote this account of my time as a United Irishman, I have become an American citizen and I have prospered in my adopted country. I settled in Philadelphia and started a business, importing exotic plants. As soon as I could afford it, I sent an expensive silver fob watch to Billy the Orangeman, to repay his charity to me. I brought over my mother to live out her declining years in the comfort of my new home, modest by American standards but as grand as that of any Belfast merchant.

Eliza and I exchanged some tear-sodden letters. We ran out of things to say. The last I heard she married and bore several children. I am happy about that. I never married myself.

The French came again, but it was too little, too late. Wolfe Tone was captured trying to lead a French force to Donegal and took his own life. Samuel Neilson gave information about the United Irishmen in return for other prisoners' lives and was released after four years. He came to New York where he died of yellow fever before we had a chance to meet. It was just as well. I want to remember him as the courageous, radical editor of the *Northern Star*, taking on the Castle junto from his little office in High Street. Thomas Russell returned to the north with Jemmy Hope in 1803 to reignite the fires of revolt, but there was no appetite in Down or Antrim for another effort at 'catching cannonballs with pitchforks' as someone put it. He went on the run, and his friend, the bold hypocrite Dr James MacDonnell, subscribed fifty guineas to an award for his arrest. Tom was caught and hanged at Downpatrick jail. Please God that his dying hope will one day prevail. Jemmy Hope returned to live in Antrim, never giving up the principles in which he believed. William Putnam McCabe went to France and established a cotton mill in Normandy. The last I heard of Charles Teeling, he had settled in Dundalk as a linen bleacher.

Eliza's brother, Andrew, served in the British military in Martinique but escaped and made it to New York. The Revd Birch settled in Pennsylvania as a preacher. The Revd Steel Dickson became minister in Keady, County Armagh. Tom Storey returned to Belfast and prospered. Lord Moira, a decent soul, sold Montalto House and washed his hands of Ireland.

I keep in touch with some of my dearest friends from rebel days, in particular David Bailie Warden, who entered service with the American government and was sent by President Thomas Jefferson to Paris as American consul. Davy represented America at the Congress of Vienna in 1815 where he again encountered Castlereagh, who attended as British foreign secretary.

Using bribery and threats, Castlereagh got an Act of Union through the Irish Parliament in 1800 and the corrupt Dublin parliament was abolished. Now Britain and Ireland are one entity, doomed to an unhappy marriage. As Slender put it in *The Merry Wives of Windsor*, 'If there be no great love in the beginning, yet heaven may decrease it upon better acquaintance.' There is less love and greater hatred within Ireland itself. Daniel O'Connell, the young Catholic lawyer about whom O'Connor warned us, has made the cause of Ireland a Papist cause, and on our side, demagogues like the Revd Henry Cooke stir up the Presbyterians against the Roman Catholics.

Castlereagh shipped the set of chairs used by the delegates at the Congress of Vienna to Mount Stewart where they are on display. I am sure no mention is ever made in that grand edifice that the rebel Davy Warden, son of a tenant, sat on one of these chairs, on equal terms as America's representative, deciding the fate of the world. Castlereagh's name will forever be associated with the bloody repression of revolt on both sides of the Irish Sea. He died by his own hand. Byron captured what many felt:

Posterity will ne'er survey,
A nobler grave than this:
Here lie the bones of Castlereagh:
Stop, traveller, and piss.

We were undone by informers, the curse of Ireland. It turned out that the bookseller John Hughes was all along in receipt of the King's shilling;

he emigrated to America in 1802 and became a slave owner. A Saintfield Catholic called Nicholas Mageean penetrated our top ranks and kept Nugent informed all the time of our plans – how ironic that a Papist should betray his Presbyterian friends who were fighting for Roman Catholic rights. He ended up a drunk in the debtors' prison. Edward Newell, as we know, met a watery grave. The Revd William Cleland, 'master of the croppy hounds', amassed a fortune in blood money and built a castle at Stormont. I'm told that the couple I cursed for betraying Harry and me were shunned thereafter and the wife became a beggar woman.

Betrayal, defeat and exile have not extinguished the flame inside me for the ideals that inspired us, liberty and justice, but sometimes I despair of human nature.

Betsy Gray has become a heroine at home through fighting and dying for the rights of her gravely wronged kinfolk. She is tremendously admired even by those who now enthusiastically embrace the union. Not long after she died, the poet Mary Balfour from Limavady wrote these lines:

The star of evening slowly rose,
Through shades of twilight gleaming.
It shone to witness Erin's woes,
Her children's life-blood streaming:
'Twas then, sweet star, thy pensive ray,
Fell on the cold unconscious clay,
That wraps the breast of Betsy Gray,
In softened lustre beaming.

Betsy lives on in my memory and that of my kinfolk. I still have the strands of her hair in my watch case. She is Ireland to me. I sometimes glimpse her in my dreams; a red-haired beauty, wearing my earrings, laughing and teasing, full of fire and patriotism, and, I believe, secretly in love with her rebel *Star* man.

My love for her, for Ireland, was never requited. That is my fate.

POSTSCRIPT

William Kean merits a number of mentions in academic books, letters and archives. We know that he was a Presbyterian, born in Moira and educated in business at the academy in Belfast and that he started work as a clerk in the *Northern Star* in 1792 and was still employed there when it was suppressed in 1797. He joined the United Irishmen (Divisional Committee No. 69 in Belfast) and was promoted to membership of the secret military committee. In 1797 he was betrayed by the informer Newell, who identified Kean in a raid on Alexander's tavern in Belfast. He was imprisoned in Kilmainham for thirty-two weeks. His mother unsuccessfully petitioned for his freedom. He was released with several others on 24 November 1797. His name next crops up in a United Irish communication in April 1798 stating he had been in Dublin and had been provided with information on how the insurgents in the north should act when the rising occurred. He took part in the early stages of the Battle of Antrim. That same day he made his way by boat across Belfast Lough, bringing news that the rising had started in Antrim. He is subsequently referred to in court papers as aide-de-camp to General Monro at the Battle of Ballynahinch. After the defeat on 13 June 1798, Monro and Kean fled together but were betrayed and captured. Kean was taken to Belfast and lodged in the Donegall Arms Hotel, which served as a temporary prison. He was tried on 1 July. Four witnesses testified as to his role in the Battle of Ballynahinch and he was sentenced to be hanged the following day. That evening he made a dramatic escape (three different second-hand accounts exist) from the Donegall Arms. A government notice, published in the *Belfast News-Letter*, threatened anyone who harboured William Kean with death. He was sheltered by a Belfast Orangeman (a less credible account has him hiding in his mother's house) and after six weeks smuggled aboard a ship called *Harmony* in Belfast harbour. It set sail for New York on 16 August 1798 carrying many of his comrades. He is last heard of in Philadelphia where he is mentioned as a wealthy and respected citizen.

All this is factual. William Kean's thoughts, emotions, conversations and meetings are otherwise imagined by me. No major character or event is invented, but since this is a historical novel and not a history book, I have taken some liberties, intertwining our hero's life with those of other notable figures of the time and placing him at important events to tell the story of that tumultuous decade.

I have drawn on more than one hundred history books, biographies and pamphlets, as well as contemporary letters and government records, to make the narrative as historically accurate as possible within the scope of a novel. The most important of these were the three-volume *Drennan-McTier Letters 1776-1819* (IMC Women's History Project) edited by Jean Agnew, *Betsy Gray or Hearts of Down* by W.G. Lyttle (*Mourne Observer*), *1798: Rebellion in County Down* edited by Myrtle Hill, Brian Turner and Kenneth Dawson (Colourpoint), and the hard-copy files of the *Northern Star* held in the Linenhall Library in Belfast.

A number of people helped me piece together the story of those extraordinary years, principal among them the unassuming and exacting Ballynahinch historian, Horace Reid, who was my guide and mentor throughout the process of research and discovery and who more than once saved me from egregious errors. I am also indebted to Ken Dawson, Head of History and Vice Principal at Down High School, Downpatrick, for his advice and encouragement. Thanks also to Maurice Brick, Jim Gorry, Paul Caffrey, Marie Hewitt, Cathy O'Clery, Joan O'Clery, Michael O'Clery, Michael O'Farrell, Matthew Jebb, the staff of the Linenhall Library and the Northern Ireland Records Office in Belfast and of the Public Records Office and the National Library of Ireland in Dublin. I am more than grateful to my wise and gracious agent Jonathan Williams for his suggestions and edits, and to Zhanna O'Clery for her meticulous help with the manuscript, and not least for her forbearance while her husband was off time-travelling with the men and women of '98.